MAPS

ICELAND

NORWAY

Nidaros/
Trondheim

FAEROES

Orkney

Uppsala

Clontarf

SCOTLAND

ENGLISH
SEA

IRELAND

Dublin

York

ENGLAND

DENMARK

BALTIC SEA

Bremen

Rouen

Normandy

Lotharingia

Burgundy

FRANKIA

Aquitaine
Auvergne

Rome

GREAT

Traina

Catania
Augusta
Syracuse

SICILY

Kairouan

LIBYA

Thorgil's Journeys

- - - - - - - - - Constantinople – Holy Land – Constantinople
———————— Constantinople – North Lands

SKRIDFINNI

KARELIA

Aldeigjuborg

RUS

GARDARIKI

Kiev

Pontic Sea

Constantinople/
Miklagard

Propontis

Prokonnesos

Lemnos

Abydos

SYRIA

Baghdad

Cape Taenarum

HOLY
LAND
Ramla

SEA

Joppa

Jericho

Jerusalem

SERKLAND

EGYPT

Thorgil's Journeys

------- Norway – Scotland
———— Norway – Duke William's court
··········· Normandy – Harald's last battle

ICELAND

FAEROES

Orkney

Caithness
Firth of Moray
The Mounth
Birnam

Clontarf

IRELAND

Dublin

Northumbria

York

Stamford Bridge

London

Hastings

ENGLAND

NORWAY

Nidaros/
Trondheim

Upplands

Vaner
Lake

Uppsala

Vaster
Gotland

ENGLISH
SEA

DENMARK

BALTIC SEA

Bremen

Flanders

St Valéry
Fécamp
Dives

Boulogne
Ponthieu

Rouen
Jumieges

Normandy

Auxerre

Burgundy

Cluny

FRANKIA

VIKING:
KING'S MAN

To my holy and blessed master, Abbot Geraldus, in humble obedience to your wish, I send this, the third and last packet of the writings of the false monk Thangbrand. Inauspicious was the day when I first found these pages in our library! May I be forgiven for reading them with my sinful eyes, for I was urged on by my imagination and impatience.

Here I have found false witness artfully woven into a tale intended to beguile the credulous. This serpent in our bosom levels vile and wicked allegations against our brothers in Christ, and shamelessly admits piracy and the desecration of hallowed relic. Even when among the schismatics of the East he cannot restrain his viper's tongue.

Nothing has grieved me more than to learn that this false monk made a journey to the Holy Land, a pilgrimage which is the greatest desire of those who are as poor and unworthy as I. Yet he besmirches his witness with profane mistrust, and thereby seeks to undermine the faith of all those who believe in the Incarnation of the Word. As scripture avers, to an evil, unbelieving man, the truth becomes a lie.

His spew of corruption is the more disturbing, for it touches on high matters of state. Questioned is the very ascent to the throne of England itself, and his words must surely be judged treasonable by those who have competence in these matters.

We will speak no further of this matter, but will leave the pious labours of the faithful to be rewarded and paid for by the Just Judge.

Will there ever be an end to the deceit and mendacity of this impostor? I pray for his salvation in the fear of God, for is it not said that even one sparrow cannot fall into a snare without his providence, and that when God wills the end may be good?

Aethelred
Sacristan and Librarian
Written in the month of January in the Year of our Lord One Thousand and Seventy-two

ONE

THE EMPEROR WAS pretending to be a whale. He put his head under water and filled his mouth, then came back up to the surface and squirted little spouts across the palace plunge pool. I watched him out of the corner of my eye, not knowing whether to feel disdainful or sympathetic. He was, after all, an old man. Past seventy years of age, he would be relishing the touch of warm water on his blotchy skin as well as the feeling of weightlessness. He was afflicted with a bloating disease which had puffed up his body and limbs so grossly that he found walking very painful. Only the week before I had seen him return to the palace so exhausted after one of the endless ceremonials that he had collapsed into the arms of an attendant the moment the great bronze doors closed behind him. Today was the festival the Christians call Good Friday, so in the afternoon there was to be yet another imperial ceremony and it would last for hours. I decided that the emperor deserved his moment of relaxation, though his whalelike antics in the pool might have surprised his subjects as the majority of them considered him to be their God's representative on earth.

I shifted the heavy axe on my shoulder. There was a damp patch where the haft had rested on my scarlet tunic. Beads of sweat were trickling down under the rim of my iron helmet with its elaborate gold inlay, and the heat in the pool room was making me drowsy. I struggled to stay alert. As a member of the Hetaira, the imperial household troops, my duty was to protect the life of the Basileus Romanus III, ruler of Byzantium, and Equal of the Apostles. With five hundred fellow members of his personal Life Guard, the palace Varangians, I had sworn to keep the emperor safe from his enemies, and he paid us handsomely to do so. He trusted us more than his fellow countrymen, and with good reason.

At the far end of the baths were clustered a group of the emperor's staff, five or six of them. Sensibly they were maintaining their distance from their master, not just to give him privacy, but also because his advancing illness made him very tetchy. The Basileus had become notoriously short-tempered. The slightest wrong word or gesture could make him fly into a rage. During the three years I had served at the palace, I had seen him change from being even-handed and generous to waspish and mean. Men accustomed to receiving rich gifts in appreciation from the imperial bounty were now ignored or sharply criticised. Fortunately the Basileus did not yet treat his Life Guard in a similar fashion, and we still gave him our complete loyalty. We played no part in the courtiers' constant plotting and scheming as various factions sought to gain advantage. The ordinary members of the guard did not even speak their language. Our senior officers were patrician Greeks, but the rank and file were recruited from the northern lands and we continued to speak Norse among ourselves. A court official with the title of the Grand Interpreter for the Hetaira was supposed to translate for the guardsmen, but the post was in name only, another high-sounding title in a court mesmerised by precedence and ceremonial.

'Guardsman!' The shout broke into my thoughts. One man in the group was beckoning to me. I recognised the Keeper of the Imperial Inkwell. The post, despite its pompous name, was one of real importance. Officially the keeper proffered the bottle of purple ink whenever the Basileus was ready to sign an official document. In reality he acted as secretary of the emperor's private office. The post gave him open access to the imperial presence, a privilege denied even to the highest ministers, who had to make a formal appointment before being brought before the Basileus.

The keeper repeated his gesture. I glanced across at the Basileus. Romanus was still wallowing and spouting in the pool, eyes closed, happy in his warm and watery world. The pool had recently been deepened in its centre, yet was still shallow enough for a man to stand upright and keep his head above the surface. There seemed no danger there. I strode over towards the keeper, who held out a parchment. I caught a glimpse of the imperial signature in purple ink even as the keeper indicated that I was to take the document to the adjacent room, a small office where the notaries waited.

It was not unusual for a guardsman to act as a footman. The palace officials were so preoccupied with their own dignity that they found it demeaning to carry out the simplest tasks like opening a door or carrying a scroll. So I took the parchment, cast another quick look over my shoulder and walked to the door. The Basileus was still blissfully enjoying his swim.

IN THE NEXT room I found the Orphanotrophus waiting. He was in charge of the city orphanage, an institution financed from the royal purse. Once again the title was no reflection of his real importance. John the Orphanotrophus was the most powerful man in the empire, excluding only the Basileus. Thanks to a combination of raw intellect and shrewd application, John had worked his way up through the various grades of the imperial hierarchy and was prime minister of the empire in all but name. Feared by all, he was a thin man who had a gaunt face with deep-sunk eyes under startlingly black eyebrows. He was also a beardless one, a eunuch.

I came to attention in front of him, but did not salute. Only the Basileus and the immediate members of the imperial family

warranted a guardsman's salute, and John the Orphanotrophus
was certainly not born to the purple. His family came from
Paphalagonia on the Black Sea coast, and it was rumoured that
the family's first profession when they came to Constantinople
was to run a money exchange. Some said that they had been
forgers.

When I handed over the parchment, the Orphanotrophus
glanced through it, and then said to me slowly, pronouncing each
word with exaggerated care, 'Take this to the logothete of
finance.'

I stood my ground and replied in Greek, 'My apologies, your
excellency. I am on duty. I cannot leave the imperial presence.'

The Orphanotrophus raised an eyebrow. 'Well, well, a guardsman who speaks Greek,' he murmured. 'The palace is finally
becoming civilised.'

'Perhaps someone could call a dekanos, ' I suggested. 'That is
their duty, to carry messages.' I saw I had made a mistake.

'Yes, and you should do yours,' the Orphanotrophus retorted
acidly.

Smarting at the rebuff, I turned on my heel and marched back
to the baths. As I entered the long chamber with its high, domed
ceiling and walls patterned with mosaics of dolphins and waves, I
knew immediately that something was terribly wrong. The Basileus was still in the water, but now he was lying on his back,
waving feebly with his arms. Only his corpulence was keeping
him from sinking. The attendants who had previously been in the
room were nowhere to be seen. I dropped my axe to the marble
floor, wrenched off my helmet and sprinted for the pool. 'Alarm!
Alarm!' I bellowed as I ran. 'Guardsmen to me!' In a few strides
I was at the edge of the pool and, fully clothed, dived in and
swam as fast as I could manage towards the Basileus. Silently I
thanked my own God, Odinn, that we Norse learn how to swim
when we are still young.

The Basileus seemed unaware of my presence as I reached
him. He was barely moving and occasionally his head slipped

underwater. I put one hand under his chin, lowered my legs until I could touch the bottom of the pool, and began to tow him towards the edge, taking care to keep his head on my shoulder, clear of the water. He was limp in my arms, and his scalp against my chin was bald except for a few straggly hairs.

'Guardsmen to me!' I shouted again. Then in Greek I called out, 'Fetch a doctor!'

This time my calls were answered. Several staff members — scribes, attendants, courtiers — came running into the room and clustered at the edge of the pool. Someone knelt down to grab the Basileus under the armpits and haul him dripping out of the water. But the rescue was clumsy and slow. The Basileus lay on the marble edge of the pool, looking more than ever like a whale, a beached and dying one this time. I clambered out and pushed aside the courtiers.

'Help me lift him,' I said.

'In Thor's name what's going on?' said a voice.

A decurion, the petty officer of my watch, had finally arrived. He glowered so fiercely at the gawking courtiers that they fell back. The two of us picked up the emperor's limp body and carried him towards a marble bench. One of the bath attendants had the wit to spread a layer of towels over it before we laid down the old man, who was moving feebly. The decurion looked round and ripped a brocaded silk gown off the shoulders of a courtier and laid it over the emperor's nakedness.

'Let me through, please'.

This was one of the palace physicians. A short, paunchy man, he lifted up the emperor's eyelids with his stubby fingers. I could see that he was nervous. He pulled his hands back as if he had been scalded. He was probably frightened that the Basileus would expire under his touch. But the emperor's eyes stayed open and he shifted his head slightly to look around him.

At that moment there was a stir among the watching courtiers, and their circle parted to allow a woman through. It was Zoë, the empress. She must have been summoned from the gynaeceum, the women's quarters of the palace. It was the first time I had seen her close to, and I was struck by her poise. Despite her age she held herself with great dignity. She must have been at least fifty years old and had probably never been a beauty, but her face retained that fine-boned structure which hinted at aristocratic descent. She was the daughter and granddaughter of emperors, and had the haughty manners to prove it.

Zoë swept through the crowd, and stepped up to within an arm's length of her husband where he lay on the marble slab. Her face showed no emotion as she gazed down at the emperor, who was ashen pale and breathing with difficulty. For a brief moment she just stared. Then, without a word, she turned and walked out of the room.

The courtiers avoided looking at one another. Everyone, including myself, knew that there was no love between the emperor and his wife. The previous Basileus, Constantine, had insisted that they marry. Zoë was Constantine's favoured daughter, and in the last days of his reign he had searched for a suitable husband for her from among the ranks of Constantinople's aristocracy. Father and daughter had both wanted to ensure the family succession, though Zoë was past childbearing age. That had not prevented her and Romanus when they ascended the throne together from attempting to found their own dynasty. Romanus had dosed himself with huge amounts of aphrodisiacs – the reason for his hair loss, it was claimed – while his elderly consort hung herself with fertility charms and consulted quacks and charlatans who proposed more and more grotesque ways of ensuring pregnancy. When all their efforts failed, the couple slid into a mutual dislike. Romanus had taken a mistress and Zoë had been bundled off to the gynaeceum, frustrated and resentful.

But that was not the whole story. Zoë had also acquired a lover, not two years since. Several members of the guard had come across the two of them coupling together and turned a blind eye. Their tact had not been out of respect for the empress – she conducted her affair openly – but because her consort was the younger brother of John the Orphanotrophus. Here was an area where high politics mingled with ambition and lust, and it was better left alone.

'Stand back!' ordered the decurion.

He took up his position a spear's length from the Basileus's bald head, and as a reflex I stationed myself by the emperor's feet and also came to attention. My axe was still lying somewhere on the marble floor, but I was wearing a dagger at my belt and I dropped my hand to its hilt. The doctor paced nervously up and down, wringing his hands with worry. Suddenly Romanus gave a deep moan. He raised his head a fraction from the towel that was his pillow and made a slight gesture with his right hand. It was as if he was beckoning someone closer. Not knowing whom he gestured to, no one dared move. The awe and majesty of the imperial presence still had a grip on the spectators. The emperor's gaze shifted slowly, passing across the faces of his watching courtiers. He seemed to be trying to say something, to be pleading. His throat moved but no sounds emerged. Then his eyes closed and his head fell back and rolled to one side. He began to pant, his breath coming in short shallow gasps. Suddenly, the breathing paused, and his mouth fell open. Out flowed a thick, dark brown substance, and after two more choking breaths, he expired.

I stood rigidly to attention. There were the sounds of running feet, of tumult, and in the distance a wailing and crying as news of the emperor's death spread among the palace staff. I took no notice. Until a new Basileus was crowned, the duty of the guard was to protect the body of the dead emperor.

'Thorgils, you look like the village idiot standing there in your soaking uniform. Get back to the guardroom and report to the duty officer.'

The instructions were delivered in Norse and I recognised the voice of Halfdan, my company commander. A beefy veteran, Halfdan had served in the Life Guard for close on ten years. He should have retired by now, after amassing a small fortune from his salary, but he liked the life of a guardsman and had cut his ties with his Danish homeland, so he had nowhere else to go.

'Tell him that everything is under control in the imperial presence. You might suggest that he places a curfew on the palace.'

I squelched away, pausing to collect my helmet and the spiked axe which someone had obligingly picked up off the floor and leaned against the wall. My route to the guardroom lay through a labyrinth of passages, reception rooms and courtyards. Romanus III could have died in any one of his palaces – they all had swimming pools – but he had chosen to expire in the largest and most sprawling of them, the Great Palace. Standing close to the tip of the peninsula of Constantinople, the Great Palace had been extended and remodelled so many times by its imperial occupants that it had turned into a bewildering maze of chambers and anterooms. Erecting ever grander buildings was a fascination bordering on mania for each occupant of the purple throne. Every Basileus wanted to immortalise his rule by leaving at least one extravagant structure, whether a new church, a monastery, a huge palace, or some ostentatious public building. Romanus had been busily squandering millions of gold pieces on an immense new church to the mother of his God, though it seemed to me that she already had more than enough churches and monasteries to her name. Romanus's new church was to be dedicated to her as Mary the Celebrated, and what with its surrounding gardens and walkways and fountains – and the constant changes of design, which meant pulling down half-finished buildings – the project had run so far over budget that Romanus had been obliged to raise a special tax to pay for the construction. The church was not yet finished and I suspected it never would be. I surprised myself by realising how easily I was already thinking of Romanus in the past tense.

'Change into a dry uniform and join the detail on the main gate,' the duty officer ordered when I reported to him. No more than twenty years old, he was almost as edgy as the physician who had attended the dying emperor. A Greek from one of Constantinople's leading families, his family would have paid handsomely to buy his commission in the Life Guard. Merely by placing him inside the walls of the palace, they hoped he might attract the attention of the Basileus and gain preferment. Now their investment would be wasted if a new Basileus decided, out of concern for his own safety, to replace all the Greek officers. It was another deception so characteristic of palace life. Byzantine society still pretended that the Hetaira was Greek. Their sons prided themselves on being officers of the guard, and they dressed up in uniforms which denoted the old palace regiments – the Excubia, the Numeri, the Scholae and others – but when it came to real work our Basileus had trusted only us, the foreigners, his palace Varangians.

I joined twenty of my comrades at the main gate. They had already slammed the doors shut without asking permission of the keeper of the gate, whose duty it was to supervise the opening of the main gate at dawn, close it again at noon, and then reopen it for a few hours in the early evening. But today the death of the emperor had removed his authority and the keeper was at a loss to know what to do. The decurion decided the matter for him. He was refusing to let anyone in or out.

Even as I arrived, there was a great hubbub outside the gate, and I could hear thunderous knocking and loud, impatient shouts.

'Glad you've got here, Thorgils,' said the guard commander. 'Maybe you can tell me what those wild men out there want.'

I listened carefully. 'I think you had better let them in,' I said. 'It sounds as though you've got the Great Patriarch outside, and he's demanding admittance.'

'The Great Patriarch? That black-clad old goat,' grumbled the guard commander, who was a staunch Old Believer. 'Lads, open the side door and allow the monks through. But hold your breath. They don't wash very often.'

A moment later a very angry group of monks, all with chest-length beards and black gowns, stormed through the gap between the doors, glared at us, and hurried off down the corridor with a righteous-sounding slap of sandals and the clatter of their wooden staffs on the marble floor slabs. In their midst I saw the white-bearded figure of Alexis of the Studius, the supreme religious authority of the empire.

'Wonder what's brought them down from their monastery in such a hurry,' muttered a Varangian as he pushed shut the door and dropped the bar back in place.

His question was answered later, when we came off duty and returned to the guardroom. Half a dozen of my colleagues were lounging there, smirking.

'The old bitch has already got herself a new husband. The moment she was sure that old Romanus was definitely on his way out, she sent someone to fetch the high priest.'

'I know, we let him and his crows in.'

'Well, she certainly didn't summon them to give her beloved husband the last rites. Even while the priests were on their way, the old lady called an emergency meeting of her advisers, including that foxy creep, the Orphanotrophus. She told them that she wanted her fancy-boy to be the new Basileus.'

'Not the handsome rattle-brain!'

'She had it all worked out. She said that, by right of imperial descent, she represented the continuity of the state, and that it was in the best interests of the empire if "my darling Michael", as she called him, took the throne with her.'

'You must be joking! How do you know all this?'

The guardsman gave a snort of derision. 'The Orphanotrophus had ordered four of us to act as close escort for the empress in case there was an attempt on her life. It was a ruse, of course. When the other courtiers showed up to dispute the idea of Michael's succession, they saw the guard standing there, and came to the conclusion that the matter had already been settled.'

'So what happened when the high priest arrived?'

'He plunged straight into the wedding ceremony for the old

woman and her lover-boy. She paid him a fat bribe, of course, and within the hour they were man and wife.'

This bizarre story was interrupted by the arrival of another of our Greek officers, who scuttled into the room, anxiously demanding a full sovereign's escort. We were to don our formal uniforms and accompany him to the Triklinium, the grand audience chamber. He insisted that there was not a moment to be lost.

Thirty of us formed up and marched through the passageways to the enormous hall, floored with mosaics, hung with silk banners and decorated with rich icons, where the Basileus formally received his ministers, foreign ambassadors and other dignitaries. Two ornate thrones stood on a dais at the far end of the hall and our officer led us straight to our positions – to stand in a semicircle at the back of the dais, looking out across the audience chamber. A dozen equerries and the marshal of the Triklinium were busily making sure that everything was in order for the arrival of their majesties. Within moments the Empress Zoë and Michael, her new husband, entered the room and hurried up to the thrones. Close behind came the Orphanotrophus, some high-ranking priests, and a gaggle of courtiers associated with the empress's faction at court. Zoë and Michael stepped up on the dais, our Greek officer hissed a command, and we, the members of the Life Guard, obediently raised our axes vertically in front of us in a formal salute. The empress and emperor turned to face down the hall. Just as they were about to sit down there came a tense moment. By custom the guard acknowledges the presence of the Basileus as he takes his seat upon the throne. As the emperor lowers himself on to his seat, the guards transfer their axes from the salute to their right shoulders. It is a signal that all is well and that the business of the empire is continuing as normal. Now, as Zoë and Michael were about to settle on their throne cushions, my comrades and I glanced at one another questioningly. For the space of a heartbeat nothing happened. I sensed our Greek officer stiffen with anxiety, and then, raggedly, the guard placed their axes on their shoulders. I could almost hear the sigh of relief from Zoë's retinue.

That crisis safely past, the proceedings quickly took on an air of farce. Zoë's people must have sent word throughout the palace, summoning the senior ministers and their staff, who came in one by one. Many, I suspected, arrived thinking that they would be paying their respects to the body of their dead emperor. Instead they were confronted with the astonishing spectacle of his widow already remarried and seated beside a new husband nearly young enough to be her grandson. No wonder several of the new arrivals faltered on the threshold, dumbfounded. The matronly empress and her youthful consort were clutching the emblems of state in their jewelled hands, their glittering robes had been carefully arranged by their pages, and on Zoë's face was an expression which showed that she expected full homage. From the back of the dais I watched the courtiers' eyes take in the scene – the aloof empress, her boyish husband, the waiting cluster of high officials, and the sinister, brooding figure of John the Orphanotrophus, Michael's brother, noting how each new arrival responded. After a brief moment of hesitation and calculation, the high ministers and courtiers came forward to the twin thrones, bowed deeply to the empress, then knelt and kissed the ring of her bright-eyed husband, who, less than six hours earlier, had been known as nothing more than her illicit lover.

The next day we buried Romanus. Overnight someone – it must have been the supremely efficient Orphanotrophus – arranged for his swollen corpse to be dressed in official robes of purple silk and laid out on a bier. Within an hour of sunrise the funeral procession had already assembled with everyone in their correct place according to rank, and the palace's main gates were thrown open. I was one of the one hundred guards who marched, according to tradition, immediately before and after the dead Basileus as we emerged on to the Mese, the broad main avenue which bisects the city. I was surprised to see how many of the citizens of Constantinople had left their beds this early. Word of the Basileus's sudden death must have spread very fast. Those who stood at the front of the dense crowd lining the route could see for themselves the waxen skin and swollen face of the dead emperor, for his head and hands had been left uncovered. Once or twice I heard someone shout out, 'Poisoned!', but for the most part the crowd remained eerily silent. I did not hear a single expression of sorrow or regret for his passing. Romanus III, I realised, had not been popular in Constantinople.

At the great Forum of Amastration we wheeled left, and half a mile further on the cortège entered the Via Triumphalis. Normally an emperor processed along this broad avenue to the cheers of the crowd, at the head of his victorious troops, as he displayed captured booty and files of defeated enemy in chains. Now Romanus was carried in the opposite direction in a gloomy silence broken only by the creaking wheels of the carriage which carried his bier, the sound of the horses' hooves and the muted footfalls of hundreds upon hundreds of the ordinary citizens of Constantinople, who, simply out of morbid curiosity, joined in behind our procession. They went with us all the way to the enormous unfinished church of Mary the Celebrated that was Romanus's great project, and where he was now the first person to benefit from his own extravagance. Here the priests hurriedly placed him into the green and white sarcophagus which Romanus had selected for himself, following another curious imperial custom that the Basileus should choose his own tomb on the day of his accession.

Then, as the crowd was dispersing in a mood of sombre apathy, our cortège briskly retraced its steps to the palace, for there was no a moment to be lost.

'Two parades in one day, but it will be worth it,' said Halfdan cheerfully as he shrugged off the dark sash he had worn during the funeral and replaced it with one that glittered with gold thread. 'Thank Christ it's only a short march this afternoon, and anyhow we would have to be doing it anyway as it's Palm Sunday.'

Halfdan, like several members of the guard, was part-Christian and part-pagan. Superficially he subscribed to the religion of the White Christ – and swore by him – and he attended services at the new church to St Olaf recently built near our regimental headquarters down by the Golden Horn, Constantinople's main harbour. But he also wore Thor's hammer as an amulet on a leather strap around his neck, and when he was in his cups he often announced that when he died he would much prefer to feast and fight in Odinn's Valholl than finish up as a bloodless being with wings like a fluffy dove in the Christians' heaven.

'Thorgils, how come you speak Greek so well?' The question came from one of the Varangians who had been at the palace gate the previous day. He was a recent recruit into the guard.

'He licked up a drop of Fafnir's blood, that's how,' Halfdan interjected. 'Give Thorgils a couple of weeks and he could learn any language, even if it's bird talk.'

I ignored his ponderous attempt at humour. 'I was made to study Greek when I was a youngster,' I said, 'in a monastery in Ireland.'

'You were once a monk?' the man asked, surprised. 'I thought you were a devotee of Odinn. At least that is what I've heard.'

'I am,' I told him. 'Odinn watched over me when I was among the monks and got me away from them.'

'Then you understand this stuff with the holy pictures they carry about whenever we're on parade, the relics and bits of saints and all the rest of it.'

'Some of it. But the Christianity I was made to study is different from the one here in Constantinople. It's the same God, of course, but a different way of worshipping him. I must admit that until I came here, I had never even heard of half of the saints they honour.'

'Not surprising,' grumbled the Varangian. 'Down in the market last week a huckster tried to sell me a human bone. Said it came from the right arm of St Demetrios, and I should buy it because I was a soldier and St Demetrios was a fighting man. He claimed the relic would bring me victory in any fight.'

'I hope you didn't buy it.'

'Not a chance. Someone in the crowd warned me that the huckster had sold so many arm and leg bones from St Demetrios that the holy martyr must have had more limbs than a centipede.' He gave a wry laugh.

Later that afternoon I sympathised with the soldier as we marched off for the acclamation of our young new Basileus, who was to be pronounced as Michael IV before a congregation of city dignitaries in the church of Hagia Sophia. We shuffled rather than marched towards the church because there were so many slow-moving priests in the column, all holding up pictures of their saints painted on wooden boards, tottering under heavy banners and pennants embroidered with holy symbols, or carrying precious relics of their faith sealed in gold and silver caskets. Just in front of me was their most venerated memento, a fragment from the wooden cross on which their Christ had hung at the time of his death, and I wondered if perhaps Odinn, the master of disguise, had impersonated their Jesus. The Father of the Gods had also hung on a wooden tree, his side pierced with a spear as he sought to gain world knowledge. It was a pity, I thought to myself, that the Christians were so certain that theirs was the only true faith. If they were a little more tolerant, they would have admitted that other religions had their merits, too. Old Believers were perfectly willing to let people follow their own gods, and we did not seek to impose our ideas on others. But at least the Christians of Constantinople were not as bigoted as their brethren further north, who were busy stamping out what they considered pagan practices. In Constantinople life was tolerant enough for there to be a mosque in the sixth district where the Saracens could worship and several synagogues for the Jews.

A hundred paces from the doors of Hagia Sophia, we, the members of the guard, came to a halt while the rest of the procession solemnly walked on and entered the church. The priests had no love for the Varangians, and it was customary for us to wait outside until the service was concluded. Presumably it was thought that no one would make an attempt on the life of the Basileus inside such a sacred building, but I had my doubts.

Halfdan let my company stand at ease, and we stood and chatted idly among ourselves, waiting for the service to end and to escort the acclaimed Basileus back to the palace. It was then that I noticed a young man dressed in the characteristic hooded gown of a middle-class citizen, a junior clerk by the look of him. He was approaching various members of the guard to try to speak to them. He must have been asking his questions in Greek, for they either shook their heads uncomprehendingly or ignored him. Eventually someone pointed in my direction and he came over towards me. He introduced himself as Constantine Psellus, and said he was a student in the city, studying to enter the imperial service. I judged him to be no more than sixteen or seventeen years old, about half my age.

'I am planning to write a history of the empire,' he told me, 'a chapter for each emperor, and I would very much appreciate any details of the last days of Basileus Romanus.'

I liked his formal politeness and was impressed by his air of quick intelligence, so decided to help him out.

'I was present when he drowned,' I said, and briefly sketched what I had witnessed.

'You say he drowned?' commented the young man gently.

'Yes, that seems to have been the case. Though he actually expired when he was laid out on the bench. Maybe he had a heart attack. He was old enough, after all.'

'I saw his corpse yesterday when it was being carried in the funeral procession, and I thought it looked very strange, so puffed up and grey.'

'Oh, he had had that appearance for quite some time.'

'You don't think he died from some other cause, the effects of a slow-acting poison maybe?' the young man suggested as calmly as if he had been discussing a change in the weather. 'Or perhaps you were deliberately called away from the baths so someone could hold the emperor underwater for a few moments to bring on a heart attack.'

The theory of poisoning had been discussed in the guardroom ever since the emperor's death, and some of us had gone as far as debating whether it was hellebore or some other poison which was being fed to Romanus. But it was not our job to enquire further: our responsibility was to defend him from violent physical attack, the sort you block with a shield or deflect with a shrewd axe blow, not the insidious assault of a lethal drug in his food or drink. The Basileus employed food-tasters for that work, though they could be bribed to act a sham, and any astute assassin would make sure that the poison was slow-acting enough for its effect not to be detected until too late.

But the young man's other suggestion, that I had been lured away to leave Romanus unguarded, alarmed me. If that was the case, then the Keeper of the Inkwell was certainly implicated in the Basileus's death, and perhaps the Orphanotrophus as well. I remembered how he had tried to send me on to the logothete of finance with the parchment. That would have delayed me even more. The thought that I might have been a dupe in the assassination of the Basileus brought a chill to my spine. If true, I was in real danger. Any guardsman found to be negligent in his duty to protect the Basileus was executed by his company commander, usually by public beheading. More than that, if Romanus had indeed been murdered, I was still a potential witness, and that meant I was a likely target for elimination by the culprits. Someone as powerful as the Orphanotrophus could easily have me killed, in a tavern brawl, for example.

Suddenly I was very frightened.

'I think I hear the chanting of the priests,' said Psellus, interrupting my thoughts and fidgeting slightly. Maybe he realised he had gone too far in his theorising, and was close to treason. 'They must have opened the doors of Hagia Sophia, getting ready for the emergence of our new Basileus. It's time for me to let you

go. Thank you for your information. You have been most helpful.'
And he slipped away into the crowd.

We took up our positions around Michael IV, who was
mounted on a superb sorrel horse, one of the best in the royal
stables. I remembered how Romanus had been a great judge of
horseflesh and had built up a magnificent stud farm, though he
had been too sick to enjoy riding. Now I had to admit that the
youthful Michael, though he came from a very plebeian background, looked truly imperial in the saddle. Perhaps that was
what Zoë had seen in him from the beginning. Halfdan had told
me how he had been on duty when Zoë had first gazed on her
future lover. 'You would have been an utter dolt not to have
noticed her reaction. She couldn't take her eyes off him. It was
the Orphanotrophus who introduced him to her. He brought
Michael into the audience chamber when Zoë and Romanus were
holding an imperial reception, and led him right up to the twin
thrones. Old Romanus was gracious enough, but Zoë looked at
the young man as if she wanted to eat him on the spot. He was
good looking, all right, fresh-faced and ruddy-cheeked, likely to
blush like a girl. I reckon the Orphanotrophus knew what he was
doing. Set it all up.'

'Didn't Romanus notice, if it was that obvious?' I asked.

'No. The old boy barely used to look at the empress by then.
Kept looking anywhere except in her direction, as though her
presence gave him a pain.'

I mulled over the conversation as we marched back to the
Grand Palace, entered the great courtyard and the gates were
closed behind us. Our new Basileus dismounted, paused for a
moment while his courtiers and officials formed up in two lines,
and then walked down between them to the applause and smiles
of his retinue before entering the palace. I noted that the Basileus
was unescorted, which seemed very unusual. Even stranger was
the fact that the courtiers broke ranks and began to hurry into the
palace behind the Basileus, almost like a mob. Halfdan astonished
me by rushing off in their wake, all discipline gone. So did the

guardsmen around me, and I joined them in pushing and jostling as if we were a crowd of spectators leaving the hippodrome at the end of the games.

It was unimaginable. All the stiffness and formality of court life had evaporated. The crowd of us, ministers, courtiers, advisers, even priests, all flooded into the great Trikilinium. There, seated up on the dais, was our young new emperor, smiling down at us. On each side were two slaves holding small strongboxes. As I watched, one of the slaves tilted the coffer he held and a stream of gold coins poured out, falling into the emperor's lap. Michael reached down, seized a fistful of the coins, and flung them high into the air above the crowd. I gaped in surprise. The shower of gold coins, each one of them worth six months' wages for a skilled man, glittered and flashed before plummeting towards the upstretched hands. A few coins were caught as they fell, but most tumbled on to the marble floor, landing with a distinct ringing sound. Men dropped to their hands and knees to pick up the coins, even as the emperor dipped his hand into his lap and flung another golden cascade over our heads. Now I understood why Halfdan had been so quick off the mark. My company commander had shrewdly elbowed his way to a spot where the arc of bullion was thickest, and was clawing up the golden bounty.

I, too, crouched down and began to gather up the coins. But at the very moment that my fingers closed around the first gold coin, I was thinking to myself that I would be wise to find some way of resigning from the Life Guard without attracting attention before it was too late.

TWO

THE THOUGHT THAT Romanus had been murdered nagged at me in the weeks that followed. I brooded on the possible consequences of my unwitting participation in a regicide and began to take precautions for my personal safety. I only ate mess food prepared by the army cooks, and I did not leave the barracks unless I was on duty or in the company of two or three of my colleagues, and then I only visited places I knew to be safe. Had my companions realised my fears, they would have scoffed at my timidity. Compared with the other cities I had known – London for example – Constantinople was remarkably peaceful and well run. Its governor, the city eparch, maintained an efficient police force, while a host of civic employees patrolled the marketplaces, checking on fair trade, cleanliness and orderly behaviour. Only at night, when the streets were given over to prostitutes and thieves, would my colleagues have bothered to carry weapons to defend themselves. But I was not reassured. If I was to be silenced for what I had witnessed in the imperial swimming pool, then the attack would come when I was least expecting it.

The one person to whom I confessed my fears was my friend Pelagia. She ran a bread stall on the Mese, and I had been seeing her twice a week to practise my conversational Greek because the language I had learned in the Irish monastery was antiquated and closer, coincidentally, to the language spoken in the imperial court than koine, the language of the common people. An energetic, shrewd woman with the characteristic dark hair and sallow skin of someone native to the city, Pelagia had already provided me with a lesson in the tortuous ways of Byzantine thinking, which often succeeded in extracting advantage from calamity. She had started her business just days after her husband, a baker, had burned to death in a blaze which had started when the bread oven cracked. A city ordinance banned bakeries from operating in close proximity to town houses, otherwise the accident would have sent the entire district up in flames. The ashes of the fire were barely cold before Pelagia had gone to her husband's former business competitors and worked on their sympathy. She coaxed them into agreeing to supply her stall at a favourable discount, and by the time I met her she was well on her way to being a wealthy woman. Pelagia kept me up to date with all the latest city rumours about palace politics – a favourite topic among her many clients – and, more important, she had a sister who worked as a seamstress for the empress Zoë.

'No one doubts that Zoë had a hand in Romanus's death, though it's less certain that she actively organised what happened in the bathhouse,' Pelagia told me. We had met in the spacious rooms of her third-floor apartment. Astonishing to people like myself from lands where a two-storeyed building is unusual, many of Constantinople's houses had four or even five floors. 'My sister tells me that poisons of every sort are readily available in the empress's quarters. They are not even kept locked up for safety. Zoë has a mania for creating new perfumes and unguents. Some say it's a hangover from the days when she was trying to rejuvenate herself and bear a child. She keeps a small army of women servants grinding, mixing and distilling different concoctions, and several of the ingredients are decidedly poisonous. One young girl fainted the other day merely from inhaling the fumes from one of the brews.'

'So you think Zoë was the poisoner, but not the person who

arranged for Romanus to have an accident during his swim,' I asked.

'It's hard to say. If the empress did plot with her lover to do away with Romanus and rule the empire through him, she's been disappointed. Michael, my sister tells me, has been acting as if he alone is in charge. She is not consulted on matters of state – they are all taken care of by his brother, the Orphanotrophus. So if Zoë had nothing to do with the murder, she may well bring an accusation against the new Basileus in order to overthrow him. Either way, you are in real danger. If there is an enquiry, the investigating tribunal will call witnesses to Romanus's death, and their usual way of interrogating witnesses is to torture them.'

'I don't follow you,' I said. 'Surely if there was a conspiracy between Zoë and Michael, neither party would want to risk it being discovered. And if only Michael is guilty, and perhaps the Orphanotrophus as well, then Zoë would be unlikely to harm the man with whom she is infatuated.'

'You don't know what a silly and capricious woman Zoë can be, despite her age and position,' Pelagia replied witheringly. 'My sister has been talking to some of the people who look after Zoë's wardrobe. Apparently Zoë feels that she is a woman scorned. Michael has banished her to the gynaeceum, and doesn't even visit her bedchamber as often as when she was still married to Romanus. Now there is even a rumour that Michael has some sort of incurable sickness and that the Orphanotrophus deliberately hid that fact from Zoë when he first introduced him to her.'

The intrigues of the court were beyond normal comprehension, I thought to myself. Never would I be able to untangle the subterfuges of those who seek or wield absolute power. It would be better for me to make myself as unobtrusive as possible and place my trust in the protection of Odinn, the arch-deceiver. I promised myself that next time my Christianised comrades in the guard went off to pray in the new church to St Olaf, I would find a quiet spot and make an offering to the All Wise. Perhaps the God of Cargoes would show me a way out of my predicament.

It turned out that Odinn answered even before I made the sacrifice. But first he gave me a fright I was to remember for the rest of my days in the service of the Basileus.

Early in June Pelagia told me that a report was sweeping the city that a force of Rus were about to attack Constantinople. A war fleet had been sighted making its way down the great river which leads from the kingdom of Kiev.

'Of course you know that route yourself, Thorgils. That's the way you came to Constantinople,' Pelagia said. She was standing in the shade of the portico behind her bread stall, chatting with a group of her fellow traders while her assistant sold the loaves off the counter.

'No, I came by a different route, along another river further east. But it's much the same thing: all paths lead to Constantinople.'

'Just as all Rus are much the same thing – violent, hairy barbarians who worship idols.' The jibe came from one of Pelagia's fellow stallholders, another bread-seller who had the chirpy swagger of a true city-dweller. Over his stall hung a crudely sketched picture of the White Christ issuing loaves and fishes to the multitude, so I knew him to be a vehement Christian.

'Well, not exactly,' I corrected him mildly. 'The people you lump together as Rus are all sorts and types – those who come from Kiev are Christians and acknowledge your own Great Patriarch. Others like myself are from the lands of the northmen and, while we follow our own gods, we come to trade not to fight. Half your churches would be in darkness if those so-called barbarians didn't bring beeswax from the northern forests for you to turn into candles to illuminate your painted saints while you adore them.'

The stallholder was not to be placated. 'This city can defend itself whatever that scum throws at it. You would have thought they had learned their lesson last time.' He saw I had missed his point. 'My grandfather loved telling me how we dealt with those ignorant savages the last time they dared to assault the Queen of

Cities. They showed up with their fleet expecting to swarm in and put the place to the sack. But Blessed Mary and our Basileus protected us. The enemy never even got past the city walls – much too strong for them. So they muddled about, went here and there in their stupid, mindless way, raiding and raping in small settlements along the coast. But all the while our Basileus was biding his time. He waited until the Rus were off guard, and then sent out our ships and caught them fair and square. We burned them to cinders with the Fire. They never knew what hit them. Less than a hundred of them returned home. It was a massacre. My grandfather told me that burned bodies were washing up on the shore, and you could smell the stench of burned flesh . . .' At that moment he must have remembered how Pelagia's husband had died, for his voice trailed away in embarrassment and he looked down at his feet before finding an excuse to turn away and attend to the display on his stall.

I was about to ask Pelagia what the man had meant by 'the Fire', when I heard my name called out, and turned to see Halfdan pushing through the crowd towards me. Close behind him was a palace messenger.

'There you are, Thorgils. Thought I might find you here with Pelagia,' Halfdan exclaimed, though without the innuendo that normally accompanied his mention of Pelagia's name. 'There's some sort of flap on at the palace, and it involves you. You are to report at once to the office of the Orphanotrophus. It's urgent.'

Panic gripped me as I glanced across at Pelagia. There was no mistaking the alarm in her expression too.

I quickly followed the messenger to the palace. He brought me to the office of the Orphanotrophus, where I noticed that the emperor's eunuch brother had appropriated for himself the chambers immediately beside the staterooms of the Basileus. My colleagues who were on duty glanced at me curiously as I passed them. Never before had any of them seen a mere guardsman summoned in this way.

A moment later my stomach was churning with anxiety as I

stood in front of John. He was sitting at an ornate desk, reading through a document, and when he raised his head to look at me, I thought how very tired he seemed. His eyes were sunk even deeper than usual. Perhaps the cares of state were weighing more heavily than he had expected, or maybe the rumours in the marketplace were true: that the Orphanotrophus never slept, but in the night dressed up as a monk and walked the streets of the city, eavesdropping on conversations, questioning ordinary citizens and learning the mood of the people. It was little wonder that people feared him. Certainly I felt sick with apprehension as I waited for him to speak. And his first words told me that he remembered exactly who I was.

'I have summoned you because you speak excellent Greek as well as Varangian,' he said. 'I have a mission for you.'

The tight knot in my stomach began to relax, but only for a moment. Was this another court deceit? Was the Orphanotrophus putting me at ease before revealing his true intention?

'My agents tell me that a large force of Rus is approaching. It appears that there are about five hundred of them travelling in monocylon, the vessels which traders from Rus normally use, and they are coming by the same route.'

Five hundred Rus did not amount to an invading force, I thought to myself. The market rumour was greatly exaggerated. It would take at least ten times that number to pose a threat to Constantinople's well-tried defences.

As though reading my mind, the Orphanotrophus added, 'I'm not concerned about the safety of the city. What does interest me is that my informants tell me these men are not merchants. They do not carry trade goods, they are heavily armed and there is a report that their leader is some sort of prince or nobleman. His name is Araltes, or something like that. Do you know anyone by this name?'

'No, your excellency,' I replied. 'It's not a name that I am familiar with.'

'You soon will be,' the Orphanotrophus replied dryly. 'I have given orders that the foreigners are to be intercepted at the entrance to the straits. They will be escorted to the district of St Mamas on the opposite side of the Golden Horn and held there, well away from the city, pending an investigation of their intentions. That is where you come in. I want to know who they are and why they have come here. If they are Rus, you will understand their language when they speak among themselves, and you seem to be an intelligent man who can make his own judgements and ask the right questions. Afterwards you come back to me and report your impressions in person.'

'Yes, your excellency,' I answered, beginning to think that I had been unnecessarily suspicious of John. 'When do you expect the foreigners to arrive?'

'In three days' time,' he answered. 'Now go and report to my chief chartularius. He will write out your instructions. Officially you will be serving as escort to the deputation from the office of dromos.' He paused, and then said something which – as intended – reminded me of the words I had used when delivering the message that lured me from my duty to guard the Basileus. 'As I'm sure you are aware,' the eunuch continued softly, 'the logothete of the dromos is responsible for foreign relations, secret intelligence and embassies, as well as the imperial postal system – a curious mixture, don't you think? – while the dekanos are the palace messengers. So the men from the dromos will manage the official contact with these five hundred barbarians, but you are my eyes and ears. I want you to eavesdrop on the foreigners for me.'

My interview was at an end. I looked into the hooded eyes of the Orphanotrophus and, with numbing certainty, understood why he was so confident that I would act as his spy, even against my own people. It was just as Pelagia had said: it did not matter whether John had plotted to put his brother Michael on the throne. Basileus Romanus had died during my watch, when I had been responsible for his safety. John had witnessed my dereliction of duty and he could bring me to account at any time he chose. I was at his mercy. Yet he was too subtle to mention that fact

outright. He preferred to rely on my fear and make me his
creature.

So it was that three days after my interview with the Basileus's
sinister brother I was aboard a small ferry boat, being rowed
across the choppy waters of the Golden Horn towards the landing
place at Mamas. With me were two dour-looking officials from
the secretariat of the dromos. To judge from their manner, they
thought it was a vile imposition to be plucked from the calm
shelter of their offices and sent to interview a gang of uncouth
barbarians from the north. One of the officials wrinkled his nose
with distaste as he clutched his robe so that the hem did not get
soaked by the slop of bilge water. Since they were on official
business, both he and his colleague were wearing formal costumes
which denoted their bureaucratic rank. His cloak had a green
border, so I knew he was a high-ranking civil servant, and I
wondered whether he too spoke Norse. The office of the dromos
maintained a college of trained interpreters and it would be typical
of the Orphanotrophus to send not one but two spies so he could
cross-check their impressions.

As our little boat approached the landing stage, the sight of
the moored flotilla of a dozen or so boats suddenly made me
homesick for the northern lands. The monocylon, as John had
called them, were a smaller version of the curved seagoing ships I
had known all my life. The boats docked at Mamas were less well
built than genuine ocean-going vessels, but they were handy
enough for short sea crossings and very different from the tubby
hulls favoured by the Greeks. My nostalgia grew as I scrambled
up on to the quay and walked across the open ground where the
foreigners had been given permission to pitch their tents. There
were piles of flax sails, wooden kegs, spars, coils of rope, anchors
and other ship's gear, all so familiar to me. I could smell the tar
on the ropes and the grease on the leather straps of the steering
blades. Even the stacked oars were of the same pattern I had used
when I was a youngster.

The encampment, with its neat rows of tents, had a vaguely

military feeling, and I understood why the imperial spies had reported their unease. This large assembly of travellers had definitely not come to Constantinople to buy and sell goods. The men strolling around the camp, hovering over the cooking pots, or simply lazing in the sun, all had the look of warriors. They were big and self-confident and they were Norse – that was sure. They had the blond colouring of the Norse, the long hair and luxuriant beards, and they wore the characteristic heavy leggings and cross-garters, though their tunics were a motley of colours and cloths, ranging from linen to leather. One or two even wore sheepskin jerkins, which were highly unsuitable in Constantinople's sunshine.

I scarcely attracted a glance from these burly strangers as I headed for a tent, larger than the others, which stood apart. I recognised it at once as a command tent, and did not need to be told that this was where we would find the leaders of this unknown group.

Gesturing to my two companions that they should wait outside, I pushed open the door flap. As I entered, it took a moment for my eyes to adjust to the subdued light. Around a trestle table stood a group of four or five men. Observing that I was a stranger and dressed in a foreign uniform – for I wore the guards' scarlet tunic – they waited impassively for me to explain what I wanted. But one man, thickset, with bushy grey hair and a heavy beard, reacted differently. He stared hard at me.

There was an awkward silence while I wondered how I should introduce myself, and what tone I should adopt. Then the silence was broken. 'Thorgils Leifsson! By all the Gods, if it isn't Thorgils!' the grey-haired man exclaimed loudly. He spoke with an unmistakable Icelandic accent, and I could even pick out which region of Iceland he came from: he was a man from the west fjords. His voice also gave me the clue to his identity, and a moment later I placed him. He was Halldor Snorrason, fifth son of Snorri Godi, with whose family I had stayed in Iceland as a

young man. In fact, Halldor's sister Hallbera had been the first
girl with whom I had fallen in love, and Halldor's father had
played a crucial role in my teenage years.

'What's that fancy uniform you're wearing?' Halldor asked,
striding across to clap me on the shoulder. 'The last we heard,
you were headed off into Permia to buy furs from the ski-runners.
Don't tell me that Thorgils, former associate of that outlaw
Grettir the Strong, is now a member of the imperial Life Guard.'

'Yes, I'll have been a guardsman three years this autumn,' I
said, and here I dropped my voice in case the men from the
dromos could hear me through the tent cloth. 'I've been sent to
find out what you and your comrades are doing, and why you
have come to Constantinople.'

'Oh, that's no secret. You can go back to your chief and tell
him that we've come to offer our services as fighting men to the
Emperor of Miklagard,' Halldor replied cheerfully. 'We hear that
he pays very well and the chances of loot are excellent. We want
to go home as rich men!' He laughed.

I had to smile at his enthusiasm. 'What? All of you want to
join the Life Guard? I'm told that there are five hundred of you.
A recruit only joins when there is a vacancy and there is a long
waiting list.'

'No,' said Halldor. 'We don't want to join the guard. Our
plan is to stay together as a single fighting unit.'

The idea was so unexpected that for a moment I was silenced.
Norsemen did not usually form themselves into disciplined warrior
brigades, particularly when they were roving freebooters hoping
to loot and plunder. They were far too independent-minded.
There had to be another factor.

Halldor saw my puzzlement. 'Every one of us has already
pledged allegiance to one man, a single leader. If he finds service
with the Basileus, then we follow him.'

'Who is that man?' I asked.

'I am,' said a deep voice, and I turned to see a tall, soldierly figure stooping in under the door flap at the far end of the tent. He straightened up to his full height, and in that instant I knew that Odinn had answered my profoundest hope.

Harald Sigurdsson – as I soon knew him to be and that was long before he became known as Hardrada, 'Hard Ruler' – stood a little under six and a half feet tall, and in the half light of the tent he was like a hero emerging from the shadowy world of the earliest sagas. Broad-shouldered and muscular, he moved with an athletic grace, towering over the other men. When he came closer, I imagined for a moment that I was looking up into the face of someone I had heard described in a fireside tale when I was a child. He had the fierce look of a sea eagle. His prominent nose was like a beak, while his close-set bright blue eyes had an intense, almost unblinking stare. His thick yellow hair, too, resembled the ruff of long feathers around a sea eagle's neck, for it hung down to his shoulders, and he had a quick way of turning his head, like a bird of prey seeking a victim, so that the hair shifted on his shoulders like an eagle's ruff. His moustache was even more spectacular. It was dressed in a style long out of fashion: two thick strands of moustache hung down on either side of his mouth, like blond silk cords, and dangled against his chest.

'And who are you?' he demanded.

I was so stunned by his appearance that I faltered in my reply, and Halldor had to fill the gap for me.

'He is Thorgils, son of Leif the Lucky,' said the Icelander. 'He used to stay at my father's place in Iceland when he was a teenager.'

'He's your foster brother?'

'No – my father took an interest in him because he was what you might call gifted. He has, or had, the second sight.'

The giant Norseman turned towards me, and his eyes searched my face, judging me. I sensed that he was calculating whether I could be useful to him.

'Is that the uniform of an imperial Life Guard?'

'Yes, my lord,' I replied. Calling him 'my lord' seemed utterly natural. If ever I had seen a born aristocrat, it was this tall, proud stranger. I guessed he was about fifteen years younger than me, but there was no question who was owed respect.

'I suppose they've sent you as a spy,' he said bluntly. 'Tell your master that we are exactly what we seem to be – a war band – and that its leader is Harald Sigurdsson of Norway, half-brother of St Olaf. Tell him that I have come to place my myself and my men at his disposal. Tell him also that we are veteran fighters. Most of us have already seen service in the household of King Jaroslav of Kiev.'

Now I knew exactly who he was: scion of one of the most powerful families in Norway. His half-brother Olaf had ruled Norway for a dozen years before being toppled by jealous chieftains. 'I'm only a duty escort, my lord,' I said meekly. 'You need to talk to the two officials waiting outside. They are from the seketron – from the office which looks after foreign envoys. They will handle the arrangements.'

'Then don't let's waste time,' Harald said briskly. 'Introduce me.' And he turned on his heel and left the tent. I hurried after him just in time to see the expressions on the faces of the two bureaucrats as this imperious giant of a man bore down on them. They looked alarmed.

'This is the leader of the, er, barbarians,' I said in Greek. 'He is very high-born. In his own country he's a nobelissimus. He has spent some time in the court of Kiev and now wishes that he and his men enter the service of the great Basileus.'

The two civil servants had regained their composure. They produced parchment and reed pens from the small ivory work cases they carried and waited expectantly.

'Please repeat the name of the nobelissimus,' said the man whom I took to be the senior.

'Harald, son of Sigurd,' I answered.

'His rank and tribe?'

'No tribe,' I replied. 'From his family have come the kings of a far northern country called Norway.'

The civil servant murmured something to his colleague. I could not hear what he said, but the man nodded.

'Is his father the current king of his people?'

This was becoming embarrassing. I had no idea of Harald's current status, and was too nervous to ask him directly, so I translated the question to Halldor, who had joined us. But it was Harald himself who replied.

'Tell him that my country was ruled by my half-brother until he was killed in battle by his enemies and that I am the rightful heir.'

Harald, I thought to myself, had a very clear idea of his own worth. I translated his statement and the official wrote it down carefully. He was clearly feeling more comfortable now that he could reduce everything to the written word.

'I will need an exact roster of the people in his company – their names, ages, rank and places of origin. Also a full inventory of any goods they are carrying: type, size and description of their weapons; number and condition of the sea craft they have; whether there has been any sickness during the journey from Kiev . . .'

I sensed that Harald, beside me, was losing patience.

'Making lists, are they?' he interrupted.

'Yes, my lord. They have to report back to their office with a full description of your war band and all its equipment.'

'Excellent,' he said. 'Tell them to make a second copy for me. It could be useful for my quartermasters.' Then he turned on his heel and strode away.

Fortunately one of the Rus guides who had brought Harald and his men downriver from Kiev spoke adequate Greek and volunteered to relieve me of the chore of translating as the bureaucrats from the dromos patiently went about their task. I took the chance to draw Halldor to one side and ask him about Harald.

'What's this about him being the rightful heir to the throne of Norway?' I asked. 'And if he is the rightful heir, why has he been spending time at the court of King Jaroslav in Kiev?'

'He had to flee Norway when his half-brother was defeated and killed in battle while trying to regain the throne. He found refuge with King Jaroslav, as did many other Norwegians who backed the wrong side in the civil war. He spent three years in Kiev as a military commander and was so outstanding that he asked the king if he could marry his daughter Elizabeth.'

It seemed that there was no limit to the self-confidence of Harald Sigurdsson.

'So what was the king's answer?'

'He didn't need to say anything. The Princess Elizabeth told Harald to come back when he had riches and renown, and as Harald is not one to let the grass grow under his feet, he retorted that he would win his fortune in the service of the Basileus. Anyone who wanted to join him could do so if they were good warriors and swore allegiance to him. Then he left Kiev with his war band.'

'Well, what about you? Was Harald's boast enough to make you join up?'

'It's just as I said, Thorgils. I want to be rich. If there's anyone on this earth who's going to win plunder, it's Harald Sigurdsson. He's ambitious, he's energetic, and, above all, he's got battle luck.'

There was one more question which I had to ask, and I dreaded the reply.

'Is Harald a follower of the White Christ,' I asked, 'or does he follow the Old Ways?'

'That's the odd thing,' replied Halldor. 'You would have thought Harald would be as Christian as his half-brother King Olaf, whom many are now calling "St Olaf". Yet, I've never seen Harald go out of his way to attend a church service or say a prayer to Christ. He serves just one God – himself. He knows exactly what he wants: to win the throne of Norway, and he will follow any God or belief that will help him achieve his ambition.'

It was that statement which, in due course, convinced me to throw in my lot with Harald Sigurdsson. Later I was to join him, not for riches, but because I believed that I had finally met the one man capable of restoring the fortunes of the Old Ways. If I could help Harald to gain his throne and show that Odinn and the Old Gods had favoured him, then he might return his kingdom to the Elder Faith. My scheme was refined and shaped in my mind over the weeks and months to come, but it began on the day that Halldor Snorrason told me of Harald's ambition.

'You should know that Harald's more than just a bold warrior,' Halldor went on, unaware that his every word was adding to my certainty that Odinn himself had groomed Harald as his champion. 'He's a great patron to skalds. He can judge their poetry because he knows the ancient lore as well as any man alive, and gives a handsome reward to any skald who skilfully portrays the world of the Gods. And he's more than just a critic. He composes good verse himself. Most of us in his war band can quote the couplet he composed as he fled from the battle that killed his half-brother – ' Here Halldor paused. Then he took a breath and recited:

> 'Now I go creeping from forest
> To forest with little honour;
> Who knows, my name may yet become
> Renowned far and wide in the end.'

'Not bad for a fifteen-year-old wounded while fighting on the losing side of a battle that decides a throne,' he commented.

Yet again I felt that Odinn was pointing the way. I too had been fifteen years old when I fought and was wounded in a great battle that had decided a kingdom, the throne of Ireland. The Norns, who determine men's destiny, had woven the same patterns into the lives of Harald Sigurdsson and myself. Now Odinn had brought us to where our paths crossed.

The sound of a footfall behind me made me turn, and there was the man himself. With the sunshine falling full on his sea eagle's face, I saw something that I had not noticed before: his features were regular and well made, and he was a very handsome man, except in one strange detail – his left eyebrow was very much higher than the other. I took it to be a shadow of Odinn's lop-sided mark, Odinn the one-eyed.

'So what did you make of this Araltes?' asked John the Orphanotrophus when I reported back to him the following day. I noted a sheet of parchment on the desk in front of him, and guessed that it was the written report from the office of the dromos. It was widely acknowledged that the imperial bureaucracy had never operated so efficiently as when John had taken over the running of the state.

'He seems genuine, your excellency. In Norse his name is Harald, son of Sigurd,' I answered, standing to attention and staring fixedly at a semicircle of gold paint. It was a saint's halo in an icon fixed to the wall behind the Orphanotrophus's head. I was still frightened of the man and I did not want him looking into my eyes and reading my thoughts.

'What about this tale that he is some sort of nobleman?'

'It is correct, your excellency. He is related to the royal family of Norway. He and his men have come to offer their services to his majesty, the Basileus.'

'And what would you say is the status of their morale and equipment?'

'First-class morale, your excellency. Their weaponry is work-manlike and well maintained.'

'Their ships?'

'In need of some overhaul, but seaworthy.'

'Good. I see that you kept your wits about you. My pedantic colleagues in the dromos have taken care to remind me of the regulation that no foreign prince may serve in the imperial Life Guard. Too risky, it seems. In case he gets ideas above his station. But I believe I have a use for these barbarians. I am sending a note to the akolouthos, the commanding officer of the guard, telling him that you are detached for special duties. You are to be the liaison between my office and Araltes and his force. You will receive a bonus above your regular guard's pay and, unless you are employed otherwise by me, you will continue to perform your normal guard duties. That is all.'

I left the room and was immediately intercepted by a secretary. He handed me a scroll and I opened it to see that it contained my written orders. It seemed that the Orphanotrophus had decided on his course of action before I even reported to his office. I read that I was to prepare 'the visitor Araltes' for an audience with his imperial majesty, the Basileus, at a date yet to be decided. Until that time I was to assist in familiarising Araltes with the organisation and operational structure of the imperial navy. I reread this sentence, as it was not what I had anticipated. The imperial navy was very much the junior branch of the imperial forces, though it possessed the most powerful fleet in the Great Sea. I had expected Harald and his men to be recruited into the Varangians-without-the-walls, the brigade of foreign mercenaries which included Armenians, Georgians, Vlachs and the like. But instead Harald and his men were to be marines.

When I next visited the camp at Mamas, I explained these orders to Halldor, who merely grunted. 'Makes sense,' he said. 'We're used to sea fights. But what's all this about preparing us for reception by the Basileus?'

'You've got to get the details absolutely right,' I told him. 'Nothing angers the emperor's councillors more than mistakes in court etiquette. It reinforces their view that anyone unfamiliar with court procedures is an ignorant savage, utterly uncouth and not worth dealing with. They've been known to turn down the requests of foreign ambassadors simply because of some minor transgression of court protocol. For example, a visiting ambassador who uses the wrong title to address the Basileus will be refused further audiences with the emperor, have his ambassadorial privileges withdrawn, and so on.'

'So what should Harald call the Basileus?'

'Emperor of the Romans.'

Halldor looked puzzled. 'How's that? This is Constantinople, not Rome, and anyhow isn't there a German ruler who calls himself the Holy Roman Emperor?'

'That's what I mean. The Basileus and his entire court are convinced that they are the true heirs of the Roman empire, that they represent its true ideals and continue its glory. They are prepared to grant that the German is the "the king" of the Romans, but not "the emperor". Just the same way that their own holy men claim that their Great Patriarch is the high priest of White Christ worship, not the person in Rome who calls himself the pope. It also explains why there's such a confusing mix of Latin and Greek in their military ranks – they speak of decurions and centurions as if they were soldiers in a Roman army, but the higher ranks nearly all have Greek titles.'

Halldor sighed. 'Well, I just hope you can persuade Harald to use the right phrases and do the right thing. I'm not sure he will like grovelling to the Basileus. He's not that sort.'

Halldor's worries were needless. I found that Harald Sigurdsson was fully prepared to rein in his usually arrogant behaviour if it was to be to his advantage, and because I desperately wanted the Norwegian prince to succeed, I worked hard at tutoring him in exactly how to behave during his visit to the Great Palace. The emperor's subjects, I told him first, thought it such a great privilege to be allowed to meet the Basileus in person that they would wait for years to be granted an audience. For them it was the equivalent of meeting their God's representative on earth, and everything inside the palace was regulated to enhance this impression.

'Think of it, my lord, like a service in the most lavish White Christ church,' I said. 'Everything is ceremony and pomp. The courtiers wear special silken robes, each man knows his exact duties, the spot where he must stand, the exact gestures to use, the correct words to say. Everything focuses on the emperor himself. He sits on his golden throne, wearing the jewel-encrusted costume they call the chlamys. Across his shoulders is the loros, the long stole that only the emperor may wear, and on his feet are the tzangia, the purple boots exclusive to his rank. He will be motionless, gazing down the hall towards the door where you enter. You will be ushered in and then must advance down the hall and perform proskynesis.'

'What's proskynesis?' Harald asked, leaning forward on his stool.

I realised that I had got carried away with the splendour of the ceremony, and hesitated because I did not know how Harald would react to my explanation.

'Proskynesis is the act of homage,' I said.

'Go on.'

I swallowed nervously. 'It means lying prostrate on the floor, face down, and staying there until the word comes from a courtier for you to rise.'

There was a long pause as Harald thought this over. I feared that he was about to refuse to debase himself this way, but instead he asked, 'How far am I from the throne when I have to do this lying-down performance?'

I had been holding my breath, and let it out gently. 'As you walk down the hall towards the Basileus, look downward and you will see that there is a purple disc set in the marble floor. That marks the spot where you should lie down.'

Harald asked promptly, 'How do you know all this?'

'Because a detail of the guard stands behind the emperor's throne during the ceremony, and I have watched it happen many times. The guardsmen get to know the little tricks which make the ceremony seem more impressive. In fact sometimes it is difficult to keep a straight face.'

'Like when?'

'If the court chamberlain thinks the visitor is impressionable enough, the Basileus's throne is made to elevate during the proskynesis. While the supplicant is face down on the floor, a team of operators winds a lifting jack hidden behind the throne so that when the supplicant lifts his head he sees the emperor seated higher than before. The look of astonishment on the supplicant's face can be very entertaining. But,' I added hurriedly, 'I don't think they will try that ruse on the day you have an imperial audience.'

Recalling my first conversations with Harald, it occurs to me now that I was possibly making a mistake. I thought I was merely preparing him for his meeting with the Basileus, but I fear that Harald was in fact learning a very different lesson: the importance of establishing dominion over others, how to dazzle them. If so, in my enthusiasm for Harald's success I was preparing the seeds for my own later disappointment.

The Orphanotrophus had also instructed me to familiarise the Norwegian prince with the imperial navy, so I took Harald to the naval arsenal on the Golden Horn. There the eparch of the dockyard, fearing espionage, received us coolly and insisted that an official from the dromos as well as his own deputy accompany us on our tour. I showed Harald rank upon rank of slipways, where the warships were built and repaired, warehouses filled with naval stores, mast sheds and sail lofts, and I explained how most of the seamen were recruited from the coastal peoples across the straits in Asia Minor. Harald, who had an expert eye for ship-wright's skills, asked such probing questions of the master carpenters that I was sometimes at a loss for the right words as I translated into Greek. Then he demanded to inspect a warship in commission. When the eparch's deputy hesitated, Harald insisted. If his men were to serve on the imperial ships, then at least they should know what to expect. He pointed at a dromon of the largest size, a three-masted fleet battleship which lay at anchor in the Golden Horn, awaiting orders. He would like to inspect that vessel, he said. As I was to notice many times later, when Harald Sigurdsson put a request, it sounded more like a command.

A naval pinnace rowed us out. Close up, the dromon was even larger than I had expected. I had never been aboard one before, and she was immense, at least half as long again as the largest longship that I had seen in the past and two or three times as broad. But what really made her seem imposing was her height above the water. Our Norse warships are low and sleek, but the imperial battleships are built upwards from the waterline. The intention is to overawe the enemy and give a superior platform from which archers can shoot downwards. So the dromon loomed over us as we approached, her height increased by a castle-like structure built amidship. We clambered up her side and on her deck immediately came face to face with her kentarchos, her sailing master. Angrily he demanded to know who this strange-looking foreigner with the long moustaches was who came climbing aboard his ship as though he owned her. When the man from the dromos explained that Harald had a letter from the sekreton of the Orphanotrophus, the kentarchos glowered, then accompanied us at every pace around her deck, watching us suspiciously.

Harald missed nothing. Fascinated by this unknown design of war vessel, he asked how the dromon handled in a seaway, how her sails were set and reefed, how nimbly she could alter course, how fast she went when all two hundred oarsmen were at the benches and for how long they could keep up a cruising pace. The kentarchos answered reluctantly. To him a bearded Norseman was a natural foe. Time and again I had to remind our guide that it was the Orphanotrophus's order that Harald should be familiar with the imperial war fleet, and one day Harald's men might be aboard as his marines. The kentarchos looked as if he would prefer to scuttle his vessel.

Finally we reached the forecastle in the dromon's bows.

'And what is that?' asked Harald.

A bronze tube protruded through a metal plate, pointing forward like a single nostril. Close behind the tube stood two metal baths, joined by copper pipes to an apparatus that looked like a pump.

'That's the vessel's siphon,' said the man from the dromos.

The kentarchos glared at him, then rudely walked in front of Harald, deliberately blocking his view.

'Not even the emperor's direct command allows me to tell you more,' he growled. 'Now get off my ship.'

To my surprise, Harald obeyed.

Much later, when we were safely back outside the arsenal and no officials were in earshot, Harald muttered, 'So that's how they launch the Fire. But how do they create it?'

'I don't know,' I said. 'I'm not even sure what it is.'

'When I was in Kiev I heard people describe how it destroyed a war fleet in their grandfathers' time,' Harald said. 'People marvelled how the Fire ignites in the air, turning to cinders anything it touches. It even burns underwater. It's amazing.'

That evening, when I asked Pelagia about the Fire, my normally reliable source of information was little help. She told me that only a handful of technicians knew how to create it, and that the ingredients were among the most closely guarded state secrets. Rumour had it that the Fire was made of quicklime mixed with an oil that comes from the earth. I told her about the strange bronze tube aboard the dromon and she laughed. She said that there were foreign sailors who believed the imperial navy had a breeding programme of fire-breathing dragons, which they stowed below decks before setting out on a campaign and then let loose in the bows of their ships just before a fleet action.

Shortly after the feast day of the Transfiguration, one of Constantinople's major festivals, and two months after his arrival Harald finally had his audience with Michael. It took place in yet another of the splendid halls within the Great Palace, the Magnaura, which was often used for greeting foreign ambassadors, and as luck would have it I was a member of the imperial escort. As I took up my position behind the throne and rested my axe on my shoulder, I felt like a nervous schoolmaster who waits to see how his star pupil will perform. The interior of the hall was like a vast church, with columns and galleries and high windows glazed with coloured glass. The far end opened on to a wide courtyard planted with trees, and there the supplicants were assembled. Among them I could see Harald, standing a full head taller than his colleagues. In the foreground stood a host of court dignitaries waiting for the signal from the master of ceremonies. Even after witnessing dozens of such ceremonies, I still marvelled at the splendour of the occasion. The courtiers and dignitaries were dressed according to their seniority and the office they held. There were senators and patricians in blue and green, Greek officers of the Hetaira in white tunics with gold bands, magistrates and high officials dressed in shimmering patterned silk and holding their insignia – golden staffs, ivory wands, court swords in scabbards ornate with enamel plaques, jewelled whips, tablets and illuminated scrolls. Many of the costumes were so stiffly sewn with gold and silver embroidery, as well as precious stones and pearls, that their wearers could barely move. But that was also part of the ritual. All the assembly was expected to stay motionless, or at least nearly so. Any movement must be slow and dignified.

A trumpet blast announced that the ceremony was to begin, and the assembly, facing towards Michael on his throne (Zoë had not been invited), raised the customary paean in honour of the Basileus. After several minutes of praise and acclamation I saw in the distance the ostiarios, the palace eunuch whose duty was to introduce dignitaries to the emperor, approach Harald and indicate that he was to walk forward. The crowd had now parted, leaving an aisle which led towards the throne. On the marble floor, in the open space before the throne, I could see the purple disc where Harald was to lie face down and perform proskynesis. At that moment I suddenly realised that I had failed to warn Harald about the automata. I had told him of the elevating throne, but forgotten that in the Magnaura, on each side of the purple disc, stood the lifelike bronze statue of a lion. The statues were hollow and articulated; by an ingenious system of hidden air pumps the animals could be made to lash their tails, open their jaws and let out a roar. The operators of the automata, concealed in the crowd, were instructed to make the beasts roar at the very moment the supplicant was about to prostrate himself before the throne.

I watched Harald as he stalked down the great hall between the lines of watching courtiers. He was bare-headed and wearing a velvet tunic of dark green with loose silk pantaloons. His only jewellery was a plain gold torc on each arm. In such a glittering and flamboyant assembly he should have been inconspicuous, but his presence dominated those around him. It was not just his height and obvious physical strength which impressed the onlookers, it was that Harald of Norway walked the length of Magnaura as if the ceremonial hall belonged to him, not the Basileus.

He approached the purple disc and halted in the open space before the throne, clear of the watching crowd. There was a pause, a long moment of silence, as he faced the emperor. At that moment the hidden operators of the automata opened the valves and the mechanical beasts lashed their tails and roared. If the audience had been expecting Harald to flinch or look startled, they were disappointed. He turned his head to look into the open jaws, first of one beast, then the other. He seemed thoughtful, even curious. Then, nonchalantly, he lay down on the marble floor and performed proskynesis.

Much later he told me that it was as he stared into the open mouths of the bronze lions and heard the hiss of the air pumps that made them move and roar that he understood the Fire.

THREE

I DID NOT SEE Harald again for nearly four months. After his proskynesis to the Basileus, he and his men left Constantinople. The Orphanotrophus had given them the task of dealing with the growing menace from Arab pirates who regularly attacked ships sailing from Dyrrachium on the west coast of Greece. The port of Dyrrachium was a vital link in the empire's communications. Through its harbour passed imperial couriers, troops and merchandise on their way to and from Constantinople and the colonies in southern Italy. Recently the raiders had been so bold as to establish bases in the nearby Greek islands, from where their fast galleys pounced on passing ships. The Orphanotrophus's original plan was to send to the area additional units of the imperial navy with Harald's men aboard. But, according to my colleagues in the guard, the drungarios, the admiral of the fleet, refused. He baulked at taking so many barbarians on board his ships, and Harald had made matters worse by stating that he would not take orders from a Greek commander. The deadlock was resolved when Harald offered to use his own vessels, the light monocylon, and base them at Dyrrachium. From there he would send them out as escorts for the merchant ships and to patrol against the enemy.

With Harald gone, I returned to my previous duties with the guard and found that the whispers about Michael's ill health were true. The young emperor was afflicted by what the palace physicians tactfully called 'the holy sickness'.

I first noticed the symptoms when Michael was dressing for the festival which celebrates the birth of the White Christ. With five other members of the bodyguard, I had escorted Michael to the imperial robing chamber. There the vestitores, the officials who solemnly place the imperial regalia on the Basileus, ceremonially opened the chest containing the royal garb. The most junior of the officials took out the cloak, the chlamys, which he solemnly handed to the next most senior in rank. From hand to hand the garment was passed until finally it reached the senior vestitor, who reverently approached the waiting Basileus, intoned a prayer, and settled the cloak on the emperor's shoulders. There followed the pearl-encrusted stole, the jewelled gloves, the chest pendant. All the time the Basileus stood motionless until the crown was presented to him. At that moment, something went awry. Instead of leaning forward to kiss the cross on the crown, as ritual demanded, Michael began to tremble. It was only a slight movement, but standing behind him we, the members of the escort, could see that his right arm was shaking uncontrollably. The vestitor waited, still proffering the crown, but Michael was paralysed, unable to move except for the trembling of his arm. There was complete silence as the interval lengthened and everyone in the room stood still, as if frozen in place, the only movement the rapid shaking of Michael's right arm. Then, after the time it takes for a man to empty his lungs slowly seven or eight times, the arm slowly grew still, and Michael resumed full control of his body. Later that day, as if nothing had happened, he joined the procession along the garlanded streets to a service at the church of Hagia Sophia, then held several formal receptions in the Great Palace at which senior bureaucrats received their Nativity gifts, and in the evening appeared at a great banquet in the lausakios, the dining hall of the Great Palace. But the Orphanotrophus must have been advised of the emperor's brief moment of paralysis, because the normal seating arrangements had been modified. Michael was seated alone at a separate ivory table, on view to all his noble guests, but no one could come close to him.

'They say this kind of sickness is caused by demons in the brain,' Halfdan commented to me as we were removing our ceremonial armour later that evening in the guardroom.

'Maybe,' I replied. 'Yet some people see it as a gift.'

'Where's that?'

'Among the ski-runners in Permia,' I said. 'I spent the winter with the family of one of their wise men, who sometimes behaved in the same way as the emperor, only it was more than just his arm trembling. Often he would fall on the ground and lie without moving for as long as an hour. When he woke up again, he told us how his spirit had been visiting the otherworld. It could happen with the Basileus.'

'If it does, the Christians won't believe he visited any spirit world,' Halfdan grumbled. 'They don't hold with that sort of thing. Their saints show up on earth and perform miracles, but no one travels in the opposite direction and comes back.'

My analysis turned out to be correct. As the weeks passed, Michael's eccentric behaviour became more pronounced and the episodes lasted longer. Sometimes he would sit mumbling to himself, or begin chewing rhythmically though there was no food in his mouth. On other occasions he would suddenly start to wander about the palace in a state of confusion until, abruptly, he came to his senses and looked about him trying to identify where he stood. The duty guardsmen escorted him as best they could, walking behind the dazed Basileus while someone sent hastily for a palace physician. If there was an encounter with someone who did not know about the emperor's state of health, then the guardsmen had orders to form a circle around the Basileus and shield him from view. The handful of doctors who were privy to Michael's condition tried doses of opium and rose oil, and induced him to drink muddy concoctions of earth gathered in their Holy Land and dissolved in holy water from a sacred well in a church

at Pege just outside the city walls. But the emperor's behaviour
did not return to normal. Rather, it grew ever more extreme and
unpredictable.

By contrast, as this crisis gradually developed, my own
troubles seemed to recede. Having successfully obeyed the
Orphanotrophus's instructions in dealing with Harald and his
men, I calculated that John would keep me as a go-between as
long as Harald proved loyal. Pelagia encouraged me in this
thinking. I was spending more and more time with her, and in the
evenings when off duty I would go to dine at her apartment – she
always brought back fresh delicacies from the market where she
kept her bread stall – and we would sit and chat together,
ostensibly to practise my Greek but more and more because I
found her company to be a pleasant change from regimental life
and because I valued her shrewd commentary on the power play
that I was observing in the palace.

'As long as you might prove useful to the Orphanotrophus,'
she said, 'you should be safe. He's got much to worry him now
that his brother is showing signs of ill health.'

'So news of the emperor's condition has leaked out?'

'Naturally,' she replied. 'There's not much that goes on in the
palace that doesn't eventually become gossip in the marketplace.
There are too many people employed in the palace for there to be
secrets. Incidentally,' she added, 'your bearded northern friends
who went off to Dyrrachium with their ships must be doing well.
That cheese I served with the first course this evening comes from
Italy, and until recently it was almost impossible to get. The
Italian cheese-makers were reluctant to send their produce when
so many of the merchant vessels were falling into the hands of the
Arab pirates. Now the cheese has reappeared in the market. That's
a good sign.'

I remembered our conversation when I received my next
summons from the Orphanotrophus. This time I found he was
not alone. The fleet admiral, the drungarios, was in his office, as
well as a naval kentarchos, by coincidence the same man who had

turned Harald and myself off his dromon. Both men looked surprised and resentful that I had been called to the meeting, and I made sure I stood respectfully, eyes fixed once again on the golden halo of the icon, but listening with close attention to what the Orphanotrophus had to say.

'Guardsman, I've received an unusual request from war captain Araltes, now on anti-piracy patrol. He wants you to accompany the next pay shipment for our army in Italy.'

'As your excellency orders,' I answered crisply.

'It is not that straightforward,' said the Orphanotrophus, 'otherwise I would not have summoned you in person. This shipment could be a little different from usual. Araltes – or Harald as you told me your people call him – has been very effective. His men have destroyed several pirate bases and captured or sunk a number of the Saracen vessels, but not all of them. One particularly dangerous vessel remains at large. Araltes reports that the vessel's base is in Sicily and therefore beyond the operational range of his monocylon. The drungarios here agrees with this assessment. He also tells me that several of his warships have attempted to hunt down this corsair but so far have failed.'

'The vessel has been too quick for them,' explained the drungarios in self-defence. 'She is powerful and well manned and she has been able to outrun my dromons.'

The Orphanotrophus ignored the interruption. 'It is vital that our troops now on campaign in southern Italy receive their pay in the next few weeks. If they do not, they will lose heart. They have not been paid for half a year as both the last two pay shipments were lost. We believe the vessels carrying the payments were intercepted by the same cruising pirate, who has yet to be accounted for. It was either a remarkably bad stroke of luck for the raider or, as Araltes suggests, the pirate was informed in advance when and where the shipments were being made.'

I waited impassively to hear what the Orphanotrophus would say next. So far he had not mentioned anything which explained why Harald wanted me to accompany the next shipment.

'War captain Araltes has suggested a ruse to ensure that the next payment does get through. He proposes that the army's pay is not sent in the usual way, by the imperial highway from the capital to Dyrrachium and there trans-shipped for Italy. He proposes that the money is delivered by sea all the way, aboard a fast ship sailing from Constantinople, around Greece and then directly across to Italy.'

'That plan is madness, your excellency. Typical of a barbarian,' protested the kentarchos, 'What is there to say that the merchant ship would not equally be intercepted by the pirate. Unarmed, the vessel would be helpless. It would be an even easier target.'

'There is a second part to the plan,' said the Orphanotrophus smoothly. 'Araltes suggests a fake pay shipment is also sent, at the same time and along the normal route, to distract the raider. This shipment is to be of lead bars instead of the usual gold bullion. It will be fully escorted as if it were the real consignment, taken to Dyrrachium, and loaded aboard a military transport carrying extra fighting men supplied by Araltes. This decoy vessel will then set sail for Italy. If the pirate's spies tell him about this vessel, he will intercept it, and this time he may be destroyed. Meanwhile the real shipment will have slipped through.'

'If it please your excellency,' the kentarchos interjected, 'the shipment can go all the way by sea, but why not aboard a dromon? No pirate would dare attack.'

'The drungarios assures me that this is impossible. He cannot spare a battleship,' replied the Orphanotrophus. 'Every dromon is already committed.'

Out of the corner of my eye I watched the drungarios. He looked towards his kentarchos and gave a shrug. The drungarios, I thought to myself, was as much a courtier as a seaman. He did not want the risk of the imperial navy losing another bullion shipment, nor did he want to contradict the Orphantrophus.

'Guardsman, what is your opinion?'

From the tone of his voice I knew the Orphanotrophus had

directed his question at me, but still I dared not look directly into his face, and kept my gaze fixed on the icon on the wall behind him.

'I am not an expert on naval matters, your excellency,' I said, choosing my words carefully, 'but I would suggest that, just as a precaution, two of the monocylon escort the bullion vessel through the zone where the pirate ship is most likely to be operating, at least to the limit of their range.'

'Strange you should mention that,' observed the Orphanotrophus. 'That is just what Araltes also proposes. He says he can send two of the monocylon to a rendezvous off the south cape of Greece. That is why he asks that you be aboard the bullion ship. So that there are no misunderstandings when the captain of the Greek ship meets up with the Varangian captains.'

'As your excellency wishes,' I replied. Harald's deception plan was the sort of strategy which would appeal to the Orphanotrophus.

'Araltes asks one more thing. He requests that we send him an engineer and materials for the Fire.'

Beside me the kentarchos almost choked with astonishment. John noted his reaction.

'Don't worry,' he said soothingly. 'I have no intention of allowing the Fire to be made available to barbarian vessels. At the same time I don't want to snub Araltes. He is evidently someone who takes offence easily. He says nothing about requiring a siphon to dispense the Fire. So I'll send him the engineer and the materials, but no siphon. It will be a genuine mistake.'

It took three weeks to prepare the plan. First the bureau of the logothete of the domestikos, the army's secretariat, had to draw up two sets of orders: the official one for the false shipment and a second, secret set of instructions for the genuine consignment. Then their colleagues in the office of the logothete of the dromos, responsible for the imperial highways, had to make their preparations for an escorted convoy to go overland from Constantinople to Dyrrachium. The managers of the way stations were warned to be ready with changes of pack mules for carrying the payment, as well as horses for the mounted troopers. The eparch of the palace treasury received his instructions direct from the Orphanotrophus: he was to cast eight hundred bars of lead to the same weight as the thousands of gold nomisma, the imperial coins with which the troops were paid. Last, but not least, the navy had to find a suitable merchant ship to carry the genuine shipment around the coast.

When I went to the Golden Horn to view the chosen vessel, I had to admit that the kentarchos, who had been given this responsibility, knew his job. He had picked a vessel known locally as a dorkon or 'gazelle'. Twenty paces in length, the vessel was light and fast for a cargo carrier. She had two masts for her triangular sails, a draught shallow enough to allow her to work close inshore, and extra oar benches for sixteen men so she could make progress in a calm as well as manoeuvre her way safely in and out of harbour. Her captain also inspired me with confidence. A short, sinewy Greek by the name of Theodore, he came from the island of Lemnos, and he kept his ship in good order. Once he had made it clear to me that he was in charge and I was to be only a supercargo, he was polite and friendly. He had been told only that he was to sail to Italy by the direct route and expect a rendezvous at sea with auxiliary ships of the imperial navy. He had not been told the nature of his cargo. Nor did he ask.

I next saw Theodore on the night we left harbour. In keeping with the secrecy of our mission, we sailed within hours of the chests of bullion being carried aboard. The water guard were expecting us. They patrolled the great iron chain strung across the entrance to the Golden Horn at dusk to hinder smugglers or enemy attack, and they opened a gap so that the dorkon could slip out and catch the favourable current to take us down towards the Propontis or inner sea. As I looked towards the towering black mass of Constantinople spread across its seven hills, I recalled the day when I had first arrived. Then I had been awed by the sheer scale and splendour of Miklagard. Now the city was defined by the pinprick lights of the apartment blocks where thousands upon thousands of ordinary working citizens were still awake. Closer to hand, the steady beam of Constantinople's lighthouse shone out across the water, its array of lanterns fuelled by olive oil and burning in great glass jars to protect the flames from the wind.

The dorkon performed even better than I had anticipated. We set course directly across the Propontis, and this in itself was a measure of our captain's competence. Greek mariners normally stopped each evening and anchored at some regular shelter or pulled into a local port, so they hugged the coast and were seldom out of sight of land. But Theodore headed directly for the lower straits which led into what he called the Great Sea. Nor did he divert into the harbour at Abydos, where the empire maintained a customs post and all commercial vessels were required to stop and pay a toll. A patrol boat, alerted by signals from the customs post, managed to intercept us but I showed the written authority that the Orphanotrophus's chief chartularius had given me, and they let us proceed. The document stated we were on urgent imperial business and not to be delayed. John, I noted, had even taken to signing his name in the purple ink.

I was rolling up the scroll with its lead seal and about to return it to my satchel when the wind plucked a folded sheet of parchment from the bag and blew it across the deck. Theodore deftly caught the paper before it disappeared overboard, and as he returned it to me he gave me a questioning glance. He had obviously recognised some sort of map. I had been planning to show it to him later, but now seemed an opportune moment.

'The commander of the vessels which will join us later as our escort provided me with this,' I said, spreading out the page. 'He sent it by courier from Dyrrachium to the office of the dromos in Constantinople to be passed on to me. It shows where we can expect to rendezvous with our escort.'

The Greek captain glanced down at the outline drawn on the

parchment and recognised the coastline immediately. 'Just beyond the Taenarum cape,' he said, then shrugged. 'Your commander need not have troubled himself. I know that coastline as well as my home port. Sailed past it more times than I can remember.'

'Well, it's best to be sure,' I said. 'He's marked where his ships will be waiting for us.' I placed my finger next to a runic letter drawn on the parchment. Recalling what Halldor had told me about Harald's knowledge of the ancient lore, I recognised it as a private code.

'What's that sign?' asked Theodore.

'The first letter of what might be described as the alphabet my people use. It's called fehu – it represents livestock or wealth.'

'And that one?' asked the captain. A vertical stave line with a single diagonal bar had been drawn near the coast a little further north.

'That's nauthiz, the letter which signifies need or distress.'

The Greek captain examined the map more closely and remarked, 'What's it put there for? There's nothing along that stretch of coast except sheer cliffs. Not a place to be caught in an onshore gale either. Deep water right up to the land and no holding ground. You'd be dashed to pieces in an instant. Wiser to give the place a wide berth.'

'I don't know the reason,' I said, for I was equally puzzled.

With each mile that our ship travelled, I noticed the difference between sailing in the Great Sea and the conditions I had experienced in colder northern waters. The water had a more intense blue, the wave crests were whiter and more crisp against the darker background, and the waves themselves more lively. They formed and re-formed in a rapid dance, and seemed never to acquire the height and majesty of ocean rollers. I commented on this to Theodore, and his reply was serious.

'You should see what it is like in a storm,' he warned. 'A sort of madness. Steep waves falling down on themselves, coming from more than one direction to confuse the helmsman. Each big enough to swamp the boat. And no hint before the tempest strikes. That's the worst. It sweeps in from a cloudless sky and churns the sea into a rage even before you've had time to shorten sail.'

'Have you ever been shipwrecked?' I asked.

'Never,' he said and made the sign of the cross. 'But don't be lulled into complacency – the Great Sea has seen more than its share of shipwrecks, from the blessed St Paul right back to the times of our earliest seafarers, to Odysseus himself.'

The dorkon was sailing close inshore at the time, passing beneath a tall headland, and he gestured up towards its crest. High up, I could see a double row of white columns, close spaced and crowned with a band of white stone. The structure gleamed, so brilliant was its whiteness.

'See that there. It's a temple to the old Gods. You'll likely find one on every major headland – either that or some sort of burial mound.'

For a moment I thought he was talking about my Gods and the Elder Way, but then realised he meant the Gods whom his people had worshipped before they believed in the White Christ.

'They were built where they could be seen by passing sailors,' the captain went on. 'I reckon that in former times the mariners prayed when they saw those temples, asking their heathen gods to give them safe passage, or thanking them for a voyage safely completed. Like today I lit a candle and said a prayer to St Nicholas of Myra, patron saint of mariners, before I embarked.'

'Who were those older Gods?' I asked.

'Don't know,' he answered. 'But they seem to have been some sort of family, ruled over by a father god, with other Gods responsible for the weather for crops, for war and such like.'

Much like my own Gods, I thought.

Our vessel was far ahead of the most optimistic schedule, and when we rounded Taenarum cape and reached the place where Harald's two ships were due to meet us, I was not surprised that the sea was empty. There was no sign yet of the two monocylon, and I had some difficulty in persuading Theodore that we should wait a few extra days. He was well aware that we were entering the area where piracy was rife, but he was also worried by the risk of dawdling off a dangerous shore.

'As I told you,' he said, gesturing towards the distant horizon where we could see the faint line of the coast, 'there's no harbour over there, and if the wind swings round and strengthens we could be in trouble.'

In the end he agreed to wait three days, and we spent them tacking back and forth, then drifting each night with sails furled. Each morning we hoisted our lookout, seated on a wooden cradle, to the masthead, and there he clung, gazing to the north, the direction from which we expected Harald's ships to arrive.

At dawn on the third day, as he was being hauled up to his vantage point and glancing around, the lookout let out a warning shout. A vessel was approaching from the south-west. Theodore jumped up on the rail, gazed in that direction, then leaped back on deck and came striding towards me. Any hint of his usual friendliness was gone. Fury was mingled with suspicion in his expression.

'Is that why you wanted us to wait?' he shouted, seizing me by the arm and bringing his face up close. His breath smelled overpoweringly of garum, the rotten fish sauce the sailors relished. For a moment I thought he was going to strike me.

'What do you mean?' I asked.

'Over there,' he shouted, waving towards the distant sail. 'Don't tell me you weren't expecting that. I should have known it all along. You treacherous savage. You lied about waiting for an escort. That's a Saracen ship twice our size, and you're the reason why she turned up here so conveniently.'

'How can you be so sure she's an Arab vessel? No one can tell at this distance,' I defended myself.

'Oh, yes I can,' the captain snarled, his fingers digging deeper into my arm. 'See how she's rigged. Three triangular sails on three masts. She's an Arab galea out of Sicily or—'

'Keep calm,' I interrupted. 'I've no idea how that ship happens to be here just now. Even if you don't believe me, we're wasting time. Set all sail, get your oarsmen to stand by, steer north. I'm sure our escort ships are well on their way, and we should meet up with them before the Saracens catch us.'

The Greek captain laughed bitterly. 'No chance. If that Saracen ship is the one I think she is, we won't get far. You know what "galea" means. It's our word for a swordfish, and if you've ever seen a swordfish racing in for the attack, you'd know she'll catch us. Probably by noon, and there's no way out. There isn't even a friendly harbour where we can seek refuge.'

His words reminded me of the map Harald had sent. I fumbled in my satchel and pulled out his chart. 'Here, what about this?' I tapped the nauthiz rune. 'Isn't that the reason for this mark. It's a place to go if we're in distress.'

The captain looked at me with dislike. 'Why should I trust you now?' he said grimly.

'You don't need to,' I replied, 'but if you're right, and that Arab vessel is as fast and dangerous as you say, you've no other choice.'

He thought about it for a moment, then angrily spun on his heel and began yelling at his crew to set all sail, then get themselves to the oar benches. Taking the helm, he steered the dorkon on a slanting course towards the distant coast. He didn't even look at me, but set his jaw and concentrated on getting the best speed from his ship.

Even the most ignorant sailor would have seen that our vessel was no match for the Arab galea. We were light and quick for a merchant vessel, but the Arab had been designed as a pure seagoing hunter. She carried far more sail than we did and was expertly handled. Worse, the southerly breeze suited her to perfection and she began to overhaul us so rapidly, her bow slicing through the sea and sending up a curl of white foam, that I wondered if we would even get as far as the coast. I had been in a sea chase years earlier, pursued by longships, and we had gained temporary advantage by running across a sandbar into waters too shallow for our enemies. But this was not an option now. As the coast ahead drew nearer, I saw that it was utterly forbidding, a rampart of cliffs directly ahead of us.

The Arab ship was undoubtedly a pirate. As she closed on us we could make out that she carried at least eighty men, far more than any trading ship would require, and they were chillingly professional in the way they went about their duties. They adjusted the three huge sails to perfection, then moved across the deck and lined the windward side to trim their vessel and waited there. They did not shout or cheer, but remained poised and silent, certain of the outcome of the pursuit. Up in her bows I saw the archers, sitting quietly with their weapons, waiting until we were in range.

Theodore knew our situation was hopeless, yet he passed from panic to a sense of defiance. Every time he turned and saw how much the gap between the ships had closed, he did not change expression but merely looked up to see that our sails were at their best, then turned back to face towards the cliffs as they drew closer. After three hours' chase we were no more than a mile from the coast, and I could see that Theodore had been right. The sheer rock face extended in each direction for mile after mile, yellow-brown in colour, sun-baked and utterly desolate. The dark sea heaved against the boulders along their base. Either the pursuing galley would overtake and its crew board us, or we would simply crunch against the rocks. Fifty paces from the cliff, our captain pushed across the helm and our vessel turned and began to run parallel to the precipice, so close that I could hear the cries of the sea birds nesting on the high ledges. Here the wind was fluky, bouncing off the rock face so that our sails began to flap and we lost speed.

'Get out your oars and row!' bellowed Theodore.

The crew stabbed at the water and did their best, but it was almost impossible to get a grip on the choppy water and they were not professional galley rowers. They looked shocked and frightened, but to their credit they remained almost as silent as the chasing pirates. Only occasionally did I hear a sob of effort or despair as they tugged on the looms of the oars.

Of course I joined them on the oar bench. I had rowed a longship and knew how to handle an oar, but it was only a gesture. Our sole hope was that Harald's two monocylon would suddenly appear, sweeping down from the north. But each time I looked over my shoulder the sea remained empty. To one side of us, and almost level now, the Arab galea kept pace. Her captain had reduced sail so he did not overshoot his victim. Half his oarsmen, perhaps forty men, were rowing to hold their position steady. He was, I realised, worried that he might come too close to the cliffs, and did not want to risk damaging his vessel. I judged that he would bide his time until we were in more open water, then close in for the kill.

We were approaching a low headland which jutted from the line of cliffs, obscuring what lay further up the coast.

'Listen, men,' shouted our captain. 'I'm going to beach the ship if I see a suitable spot. When I do that, it's every man for himself. Drop your oars, leap out and make a run for it. So keep up the pressure now, row as best you can, and wait until I give the word.'

Soon the dorkon was lurching past the headland, so near that I could have thrown a pebble on to the rocks. Now the pirate galley closed the range. One or two arrows flew. The archers were hoping for a lucky strike, to maim a few of our oarsmen. Not too many, of course, because crippled slaves fetched a lower price.

Past the headland the coastline opened up ahead. To our right was a wide, shallow bay, but the beach itself was a mass of stones and rock. There was no place where we could run ashore. Theodore jerked his head at me and I left my oar to join him at the helm. He seemed almost calm, resigned to his fate.

'This is the spot marked on your map where we should be in case of need. But I don't see anything.'

I looked around the sweep of the bay. Ahead of us, perhaps

half a mile, I saw a narrow break in the cliffs which rose again on the far side. 'Over there,' I said, pointing. 'Perhaps in there we will find a landing place. And maybe the entrance is too narrow for the Arab ship to follow us. If we can squeeze in, we might have a few moments to abandon ship and run clear.'

'It's worth a try,' grunted the captain, and altered course.

We laboured ever closer, heading for the cleft. But as we approached, I saw that I had misjudged it. The gap was wider than I had supposed, which meant our dorkon could slip in, but so too could the pirate ship if her steersman was bold enough. The skipper of the Arab craft must have thought the same, for he did not harry us as we crept closer to where two low reefs reached out, leaving a narrow gap between. Our pursuer even had the confidence to stop rowing: I saw the regular beat of the sweeps come to a halt. They waited and watched.

Sails flapping, our dorkon glided through the gap. As we entered, I knew we were doomed. We found ourselves in a natural harbour, a small cove, almost totally landlocked. Sheer cliffs of yellow rock rose on each side, banded with ledges. They enclosed a circular sea pool, some forty paces across. Here the colour of the water was the palest blue, so clear that I could see the sandy bottom, no more than ten feet below our keel. Despairingly I realised that the water was deep enough for the Arab galley to float. There was not a breath of wind. The cove was so tightly surrounded that the cliffs overhung the water in places, and if the lip of the precipice crumbled, the rocks would fall straight on to our deck. We had found the refuge marked on the map, and had we reached it earlier, even by a day, we could have concealed ourselves here and waited in safety for Harald's monocylon to appear. I had failed.

'We're trapped,' said Theodore quietly.

In the distance I heard a shout. It must have been the voice of the Arab captain prowling outside, ordering his men to furl sail and prepare to row their larger ship through the entrance. Then I heard the creak of ropes in wooden blocks and supposed that the

Arabs were lowering the spars as well. They were taking their
time, knowing that they had us at their mercy.

'Every man for himself!' called Theodore, and his crew needed
no urging. They began to jump into the clear water – it was no
more than a few strokes for them to swim ashore. At the back of
the cove was a ledge of rock where a man could haul himself out.
From there the faint line of a goat path meandered up the cliff
face. If we scrambled up fast enough, maybe we could get clear
before the slave-catchers arrived.

'I'm sorry—' I began to say, but Theodore interrupted.

'It's too late for that now. Get going.'

I threw myself overboard and he jumped a moment later. We
were the last to abandon the ship, leaving her bobbing quietly in
the placid water.

I hauled myself out on to the rock ledge, reached down and
gave Theodore a hand, pulling him ashore. He followed the line
of wet footprints where his crew had scrambled for the goat path.
Up above me I heard the clattering of falling stones as they
clambered upwards as fast as possible.

Glancing back, I saw the Arab ship was nosing in cautiously
through the gap between the rocks. Her hull almost filled the
entrance, and her oarsmen had scarcely enough room to row.
Several of the pirates stood on deck and were using the long
sweeps to push the vessel into the cove.

I turned and climbed for my life. I had kicked off my boots
before I swam, so I felt the sharp rocks cut and bruise my bare
feet. I slipped and grabbed for handholds while I looked upwards
trying to locate the path. Dirt and small pebbles dislodged by the
Greek captain rained down on me. I was less than halfway up
the cliff face when I caught up with Theodore. There was no
room to overtake him, so I paused, panting with exhaustion, the
blood roaring in my ears, and stared back down into the cove.

The Arab galea now lay alongside our abandoned ship, with
about a dozen looters already on the dorkon's deck. They were

levering up the hatch cover, and soon they would reach the bullion chests lying in the hold. Shouts from below told me that the Arab captain — I could clearly identify him by his red and white striped turban — was ordering some of his men to pursue and capture us. Two or three of them were already swimming ashore.

Suddenly, a speck dropped past the cliff face on the far side of the cove. At first I thought it was a fault in my eyesight, a grain of dirt in my eye or one of those black spots which sometimes swims across one's vision when one is panting for breath. Then two more dark specks followed, and I saw the splashes where they hit the water. Something was falling from the lip of the cliff. I looked across and glimpsed a sudden movement in the fringe of scrub and bushes. It was an arm, throwing some sort of object. The projectile travelled through the air, curving far out and gathering speed until it struck the deck of the galea. It burst on impact. I watched in amazement. Several more of the missiles sped through the air. Whoever was throwing them had found their range. One or two of the missiles splashed into the water, but another four or five landed on the pirate vessel.

From below me came shouts of alarm. The men who had boarded the dorkon began to scramble back aboard their own ship, while their captain raced towards the stern of his vessel. He was shouting at his crew and waving urgently. One of the Arabs picked up from the deck a missile which had failed to burst and threw it overboard. I saw it was some sort of round clay pot, the size of a man's head. The Saracens kept their discipline, even though they had been taken totally by surprise. Now, those who had been swimming ashore turned back towards their vessel. Others hacked through the ropes binding the galea to the captured dorkon and began to push clear. Most of the crew found their places on the benches again and set their oars in place, but they were hampered by the confines of the little cove. There was little room to row and not enough space to turn the galley. The Arab

captain yelled another command and the oarsmen changed their
stroke. They were backing water, now attempting to reverse the
galea out through the narrow gap.

Meanwhile the clay pots continued to rain down. From several
came spouts of flame as they struck. Fire broke out on the galea's
cotton sails, neatly furled on their spars. The rolled-up cloth
served as enormous candle wicks, and I watched the flames run
along the spars, then catch the tarred rigging and race up the
masts. More fire pots struck. As they burst, they spilled a dark
liquid which splashed across the wooden deck. Sometimes the
liquid was already ablaze as it spread. At other times it oozed
sideways until it touched a living flame and then burst into fire.
Within moments the deck of the galea was ablaze with pools of
fire expanding towards one another, joining and growing fiercer.

The Saracens began to panic. Rivulets of flaming liquid spilled
down and ran below the galley benches. An oarsman leapt up,
frantically beating at his gown, which had caught fire. His
companions on the bench abandoned their task and tried to help
put out the flames. They failed, and I saw the desperate oarsman
fling himself overboard to douse himself.

Then I saw something else which I would not have believed
was possible. The burning liquid from the fire pots dripped from
the galea's scuppers and ran down the hull, then spread across the
surface of the pool and *the liquid continued to blaze*, even on the
water. Now I knew I was witnessing the same terrible weapon
that had destroyed the Rus fleet when it attacked the Queen of
Cities two generations earlier. This was the Fire.

As the Fire took hold, there was no stopping or extinguishing
or diverting it. The blazing liquid spread across the galea's deck,
sought out her hold, ran along the oar benches and surrounded
the vessel in flickering tongues of flame. The expanding fire licked
the sides of the abandoned dorkon, and soon that vessel too was
alight. Smoke was pouring up from the two burning vessels. The
column of smoke twisted and roiled. Its base expanded and shifted,
enveloping the wretched Saracens. Some wrapped their turbans

around their faces to protect themselves, and tried uselessly to beat back the flames. The majority jumped into the fiery water. I watched them try to duck beneath the floating skin of Fire. But when they surfaced for air they sucked the Fire down into their lungs and sank back down, not to rise again. A handful managed to swim towards the open sea, heading towards the gap between the reefs. They must have dived down and swum underwater to get beyond the reach of the floating Fire. But their escape was blocked. Now their attackers showed themselves.

Along the arms of the two reefs scrambled armed warriors. Big and heavily bearded, wearing cross-gartered leggings and jerkins, I recognised them at once: they were Harald of Norway's men. They carried long spears and took up their positions on the rocks where their weapons could reach the swimmers. I was reminded of the fishermen in the northern lands who wait on riverbanks, on shingle spits, or at weirs, ready to spear the migrating salmon. Only this time it was men they speared. Not a single swimmer escaped through the gap.

Just five of the pirates managed to reach the rocky ledge below me and haul themselves ashore. Suddenly I was knocked aside by a Norseman leading ten of his fellows down the goat track to the ledge. This time they did not kill their enemy, because the Arabs sank down on their knees and begged to be spared.

'Hey, Thorgils, time to come on up!' It was Halldor's voice, shouting cheerfully. I saw him on the far lip of the cliff waving to me. I turned away from the massacre, a picture of those dying men seared into my mind. Weeks earlier, in Constantinople, I had come across one of the White Christ fanatics haranguing a crowd in the marketplace. To me he had seemed half mad as he threatened his listeners with terrible punishment if they did not repent of their sins. They would fall into an abyss, he screamed at them, and suffer terrible horrors, burning in torment. That image came very close to the scene I had just witnessed.

'You used us as bait!' I accused Halldor after I had climbed to the top of the cliff and found some forty Norsemen gathered,

looking very pleased with themselves. Concealed in a fold in the
ground some distance away was their camp, a cluster of tents
where they had established themselves as they waited to spring
the trap.

'And very good bait you made,' answered Halldor, a grin of
triumph showing his teeth through his beard.

'You could at least have warned me,' I said, still disgruntled.

'That was part of the plan. Harald calculated that you would
understand the meanings of the rune symbols on the map, and be
so pleased with yourself for having worked them out, that you
wouldn't think of anything else but carrying out the message.
That would make the scheme all the more effective.'

His answer made me feel even worse. I, as well as the Arab
pirate, had been hoodwinked.

'And what would have happened if our ship had got here
earlier, or the Arab pirate had showed up later? Your elaborate
scheme would have collapsed.'

Halldor was not in the least contrite. 'If the Arab had shown
up late, then the bullion shipment would have got through safely.
If you were very early and tucked yourselves away in the cove,
he would have come looking for you. Naturally we would then
have helped him, sending up smoke from a cooking fire or some
other way of guiding him to the spot.'

I looked round the group of Norsemen. There were very few
of them to have destroyed the most powerful Saracen vessel in
the region.

'Don't you see the genius of it?' Halldor went on, unable to
conceal his satisfaction. 'Both the pirate and that eunuch minister
in Constantinople thought this was a double deception. The
minister believed we would lure in the pirate to the fake shipment
and the real bullion would get through. The pirate thought he had
seen through that plot and would pounce upon an easy prize. But
Harald was playing a triple game. He reckoned on using the real
shipment as the genuine bait, and look how well it turned out.'

'And if the galea had overhauled us at sea, and captured us and the gold?'

Halldor shrugged dismissively. 'That was a risk Harald was prepared to take. As I told you, he has battle luck.'

I looked around. 'Where's Harald now?'

'He entrusted the ambush to me,' said Halldor. 'We stumbled on the cove when we were searching for pirate bases along the coast. Harald immediately saw how it could provide the perfect location for an ambush. But he thinks the imperial bureaucracy is so riddled with spies and traitors that he had to take every precaution. He sent only a handful of men to set up the ambush so their absence would not be noticed in Dyrrachium, while he himself stayed with our ships. They should be here in a day or two, and Harald will be aboard.'

I must still have looked resentful because Halldor added, 'There's another benefit. Harald's cunning has exposed the source of the pirates' information. It must be the office of the dromos. Someone there who makes the practical arrangements for the bullion shipments was informing the Saracens where and when to strike. Harald suspected this, so when he sent that map with the rune signs he set another trap.'

I remembered the officials from the dromos who had accompanied me on my first visit to Harald's camp at Mamas. Even then I had wondered if one of them had learned to speak Norse in the dromos's college of interpreters.

'You mean the spy had to be able to read rune signs if he was to understand the significance of the map,' I said. 'And only someone in the dromos office would have that skill.'

Halldor nodded. 'Tell that to your castrated minister when you get back to Constantinople.'

Harald himself arrived with his patrol ships just as Halldor and his men were beginning the task of salvaging the cargoes of the two burned-out wrecks. The water in the cove was so shallow that it was easy to recover the bullion chests from the dorkon.

Their contents were unharmed. Halldor's divers then turned their attention to seeing what had sunk with the galea. To everyone's delight it turned out that the ship was packed with booty the pirates had taken earlier. Many of the valuables had been damaged by the Fire and seawater had ruined much of what remained, but there was still a good deal worth salvaging. The finest items were church ornaments, presumably looted from raids on Christian towns. They included dishes and bowls of silver as well as altar cloths. The fabric was a blackened mass, but the pearls and semi-precious stones which had once been stitched to the cloth were unharmed. They too were added to the growing pile of valuables.

'One-sixth goes to the imperial treasury as the emperor's share, the rest is for us. That's the rule,' gloated Halldor as another dripping mass of plunder was brought to the surface.

Harald, I noticed, kept a very close eye on what was being recovered. He trusted his men to carry out an ambush unsupervised, but when it came to division of the spoils he made sure that every single item was precisely accounted for. He stood beside the makeshift table on which each piece of salvage was examined, and watched as its value was calculated. When a mass of silver Arab dinars was brought up, the coins melted together as a lump of metal by the Fire's heat, he ordered it to be weighed three times for value before he was satisfied.

Watching him, I could not help but wonder about his inner thoughts. I had seen him lie full length on the marble floor before the Basileus, who claimed to be the White Christ's representative on earth, and I feared that this lucky outcome for his allegiance might prove a step along the path that would lead Harald to favour the Christian faith. It would be easy for him to be seduced by the wealth and luxury. Standing with a group – Harald, Halldor, and several of his councillors – I was on hand when the most precious of all the objects recovered from the galea was laid upon the table. A Christian cross, it had no doubt been stolen from some rich monastery or church. Each arm was at least three spans in length, as thick as a man's finger, and embellished with patterns moulded on its surface. I knew from my days as a novice in an Irish monastery that to create such an exquisite piece was itself an act of great devotion. The magnificent cross lay upon the bare wood, giving off the dull sheen that only pure gold will give.

Halldor ran his fingers over the workmanship with admiration. 'What's that worth?' he wondered aloud.

'Weigh it and we'll find out,' came Harald's blunt instruction. 'There are seventy-two nomisma to every pound of gold.'

If Harald was naturally inclined to follow any god, I thought to myself, it was not the White Christ but Gullveig from my own Elder Faith. Thrown into the fire to be destroyed, Gullveig, whose name meant 'gold draught', always emerged more radiant than before, the very personification of thrice-smelted gold. But she was also a treacherous and malignant witch-goddess, and suddenly I felt a twinge of foreboding that Harald's gold thirst would lead to his downfall.

FOUR

'YOUR EXCELLENCY, HARALD plans to return to Constantinople now that the pirate menace is dealt with,' I reported to John the Orphanotrophus when I got back to the capital. 'He has already transferred the bullion shipment to Dyrrachium, where he intends to purchase a replacement ship for the Greek captain Theodore so that he can continue on to Italy with the army's pay. They may even have received it by now.'

'This Araltes acts without waiting for orders,' commented the Orphanotrophus.

'It is his nature, your excellency.'

The Orphanotrophus was silent for several moments. 'Corruption is everywhere in the bureaucracy,' he said, 'so the information that the pirate had a spy in the office of dromos is useful, though hardly surprising.'

His words had an undertone which made me wonder if the discovered spy was to be added to the minister's schemes. John was as likely to blackmail the informant into working for him as to punish the man. I felt sympathy for the victim. His position was not so different from my own.

'Does Araltes trust you?' the eunuch asked abruptly.

'I don't know, your excellency. He is not someone who gives trust easily.'

'Then I want you to win his trust. When he arrives back here, you are to assist him in any way you think will earn his confidence.'

When I told Pelagia about my new assignment that evening, she was apprehensive.

'Thorgils, it looks as if you can't untangle yourself from affairs of state, however much you try. From what you've told me about Harald, he is a remarkable man, but dangerous also. In any conflict of interest between him and the Orphanotrophus, you will be caught in the middle. Not an enviable position. If I were you I would pray to your Gods for help.'

Her remark prompted me to ask if she knew anything about the older Gods who were worshipped by the Greeks before they began to follow the ways of the White Christ.

'Theodore, the Greek captain I sailed with,' I told her, 'pointed out to me a ruined temple up on one of the headlands. He said the old Gods were like a family. So I'm wondering if they were the same Gods we worship in the northern lands.'

Pelagia shrugged dismissively. 'I'm not the right person to answer that. I'm not devout. Why would I be when I am named after a reformed prostitute?' She saw she had to explain herself and continued wryly. 'St Pelagia was a streetwalker who took the faith and became a nun. She dressed up as a eunuch and lived in a cave on the Mount of Olives in the Holy Land. She's not the only harlot to have done her bit for the Christians. The mother of Constantine, who founded this city, previously ran a tavern where she provided her clients with more than cheap wine and stale bread. Yet she was the one who found the True Cross and Christ's tomb in the Holy Land.'

Seeing that I genuinely wanted to know more about the older beliefs, Pelagia relented.

'There's a building called the Basilike on the Mese, close to the Milion. It's stuffed full of old statues which no one knows what to do with. Some of them have been stored there for centuries, and among them you may be able to find a few statues of the old Gods. Though whether anyone can identify them for you is another matter.'

The following day I located the Basilike without difficulty and gave the elderly doorkeeper a few coins to let me look around. My intention, of course, was to discover who the old Gods were and why they had been replaced. I hoped to learn something which might save my Gods of the North from the same fate.

The interior of the Basilike was dark and depressing. Hall after hall was filled with dusty statues, placed with no sense of order. Some were damaged, others lay on their sides or had been leaned casually against one another by the workmen who had brought them there. The only sunlight was in the central court-yard, where the larger pieces had been dumped. All were crammed so close together that it was difficult to squeeze through between them. I saw busts of former emperors, sections of triumphal columns, and all manner of marble odds and ends. There were heads which lacked bodies, faces with broken noses, riders without horses, warriors missing shields or holding broken swords and spears. Every few paces I came across inscribed marble panels which had been prised from their original locations. Cut in different sizes and thicknesses, the panels had once identified the statues to which they had been fixed. I read the names of long-dead emperors, forgotten victories, unknown triumphs. Some-where in the jumble of statuary, I imagined, were many of the originals to which the inscriptions had once belonged. To reunite them would be impossible.

I was standing in front of a marble panel trying to decipher the worn letters when a wheezing voice said, 'What size are you looking for?'

I turned to see an old man who had shuffled out from the maze of figures. He was wearing a shapeless woollen mantle with a frayed hem.

'The best pieces go quite quickly, but there are some large ones at the back which have cracks in them. If you cut away the damaged areas, they're still usable.'

I realised that the old man had mistaken me for someone searching for scrap marble. Pelagia had mentioned that marble-work in the city was now made mostly from pieces of salvaged material.

'I had no idea there was so much derelict statuary in store,' I said.

The old man sniffled; the dust was getting in his nose as well as his eyes.

'The city authorities need the display space,' he explained. 'Every time there's a new monument, the sponsors want to put it in the city centre where most people will see it. But the city centre is full up. Not surprising when they've been erecting public monuments there for seven hundred years. So they tear something down and, if they're trying to save money, reuse the plinth. Half the time no one can remember who or what the original statue commemorated. And that's not to mention the statues and monuments which get pulled down when someone wants to build a new apartment block, or which topple over due to neglect or during an earthquake. The city council doesn't want to spend money on putting statues back on their feet.'

'I came here to look at the older statues,' I said cautiously. I did not want to arouse any suspicions that I was a heathen. 'Maybe I can find a representation of one of the ancient Gods.'

'You're not the first person to do that ' said the old man, 'though I doubt if you'll have much luck. Difficult to turn an old God into a new man.' He cackled. He still believed that I was a monumental sculptor looking for a cheap and quick way to carry out a commission by remodelling an earlier statue.

'Can you tell me the best place to look?'

The old man shrugged. 'Can't help you there,' he replied curtly. 'Could be anywhere.' As he turned away with complete lack of interest, I reflected that when the old Gods were discarded, they fell into oblivion.

I spent the next few hours nosing around the Basilike. Nowhere did I find a statue that resembled the Gods I believed in, though I did find what was obviously a sea god, for he had a fishy tail and carried a seashell in one hand. But he was not Njord, my own God of the Sea, so I presumed he belonged to a different faith. In one corner I saw a well-muscled statue sporting a bushy beard, and thought I had stumbled across Thor. But, looking more closely, I changed my mind. The unknown God carried a club, not a hammer. No True Believer would have failed to show Mjollnir, or Thor's iron gloves and strength-giving belt. The other effigy which raised my hopes was the contorted figure of a man pinioned to a rock. The writhing figure was obviously in torment, and I thought it might be Loki the trickster whom the Gods punished by tying him to a rock, using the entrails of his own son as his bonds. But I could see no trace of the serpent whose venom would fall on Loki's face if it was not collected in a bowl by his faithful wife Sigyn, nor a statue of Sigyn herself. The carving remained a mystery, and I was disappointed that I found no trace whatever of the God whom I expected to be there – Odinn. And among all the inscriptions I saw not a single rune letter.

I had reached the very back of the last storage hall when I finally came across one image that I could identify for certain. The carving was done on a panel, and there were holes drilled for the attachment points where it had been fixed on public display. It was a picture of the three Norns, the women who weave the fate of all beings. One of them was spinning, another measuring, and the third held scissors. As I gazed at the panel, it occurred to me that here, perhaps, was a message that I should heed. Not even the Gods themselves can alter the destiny that the Norns have woven, so there was nothing that I could do to change the ultimate fate of the Elder Way. It was better that I should try to understand what was replacing it.

Perhaps Odinn put that thought into my head, because he soon arranged for me to fulfil my wish. On my return to the guards barracks, a message was waiting for me from John's sekreton. It informed me that I had been seconded to the staff of

Araltes, and my duty was to act as his interpreter with proto-maistor Trdat on a mission of great importance. When I showed the message to Pelagia and asked her if she knew about this Trdat, what he did or where he was going, she seemed baffled.

'A lot of citizens would know the name of Trdat,' she said, 'but it can't be the same man. He was the protomaistor, the master builder, who repaired the church of Hagia Sophia, the Holy Wisdom, after it had been damaged in an earthquake. But that was in my grandparents' time. That Trdat must be long dead by now. He was an Armenian, a genius as an architect. It is said that no one else had the talent to make such an elegant repair. Maybe this Trdat is his grandson, or his great-nephew. The role of protomaistor passes down through families.'

'And what about this mysterious mission of great importance the Orphanotrophus mentions? Does the gossip in the marketplace have any clues as to what that might be?'

'No doubt it has something to do with the Basileus,' she answered. 'His sickness – even though you still don't want to call it that – isn't getting any better. In fact it has been growing worse. It now affects him almost daily. The doctors are unable to halt the progress of the illness, so Michael has turned to the priests. He's becoming more and more religious, some would say morbid. He thinks that he can obtain a cure from God by prayer and religious works.'

'There's something else I need to ask you before Harald gets back to Constantinople,' I said. 'I didn't mention this to the Orphanotrophus, but Harald asked me to find out the best way of converting his booty from the pirate ambush into cash or bullion. And he would like to make the arrangement discreetly so that the authorities do not know.'

Pelagia gave a thin smile. 'Your Harald is already acquiring some of the habits of this city. But, as I said, you had better be careful. If the Orphanotrophus gets to hear that you are acting for Harald in the conversion of loot into cash on the black market, and not keeping him informed, you will suffer for it.'

'I will say that I was carrying out his instructions to win Harald's confidence. What could be more helpful than acting as his money agent?'

'What sort of loot does Harald have on offer?' Pelagia asked bluntly, and I reminded myself that she was a woman of business.

'Silver and gold items mostly,' I replied. 'Plate, cups, jugs, that sort of thing, foreign coins of various countries, some jewellery, a few pearls. The pirate was making shore raids as well as seizing merchant ships before he was caught. His galea had a very mixed haul of booty. Our divers brought up a small clay jar from the burned-out wreck. It was packed in straw and carefully crated so it had survived unbroken. Our Greek captain was most excited when he saw it. He read the marks and told us that it was a dye shipment on its way to the imperial silk factory.'

'If that was a jar of purple dye, then he had every reason to be excited,' Pelagia told me. 'The dye comes from seashells, and the extract of twelve thousand shells is needed to colour a single imperial robe. By weight that dye is far more precious than fine gold.'

'Where could Harald dispose of such things without attracting attention?'

Pelagia thought for a moment, then said, 'He should deal with a man called Simeon. Officially he's an argyroprates, a seller of silver. But he also handles gold and precious stones. In fact he has another string to his bow as a moneylender. He's not supposed to be in that business, but he can't resist the eight per cent interest. The bankers' guild probably knows what he is up to, but they let Simeon operate because they find it useful to have someone who can do the occasional deal for them off the books. But it would be best if I contact Simeon first. He has a money changer's table on the Milion, not so far from the bread market, and we know each other by sight. If I make the connection successfully between Simeon and Araltes, I will want an introduction fee of, say, half a per cent.'

Pelagia was as good as her word, and it turned out that the half per cent was a bargain for the services that Simeon was to provide Harald with. The argyroprates always contrived to find someone willing to pay silver or gold for brocades, silks, boxes of spices, holy artefacts, even on one occasion a pair of lion cubs. In that particular transaction the keeper of the Basileus's menagerie in the Great Palace paid a premium price.

Harald came back to Constantinople shortly before Ascension Day, and barely had time for one private meeting with Simeon — at which I acted as the interpreter — before he received the details of his new assignment. His war band was to be sworn in as a unit of the Varangians-without-the-walls and receive regular army pay and accommodation. Harald himself was to select twenty of his best men and report aboard a warship loading stores and materials in the harbour of Bucephalon.

A copy of his orders had been sent to me, with a note penned in the margin by the chief secretary to the Orphanotrophus telling me that I was to accompany Araltes. I had lived long enough in Constantinople to know that Bucephalon harbour was reserved for vessels used by the imperial family. The only warship stationed, as far as I was aware, was the fast dromon assigned for the use of the Basileus himself. I had no idea why Harald and his men should be on board.

The intelligent-looking young man who greeted me on the dromon's deck quickly explained the situation. A civilian, he was slightly chubby with a glossy mass of curly black hair, and he had the look of a man always ready to find an excuse to smile or make a joke.

'I'm Trdat,' he said genially. 'Welcome aboard. I gather that you are to be the interpreter for my military escort. Though why I need one is beyond me.' He spoke with such lack of formality that I wondered what he was doing on board the Basileus's personal dromon.

Trdat waved his hand casually at the taut rigging of the

immaculate warship, the scrubbed decks and gilded detailing, the smartly dressed officers. Even the blades of the thirty-foot rowing sweeps were picked out in imperial purple and gold.

'Quite a ship, don't you think? Couldn't imagine anything finer for a gentle sea voyage in the best season of the year.'

'Where are we going?' I asked. 'And why?'

'Those stuffy bureaucrats haven't told you? Just like them. Always priding themselves on their discretion when there's no need for secrecy, yet willing to sell classified information if it swells their purses. We are bound for the Holy Land to see what can be done about the state of Golgotha. It's a mission for His Majesty the Basileus. By the way, I'm an architect, a protomaistor.'

'But I was told that protomaistor Trdat restored the Church of Holy Wisdom more than forty years ago.'

'That would be my grandfather,' the architect replied cheerfully. 'And he did a very good job too. That's why I've been picked for this commission. The Basileus hopes I can do as well as my grandfather. This is to be another restoration project.'

'Perhaps you could tell me exactly what is involved so I could explain it to your escort when they arrive.'

'I don't want to bore you with the details, and I can hear by your accent that you are a northerner – don't be offended, I'm Armenian by origin – so you may not even be a Christian. But the spot where the Christ died and was buried is one of the truly sacred places of our faith. A magnificent basilica was erected there not long after the blessed Augusta Helena discovered the True Cross and her people identified the cave where the Christ's body was interred. For centuries the sanctity of the sepulchre was respected, even when it fell into the hands of the Muslims. Unfortunately times have changed. In my father's day a Caliph, who justly earned the title of Murad the Mad, gave orders for both the basilica and the sepulchre to be destroyed. He told the local governor that no stone was to be left upon another. The governor was also ordered to close all the other Christian churches in the province and turn away Christian visitors. Since then we have had no reliable information as to how bad was the destruction of the sepulchre – the Anastasis or Resurrection, as it is known – nor what the ruins look like today. Murad the Mad went to meet his maker sixteen years ago. He was assassinated by a religious zealot – rather appropriate, don't you think? – and our Basileus is currently negotiating with his successors for permission to rebuild the basilica and repair the sanctuary. That's where I come in. I have been commissioned to assess the present condition of the buildings and make on-the-spot repairs. Those civil servants may be venal idlers, but they are good at keeping archives, and I've managed to locate the plans of the original basilica. But if the shrine is so badly wrecked that it cannot be restored, then I am to design an entirely new building worthy of the site.'

'That's quite a responsibility,' I observed.

'Yes, the emperor sets great store by the scheme. He believes it will show the depth and extent of his devotion, and he hopes he will be rewarded with an improvement in his health. I presume you are familiar with the problems he has been having in that regard. That's also why he placed the imperial dromon at my disposal. It shows his level of concern.'

To my surprise Trdat had not bothered to lower his voice when he spoke of the state of Michael's health.

He breezed on. 'Perhaps you could pass word to your military friends that we will be ready to sail as soon as I've loaded the last of the paints and tesserae – those are the little cubes we use for making mosaics. It should be no later than the day after tomorrow. My own staff – the mosaicists, plasterworkers, painters and the rest – are already on standby. Though whether they will actually have any work to do when we get to the Holy Land remains to be seen.'

When I relayed all this information to Harald, he seemed pleased. I supposed he thought that the personal vessel of the Basileus was exactly the sort of transport that he merited. Certainly when Harald and his men, including Halldor, whom I was glad to see, arrived at the Bucephalon, the Norwegian prince walked up the gangplank as though he was the owner of the vessel, not just the escort commander for an architect.

'Tell your Varangians that we'll be making just one stop en route,' Trdat said to me. 'We need to put in to the island of Prokonnesos to pick up some marble in case we can patch up the place of resurrection.'

Already the dromon was moving out to sea under oars, every stroke closely supervised by the protokarabos, the officer responsible for the rowing. He was very conscious that people were watching from the windows of the Great Palace, and he wanted as smart a departure as possible.

It occurred to me that the protomaistor might well know something about the derelict statues in the Basilike, and I asked him if he had ever visited the place.

'Of course,' he answered. 'My father and grandfather, while he was alive, put me through all the hoops. They made me study everything an architect needs to know and more – geometry, arithmetic, astronomy, physics, building construction, hydraulics, carpentry, metalwork, painting. There seemed no end to it. Luckily I enjoyed the work, particularly drawing. I still get satisfaction from preparing diagrams and elevations. They positively encouraged me to visit the old temple sites, took me round the Basilike, and never lost the chance to point out the remnants of the old statuary on display in Constantinople. It's still there if you know what you are looking at. That tall bronze statue of a woman in the Forum of Constantine, for example. Everyone thinks it's a former empress or perhaps a saint. In fact, it's an early Greek goddess. And have you ever noticed the figure on top of the Anemodoulion?'

'The monument near the Forum Tauri, the pyramid with a bronze figure of a woman at the top, which turns and points with the slightest breath of wind? We have similar wind vanes on our ships and houses in the north lands, but they are much smaller and simpler in design.'

'Yes, that's right,' said Trdat, 'But how many people know

that when they look up at the Anemodoulion to check the wind direction, they are actually consulting a bygone pagan goddess? But we'll talk more about this during the voyage. I expect it will take us at least three weeks to reach the Holy Land, even aboard the fastest dromon in the fleet.'

Trdat's company turned our trip into one of the most informative sea journeys I have ever undertaken. The Armenian loved to talk and he was free with his knowledge. He pointed out details about coastlines, described his upbringing in a family of famous architects, and introduced me to some of the techniques of his profession. He took me down into the hold to open up sacks of tesserae and showed me the little cubes of marble, terracotta, different-coloured glass and mother-of-pearl. He demonstrated how they would be stuck into a bed of soft mortar to make portraits or patterns on a wall or on the floor, and told me that a skilled mosaicist, working flat out, could complete in one day an area as wide as a man could spread his arms in each direction.

'Imagine how long it took to decorate the inside of the apse in the church of the Holy Wisdom. Grandfather Trdat calculated that it required two and a half million tesserae.'

When we reached the marble island of Prokonnesos halfway across the Propontis Sea, he also invited me to go ashore with him as he visited the quarries where miners were cracking open the rock and splitting away sheets of marble ready to be sawn and carved to shape.

'Prokonnesos marble is so widely used that I find it rather boring,' he confessed. 'You see it everywhere – the same white stone with blue-grey veining. But it's readily available, and the supply seems inexhaustible.'

'I thought that most of the new marblework was made from salvage.'

'True. Yet many of those salvaged pieces came from Prokonnesos in the first place, and the quarry owners have been shrewd enough to pander to the builders' laziness. They prepare the marble pieces here on the island, carving out the shapes and patterns, and have them ready and waiting on the quay. You simply pick up ready-made segments for columns, and capitals and pediments in stock designs, but it restricts an architect's creative skill if he has to work with such stuff just because his client wants to save money. I know of at least nineteen different varieties of marble, yet if you were to walk around Constantinople you would think there was only one – Prokonessos. I love it when I have the chance to work with dark red porphyry from Egypt, serpentine from Sparta, green from Thessaly, or rose red from Syria. There's even a black and white marble that can be brought from the far end of the Great Sea.'

In the end my new-found friend selected only a few plain slabs of the Prokonnesos marble which, as he put it, 'were good enough to put down as paving around Christ's tomb if the flooring has been ripped up at Mad Murad's command'.

Harald, Halldor and the other Varangians kept to themselves throughout the trip, though I sensed they were itching to take the helm or adjust the dromon's sails. Her captain was a palace appointee with no apparent seafaring skills, and he had the good sense to leave the running of the vessel to the protokarabos and his assistants. Navigation presented few challenges as they could set the course from one island to the next, watching for each new sea mark to come up over the horizon ahead even as the last island peak dropped out of sight behind us.

As we were steering toward the distant loom of an island, Trdat made a comment which caused a jolt of memory. Squinting at the high ground taking shape ahead, he remarked, 'That must be the lame smith's favourite haunt.'

His words brought back an image of my first tutor in the Old Ways, Tyrkyr the German. He had been heating and shaping iron in his forge when he told me how Volund the master metalworker had been deliberately crippled by the evil King Nidud and left on an island where he was forced to work for his captor.

'A lame smith on that island. What was his name?' I asked Trdat. 'Hephestus the smith God,' he replied. 'That island over there is Lemnos. Legend says that it was the place where Hephestus resided. There's a shrine to him there and a cult still flourishes, so I'm told, though it operates in secret.'

'Why was Hephestus lame? Was he mutilated deliberately?'

'No,' Trdat replied. 'As far as I know, he was born lame, and he was ugly enough as well. But he was a magnificent metalworker, the finest ever known. He could make anything. He even fashioned a metal net, which he hung over his bed when he suspected his wife of adultery with another God. He pretended to leave home, then crept back, and when his wife and her lover were in action, Hephestus dropped the net on them as they lay stark naked. Then he called the other Gods to visit him and have a laugh at their embarrassment. It's said to have happened over on that island, inside a burning mountain.'

'Strange,' I said. 'We also have the story of a lame metalworker who took his revenge on his enemy. Though it was by murdering his sons and making drinking cups of their skulls and jewels from their eyes and teeth, which he presented to their unknowing parents.'

Trdat grimaced. 'Bloodthirsty lot, your Gods,' he said.

'I suppose so,' I replied. 'They could be cruel, but only when it was deserved. Like Loki, whom they punished for his endless deceit by tying him to a rock with the entrails of his own son. The earth shakes when Loki struggles to free himself. I saw Loki's statue in the Basilike.'

Trdat laughed out loud. 'That wasn't Loki or whatever you call him. I remember that statue. It used to be in the Forum of Constantine until someone needed the space and it was taken away and dumped in the Basilike. It's one of the earlier Gods – well, he was the son of what they called a Titan – by the name of Prometheus. He was a trickster who angered Zeus, the chief of the Gods, once too often. Zeus punished him by telling Hephestus to nail him to a rock. Then Zeus sent an eagle each day to eat Prometheus's liver, which grew again during the night. So he was in endless torment.'

'Sounds as if your old Gods were just as cruel as mine,' I said.

'Equally human, I would say,' was Trdat's response. 'Or perhaps inhuman, if you want to put it that way. Depends how you look at it.'

'Was I also mistaken in thinking that there's a marble panel in the Basilike which shows the Norns?'

'Never heard of them. Who are they?'

'The women who decide our destiny when we are born,' I said. 'They know the past, present and future, and they weave the pattern of our lives.'

'I can't remember seeing that panel, but you must be talking about the three Fates,' Trdat answered after a moment's thought. 'One spins the thread of a man's life, another measures it and the third cuts it. Norns or Fates, the message is the same.'

We reached our destination, the port of Joppa on the coast of Palestine, to find that the local governor knew nothing about our mission. For three days we sweltered in the summer heat, confined aboard the dromon while the governor checked with his superiors in the capital at Ramla if we could be allowed to land.

Finally Harald, rather than the easy-going Trdat, took command of the situation. He stormed ashore and I went with him to the governor's residence, where the anger of the towering northerner with his long moustaches and strange lopsided eyebrows cowed the governor into agreeing that a small advance party could go ahead to inspect the Anastasis while the majority of Trdat's technicians and workmen stayed behind. As we left the governor's office, we were surrounded by a clamouring crowd of elderly men, each offering to act as our guide. For years they had made their living by taking devout Christians up to see their holy places, but the prohibitions of Murad the Mad had destroyed their trade. Now they offered to hire us carts, tents, donkeys, and all at a special price. Brusquely Harald told me to inform them that he did not ride on carts and certainly not donkeys. The first person to come to the dockside with two dozen horses would be employed.

The horses that were brought were so small and scrawny that I thought for a moment Harald would take it as an insult. But their owner, as lean and malnourished-looking as his animals, assured me that the creatures were adequate to the task, and it was only two days' easy ride to our destination. Yet when Harald got into the saddle, his feet almost touched the ground on either side, and the other Varangians looked equally out of proportion to their mounts. So it was an undignified cavalcade that rode out of the town, crossed a narrow, waterless, coastal plain, and began to climb into the rocky hills of what our guide enthusiastically called the Promised Land.

I have to admit that I had expected something better. The landscape was bleached and bare with an occasional small field scratched out of the hillside. The few settlements were meagre clusters of small, square, mud-walled houses, and the inn where we stayed that night was crumbling and badly run-down. It offered only a dirty courtyard where we could stable the horses, a dreary meal of pea soup and flat bread, and flea-infested bed mats. Yet if we were to believe our guide, who was very garrulous and spoke Latin and Greek with equal ease, the sere brown land we were crossing was fortunate beyond all others. He reeled off lists of the holy men or miraculous events associated with each spot we passed, beginning with Joppa, on whose beach, he claimed, a great fish had vomited up a prophet.

When I translated this yarn to Harald and the Varangians they looked utterly incredulous.

'And the Christians revile us for believing that the Midgard serpent lies at the bottom of the World Ocean,' was Halldor's comment. 'Thorgils, don't waste your breath translating that old fool's prattle unless he says something believable.'

In mid-afternoon on the second day we rode across a ridge and there, spreading up the slope of the next hill, was our goal: the holy city of the Christians, known to them as Jerusalem. No larger than a single suburb of Constantinople, the place was totally enclosed within a high city wall studded with at least a dozen watchtowers. What caught our attention was a huge dome. It dominated the skyline of the city. Built on rising ground, it dwarfed the buildings all around it. Most astonishing of all, it appeared to be of solid gold.

'Is that the Anastasis, the place where the White Christ was buried?' I asked our guide.

He was taken aback at my ignorance. 'No,' he said. 'It is the Holy of Holies, sacred to the followers of Muhammad and those of the Jewish faith. The Anastasis is over there,' and he pointed to the right. I looked in that direction, but saw nothing except a nondescript jumble of roofs.

We rode through the city gate, crossed a large open forum with a tall column in its centre and proceeded along a colonnaded avenue which led to the area the guide had indicated. Our exotic appearance drew curious and sometimes hostile glances from the crowds. They were an amazing mix – Saracen officials in loose white gowns and turbans, merchants dressed in black cloaks and brick-coloured sandals, veiled women, half-naked urchins.

Midway along the avenue we came to a great gap in the line of buildings, and the guide announced, 'Here is the place.'

Trdat looked aghast. The space ahead of us was a scene of utter devastation. Massive building blocks, broken and dislodged, marked the lines of former walls. Heaps of smashed tiles were all that remained of roofs. Charred beams showed where the destruction had been hastened by fire. Everywhere was rubble and filth. Without a word, Trdat leaned down and picked up a small stone from among the weeds that were growing over the rubbish. Sadly he turned it over in his fingers. It was a single tessera, dark blue. It must once have graced a mosaic in the basilica that had sheltered worshippers who came to this spot. Of the church itself, nothing remained.

Our guide hitched up his loose gown and scrambled over the heaps of rubbish, beckoning us to follow. Harald and the others stayed behind. Even the hardened Norsemen were silenced by the sight of so much destruction.

I joined Trdat and the guide, just as the latter was saying, 'It was here,' as he pointed downward towards marks on the bare rock. To me it looked like the ragged scars left on Prokonnesos when the marbleworkers had prised away what they needed, only the marks of the chisels and pickaxes were random, and the spoil – the stone they had broken – was tossed to one side in a haphazard pile.

'What was here?' asked Trdat in a hushed voice.

'The tomb, the sepulchre itself. Murad's people hacked it to pieces.'

Trdat seemed numb with shock as the guide led us back through the lanes to find an inn where we could stay. The protomaistor said nothing for several hours, except to ask me to send word back to Joppa that the craftsmen waiting on the dromon should stay where they were. There was no point in them coming inland. The splendid buildings which had once stood around the Anastasis were utterly beyond repair.

'Thorgils, I never thought that I would face a challenge like this,' the architect confessed to me. 'The task is even more daunting than when my grandfather had to repair the Church of Holy Wisdom after the earthquake. At least he had something to work with. Here I have to start from scratch. I'm going to need your help.'

So it was that I, Thorgils, the devotee of Odinn, came to assist in the recreation of what our guide called the Holy Sepulchre. Partly my work was practical: I held the end of the tape as Trdat took the measurements of the area he had to work in, and I took down notes of the angles he measured. I helped him uncover the lines of the damaged walls, so that he could trace the ground plan of the earlier buildings and compare them with the architectural plans he had brought from the archives in Constantinople. I also made lists of the materials on site that might be reused – the surviving sections of columns, the larger building stones and so forth. But by far my most important contribution was assisting him in interviewing all those who had known the holy place before it was razed on the orders of Murad the Mad.

Our talkative guide was our primary source, but rumours of our enquiries spread throughout the city, and furtive figures appeared, followers of the White Christ, who were able to tell us what the shrine had looked like before its demolition. In the light of what those Christians told us, we cleared away some of the rubble and chalked out on the ground the dimensions of the tomb as they indicated. It had been a small, free-standing building, chiselled from the living rock, sheathed in marble and surmounted by a golden cross. The cave inside had been large enough for nine men to stand inside as they prayed, and at the back was the shelf on which the White Christ's body had been laid.

Trdat wanted measurements and practical details. He was told that the cave had been high enough for there to be a space of one and a half feet between the top of a man's head and the roof; the shelf was seven feet long; the entrance to the cave had faced east according to some, south according to others. Our informants told us that it had taken seven men to move the large rock rolled in front of the cave at the time of the Christ's burial, but that it had broken in half. Its two parts had been squared off and turned into altars, which had been set up within the great circular church that once covered the entire site. The man who told us that particular detail took us on a search through the rubble to see if we could find either altar, but without success.

Trdat was unperturbed. He drew a quick sketch of a squared-off stone, and showed it to the Christian. 'Is that how it looked?' he asked.

The man looked at the drawing. 'Yes, just like that,' he agreed readily.

Trdat gave me a quizzical glance and drew another altar stone, a slightly different shape this time. 'And the other one. Was it like this?'

'Oh yes, you have it perfectly,' his informant replied, so eager to please that he barely glanced at the drawing.

In our inn later that evening I asked Trdat if he really believed our informants.

He shrugged. 'It's not important if I do. People will believe what they want to. Of course I will do my best and try to reproduce the original details when I do the designs for a restoration. But as the years pass, I'm sure that those who are devout will come to believe that what they are seeing is the original, not my copy.'

All this time Harald and the other Varangians had been remarkably patient. They spent most of their hours in the inn, playing at dice, or they came to where Trdat and I were at work. The presence of these bearded warriors was useful as it kept onlookers at bay and discouraged those Saracens who shouted curses at us or threw stones. In the evenings Trdat sat at a table, ceaselessly drawing his plans or scratching out diagrams and calculations. Occasionally a Varangian might saunter over and peer over his shoulder at the work, then return to his place. But I was aware that their patience would not last for ever. I felt that without some sort of distraction, Harald and his men would want to leave.

It was our guide who proposed an excursion. He offered to show us the Christian sights in and around the city, then take us on a short trip to the nearby river, where, he said, the White Christ had undergone a ceremony of immersion. Trdat was at the stage when he was working on perspective drawings and wanted to be left alone in the inn in peace and quiet, so he readily agreed that Harald, Halldor and the others should take up the guide's suggestion, and that I should go as their interpreter.

To me that tour of the Holy Places was astonishing. There was hardly an item, a building or street corner that was not in some way associated with the White Christ or his followers. Here was Golgotha, where the White Christ was crucified, and our guide pointed to a bloodstain on the rock, which, if you were to believe him, had never been washed away. Nearby was a crack in the stone, and he assured us that if anyone put his ear to it he would hear running water, and that if an apple was dropped into the crack it would reappear in a pool outside the city wall a mile away. Eighty paces in that direction, so he claimed, was the very centre of the world. At that point rose four great underground rivers.

Next, with many backward glances to see that we were not being followed, he took us to a storeroom where he showed us a cup that the White Christ had blessed at his final meal, as well as a reed that apparently had been used to offer up a sponge of water to the Christ as he hung on the Cross, and the sponge itself, all withered and dry. The item of most interest to me was a rusty spear propped in a corner. According to our guide, it was the very lance that had been used to stab the Christ in the side as he hung on the Cross, and had been rescued from the Anastasis before Murad's men smashed up the place. I handled the spear – it seemed very well preserved to be so ancient – and I thought it strange that the followers of the White Christ would claim to find such relics, while we, the followers of the Elder Faith, never imagined we could possess the spear which pierced Odinn as he hung upon the tree of knowledge. For us, what belonged to the Gods was their own.

The catalogue of marvels outside the city walls was just as wide ranging. Here were the marks of the White Christ's knees as he knelt to pray, the stone receiving the impression as if it had been molten wax. There was the same fig tree from which a traitor by the name of Judas had hanged himself; earlier the guide had showed us the iron chain he had used for the suicide. On the Mount of Olives were more marks in the rock. This time they were footprints left behind when the White Christ was taken up to the place which was the equivalent of Valholl for his followers. Remembering my conversation with Pelagia back in Constantinople, I asked if I could see the cave where her namesake had lived, disguised as a eunuch. Without hesitation I was led to a small, dank grotto on the side of the mountain. I peered inside, but not for long. Someone had been using it as an animal pen. It smelled of goat.

The more I saw, the more baffled I became that the faith of the White Christ was so successful. Everything associated with it seemed so ordinary. I asked myself how people could believe in such obvious fictions as the suicide's fig tree, and I put the question to Harald, picking a moment when he seemed to be in good humour, because I wanted to know if he was susceptible to the White Christ's teaching.

He turned that great predatory look upon me, the sea eagle's stare, and said, 'Thorgils, you miss the point. It is not the physical things that matter: not the lance nor the sponge nor any of the other things we have been shown. The strength lies in the ideas the Christians preach. They offer hope to the ordinary people. That is their reward.'

'And for someone who is above the ordinary, my lord?' I ventured to ask.

Harald thought for a moment and then said, 'There is something there, too. Have you not noticed how obedient the Christians are to their one God. They talk about following him, and no other. That is what any ruler would want of his subjects.'

I was still thinking about Harold's reply as we collected our horses from the inn's stable and rode out of the city behind Cosmas, our guide. We left through the eastern gate, and Cosmas asked me to warn Harald and the others that some of the people we would meet along our road could prove unfriendly. The most hostile were Samaritans. They had a horror of unbelievers, whether Christian or Jew. If we wished to buy anything from a Samaritan we would have to place the coins in a bowl of water because they would receive nothing direct from our hands, considering us unclean. And after we left, they would burn straw over the hoof prints left by our horses to purify all traces of us.

I suspect that our guide was secretly pleased when, close to the river, we did encounter a group of them. The Samaritans

behaved exactly as predicted, blocking our path, spitting and
cursing, shaking their fists and working themselves into a frenzy
of hatred. Then they searched the roadside for stones which they
began to hurl at us, very accurately. At that stage Harald and the
Varangians were provoked into action. They spurred their small
horses into a canter and charged at their tormentors, smacking
them with the flat of their swords and scattering the shrieking
zealots, who fled up the hillside, surprised at such brisk treatment.

The countryside became even more desolate than before. After
crossing the plateau, our road descended through a steep-sided
gorge where the only building was a distant monastery clinging
to the rock face like a swallow's nest. A few monks still lived
there, our guide told us, because the semi-derelict building was so
difficult to access that the Saracens left it alone. Emerging from
the gorge we found ourselves riding through a wilderness of sand
and scrub completely devoid of people, except for a single party
of nomads who had set up their brown tents among the dunes.
They were burning thorn bushes for their campfire, and had
tethered their animals. I had previously seen such creatures in
the imperial menagerie − camels − and I wondered that these
beasts, which attracted so much attention in Constantinople, were
regarded here as no more unusual than an ass or donkey.

We camped on the outskirts of a ruined town. The place had
been completely levelled four years earlier by a great earthquake,
and the sight of the tumbled ruins prompted Cosmas to claim
that, long ago, its defences had similarly collapsed when an army
of besiegers had played trumpets and marched around the walls,
calling on their God to aid them.

'The din probably woke up Loki, and he squirmed in his
bonds,' muttered Halldor sarcastically. He was finding the guide's
stories more and more outrageous.

It was another disappointment when we reached the river
which we had been promised would be a marvel to behold. It was
no larger than the streams beside which I had played as a child
in Greenland. A muddy creek, it ran through reed beds, and the

water when we tasted it was gritty and unpleasant. Yet this was the river, the guide assured us, in which the White Christ had been immersed, affirming his faith. The guide showed us a set of stone steps leading down from the bank. Several of the steps were missing, others were unstable, and there was a half-rotten rope to serve as a handhold. The steps, he said, were where the faithful had come in former times to imitate the example of the White Christ.

As if on cue – indeed I suspected that Cosmas may have arranged it – a ragged priest of the White Christ appeared from a small shelter of reeds nearby. He offered to conduct just such a ceremony for a small fee, promising that anyone who did so would store up 'riches in heaven'. I translated his offer, and to my consternation Harald accepted. He removed his clothes, piled them on the river bank and, wearing only a loose gown, descended the steps and waded in. There Harald allowed the priest to splash water over him and chant a prayer. I was dismayed. Until that moment I was sure that I could sway Harald towards the Elder Faith.

Halldor saw my expression. 'Don't take it too seriously, Thorgils,' he said, 'When you've known Harald as long as I have, you'll understand that the only riches he is interested in are those on this earth. He will do anything that will help him gain them, even if it means taking a dip in a muddy river. Right now, he's probably thinking that the White Christ is fortunate to have him as a recruit.'

My consternation lasted all the way back to Aelia, as the Greeks called the Holy City, and it took Trdat's air of suppressed excitement to dispel my disappointment. The architect was positively quivering with happy anticipation.

'You can't guess what occurred in your absence, ' he said as he welcomed me. 'It's unheard of, at least since my grandfather's time.'

'What's unheard of? You look as though you've found a fortune,' I said.

'Better than that. While you were away, I went back to the
site of the Anastasis to check some details on my drawings, and
an elderly Saracen came over to see what I was doing. He was
very distinguished looking and well dressed. Of course I showed
him my work, made gestures trying to explain what I was doing,
and so forth. It turned out that he spoke a few words of Armenian
and enough Greek to tell me that he is one of the dignitaries
responsible for the upkeep of the Holy of Holies, the Golden
Dome. He has invited me to visit the place if I promise to be
discreet. Can you imagine! No Christian has been allowed to look
inside the Dome and see its wonders for years.'

'Don't talk to me about the wonders of local religion,' I said.
'I've been disappointed enough in the last few days.'

'Come on, Thorgils. This is an opportunity that won't come
again. Of course you must accompany me to visit the Dome. My
visit is scheduled for tomorrow.'

A servant collected us when the last echoes of the Saracens'
prayer call had died away, and I had to admit a sense of excitement
as Trdat and I, both wearing Saracen gowns, set off. Ahead of us
the great shining Dome glowed in the early morning sunshine,
seeming to float above the rooftops of the city. At an outer gate
to the sacred area the servant asked us to change our footwear,
providing us with slippers, then brought us across a broad
platform paved with granite slabs to where Trdat's acquaintance
was already waiting. Trdat introduced me as his architectural
assistant and then, even before our host could speak, the protomaistor had grabbed my arm and was blurting out 'the Tower of
the Winds!' To my surprise he was not staring at the magnificent
building soaring up ahead of us, but at a much smaller structure
built beside it.

'That is the Dome of the Chain,' explained our host, whose
name I gathered was Nasir. 'It's the model of the main building,
made by the original architects. They produced it so that the
caliph Abd-al-Malik, who ordered the construction, could approve

the design before building began. Nowadays we use it for storing valuables.'

But Trdat was already out of earshot, hurrying towards the smaller structure.

'Thorgils, that eight-sided base on which the Dome rests,' he called over his shoulder, 'there was one in ancient Athens just like that. That's why my grandfather made me study the classic buildings, to learn from their skills. Just as the men who designed the Dome must have done. How I wish my grandfather could have seen this.'

Trdat circled the small building excitedly. 'Do you mind if I take some rough measurements?' he asked Nasir.

The Saracen hesitated for a moment, then said, 'I suppose it can't do any harm. It will not be allowed inside the Kubbat as-Sakhra, the Dome itself. There you can only take a quick look.'

Trdat walked around the Dome of the Chain, counting his paces. Then he measured its diameter by reckoning the number of paving slabs across its width.

'Brilliant,' he breathed admiringly as he stood back to judge its height. 'It's the geometry, Thorgils. The height of the eight-sided base is the same as its width, and the height of the Dome is the same again. The result: perfect proportion and harmony. Whoever designed the structure was a genius.'

'Two of them,' said Nasir. 'A local man from the city by the name of Yazid-ibn-Sallam, and a great scholar called Abdul-ibn-Hayah.'

Trdat was squatting down and drawing with his finger across a paving slab, attempting make an outline in the dust. 'I wish I had brought wax and stylus,' he said, 'but I think I know what we will find inside the main building.'

Nasir looked at the Armenian as if he was touched in the head. 'We should not be loitering here. Just a quick glance inside is all that is permitted,' he warned, escorting us to the Golden Dome.

To me it was like a triumph of the jeweller's art, a diadem. Swathes of glittering mosaics covered the outer sides of the octagon, while the cupola above it gleamed as if solid bullion.

'How do you keep the Dome so clean?' I asked.

'In winter, when there is snow or rain, we cover it with animal skins and felt.' Nasir replied. 'The caliph had not intended that the Dome should be gilded, but the work went so well and so swiftly – it took just four years to build – that a hundred thousand gold dinars were left over from the money allocated to the architects. It was decided to melt down the coins and use them to cover the Dome in gold leaf.'

We had reached the entrance to the building, and he held up his arm to prevent us going any further, but we were close enough to see inside. At the centre, right beneath the Dome, was a honey-coloured area of bare rock which, Nasir explained, was the spot from which their prophet ascended to a Seventh Heaven. This Holy of Holies was surrounded by a circuit of marble columns which supported the great vault soaring overhead. Looking upward into the bowl of the Dome, I gasped in astonishment. Its interior was covered with gold mosaic work, and from the very centre dangled a chain on which was suspended a gigantic chandelier. The light from hundreds upon hundreds of lamps reflected and glittered off the golden surface.

'Now breathe deeply,' Nasir advised us. The air was heavy with the smell of saffron, ambergris and attar of roses. 'That's my task,' said our host proudly. 'I supervise the preparation of the perfumes which the attendants sprinkle on the sacred rock and burn in the censers. But it is time we left.'

'Double squares,' mused Trdat thoughtfully as we walked back to the inn. 'Just as I thought. That is what I was trying to work out when I was scratching in the dust. The interior of the building is based on a design of two sets of squares interlocking. The inner ones determine the circumference of the Dome itself, the outer ones provide the dimensions for the octagon. Best of all, I now know the size and shape of the dome which I will propose for the shape of the new basilica at Golgotha. I will model it on what I saw today, placing twelve pillars below, one for each of the apostles. I have all the information I need to work up my designs for the restoration of the Anastasis and the buildings around it. It is time we returned to Constantinople.'

Harald and the Varangians, when I told them the news, looked very pleased.

'Is the great Dome really solid gold?' Halldor asked.

'No, it's a hundred thousand dinars turned into gold leaf,' I answered.

'Who would have so much money to spare?' he marvelled.

'Saracen rulers are prepared to pay enormous sums for what they hold most dear,' I said casually, not realising that my comment would help Harald achieve his life's ambition – the throne of Norway.

FIVE

THE DROMON PICKED up her moorings in Bucephalon harbour after a frustrating homeward voyage. Headwinds meant that our passage back to Constantinople took much longer than anticipated, and already there was a wintry feel to the city when I said goodbye to Trdat, then accompanied Harald, Halldor and the others to the barracks of the Varangians-without-the-Walls.

We arrived in time to intervene in an angry confrontation between the Norsemen of Harald's war band and a senior Greek staff officer. The professional army, the tagmata, was soon to deploy to Italy for a campaign in the west, and the Armamenton, the imperial arsenal, had been working at full stretch to prepare weapons and supplies. Now the clerks who issued horses and weapons to the soldiers had drawn up a timetable for the troops to collect their requirements. Harald's five hundred Varangians were flatly refusing to re-equip with standard weaponry, preferring to retain their own axes and shields. Harald curtly informed the Greek staff officer that his men were a special force, recruited under his personal command, and he took instructions only from the palace or direct from the army commander, the strategos. The Greek glared at the Norwegian and snapped, 'So be it. You will find that the new strategos expects instant obedience, especially from barbarians.' Then he stalked off, seething with indignation.

'Why all this fuss about our weapons?' Halldor asked me. 'Why wouldn't they be good enough for the Greeks?'

'They are fiercely proud of their history,' I told him, 'They've been running an empire for seven hundred years and so feel they've learned how to organise things properly, whether a tax system or a military campaign. They like to do everything by the book – quite literally. During my time in the Palace Guard, our young Greek officers would arrive with their heads stuffed full of military information. They'd learned it by reading army manuals written by retired generals. Much of the advice was very helpful – how to load pack mules or scout an enemy position, for instance – but the trouble was that it was all book-learned, not practical.'

'Fighting is fighting,' grumbled Halldor. 'You don't have to read books to learn how to do it. Practising how to form up in a battle line or how to use a battle axe left-handed, that sort of thing helps. But in the end it is valour and strength that win the day.'

'Not as far as the imperial army is concerned,' I countered. 'They call themselves "Rhomai", the Romans, because their military tradition goes back to the Caesars and they've been fighting on the frontiers of empire for centuries, often against huge odds. They've won most of their battles through superior generalship or because they are better equipped or better organised or . . .' and here I thought about the scheming Orphanotrophus . . . 'because they've been able to bribe the opposing generals or create some sort of disarray in the enemy ranks with rumours and plots.'

'Too clever by half,' muttered Halldor. 'No wonder they have to hire foreigners to protect the emperor himself. They're so busy scheming that it's become a habit and they forget who their real enemies are. They finish up by stabbing one another in the back, and no longer trust their own people.'

Harald, who had been listening to us, said nothing. Maybe he already knew what I was talking about, though years later I was to remember that conversation with Halldor and wonder if, once

again, I had helped to shape the course of Harald's life. If so, then I was an unwitting agent, if not of Odinn, then of the Norns, or – as Trdat would have said – the Fates.

Leaving Harald and his men at the barracks, I lost no time in going to visit Pelagia, for I had been missing her while I was away in the Holy Land. Until now we had been friends, not lovers, but I was coming to sense that if our relationship continued to develop she might soon mean more to me than agreeable companionship and wise advice. Hoping to find her at home, I felt a pang of disappointment to discover that she was no longer living at her old address. I was redirected to a luxurious apartment in a more fashionable part of the city. When I complimented her on the move as well as the expensive furnishings of her new home, she was typically down-to-earth in her response.

'I have the coming war to thank,' she said. 'It's amazing how much money can be made from army contracts. It's such a relief not having to chase creditors in private commerce. The government always pays up, provided you grease a few palms in the commissariat.'

'Surely the army can't be buying its bread already,' I said. 'I know that army bread is rock hard and stale, but the campaign is several months away. Nothing's going to happen until spring, and by then the army will be in Italy and will be able to obtain bread locally.'

'I'm not selling them bread,' said Pelagia. 'I've got the contract to supply them with emergency rations, the sort you use on a forced march. The department of the new strategos asked for tenders, and I located someone who could supply sea onions at a good price. It was simple enough for me to assemble the other ingredients.'

'What on earth's a sea onion?' I asked.

'A plant like a giant onion. The bulb can be the size of a man's head. It's boiled, washed in water, dried and then sliced very thin. The army contract stipulated that one part of sesame

was to be added to five parts onion, and one part poppy seed to fifteen parts onion, the whole lot crushed and kneaded together with honey. Nothing that a competent baker can't organise easily.'

'What's it taste like?' I asked.

Pelagia grimaced. 'Pretty foul. But then it is only eaten in emergencies. The soldiers are issued with two olive-sized pills of it per day. The stuff is claimed to be sweet and filling, and doesn't make a man thirsty. Just the sort of thing which the new strategos would want for his troops. He's a stickler for detail.'

'That's the second time I've heard about this new strategos,' I said. 'Everyone seems to be in awe of him.'

'So they should be. Comes from somewhere on the eastern frontier where he used to be just a local town commander. He made a reputation for himself by wiping out a raiding column of Saracens when the imperial army was very low on morale. The Saracens laid siege to his town and demanded its surrender. He pretended to be scared and promised to hand over the place next morning without a fight, even sent supplies to the Saracens to show his good intentions. But he deliberately included plenty of wine in the shipment and the Saracens got themselves drunk. That night the city defenders rushed the Saracen camp and killed every one of them. He presented himself in front of the Basileus with a sack out of which he tipped a torrent of Saracen ears and noses. The emperor promoted him to corps commander on the spot. Since then he's never lost a battle. He's a brilliant tactician, and his troops would follow him anywhere.'

'He sounds very like Harald.' I said, 'Is this military paragon going to command the campaign in Italy?'

'Only the land forces,' said Pelagia. 'My sister, who's still got her job in the women's quarters at the palace, tells me that the naval contingent will be commanded by John's brother-in-law, Stephen. It's the usual set-up. The palace doesn't trust anyone enough to give them sole command, so they divide the leadership.'

'And what's the name of this general who'll command the land forces?'

'George Maniakes,' she told me.

RATHER TO MY surprise I heard nothing from the Orphanotrophus directly. I had been expecting a summons to his office to report on Harald's conduct in the Holy Land, but as my guardsman's salary continued to be paid – and I arranged for Pelagia to receive and hold the money – I presumed that I was to carry on the duties the Orphanotrophus had given me. Doubtless he had more important matters to occupy him, because the Basileus's health was showing no signs of improvement despite a frenzy of pious work. More and more of the civil administration had passed into the hands of the man the public referred to as John the Eunuch.

'You want to be even more cautious than before if you are called to his office,' Pelagia warned. 'The strain is telling on John. To relax, he organises debauches at which he and his friends get blind drunk and conduct bestial acts. But next morning his friends regret what they have done and said. The Orphanotrophus calls them in to explain any loose talk they have uttered the previous night. It's yet another of his methods of exercising control.'

'What does his brother, the Basileus, think of this behaviour?' I asked. 'I thought he was very religious.'

'More and more so. Besides sending Trdat to the Holy Sepulchre, Michael is lavishing money on monasteries and nunneries all over Constantinople. He's spending a huge sum on a church dedicated to St Cosmas and St Damian over on the east side of the city. The place is being remodelled. It's being given new chapels, an adjacent monastery, finest marble for the floors, walls covered with frescoes. You should go and see it some time. The Basileus hopes that his donations will result in his own cure because Cosmas and Damian were both physicians before they were martyred. They're known as the Anargyroi, "the Unpaid", because they never accepted any money for what they did, unlike some physicians in this city that I could think of. That's not all. The Basileus is paying for a new city hospice for beggars, and he's come up with a scheme to save all the prostitutes in the capital. He's having a splendid new nunnery built, and the public criers are circulating in the streets announcing that when the building is ready, any harlot who agrees to go and live there as a nun will be accepted. Doubtless the place will be dedicated to St Pelagia.'

The exodus of the tagmata began the week after we, the Old Believers in Harald's war band, celebrated our Jol feast, and the Christians observed the Nativity of their God. Watching the orderly departure of the troops, I had to admit that I was impressed by the efficiency of the army's organisation. First to leave the capital were the heavy weapons units, because they would move the slowest. Their petrobolla for firing rocks, the long-range arrow launchers and the cheiroballistra shaped like giant crossbows were dismantled and then loaded on to carts which ground their way out of the western gate of the city. From there they began the long overland plod to Dyrrachium, where they would be put on transports and ferried to Italy. When the column was halfway along the road, the army signallers flashed back the news along a chain of signal stations and the army despatchers released the light infantry battalions, the slingers and the archers to follow. Everything was tidy and methodical. The regiments of archers were accompanied by squads of sagittopoio, experts in repairing their bows, while the infantry had platoons of armourers who could mend or replace iron weapons. The squadron of Fire operators marched with a dedicated cavalry troop whose task was to protect the munitions wagons loaded with the mysterious ingredients for their secret weapon. Naturally each brigade also had its own field kitchen, and somewhere in the middle of the column was a team of army doctors with chests of surgical instruments and drugs.

The heavy infantry and the armoured cavalry were the last to leave. For their departure the Basileus himself attended the ceremony. It was a brilliant spectacle. The four palace regiments collected their battle standards from the church of St Stephen and the church of the Lord after the flags had been blessed by the priests, then formed up to march along the Triumphal Way. In front of them rode the heavy cavalry, coloured pennants fluttering from the tips of their lances. Each trooper wore a padded surcoat of heavy felt over his armour, and his horse was similarly protected with a jacket of stiffened leather and a mail breastplate. They looked formidable. Finally came my old regiment, the Palace Guard, on foot and surrounding the Basileus on his charger. They would proceed only as far as the Golden Gate, where the emperor would say farewell to his troops, then the Palace Guard would return with the Basileus to the Palace to carry on their duties.

Michael himself looked sickly, his face grey with fatigue and strangely bloated. I was reminded of the appearance of his predecessor, the murdered Romanus, at his funeral, which was the last occasion on which the Guard had marched along the Triumphal Way. Then there had been near silence. Now, as the imperial army set out for war, there was music. For the only time in my life I heard an orchestra on the march – drums, pipes and lyres – even as I wondered if I was seeing history repeat itself, and Basileus Michael was being slowly poisoned in some sort of labyrinthine court intrigue.

I left for Italy by sea a week later with Harald and his war band. Once again Harald's Norsemen had been assigned to serve as marines, perhaps because they had won fame for their actions against the pirates, but also as a reprimand for their Norse obstinacy about conforming to the army rule book. The result was that for the next two years we were given only a peripheral role in the campaign to regain a former jewel of the empire – the great island of Sicily.

Our enemy were Saracens from North Africa. For more than a century they had ruled the island after overrunning the Greek garrison. They had established a thriving capital at Palermo, and from their Sicilian bases they raided the empire's province of southern Italy and, of course, their ships menaced the sea lanes. Now the Basileus was determined to drive back the Saracens and restore Sicily to his dominions. George Maniakes, promoted to the rank of autokrator, was the man to do it.

He began with an invasion across the straits at Messina. Harald's war band was there to protect the southern flank of the landing, so I was a witness to the expertise of the imperial troops. The light cavalry had been rehearsing for weeks, and the attack went flawlessly. They arrived off the landing beach soon after dawn in specially built barges. Ahead of them three shallow-draught dromons, packed with archers, cruised up and down the shallows, forcing back the Saracen cavalry which had assembled to deny the landing. When the imperial landing craft touched land, the sailors lowered the sides of their barges, and the light cavalry, already mounted, clattered down the ramps. They splashed through the shallows, formed up and charged up the beach. The Saracens turned and fled. For the next ten days a steady stream of transports, barges and warships shuttled back and forth across the straits, bringing more troops and supplies, and very soon an imperial army of ten thousand men stood on Sicilian soil.

Maniakes himself crossed over on the fourth day. It was a measure of his professionalism that he saw no need to indulge in heroics by leading the attack. He and his general staff went ashore only when his command headquarters had been set up, ready to receive him. It was there, when he called a war council of his senior officers, that I first laid eyes on him.

There are times, I believe, when the Gods play tricks on us. For their amusement they create situations which otherwise would seem to be impossible. Trdat had told me that the ancient Gods of the Greeks did the same, and relished the results. The meeting between Harald of Norway and George Maniakes was one of those moments which we ordinary humans describe as coincidences, but I believe are mischievously arranged by the Gods.

How else, I ask myself, could two men so similar have been brought together, yet each man be so unusual that he was unique. Harald, as I have described, was a giant, half a head taller than his colleagues, arrogant, fierce and predatory. He struck fear into those who aroused his anger, and was a natural leader. George Maniakes was identical. He too was enormously tall, almost an ogre with his massive frame, a huge voice, and a scowl that made men tremble. He also radiated absolute authority and dominated his surroundings. When the two men came face to face for the first time in the imperial command tent, it was as if no one else was in the room. They loomed over everyone else. Neither man could have imagined he would ever meet someone so like himself, though one was blond and the other dark. There was a long moment of surprise, followed by a pause of calculation as the two men took the measure of one another. Everyone saw it. We sensed that they made a temporary truce. It was like watching two great stags who encounter one another in the forest, stop and stare, and then cautiously pass one another by, neither challenging the other, yet neither giving ground.

Harald's war band, it was confirmed at the council, was to patrol the Sicilian coast and make diversionary attacks on Saracen settlements. Our task was to discourage the local Saracen commanders from sending reinforcements to their emir, who could be expected to mass his forces near Palermo and come westward, hoping to drive the imperial army back into the sea. To meet that attack, Maniakes and the tagmata would march inland and seize the highway which linked Palermo with the wealthy cities of the east coast. Once the highway was under imperial control, Maniakes would turn south and march on Catania, Augusta and the greatest prize: Syracuse.

The Gods arranged another coincidence that day which, in its way, was a foretaste of what was to come for me and for Harald. Harald, Halldor and I were leaving the council tent when we saw four or five men coming towards us on foot. From a distance they looked like Norsemen. Indeed at first we thought they must be

Varangians; they certainly seemed to be Varangian in size and manner. We took them to be volunteers who had recently arrived from Kiev or from the lands of the Rus. It was as they drew closer that we saw differences. For one thing they were clean-shaven, which was unusual. For another their weapons and armour were not quite what we ourselves would have chosen. They carried long swords rather than axes, and though their conical helmets were very like our own, their chain-mail shirts were longer, and the skirt of the mail was split in the middle. It took a moment to understand that these warriors were dressed for fighting from horseback, not from ships. Our two groups stared at one another in puzzlement.

'Greetings! To which company do you belong?' Halldor called out in Norse.

The strangers stopped and eyed us. Clearly they had not understood Halldor's question. One of them answered in a language which, by its tone and inflection, I recognised. Yet the accent was so strong that I had difficulty in understanding. Several words were familiar, though the meaning of the sentence was confused. I summoned up the Latin that I had learned as a lad in an Irish monastery and repeated Halldor's question. This time one of the strangers understood.

'We ride with Hervé,' he said in slow Latin. 'And you?'

'Our commander is Harald of Norway. We have taken service in the army of the Basileus.'

'We also serve the Basileus,' the warrior replied. 'They call us Frankoi.'

Then I knew. The men were mercenaries from Francia, but not from the central kingdom. They were speaking the Frankish tongue with the accent of the north. They were descendants of Vikings who had settled the lands of Normannia generations earlier, and that was why they looked so familiar to us. I had heard rumours about their prowess as horse warriors, and how they sold their swords to the highest bidder. While we Varangians arrived by sea and along the rivers, the Frankoi came overland, also seeking their fortunes in the service of the emperor. There was, however, a major difference between us: Varangians wanted to return home once we were rich; the men of Normannia – or Normandy, as they themselves called it – preferred to settle in the lands they conquered.

Maniakes took the Frankoi mercenaries with him when he marched inland, and they lived up to their warlike reputation when Maniakes rebuffed the emir's forces in their counter-attack. Then the autokrator began his long, grinding campaign to regain the east Sicilian cities. The tagmata steadily advanced along the coast, laying siege to one city after another, patiently waiting for them to fall before moving on. Maniakes took no risks, and Harald and his war band grew more and more frustrated. His Norsemen had enrolled in the army of the Basileus hoping for more than their annual pay of nine nomisma: they wanted plunder. But there was little to be had, and, worse, Harald's men received a lesser share when the army's accountants divided up the booty because the Norsemen were regarded as belonging to the fleet under Stephen, the brother-in-law of the Orphantrophus, and not part of Maniakes's main force. By the second spring of the campaign, Harald and his Varangians were very restless.

By then we were besieging Syracuse. The city fortifications were immensely strong, and the garrison was numerous and ably led. Harald's squadron of a dozen light galleys had the task of occupying the great harbour so that no more supplies reached the defenders from the sea, nor could messengers slip out to summon help. From the decks of our vessels we heard the clamour of the war trumpets as Maniakes manoeuvred his battalions on the landward side, and we saw boulders and fire arrows lobbed over the defences and into the city. We even glimpsed the top of a siege tower as it was inched forward. But the walls of Syracuse had withstood attacks for more than a thousand years, and we doubted that Maniakes would succeed in capturing such a powerful except after many months of siege.

An engineer visited our flotilla. He was rowed out in a small boat and came aboard Harald's vessel. As usual I was summoned to act as interpreter, and when the engineer scrambled up the side of our ship, I thought there was something familiar about the man.

'May I introduce myself,' he said. 'My name is Nikephorus, and I am with the army technites, the engineers. I'm a siege specialist and, with your permission, I would like to investigate the possibility of building a floating siege tower.'

'What does that involve?' I asked.

'I'd like to see if we could perhaps tie up two, or maybe three, of your galleys side by side to make a raft. We would then use the raft as a base on which to build a tower which could then be floated up against the city wall.'

I translated his request to Harald, and he gave his agreement. The engineer produced a wax tablet and began making his drawings and calculations, and then I knew whom he reminded me of.

'Do you know Trdat, the protomaistor, by any chance?'

The engineer gave a broad smile and nodded. 'All my life,' he said. 'In fact we are first cousins, and both of us were students together. He studied how to build things up, I learned how to knock them down.'

'I went with Trdat to the Holy Land,' I said.

'Ah, you must be Thorgils. Trdat called you "the educated Varangian". He spoke to me about you several times. I'm delighted to make your acquaintance. We should talk some more after I've finished my arithmetic.'

In the end Nikephorus calculated that the width and stability of the makeshift raft would not be sufficient for a floating siege tower. He feared the structure would capsize.

'A pity,' he said, 'I would love to have designed something novel and to have followed in the footsteps of the great Syracusan master.'

'Who's that?' I asked.

'Archimedes the great engineer and technician, of course. He created machines and devices to protect Syracuse when the Romans were attacking. Cranes lifted their ships out of the water and dashed them to pieces, weights plunged on to their decks and sank them, and even some sort of focusing mirror, like our signal mirrors, set them ablaze. To no avail, for he lost his life when the city fell. But Archimedes is a hero to anyone who studies siege craft and the application of science to fortifications, their assault and defence.'

'I had no idea that there was so much theory to your work.'

'If you've got time,' Nikephorus suggested, 'I'll show you just how much theory there is. If your commander can spare you for a few days, you could join me on the landward side of the city, and see how the army engineers function.'

Harald agreed to let me go, and for the next few days I was privileged to see Nikephorus in action. It turned out that he had been very modest about his qualifications. He was in fact the army's chief engineer and responsible for the creation and employment of all the heavy equipment against the walls of Syracuse.

'Note how those drills are angled slightly upward. It improves the final result,' he said as he showed me around a device like a very strong wooden shed on wheels. Inside were various cogs and pulleys connected to the sort of tool that ship carpenters use for drilling holes, only the instrument was far larger. 'The shed is pushed up against the base of the city wall, where the roof protects the operators from whatever missiles and unpleasantness the defenders drop down on them. The drill opens up holes in the city wall which are then stuffed with inflammable matter and set on fire. By quenching the hot rock – urine is the most effective liquid – the stone can be made to crack. If enough holes are drilled and enough fissures result, the wall will eventually collapse.'

'Wouldn't it be safer and easier to dig a tunnel under the wall foundations so it comes down?' I asked.

Nikephorus nodded. 'Trdat was right. You should have been an engineer. Yes, if the army technites were to have a motto, it should be "Dig, prop and burn". Excavate the tunnel under the wall, put in wooden props to hold everything in place, and just before you pull out, set fire to the props and then wait for the wall to tumble down. The trouble is that tunnelling takes time, and often the enemy digs counter-tunnels to ambush your miners, then kills them like rats in a drain.'

'Is that why you preferred to build a siege tower?' I asked. 'We saw the top of it from our ships. And heard the war trumpets.'

Nikephorus shook his head. 'That was just a ruse. That particular tower was a flimsy contraption, only for show. At the start of a siege, it's a good idea to create as much commotion as you can. Make it appear that you have more troops than is the case, launch fake attacks, allow the enemy as little rest as possible. That way you dishearten the defenders and, more important, you get to see how they respond to each feint, how well organised they are, which are the strong points in their defences, and which are the gaps.'

He then took me to see the proper siege tower he was building. The structure was already massive. Eventually it would be higher than the city walls, Nikephorus explained, and when the dropbridge on the topmost level was released, it would provide a gangway for the shock troops to rush across directly on to the battlements. 'Just the job for your axe-wielding Varangians,' he added with a grin, 'but it will be several weeks before the tower is ready. As you can see, we've only got as far as putting together the main framework of the structure. We still have to install the intermediate floor, where I intend to place a platoon of Fire throwers, and the exterior will need cladding with fresh ox hides. The Saracens are accomplished in countermeasures, and I expect they will try to set the tower alight with missiles of burning pitch or oil as we approach the wall. I'm designing a system of pipes and ducts to be fitted to the tower, so that if any portion catches alight, my men stationed on the topmost level with tubs of water will be able to direct the flow of water to extinguish the flames.'

'Won't that make the tower very heavy to move?' I objected.

'Yes, that's always a problem,' Nikephorus admitted. 'But with levers and enough manpower we should be able to roll the tower slowly forward. My main concern is that the Saracens will already have prepared the ground so that the tower topples before it is in place.'

We had clambered up a series of builders' ladders and were now standing precariously on the siege tower's highest cross-beam.

'See over there?' said Nikephorus pointing. 'That smooth, level approach to the city wall? It looks like the perfect spot for the tower when we launch our attack. But I am suspicious. It's too inviting. I think the defence has buried large clay pots deep in the soil at that point. The ground is firm enough to carry foot soldiers and cavalry, but if the tower rolls over them, the amphorae will collapse and the ground cave in. Then the tower will tilt and fall, and, in addition to the loss of life, we will have wasted weeks of work.'

But the Saracens did not wait for the operation of their sunken trap, if there ever was one. Even as Nikephorus and I stood on the half-built siege tower looking down on the suspect ground, a trumpet sounded the alarm. A sharp-eyed sentry had noticed the bronze gates of Syracuse were beginning to swing open. Moments later the gap was wide enough for a troop of Saracen cavalry to ride out. There were at least forty of them, and they must have hoped to catch the imperial troops by surprise with their sudden sortie. As they charged, they nearly succeeded.

There were more trumpet calls, each one more urgent, from the tagmata's lines. We heard shouts and orders from below us, and a squad of Greek heavy infantry came running towards the base of the tower. They were menaulatos, pikemen with long weapons specially designed to fend off a cavalry attack, and they must have been on standby for just such an emergency. They formed up around the base of the tower and lowered their pikes to make a defensive hedge, for it was now clear that the siege tower was the target of the Saracen sortie.

The raiders were led by a flamboyant figure. He wore a cloak of green and white patterns over his chain mail, and a scarf of the same colour wrapped around his helmet streamed out behind him as he galloped forward. The quality of his horse, a bay stallion, carried him well clear of his men, and he was shouting encouragement at them to follow him. Even the disciplined pikemen wavered in the face of such confidence. The rider swerved into a gap between the pikes. With a deft double swing of his scimitar, first forehand and then with a backward stroke, he hacked down two of our men before his horse spun round nimbly and carried him clear.

Seeing that the siege tower was now protected, the main raiding party changed the direction of their attack and rode towards the infantry lines, where lightly armoured troops were emerging from their tents, hastily pulling on their corselets and caps. The Saracens managed to get in among their victims long enough for them to cut down a dozen or so men before wheeling about and beginning to fall back towards the city gates.

Their entire sortie had been very quick. There had been no time for the imperial cavalry to respond, with the exception of just one man. As the Saracens were about to slip back through the city gates, a lone rider came out from the tagmata's lines. He was wearing mail and a helmet, and was mounted on a very ordinary horse which, even at a full gallop, would never have caught up with the retreating Saracens. He yelled defiance, and the green-clad leader must have heard his shout, for just as he was about to ride back in through the city gates, he glanced over his shoulder and turned his stallion. The Saracen then waited, motionless, facing his challenger. When he judged the distance to be right, he spurred his mount and the animal sprang forward.

Horse and rider were superb. The Saracen wore a small round shield on his left arm, and held his scimitar in his right hand.

Scorning the use of reins, he guided his mount with his knees and raced towards his opponent. At the last moment he bent forward in his saddle and leaned his body slightly to one side. The stallion responded by changing stride and flashed past the other horse, surprising the animal so that it checked and almost unseated its rider. At the same moment the Saracen slashed out with his scimitar at his enemy. Only by chance was the blow blocked by the long shield his opponent carried.

Belatedly I had made out that the Saracen's challenger was one of the Frankoi mercenaries. He appeared cumbersome and ungainly on his horse, and his weapon was a long iron sword instead of the heavy mace that an imperial cavalryman would have carried. Hardly had the Saracen ridden past his opponent than his agile stallion turned tightly and a moment later was galloping past the Frank, this time on the opposite side. Again the scimitar swept through the air, and it was all the Frank could do to raise his sword in time to deflect the blow.

By now the walls of Syracuse were lined with cheering spectators observing the unequal contest, while below them the troops of the tagmata stood watching and waiting for its inevitable outcome. The Saracen relished the audience. He played with the Frankish rider, galloping in, swerving, feinting with his scimitar, racing past, turning and coming again at a gallop. The heavily built Frank no longer attempted to urge his horse into action. All he could do was tug on the reins and try to turn his horse so that he faced the next attack.

Finally, it seemed that the Saracen had had enough of his amusement, and, riding a little further off than normal, he wheeled about and with a halloo of triumph came racing down on his victim. The scimitar was poised, ready to slice, when the Frank abruptly leaned back over the crupper of his horse. The Saracen's blow whipped through empty air, and at that moment the Frank swung his heavy sword. It was an ugly, inelegant blow. Delivered flat, and from a man almost lying on his horse's rump, it was an awkward scything motion requiring enormous strength of the arm. The long blade swept over the ears of the racing stallion and struck its rider full in the midriff, almost chopping the Saracen in half. The green and white striped cloak wrapped around the blade, the Saracen doubled forward even as he was swept out of the saddle by the force of the blow, and his corpse crashed to the ground and lay still. The helmet with its green and white scarf rolled off across the level ground.

For one moment there was a stunned silence, and then a great shout rose from the imperial lines. The stallion, puzzled by the sudden disappearance of his rider, whickered and turned to where his master's corpse lay, nuzzled the body for a moment, then trotted quietly back to the city gate, which was opened to let the creature in. The Frank ponderously rode back to the tagmata without a word or gesture.

He earned the name Iron Arm, Fer de Bras in his Frankish tongue, for his achievement. His adversary, we later learned, was a caid or nobleman of Syracuse. His defeat in single combat severely affected the morale of the city's defenders, while, on our side, the rank and file of the Greek army regarded the burly and taciturn mercenaries from Normannia with increased respect.

SIX

MANIAKES'S TROOPS HAD little time to celebrate. Word reached us that the Saracens were massing in the interior of Sicily, ready to march on Syracuse and relieve the siege. Their new army was commanded by another emir, and he was dangerous. Abdallah, son of the ruler of Kairouan on the Libyan coast, had brought several thousand seasoned warriors across the Great Sea, and our spies estimated that his force would soon increase to more than twenty thousand men, as more recruits were arriving every day.

Maniakes reacted with typical decisiveness. He ordered the tagmata to prepare to march, but not strike camp. Each unit was to leave behind a few men who would give the impression that the siege was still in place. They were to remain as visible as possible, keep the cooking fires burning, mount patrols and follow the normal routines. At the same time the engineers and heavy weapons units were to discourage further sorties from the city by keeping up a regular discharge of missiles, and the Frankish mercenaries from Normannia were to stay behind in case of emergencies. Our harbour flotilla was stripped of men. Skeleton crews, changing from one vessel to the next, would make it look as if the blockade was still operative. Harald gave command of this minimal force to Halldor, and then he and I, with about two

hundred fellow Varangians, joined the flying column that Maniakes led inland, leaving quietly by night.

A week of forced marches across a dry and dusty landscape
brought us to the west of a mountain whose subterranean fires
reminded me of my days in Iceland, where the Gods in anger
similarly cause hot rock to flow. Here the emir had established
and fortified his base camp. He must have had warning of our
approach, because when the tagmata arrived, the Saracens had
already withdrawn within their defences and shut the gates.

Abdallah had chosen his position well. Behind the emir's
camp, and on both sides, was broken terrain unsuitable for any
direct assault against the fortifications. In front, open ground led
down to a small stream shallow enough to be crossed on foot. On
the opposite bank the land rose gently upward again to the low
ridge where Maniakes set up his own headquarters, facing across
to the Saracens. And here I watched how Maniakes's military
genius turned Abdallah's apparent advantage against him.

Nikephorus explained to me what was going on. I had been
perplexed to find the engineer included in the flying column
because his heavy equipment was much too ponderous to be
brought along. When I said as much, Nikephorus had grinned at
me and said cheerfully, 'We'll find something on the spot to make
up what is needed.' Now, as I waited near Maniakes's command
post, I saw the engineer busy by a table and went over to see
what he was doing. He had prepared a model of Abdallah's camp
and its surrounding terrain set in a bed of soft clay.

'Hello, Thorgils,' he greeted me. 'As you can see, I don't
always knock things down. I can also build them, but usually in
miniature. This is where the strategos will fight his battle.'

'You and Trdat are just the same,' I said. 'In the Holy Land
Trdat spent more time examining a model of the Golden Dome
than looking at the real thing.'

'No, no, I mean it. Victory on the battlefield often depends on
observation and timing, particularly when the enemy is so obliging
as to shut himself up and let us take the initiative. See these little

coloured markers? They represent the tagmata's forces. The grey
markers are light infantry, orange for the archers and slingers,
yellow for the heavy infantry, and red for the kataphractos, our
armoured cavalry. Note that I've placed half of the red markers
in that dip behind this ridge where they're out of sight of the
Saracen lookouts. Later I'll add markers for the Saracen forces
when I know more about them.'

'How's that possible? The Saracen forces are hidden behind
their defences.'

Nikephorus winked at me. 'Not for long. That's just a wooden
palisade, not a high city wall. Look behind you.'

I turned round to see an extraordinary structure rising from
the ground. It was like the mast of a ship, but far, far taller than
any I could have imagined. It was being hauled upright by a
complex web of ropes and angled poles. 'It's a bit makeshift,'
admitted Nikephorus, 'You can see the joints where my men have
had to lash the sections together. But it will do. Think of it as a
giant fishing rod, and that we're fishing for information.'

'What do you call it?' I asked.

'A spy pole,' he said, 'and that's only the lower section. We'll
hoist an upper section later, and then steady it with guy ropes of
twisted horsehair. There'll be a pulley at the top, and we'll use it
to haul our observer into position. He'll not be the heaviest man
in the army, of course. But he'll know his signal book, and after
he's had a good look over into the Saracen camp, he'll signal
down the information. Our scouts have already told us that
Abdallah is expecting a frontal attack. His men have sewn the
ground in front of their main gate with spikes, intending to lame
our cavalry. They know that the kataphract is our main weapon.'

We spent the next four days waiting in front of the Saracen
camp while Nikephorus and his assistants added to the coloured
markers on the sand table according to the information from the
lookouts. Each time they did so, Maniakes and his staff would
come across to review their own tactics. They shifted the markers
back and forth, discussed various possible manoeuvres, and heard

additional reports from the scouts. Twice a day the officers of the tagmata were told the latest assessment of the enemy strength, and as I watched them cluster around the table I soon differentiated between them. Infantry men wore knee-length quilted cotton coats and greaves of iron to protect their shins, while the cavalry dressed in chain-mail body armour or the jacket they called a thorax, which was made of small iron plates stitched to a leather backing. Rank was denoted by a metal band of gold, silver or copper worn on each arm. The imperial troops were recruited from a dozen different countries and spoke at least as many languages, but all had been trained to the same army standard. They observed closely the little counters as they were moved about, and it was clear that every officer was learning precisely what was expected of him. I realised how chaotic and ill disciplined our Norse contingent must have seemed by comparison, and I understood why Harald and his men had been assigned a position where we would be directly under the eye of our general.

Abdallah brought us to battle on the fifth day. Perhaps he thought his advantage in numbers was overwhelming, or maybe he was still relying on the crippling effect of the iron spikes sewn on the battlefield. He did not know that our scouts had been picking up the iron spikes under cover of darkness, and that half of Maniakes's heavy cavalry had always remained hidden behind the ridge, where the army farriers had reshod all the cavalry horses with flat iron plates to protect their hooves. Nor had the emir any benefit of surprise. Hours before the Saracen army began to emerge from its defences, our observer on the spy pole had flagged a warning, and the imperial light cavalry were poised to disrupt the Saracens from forming ranks.

Standing next to Maniakes's command post, waiting to relay his orders to Harald and the Varangians, I watched as our scorpions, as Nikephorus called them, began to fling small rocks and iron bolts into the enemy ranks. These scorpions were the army's portable artillery – long-range crossbows mounted on tripods and light enough to be carried on the march. Between their salvoes the light cavalry unleashed wave upon wave of attack. One squadron after another they cantered deliberately forward to within range, then released a first and a second flight of arrows. Then each squadron wheeled about, and as it rode away the riders turned in their saddles and released a third volley.

'Our army learned that technique generations ago, on the eastern frontier, against the Persians. It triples their effective firepower,' Nikephorus commented.

Their assault looked to me more like a war game than a serious battle, yet men were falling in the Saracen ranks when each flight of arrows rained down, and I could see the disorder which resulted.

'If you watch carefully, Thorgils,' Nikephorus added, 'you'll note that one-third of the light cavalry is engaging the enemy, one-third is preparing the next attack, and one-third is regrouping, attending to their wounded, or resting.'

Fifty paces to the rear of each cavalry squadron rode eight men. They carried no offensive weapons apart from short swords. The moment they saw a cavalryman unhorsed, one of them came dashing forward at full gallop to retrieve the downed man who, reaching up, grabbed the rider's forearm, and at the same time placed his foot in a third stirrup dangling behind the rescuer's saddle. In one smooth movement the unhorsed cavalryman was plucked off the ground, and the two men were speeding away to the rear, where the cavalryman was provided with a remount. I estimated that for every five cavalry horses struck down by Saracen arrows, four riders were back in action by the time their squadron next moved forward. The exceptions, of course, were those men who were wounded. But they were not abandoned. They were taken to where Maniakes's medical teams had set up their field hospital behind the ridge and out of sight of the enemy.

All this time Maniakes never stirred from his position on the crest of the ridge, but stood watching the conflict. The tagmata was extended in a line along the slope of the hill, facing across the shallow valley towards Abdallah's forces. The Saracens were still clumped together in a disorganised mass as they flinched from the repeated attacks of the imperial cavalry. More and more of the Saracen troops were emerging from the gates of the camp, and now they filled the space in front of the palisade until they were too closely packed to be effective. Most of them were foot soldiers, as presumably Abdallah had not been able to ship much cavalry with him from North Africa, and many seemed to be peasant levies, for they were armed with only small swords and shields, and wore leather caps instead of helmets. I saw Saracen officers trying to cajole their men into orderly lines, pushing and shoving at the troops, hoping for some formation. Meanwhile the tagmata stood calmly, regiment by regiment, scarcely moving as their company commanders watched Maniakes's signallers for their orders. I had no idea of their battle plan, and counting the superior numbers of Saracen troops I wondered what Maniakes had in mind.

I never found out, because the Gods intervened. I have mentioned that our march to the battleground was across dry and dusty ground baked under the summer sun. The soil was very loose, almost sandy. As we waited for Maniakes's instructions, I felt a puff of wind, which stirred the dust around my feet. Looking behind me I saw that a windstorm was gathering, rolling down from the distant slopes of the fiery mountain and sweeping across the dry countryside. It drove before it a cloud of fine dust. In almost the same instant Maniakes must have noticed the approaching dust storm, because he said something to a staff officer who produced a wax tablet and scribbled a note on it. Then he handed the tablet to a rider, who galloped away to the rear towards the hidden heavy cavalry. Moments later Maniakes's signallers were flapping their flags and sending orders down the infantry line. Two regiments of the heavy infantry who had been facing the centre of the enemy position moved fifty paces farther apart, leaving a clear path between them.

Glancing back towards the Saracen forces I saw that Abdallah himself had now come out from the camp. A cluster of green and yellow banners rose above what seemed to be a group of his senior officers. They were positioned directly opposite the path that the infantry regiments had now left clear.

The wind ruffled the hair on the back of my neck. I heard the sudden slatting sound of the flap of the command tent. Small twigs and dry leaves tumbled past me, and the wind brought a strange noise to my ears: it was the metallic clatter of the horseshoes of the kataphract riding up the hill behind us, still out of sight of the enemy, but heading directly for the path that led to the heart of Abdallah's army.

Moments later the dust storm was over us. Grains of sand were falling down my collar, and the hot breath of the wind pressed my leggings against the backs of my legs. The enemy vanished from sight, obscured in a brown-grey cloud. A bugle sounded, and was answered by another, then a third. Through the gloom, over to my right, I could make out the shapes of heavy cavalry riding past in a dense mass.

Then, as suddenly as it arrived, the dust cloud swept on and the air cleared. Ahead of me on the far side of the shallow valley, the Saracens were still half blinded by the trailing edge of the swirling sand; many of them had turned away to shield their eyes, or stood with heads bowed, arms raised across their faces. Those with turbans had wrapped the cloth over their mouths and eyes. All of them must have heard the triple trumpet call of the imperial heavy cavalry as they sounded the charge, and looked up to see the kataphract descending down the slope towards them like those sand devils they fear, an evil spectre spawned by the dust.

The kataphract was the cutting edge of the tagamata. As a cavalry force it was unique. Hand-picked and rigorously trained, it was the ultimate shock weapon of the imperial army. Palace regiments could be relied to fight with great bravery, but they were comparatively unwieldy on the battlefield because they were on foot. Only the heavy cavalry of the kataphract could be rapidly directed with devastating effect at a weak point in the enemy lines. Maniakes was doing just this, ignoring the military manuals which advised a field commander to be cautious about committing the kataphract. Maniakes had seen his chance, and now sent it into action very early in the battle.

Five hundred troopers, Nikephorus later told me, made up the kataphract that day. Three hundred of them were heavy cavalry, the remainder were archers. They rode in a close-packed arrowhead formation, the troopers on the outer edges protecting the bowmen in the centre as they laid down a devastating rain of arrows directly ahead of them. The advancing horses moved at a deliberate trot for they were too heavily burdened to gallop or canter. Long padded blankets hung down on each horse's sides, shielding the animal's flanks and legs. Steel plates were strapped to the horses' faces, and across each charger's chest hung a guard of chain-mail. Their riders were equally well protected. They wore steel helmets and thick body armour. Heavy gauntlets covered hands and forearms, and their legs were encased in chain mail leggings under aprons of leather reaching to their heels. The lances they had carried on parade in Constantinople had been for show. Now they held the kataphract's weapon of choice: the heavy mace. Four feet long and made of iron with a six-sided head, it was an ideal instrument to smash any enemy.

The kataphract split the Saracen forces just as a butcher's chopper cleaves a chicken carcass on the block. They rode down the slope, splashed across the shallow stream, and drove their way into the enemy ranks. I saw the leading troopers wielding their maces as though beating on anvils. The kataphract's arrowhead formation thrust deeper and deeper into the mass of their opponents, and those Saracens who did not fall under the rain of blows were thrust aside by the armoured horses. They were too far away for me to hear their cries. Many slipped and were trampled under the hooves. A platoon of disciplined pikemen might have stopped the charge of the kataphract, but the Saracens had no such defence, and their foot soldiers were too lightly armed. The only real resistance came from the Saracen cavalry, who defended their emir. There was a confused struggle as their riders fought back with swords and lances against the remorseless advance of the mace-wielding shock troops. But the impetus of the kataphract was too great. Their charge thrust far into the Saracen position, and I saw the clump of battle standards around the emir begin to waver.

Maniakes saw it, too. He growled an order, and the signallers sounded the general advance. Drums began to beat, a war cymbal clashed, its sound ringing clearly across the valley. To my right I noticed the battle standards of the four palace regiments hoisted in the air. Behind them the icons of the White Christ and his saints were lifted up on poles to encourage the men. To the steady clash of the cymbals, Maniakes's entire force, some seven thousand men, swept down the slope towards the disorganised and leaderless Saracens. They broke and ran. Within moments the battle became a rout. A Greek staff officer shouted to me to tell Harald and his Varangians that they too should join the fighting, but the Norsemen did not need me to translate. Yelling, they ran down the hill towards the combat. I was about to join them when Nikephorus held me by the arm and advised calmly, 'Stay back. Your place is here. In case the situation changes.' I looked across towards Maniakes. He still stood carefully watching the confusion and, surprisingly, I could not detect any look of satisfaction on his face. He seemed to be thinking, not of the battle just won, but of what would happen next.

Four hours later the exhausted officers of the tagmata trudged back up the slope to report total victory. In front of the palisade, the emir's army had been crushed. The majority of the Saracens had run away, throwing down their arms and fleeing into the scrubland. The rest of them were either dead or sat meekly on the ground, knowing that soon they would be sold as slaves. The tagmata had lost less than a hundred men killed, and four times that number wounded. Yet Maniakes scowled as he surveyed his officers.

'Where is the emir?' he demanded sourly. 'The kataphract's duty is to decapitate the enemy by killing or capturing their commander. Otherwise victory is nothing. The Saracens will re-group around their leader, and we will face another battle.'

Abruptly Maniakes swung round and faced me. I quailed in front of his bad temper.

'You there,' he shouted at me, 'tell your northern colleagues that now they are going to earn their pay. As soon as we get back to Syracuse, I want every galley to put to sea and blockade the coasts. Abdallah must not be allowed to escape back to Libya. I want him taken.'

He turned again towards the officers.

'The palace regiments and the kataphract will return to Syracuse. Light infantry and cavalry are to go in pursuit of the emir. Track him down. He must be somewhere. I want this matter settled for good.'

Behind me I heard someone mutter in Norse, 'What about our loot?'

Maniakes must have heard and guessed the meaning of the remark, for he stared icily over my shoulder at the Norsemen, and said, 'All loot taken from the dead bodies or found in the enemy camp is to be brought to the quartermasters. They will assess its value, and it will not be shared out until the tagmata is back in Syracuse.'

Syracuse knew of our victory long before the tagmata reached the city walls. With no hope of relief from Abdallah, the citizens opened the city gates. The Greeks in the population greeted us ecstatically, the Saracens with resignation. Naturally Harald's Norsemen were eager to know just how much reward they would receive after the great battle of Traina, and we contrived to delay our departure for the coastal patrol until Maniakes's quartermasters had made their calculations. In the end each man in Harald's war band received a bonus of thirty nomisma, more than three years' pay. Certain items, however, were kept back for distribution to the senior officers, and this led to an open quarrel between Maniakes and Hervé, the leader of the Frankish mercenaries. The object of their dispute was the same bay stallion which had carried the nobleman that Iron Arm had killed in spectacular single combat, a superlative example of that breed of horse for which the Saracens were famous. When the stallion was led forward by a groom and shown off to Maniakes, there was not a man in the watching crowd who would not have wanted to own the creature.

Unwisely, Hervé, who spoke some Greek, ventured a suggestion. 'Autokrator,' he proposed, 'the horse should given to Iron Arm in recognition of his victory over the Saracen champion.'

Maniakes took this remark as an affront and an encroachment on his absolute authority. 'No,' he said harshly. 'That horse will be placed in my stables. I keep the animal for myself.'

Hervé blundered on, compounding his error. 'Surely that is unjust,' he said. 'Iron Arm defeated his opponent in fair combat, and by custom he should receive the weapons and horse of the vanquished.'

Maniakes glared at him, his scowl of anger deepening. The two men were facing one another in the main city square. With Maniakes were a few Greek staff officers, while Hervé was accompanied by half a dozen of his mercenaries. This was a very public squabble.

'The horse is mine,' Maniakes repeated. He was now so angry that his voice had deepened to an ugly growl.

Hervé opened his mouth as if to speak, and at that moment Maniakes stepped forward and struck the mercenary full in the face. Maniakes, as I have said, was a huge man, a giant. The force of the blow knocked Hervé off his feet, though he was tall and strong enough to be capable of standing up to a normal assault. As the mercenary started to get up from the ground, his mouth bloody from a cut lip, the Greek general unleashed a kick that sent Hervé sprawling once again. Maniakes was breathing heavily, his eyes filled with rage as he watched the humiliated mercenary slowly stand upright with the help of two of his men, who hurried forward to support him. Maniakes's staff officers stayed rooted to the spot, terrified by the fury of their leader. I remembered the warning of the Greek officer back in Constantinople that the new commander-in-chief demanded instant obedience, 'particularly from northern barbarians'.

No one said anything, and the stallion and his groom stood there until into this fraught moment entered one of Hervé's mercenaries, Iron Arm himself. He detached himself from the group of onlookers and strolled across to the horse. As he walked, Iron Arm was pulling on to his right hand his heavy metal-plated gauntlet. Coming up to the stallion, the mercenary began to pet the animal, stroking the magnificent head and neck, patting his flanks and fondling his ears. The stallion responded with pleasure, turning his fine head to nuzzle the man. Then Iron Arm moved to stand directly in front of the animal, put his left hand behind his back, and clicked his fingers. The stallion's head came up, the ears pricked in curiosity, the eyes bright and questioning, wondering at the sound. In that instant Iron Arm raised his gauntleted right hand and delivered a terrific blow with his clenched right fist, right between the stallion's eyes. The stallion collapsed, his legs folding up, killed outright. Iron Arm calmly turned and walked back to join his comrades.

Next day Hervé and his entire band of mercenaries left Syracuse and returned to Italy, refusing to serve under Maniakes again.

'WHAT A PUNCH that man has got!' commented Halldor. 'The Greek general is going to regret getting on the wrong side of the Frankish mercenaries.'

We were taking our galleys out of harbour to begin our patrol, and the death of the stallion was the sole topic of conversation.

'Maniakes has been in an evil temper ever since Abdallah escaped him. I doubt that the emir will be caught now. Abdallah has had plenty of time to make his escape back to Libya. Still, if we are cruising the coast, maybe we can make a few shore raids on our own account and pick up a little booty on the side.'

Halldor's Viking instincts were to be rewarded beyond his wildest dreams. Of the five galleys in our flotilla, Harald despatched two northwards to cruise towards Palermo in case the emir was still there. Two more galleys were sent to patrol the coast, facing across to Libya and the emir's most likely escape route. The fifth galley, Harald's own, had a more free-ranging task. We would search along the south-eastern coast, examining the bays and harbours for any trace of Saracen shipping capable of carrying the emir off the island. Now that Abdallah was on the run, we knew we could rely on receiving intelligence from the Greek-speaking population who lived along the coast.

For nearly a week, we made our way slowly along the rock-bound coast, looking into creeks and harbours, interrogating fishermen and finding nothing suspicious. It seemed that Sicily was quiet again now the emir was defeated, and the populace had returned to their normal peacetime lives. We were about halfway along the coast when we came to a long beach of white sand backed with low dunes covered with tussock grass. This itself was unusual, for most of the shore that we had seen was cliff and reef. I asked the Greek fisherman who was our pilot along this stretch of coast if this beach was ever used as a landing place, and he shook his head. Apparently the nearest village was far inland, and the fishermen had no reason to come there because the fishing in the area was bad. I translated his reply to Harald, and immediately the Norwegian's predatory instinct was aroused. He scanned the beach for several moments. We could see nothing. The beach looked quiet.

'Turn for shore,' Harald ordered the helmsman. 'This needs a closer look.'

Gently we ran the galley's bows on land, and a dozen of us jumped ashore. I could hear only the slight lap of the waves on the beach. Squinting against the glare of the white sand, for the sun was blazing down, we began to walk up along the beach.

'You four,' Harald ordered a group of men next to him,

'Search in that direction as far as those low bushes in the distance. The others come with me.'

He began to walk towards the dunes. I followed him, my feet sinking in the soft sand as I tried to keep up with his massive stride. We had gone perhaps fifty paces when, suddenly, four Saracens sprang up in front of us. They had been crouched down, hiding behind a dune, and now they sprinted away inland, feet flying so I could see the soles of their bare feet. They reminded me of hares who wait until the last moment before the hunter treads on them, then start away in panic. And they were as quick, for there was no hope of catching them. We stopped and watched them growing smaller in the distance. When they were out of range of even the most ambitious archer, one of the fugitives stopped and turned, then waited there, watching us.

Harald narrowed his eyes as he looked at the distant figure. 'What does that remind you of, Thorgils?' he asked.

'My lord? I was just thinking to myself that they ran as fast as hares.'

'Not hares,' he said. 'Think of nesting birds. What do they do?'

Immediately I understood. 'Leave the nest, run off as a distraction, hoping to divert the hunter.'

'So now we look for the nest.'

But for the boy's eyes we would never have found him. He had been buried in the sand beneath the overhang of a bush. The only part of him left on the surface was his face, and even that had been covered in a light cotton rag whose colour matched the sand around him. But in breathing the boy had caused the rag to slip slightly to one side. I was walking past the bush when I saw the glint of an eyeball. I beckoned quietly to Harald, who was searching the bushes a few paces from me, and he came over to look where I pointed. The boy knew he had been found. Harald reached down, brushed away the sand and seized him by the shoulder, pulling him from his hiding place. The boy was no more than six or seven years old, slim, with a skin that was fair for a Saracen, and fine features. He was trembling with fright.

'By all the saints!' exclaimed the Greek fisherman. He had come across to see what we had found. 'That's Abdallah's son!'

'How can you be sure?' I asked.

'He rode on his father's horse the day that the emir came to visit our village. Abdallah held him up to show him off to our people and present to us our future ruler. There's no mistaking the lad. Besides, look at those clothes he's wearing. That's no peasant brat.'

I translated the fisherman's words to Harald, and, as if he was picking up a doll, the Norwegian suddenly swung the boy up in the air and held him high over his head. Then he turned to face the distant watcher, and stood there, showing off our find. After a few moments, the Saracen began to walk towards us.

'I am his tutor,' he explained, speaking good Greek with the high, quick intonation of the Saracens. He was an older man, thin, grey-bearded and clearly anguished. 'Do not harm him, I beg you.'

'Where is Abdallah, the emir?' demanded Harald.

'I do not know,' the man answered miserably. 'I was only told to bring the boy to this beach and wait for us to be picked up. But when a ship would come I had no idea. At first we thought it was your vessel. And when we realised our mistake it was too late to get away, so we tried to conceal the boy, hoping you would go away.'

'Thorgils, a word with you in private,' said Harald. 'Halldor, here, you take a hold of the lad.' Then he led me a few paces to one side and said bluntly, 'What's the boy worth?'

I was searching for an answer when Harald went on fiercely, 'Come on, think! Abdallah cannot be too far away to receive our message. What's the boy worth?'

I was so taken aback by the fierceness of his questioning that I began to stammer. 'M-m-my lord, I have no idea.'

Harald cut across me. 'What was it you said when we saw

that golden dome in the Holy Land? That the Saracens pay huge sums for those things which are most dear to them?'

'But that was a holy shrine,'

'And is not a son and heir equally precious, to a father? We don't have any time to waste, Thorgils. How much was it that the caliph or whatever he was called set aside for the gilding of the dome?'

'The sum was a hundred thousand dinars, our guide said.'

'Right. Tell the boy's tutor that if the emir pays a hundred thousand dinars, he'll see his son again, unharmed. Otherwise we hand the boy over to Maniakes. That's my message.'

'But how can the emir raise that amount of money now?' I said. 'He's a fugitive.'

'I've never heard of a ruler who doesn't take his treasure with him when he flees, provided he has the transport. And you can add a second message as a sweetener. If the hundred thousand is paid, not only will the emir get his son back, but I will make sure that my flotilla does not hinder his escape to Libya.'

I suppose I should have been shocked by Harald's double-dealing, but I was not. Perhaps the years I had spent in Constantinople had hardened me to intrigue and treachery. Certainly every Norseman in Harald's war band would have expected him to exact a price for the boy, and not one of them would want to share the ransom with the autokrator if Harald could somehow arrange it. But, even as Harald spoke, his blatant perfidy made me acknowledge to myself that my ultimate loyalty had never been to the palace in Constantinople or its appointees, but to my own people. Faced with the stark choice of serving either the Basileus or Harald, I did not hesitate.

'I will see what I can arrange, my lord,' I answered, even as I remembered just how hard-headed Pelagia could be in matters of business profit. She would certainly have advised me to extract the greatest advantage from our lucky catch.

'Good, Thorgils, do that. And be quick. If this is to succeed it must be done quickly. Three days at the most.'

The boy's tutor winced slightly when I mentioned the enormous sum, but, like a good negotiator, he avoided direct haggling. 'And how is such a large quantity of money to be delivered and the boy's well-being guaranteed?' he enquired, his eyes flicking nervously to Halldor, who still had the youngster in his grip.

'As regards the boy's safety, you will have to trust us on that,' I said. 'It's in our interest to keep him safe and well. He's not our enemy, nor is his father if he accepts this proposal. We'll keep the boy aboard ship until the ransom is paid.'

'And the payment itself? How is that transaction to be made? When so much gold is on view, men tend to lose their heads and seek more. They break their word.'

For a moment I was silent. I had never organised the paying of a ransom, and did not know how it was done so that the interests of both sides were protected. Then, perhaps with Odinn's help, I recalled my time among the ski-runners of Permia. They were a fur-trading people who mistrusted all outsiders, so they conducted any barter at arm's length. They left their furs for inspection in a deserted open place, and their customers left a similar value in payment at the same spot. Perhaps I could modify that arrangement for Harald's purposes.

'The ransom is to be brought to this end of the beach at noon on the third day from now,' I said. 'Our vessel will be in the bay close enough to watch your men place the ransom on the sand and withdraw a safe distance to a point on the dunes where they can still be seen. The only people on the beach will be the boy and myself, waiting for you at the opposite end of the beach. You will be able to see for yourselves that he is alive and well. But you are not to come any nearer. If you do so, the galley will immediately come and retrieve the boy. I will walk along the beach to inspect the ransom, and if everything is satisfactory, I will signal the galley to come and pick up the money. At that moment your people can advance and collect the boy. Neither side will be close enough to the trade to be able to take both the boy and the ransom.'

The old man looked at me and said softly, 'You I trust. But not that tall pirate who is your leader. It will be up to you to make him respect these rules. Otherwise there will be a tragedy.'

When the Saracens had left to take our message to the emir, I explained the ransom arrangement to Harald. I had never seen him so deep in thought. He chewed on his moustache as he reflected on my device, and scowled at me.

'Thorgils,' he said, 'you've lived too long among these people. You are beginning to scheme like them. Of course, if anything goes wrong, it will be you left sitting on the beach, not us.'

'I think the handover will work,' I reassured him with a confidence that I did not feel, 'though whether the emir will find so much money is another matter.'

As it turned out, the handover of the ransom went exactly as I had hoped, except for one flaw which, if I had foreseen it, might have prevented me from setting up the plan.

Shortly before noon on the third day, as our galley lay out in the bay, a file of fifteen mules approached over the sand dunes. I was seated on the far end of the beach with the young Saracen boy, who had not said a word all the time he had been with us. He was still in a state of shock. When he saw the approaching mules, his face lit up with hope, for he must have known what was going on. If I had been sensible, I should have tied his arms and legs so he could not run away when I went to examine the panniers that the muleteers dumped on the beach before they withdrew, but I did not have the heart to do so. Instead, after he had stood up and waved to his tutor, who was watching from a distance, I gestured for the boy to sit down and wait quietly, which he did. Then I walked along the sand to the pile of mule bags, unfastened the thongs that tied one or two of them, and lifted up the flaps. I had never seen so much gold coin in one place in all my life. Certainly not when I had worked for the king's moneyer in London, for he had minted silver coin, nor even when the Basileus had flung gold bounty to his courtiers in the audience hall of the Great Palace. Here were riches that were beyond my comprehension. Surprisingly, the entire payment was in coin, mostly Arab dinars, but also nomisma from the imperial mint. I could not see a single item like a gold necklace or a jewelled band whose value would have to be assessed. I had no idea what a hundred thousand dinars looked like, and there was no time to count, so I turned round and waved to the boy, gesturing for him to go. The last I saw of him he was racing up across the sand dunes to join his father's deputation.

'Thorgils, you are a genius!' exulted Harald as he came ashore, opened one of the panniers and scooped up a handful of coins. I had never seen him look so pleased. His normally harsh expression was replaced with a look of utter pleasure.

'You have the Gods to thank,' I said, seizing my chance. 'They clearly favour you.'

'Yes, the Gods,' he said. 'Freya must have wept for many nights and days.'

For a moment I did not know what he was talking about, as I had been away from my homeland for so long that my Old Beliefs were growing dim. Then I remembered that Freya, goddess of wealth, had cried tears of gold when she lost her husband.

'There's only one detail you have overlooked,' said Harald. His cautionary tone brought a sudden chill to our conversation. 'The Greek sailor who identified the emir's son for us. My own men will keep their mouths shut about this treasure when we get back to Syracuse, because they will get their share. But Greeks never hold their tongues. Even if the fisherman were handsomely rewarded, he would boast if he got back home, and Maniakes would get to hear what happened. Thorgils, I tidied up your plan a little. The Greek is dead.'

SEVEN

MANIAKES NEVER LEARNED the truth. As our vessel entered Syracuse harbour, we passed an imperial dromon beating out to sea. Twenty-four hours earlier she had arrived with an order signed in purple ink, stripping Maniakes of his command. Now the dromon was carrying the former autokrator to Constantinople to face the Basileus and his eunuch brother John. Maniakes had made the error of shaming their brother-in-law, Stephen, commander of the imperial fleet, by accusing him of allowing the emir to escape by sea. The rebuke had been made in public, Maniakes once again losing his temper and shouting at Stephen that he was useless and effeminate while he beat him about the head with a whip. Stephen had reacted like the true palace politician he was: he secretly sent word to the Orphanotrophus that Maniakes had grown overbearing with his military success and was plotting to seize the throne. Nothing was calculated to arouse the Orphanotrophus's hostility more, because John the Eunuch would do anything to maintain his family's grip on power.

We could scarcely believe our good fortune. With Stephen censured for allowing the emir's escape, our own treason was unlikely to be discovered, and Maniakes's disgrace gave Harald his excuse to declare that he too was withdrawing from the Sicilian expedition. Our flotilla, as soon as it reassembled, also set sail for

Constantinople, and from there three of our vessels continued onward for the Pontic Sea, and eventually for Kiev. In their bilges lay hidden the bulk of the emir's ransom: their crews were returning home as rich as they had dreamed of. Their departure suited Harald, as it left fewer men to let slip the truth about our faithlessness. Only a hundred of his original war band remained, and the army secretariat in Constantinople judged the number insufficient for an independent unit. So, in recognition of our contribution to the Sicilian campaign, they removed us from the Varangians-without-the-walls and attached us directly to the imperial Life Guard. To add to the irony, Harald was decorated for his services to the empire, and elevated to the rank of spatharokandidatos. This entitled him to wear a cloak of white silk and carry a jewelled court sword at ceremonials. I, of course, found myself once again an imperial guardsman.

Pelagia was dismissive of my military career. I returned to find her just as energetic and self-confident, and even more successful. She now had commercial interests in shipping and olive production as well as owning an entire chain of bakeries and bread stalls. With her newly acquired wealth she had bought a brand new substantial villa in a pleasant suburb on the Galata side of the Golden Horn, with its own garden and overlooking the straits. It was there that I found her in the main reception room, reading through bills and documents relating to her business.

'Thorgils, you come back from Sicily with a suntan but little else,' she said after I had briefly sketched in the details of my time on campaign. 'You're looking thinner, and you've got several grey hairs, but no promotion. Fortunately I've been investing your salary for you, and you'll find that you've returned to a nest egg.'

I decided it would be wiser not to tell Pelagia that I would eventually be receiving a portion of the emir's ransom money, nor that I had placed my share from the salvage from the pirate ship with Halldor to look after.

'You'll find little changed in the palace when you get back to the guardroom,' Pelagia went on. 'John is still running the government, and Michael has less and less to do with affairs of state. He's become more pious than ever. A couple of soothsayers – charlatans the pair of them – managed to convince him that he sold his soul to the devil before he married the empress Zoë in return for a glorious future, and now he punishes himself for this lapse. I'm beginning to feel sorry for the poor man. His suffering comes in waves. When it is at its worst the pain nearly drives him out of his mind, and he makes matters worse by humiliating himself.'

My colleagues in the guardroom confirmed Pelagia's sombre description.

'You'll need a strong stomach for guard duty outside the royal apartment nowadays,' I was warned by my company commander, the same Halfdan who had taken charge of the detail when the Basileus Romanus drowned. 'You should see the diseased creatures who are brought up to the imperial bedchamber – tramps picked up from the street by the nightwatch, or invalids from the hospitals. It's said Michael washes their clothes, cleans their wounds, even kisses their open sores, in emulation of his own God. He insists that they sleep in the royal bed while he lies down on the cold marble floor with a stone as a pillow so he suffers mortification. I looked in the bedchamber one morning when the Basileus and his attendants had left, and there was a stinking pile of old rags by the bed. Looked like a beggars' nest.'

My summons to the office of John the Orphanotrophus was not long in arriving, and as usual the eunuch came straight to the point.

'What's your impression of Araltes now?' he demanded. 'After two years in his company, I trust that you have won his confidence as I required.'

'I believe so, your excellency,' I replied. I was as wary of the Orphanotrophus as on the first day he had sent me to spy on Harald, but I was bold enough to add, 'He has served the Basileus well. He has been created spatharokandidatos.'

'I know, I know. But the administration of the empire rests on two pillars: honours and cash,' retorted the Orphanotrophus irritably. 'Your Araltes benefits from the honours, but what about the cash? I've been told he is gold-hungry.'

'I know nothing about that, your excellency,' I answered evasively.

'Strange that he hasn't complained about the division of booty after the fall of Syracuse, like those Frankoi mercenaries who made such an issue of it. Over a horse, I believe.'

I began to wonder if there was any limit to the eunuch's network of spies. Careful to avoid an outright lie, I told him, 'Araltes gives the impression of being content with his booty from Sicily.'

The Orphanotrophus's next words made me feel as if I had fallen through the ice of a frozen lake.

'I'm hearing that certain bullion transactions are going unreported to the city archon. One of the money changers seems to be making unusually high profits. What's his name . . .' and the eunuch made a pretence of looking down at the note on his desk, though I was sure he had no need to refresh his memory. 'A certain argyroprates named Simeon. Mention has been made that he is dealing with Varangians.'

'It could be any of the Varangian units, your excellency,' I said, trying to keep panic out of my voice, 'not necessarily those who serve Araltes.'

'Guardsman,' said the eunuch slowly and deliberately, 'if anything is going on, I want to know it.'

HARALD HAD BEEN living in his own quarters away from the Life Guard's barracks, and after the interview with John I had to restrain myself from going straight there to warn him. I suspected that I was being watched by the Orphanotrophus's agents, so I went instead to seek Pelagia's advice, and she was not reassuring.

'Simeon has been looking particularly smug these past few

months. He dresses in the latest fashions, wears expensive jewellery, and generally likes to show off how well he's doing.'

'Can't he be persuaded to be less conspicuous? If he keeps this up, sooner or later John's people will call him in for questioning.'

'I doubt it. Simeon thinks too highly of himself.'

'Couldn't Harald switch to using someone else on the Mese, a more discreet money changer, to handle the booty?'

'Simeon's the only man who would take the risk of Harald's monetary affairs.'

'What about those shifty-looking characters I sometimes see walking up and down the Mese in the financial zone, offering better rates for foreign exchange.'

Pelagia snorted with derision. 'I wouldn't advise Harald to deal with them. They're unlicensed traders. They're likely to run off with any valuables entrusted to them, or give back dud coins. And they don't have the resources to deal in the amounts that Harald brings in. Their working capital is in those grubby bags they carry about. At least Simeon has the iron table. That's what it symbolises: a metal surface on which you can bang suspect coins to hear whether they ring true. You had better tell your tall friend with the lopsided eyebrows to be very, very discreet whenever he brings any valuables to Simeon for exchanging into cash.'

My daily life, now that I was back with the Hetaira, reverted to its former pattern. There were the familiar drills and kit inspections, the regular rotation of guard duty – one week inside the Great Palace, the next week in barracks – and of course the endless parades. I found it truly tedious to spend hour after hour solemnly marching out from the palace to some great church, waiting outside for the service to finish, going back along the same route, and then having to clean up my equipment and prepare for the next ceremonial outing, which could be the next day.

Harald avoided most of this mind-numbing routine because he, Halldor and a few of his immediate followers were assigned to assist the exaktors. These were, as their name implies, the tax gatherers. How Harald got in with them is something I never learned, but later I came to realise that it was part of his own grand plan. There was certainly nothing unusual about a detachment of guards accompanying the exaktors. In fact it was a necessity. When the tax collectors set out from the capital to visit some area in the countryside that had been assessed, naturally the local inhabitants would be reluctant to pay up, so the exaktors took along an armed escort to bully the taxpayers into compliance. Few things were more terrifying to a local farmer than the menacing sight of foreign barbarians who were prepared to smash up his property if he did not pay his dues to the emperor – the arrival of a squad of Varangians was usually sufficient to loosen the purse strings. Harald, with his ferocious appearance, must have been particularly daunting, nor was he reluctant to resort to force, and that may be why he and his men were picked for the work.

Thus Harald and the others missed the bizarre event which surprised even someone as well informed as Pelagia: the proclamation that the Basileus and Empress Zoë were to have a son. Physically, of course, this was impossible. Zoë was now at least sixty years old, though as vain as ever, and Michael the Basileus was much too ill to procreate. Their son was to be by adoption. But what really stunned everyone was his identity. His only previous official role had been as commander of the Palace Guard, a purely nominal post for which he did nothing more than wear a gaudy uniform at palace ceremonials. Named Michael, just like the emperor, his father was that same Stephen who had plotted to have Maniakes recalled in disgrace, and his mother was the Basileus's sister. He was to be known by the title of Caesar, to signify that he was the heir to the imperial throne, and naturally John the Eunuch had made the choice. The Orphanotrophus knew that the sickly Basileus could die at any moment, and he was determined that the succession should stay within the family.

The actual ceremony of adoption was even more grotesque

than when the youthful Basileus had married Zoë, who was old enough to be his mother. This time the ritual took place in the church of the Blachernae Palace and culminated with the new Caesar symbolically sitting down on the ageing Zoë's lap, so he could be acclaimed by the congregation of dignitaries and high officials as her 'son'.

A few days later I was crossing a courtyard on my way to the guardroom when I passed a middle-ranking official of the chancellery. His face seemed familiar, but I would have walked right past him if he had not stopped suddenly and said, 'Excuse me, aren't you the Greek-speaking Varangian who told me how Romanus drowned?'

'That's right,' I answered, recognising the young man who had interviewed me on the day of the funeral parade. 'You're Constantine Psellus. You seem to have come a long way since you were a young student watching a funeral parade. I congratulate you.'

'You're beginning to sound like a courtier yourself. This time you must tell me your name.'

'Thorgils Leifsson.'

'Obviously you're still with the Palace Guard.'

'Back with the guard, more correctly, after service in Sicily.'

'So you know what this new Caesar is like? After all, he is, or was, your commanding officer.'

I hesitated, and Psellus said softly, 'You may speak freely. This is an opinion for posterity. I'm still compiling notes for my history of the rulers of the empire.'

Once again his frank approach won my confidence. 'Well,' I admitted, 'from the little I've seen of him, the Caesar is vindictive and shallow. His one true talent is that he is superlative at hiding his true feelings.'

'Sounds as though he was an excellent choice for the throne,' said Psellus with irony. 'I'll make a bargain with you, Thorgils. As a guardsman you sometimes see things which we outsiders never get to witness. If you'll be so kind as to keep me informed about what is going on behind the scenes, I won't forget you when the time comes – as it surely will – that you need a friend within the bureaucracy.' And he hurried on his way.

Over the next few months, there was little I could tell Psellus that he would not have observed for himself. Michael's health was in rapid decline. His limbs swelled, bloating so that his fingers became as thick as sausages. To hide his physical deterioration from public gaze, the Basileus spent less time in the city, and withdrew to his country residence. He left behind the usual intrigues inside the palace, which grew more viperish as it became evident that he did not have long to live. John the Eunuch still held the real power, but some courtiers began to pander to the young Caesar, preparing for the day when he mounted the throne. Other sycophants coalesced around his favourite uncle, Constantine, another of the Orphanotrophus's brothers. A few diehards again paid attention to the empress Zoë, though she was still confined to the gynaeceum, the women's quarters, and the Basileus had cut off her allowance so she was living in near poverty. No one trusted anyone else, and there was a growing sense that the whole structure of government was on the verge of collapse.

I came to appreciate how far the decay had spread when an official arrived in the guardroom late one December evening. He was out of breath and flustered.

'I'm looking for the guardsman Thorgils,' he announced.

'What can I do for you?' I asked.

The man looked nervously at the other off-duty guardsmen, who were watching him with open curiosity.

'You are to select one reliable colleague,' he said. 'Bring heavy cloaks, and accompany me.'

I glanced at Halfdan. 'Take Lars with you,' he ordered.

Lars was a stolid guardsman who had been with the Hetaira almost as long as Halfdan himself. Lars and I gathered up our weapons, and the official took us, half running, to the office of John the Eunuch. We found him dressed in his monk's clothes and ready to leave the palace.

'You are to accompany me as an escort in case of trouble,' said John. 'Be discreet, conceal your uniforms, and you may leave your axes behind. Swords hidden under your cloaks will be sufficient.'

We slipped out of the palace through one of the minor gates, where the doorkeepers were clearly expecting us, and hurried through the streets of the city. We kept to alleys and side streets, but I recognised the direction we were taking. It was towards the area known as the Venetian quarter because of the number of foreign merchants, mostly Italians, residing there. It was also the district of several of Constantinople's most important monasteries, and when we stopped and knocked on the wooden doors to one of them, I knew that we stood before the gate of the monastery known locally as the Kosmidion. It was the same monastery which the Basileus had funded so generously because it was dedicated to the doctor saints, Cosmas and Damian.

A grim-looking monk let us in without a word and ushered us along several stone-flagged corridors. In the background I heard chanting, and, as we turned a corner, I detected the hurried withdrawal of some cowled figures who had been waiting in the shadows, curious to see who the visitors were at such a late hour. Finally we came to the door of an ordinary monk's cell. The door stood open. Inside, on a simple cot, lay the Basileus.

I recognised him by his gross and swollen hands, for he was wearing not the clothes of an emperor, but the simple black tunic of a monk. Also, his head had been shaved in a tonsure: I could still see the nicks and cuts where the work had been done hurriedly and very recently. The Basileus looked truly ghastly, and I had no doubt that he had only a few hours left to live.

'Watch the door and passage,' snapped the Orphanotrophus. 'Let no one in.'

He appeared genuinely distressed at the sight of his sickly brother. He stepped into the room, and I had a glimpse of him dropping to his knees beside the bed and embracing the invalid before I turned my back and stared down the passageway. Behind me I heard John croon comforting words to the man whom he had manoeuvred on to the throne of the empire. I found it difficult to believe that the young and handsome courtier who had married Zoë was now the bloated and sweating wreck who lay on the cot behind me.

Nothing could be kept secret in the palace, least of all the disappearance of the emperor. At dawn we had our first visitors: the new Caesar Michael and his uncle Constantine arrived. By then the Basileus was in great pain, and the Orphanotrophus allowed them to stay only for a short time before ordering them to leave. Two physicans, one from the monastery infirmary, the other from the palace, came and attempted to relieve the patient's suffering with pain-killing drugs. Then I heard the Basileus shout aloud that he wanted to die like his Lord, in agony, and the Orphanotrophus ordered me to no longer let the physicians pass. One monk at a time was to be allowed into the cell, where he could pray for the invalid's soul. The rest of the brethren were to say their prayers for him in their chapel.

Lars and I guarded the dreary corridor for twenty hours without a break, cooped up in the heart of the monastery complex, hearing only the shuffle of feet, the moaning of the Basileus, and the muttered prayers for the sick and dying. The strangest interlude was when the empress herself appeared in the passage-way, demanding to see her husband. The doorkeepers of the monastery had let Zoë in – she was, after all, the emperor's wife – but Lars and I obeyed orders and blocked her path until John the Eunuch heard her protests and came out to see what was going on.

'Tell my husband that I want to see him,' begged Zoë.

The Orphanotrophus went back inside for a few moments, then reappeared.

'He does not wish to see you,' he said to Zoë in a flat tone. 'He asks that you go away.'

Zoë clenched her hands and looked miserable.

'Go away,' John repeated, 'otherwise I'll have the guards throw you out.'

Fortunately, for I would not have relished bundling the old woman down the corridor, Zoë turned and left. As I watched her walk away, the smell of the aged empress's musk perfume lingered in the still air of the passageway, and I remembered how she had looked upon the corpse of her first husband as he lay cold on the marble bench by the swimming pool, and wondered if she could have known that events would come to this gruesome conclusion.

At about noon the Basileus must have recovered his strength, for I heard him ask whether it was time for the midday service. He announced that, as a monk, it was his duty to attend. Then came an outburst of petulance. Trying to get up from the cot, he found that no one had provided him with the suitable monk's sandals; beside his cot were the purple boots that only the reigning emperor might wear, and he refused to put them on. Two of the monks came to fetch him, and physically carried him to the chapel, barefoot. When they brought him back an hour later, hanging between them, Michael was scarcely breathing. They took him into the cell, laid him on the bed, then left. After that there was a long silence, and then I heard nothing more. Basileus Michael had died.

John the Eunuch stayed in that cell for two more days, sitting beside his brother's corpse, mourning. It was the one truly human act I remember of a man whom, until then, I had thought of as the most cold-hearted, calculating person I had ever met. Monks came and went, washed and put new clothes on the dead emperor, and mounted a vigil in relays. The Orphanotrophus barely stirred. Officials arrived from the palace seeking instructions, and he told them that he would return to his office only when he was ready; until then they should consult the Caesar.

Finally, on the third day after his brother's death, John came out of the cell. He looked haggard.

'Guardsman,' he said as he looked straight into my eyes, 'for the second time, you've been present at the passing of a Basileus. On the last occasion you showed great discretion. That is why I chose you. These are matters of state, and the personal details are rarely dignified. They must be kept from public knowledge. A seamless transfer of power is needed; appearance is all.'

He brushed past me, and as I followed him along the passageway I promised myself that the next time I saw Psellus, I would make him swear never to reveal the source of his information.

In fact, Psellus was among the cluster of officials waiting anxiously in the outer courtyard of the palace as we came back from the monastery. Standing at the back of the group, he caught my eye. I kept my face expressionless. Now, I was just another member of the guard.

Halfdan had been hovering at the palace gate with a squad of men waiting to escort the returning Orphanotrophus to a meeting in the grand audience chamber.

'Thank the Gods you brought him back,' Halfdan hissed at me. 'The place is all in a heap. Nobody knows what's going on, or who's in charge. Everyone was waiting for the Eunuch to make decisions. What kept you?'

Before I could reply, Michael the Caesar approached. With him was his uncle, Constantine. The two men began to fawn over the Orphantrophus as we headed towards the audience chamber. They commented how tired he looked, and asked repeatedly how they might assist. It occurred to me that the two men were frightened out of their wits. They wanted to know what the Eunuch had decided for their futures, and were relying on him to guide them through the next few days until the succession of power was established. As we entered the packed Trikilinium it was evident that everyone, including the palace officials, was on edge and overwrought. Even the empress Zoë had appeared from the women's quarters. She stood there, looking at the Orphan-otrophus. She too was waiting for his decision. The atmosphere was thick with fear, ambition and duplicity.

'Now is the time to stand together, to assist one another. We should carry out the wishes of the deceased,' announced the Orphanotrophus, raising his voice so he could be heard by everyone in the waiting audience. He had recovered his composure, and his words had their usual quality of slight menace. 'We proceed with the arrangements envisaged at the time when our dear nephew, Michael – ' here he gave a thin, insincere smile – 'became Caesar. It is appropriate that he is acclaimed as Basileus at the earliest opportunity. He will, I know, value and accept the advice and support of his family.'

There was a general easing of tension in the chamber at this. The Orphanotrophus's statement was interpreted as meaning that the various factions were to share the power between them. The young Caesar would occupy the throne, but his family – John himself, his brother Constantine, and the empress Zoë – would be his silent partners. It was to be a web of alliances.

The spider at the centre of the web now stepped forward. The Caesar was a slender, sallow-complexioned young man going prematurely bald. Turning to the assembled officials, he announced that he would only accept the imperial mantle if he could share its burden and privilege with his 'revered guide and mentor the Orphanotrophus'. Here he kissed his uncle's hand. Then he walked across to his elderly adoptive mother and embraced her theatrically. 'I want all of you to bear witness,' he called out to the assembly. 'When I am crowned, there will be a second throne beside mine, occupied by my mother and mistress. I will be her slave-emperor, obedient to her commands.'

'This makes you want to puke,' muttered Halfdan near me. 'I wonder just how long that little shit will keep his word.'

Michael was crowned as Basileus by the Patriarch in a glittering ceremony the very next day. As promised, there was a second throne for the aged empress. Psellus, who watched the coronation, came away with the same opinion of the new Basileus as my company commander.

'That man reeks of hypocrisy,' he said. 'I was at a meeting of the family council taking notes, and you should have heard the way he speaks to her. Always asking her opinion, saying that he defers to her judgement, that he "is hers to command" and on and on in similar vein. He's got her quite addled. She seems to believe him.'

'It does seem odd that he should crawl to her so blatantly,' I commented. 'He's the emperor, not her.'

'Thorgils, the citizens of Constantinople are calling their new ruler "Michael the Caulker" or "The Little Twister". You may not be aware that at one time his father Stephen worked in the shipyards as a humble labourer. His job was to caulk the seams of planks with spun yarn and slop pine tar on the hulls. His family are base born, not from the sort of background that the mob respects or forgets. To the ordinary people, Zoë is the only one who has a genuine claim to wear the purple. She and her sister Theodora are true aristocrats. There's a dangerous feeling in the city that the antics of John the Eunuch and his jumped-up family have soiled the status of the Basileus, that they've gone too far with their ambitions.'

'I didn't know Zoë has a sister.'

'Hardly surprising. The two women hate one another. Zoë arranged for her sibling to be shut away in a nunnery years ago. What a pair,' the bureaucrat sighed. 'Sometimes I think the palace is like a large rock. When you roll it aside you find all sorts of unpleasant creatures creeping and crawling around underneath. At least Zoë is open in her dislike of her sister, whereas with John the Eunuch and his brother Constantine, I get the feeling that they are a pair of scorpions, tails up and circling one another warily, each always ready to deliver a fatal sting. God help us when that happens.'

Pelagia was equally alert to the impending clash. The Orphano-trophus owned a large estate very close to her villa in Galata, and he often came there to relax. Pelagia was worried that the more vicious aspects of palace politics might accompany him.

'John the Eunuch always brings an escort with him, at least

twenty soldiers. He must be expecting trouble. You couldn't
arrange for some private security guards for me, Thorgils, could
you? Perhaps half a dozen of your colleagues might like to spend
their free days here in Galata. I would pay them well, and they
would have as much wine to drink as they liked.'

'Nothing could be easier,' I replied. 'The new Basileus appointed an entirely new batch of bodyguards just last week. They
are loyal only to him. We Varangians are kept on, but we don't
have much to do. Besides, the Basileus's new Life Guards are an
odd lot, and clannish. They're Pechenegs from the north. Michael
purchased them, and every one of them is a eunuch. I'm sure that
many of my colleagues would like to get away from the atmosphere in the palace. It's becoming more and more freakish.'

IN FEBRUARY MY world came crashing down around my ears.
Harald and Halldor were arrested, as were Simeon the money
changer and three of the exaktors. All of them were accused of
swindling the state treasury. It was a simple enough fraud: they
had terrorised their victims into paying more than the official tax
assessment and pocketed the difference. One of their victims had
complained to the chancellery, and when a clerk checked the
ledgers it was clear that the tax collectors had been under-
reporting their receipts.

'What idiots,' said Pelagia when I told her. 'It's no good
stealing from the state unless you can cover your tracks properly.
All those files and written reports pile up in the archives. They
may seem a waste of effort, but if someone has the motivation
they can be used to bring down even the most powerful person.'

'What's going to happen to them?'

'The tax collectors will be dismissed from their posts, all their
private property will be seized to pay the massive fines levied on
them, and they will be lucky not to be sent to jail. As for your
Varangian friends, I don't know. They might be able to bribe
their way out of trouble and flee the country, or they might be

made an example of. Depends who their friends are. I'm sure you remember that Bulgarian who was paraded through the streets last autumn.'

Indeed I did. Like Harald, the unfortunate man had been a foreigner at court. He had decided to raise a rebellion in his native country, slipped out of the capital and gathered an army. The tagmata had crushed him, and he had been brought back to Constantinople, where he was paraded through the streets on a leading chain, his nose cut off, then strangled.

'My best guess,' Pelagia continued, 'is that the authorities will hold Harald and his associates in jail and interrogate them until they reveal where they've put the stolen money so that the treasury can try to recover it. The interrogation will be a nasty business. The interrogators pride themselves on being able to extract information without spilling blood. It's not that they're squeamish – it's a matter of having pride in their work.'

Pelagia and I were standing in her garden, overlooking the straits. The moment I had heard about Harald's arrest I had fled the city, crossing the Golden Horn on one of the public ferries to Galata. I knew very well that the Orphanotrophus would want to question me. He would ask why I had not alerted his office to Harald's conspiracy, and I was sure that Simeon would soon reveal that Harald had extorted a ransom for the emir's son. Then my failure to report truthfully to John the Eunuch would concern not theft from the state, but an act of treason.

'I can hide you here in Galata for a few days,' Pelagia offered. 'Long enough for you to find some way of escaping from the reach of the Orphanotrophus, though that will be difficult. Luckily the Eunuch has troubles of his own, and may be distracted from your case. Matters are coming to a head between him and his nephew. The Basileus has been scheming – he's fed up with doing whatever John says – and he's been playing John off against his other uncle, Constantine. No one knows who's going to win. My guess is that it will be the Orphanotrophus.'

Pelagia was wrong, and spectacularly so. The young Basileus

delivered his masterstroke right before our eyes. Several days had passed, and we were once again in the garden, overlooking the straits, when we saw a state barge about to put out from our side of the harbour and return to the city. We recognised the vessel at once: it was the boat reserved for the personal use of the Orphanotrophus, and the pennant showed that John himself was aboard.

'I wonder why he's going back so soon?' Pelagia mused. 'My servants tell me that the Eunuch only came here last night, and in a towering rage. The Basileus had publicly snubbed him at court, refused to grant him an audience, and went to consult with Constantine instead. If the Orphanotrophus is being summoned back to the Great Palace, it must be to arrange some sort of truce between the family factions.'

We watched the barge cast off from the landing stage below us. A small cluster of brilliantly dressed officials stood amidships, among them the soberly dressed figure of the Eunuch himself. It was a bright sunny day, with a gentle breeze, and the personal standard of the Orphanotrophus rippled prettily. Everything seemed peaceful and normal. A few fishing boats had their nets down in the bay, a couple of merchant ships were on passage down the straits, and an imperial dromon was heading into the Golden Horn. I guessed she was on her way to the naval arsenal to pick up stores.

We saw the gap widening between the dock and the departing barge. Down on the quayside the bodyguard of Varangians which had accompanied the Orphanotrophus to his embarkation turned and began to march back up the hill to his residence.

'I wonder what the Basileus has got to say to him, and whether he'll manage to patch up his quarrel with his brother Constantine,' Pelagia mused.

Even as she spoke, a bright flash came from high up on the walls of the Great Palace. At first I thought it was the sunlight reflecting off a polished metal shield or a pane of glass in one of the palace rooms, but then the flash was repeated, and I knew it was a signal mirror. Someone in the palace was sending a message across the water. Even as the mirror stopped flickering I saw the dromon, inbound to the arsenal, suddenly change course. Her oars began to thrash the water as her rowers were urged into action, and their blades left a line of small whirlpools in her wake as the warship accelerated. Her target was the Orphanotrophus's barge which was making its way sedately across the harbour. Capture was inevitable. Within moments, the dromon had laid alongside the slow-moving barge and grappled with her. A boarding party from the dromon – I guessed it must be a squad of the Basileus's Pechenegs – rushed across the barge's deck. In a few strides they had surrounded the Orphantrophus and his entourage, who were so astonished that they offered no resistance. For ten years no one had dared challenge the Eunuch's authority, let alone lay hands on him.

I could just make out that the Pechenegs had seized the Orphanotrophus and were carrying him back aboard the dromon, then saw that the warship cast off her lines. She pulled away rapidly from her victim and set course out of the bay, southwards towards the horizon, carrying John with her. The entire operation had lasted less time than the Orphanotrophus's bodyguards took to return back up the hill to his house. The most powerful man in the empire until now had been kidnapped.

'His eyes have almost certainly been put out,' said Psellus with a grimace when I managed to get an appointment with him at his office in the chancellery a week later. 'He may even have been executed. The rumour in the palace is that the Basileus himself stood on the battlements and gave the signal for the Orphanotro-phus to be carried off.'

His remark made me realise how lucky I was. I could have been similarly maimed if the Eunuch had set his interrogators on me.

'I've come to ask for your assistance,' I told Psellus. 'Can anything be done to extricate the spatharokandidatos Harald and his colleagues from jail, now that the Orphanotrophus is out of the way? They were put there on his orders.'

To my disappointment, Psellus shook his head. 'I can't risk anything at this time. Not until I know who really holds the reins of power now. Is it the Basileus or is it his uncle Constantine? And what's going to happen to Zoë? Is she still going to be treated as the Empress Mother, as her "son" promised? It's better to wait for things to settle down. There's no need to be distressed about the prison conditions for your friends. I've heard that Araltes has been very generous, spreading his money around, so that he and his companions are living very comfortably. No dark dungeons, heavy chains and that sort of thing. They're being held in the Prandiara prison, and have their own suite of rooms. He has even hired his own staff. Your Araltes lives like a prince.'

'That's what he is, in his own country.'

'My advice to you is to act normally, as if nothing has happened. Carry on with whatever duties are allocated to the Varangians, and not to those Pecheneg ruffians whom Michael brought in as his enforcers. I'll contact you as soon as I see an opportunity to get Araltes's case reviewed by the officials in the Treasury. However, I must warn you that there's no way of knowing when that will be. The civil administration is in paralysis. Everyone believes that the arrest of the Orphanotrophus heralds the start of the power struggle. It has shown that our new Basileus Michael is capable of lashing out suddenly. Who the next victim will be is anyone's guess. Yet as fast as he cuts down his rivals, he makes enemies for himself, not least among the priests. Our religion tells us that the Basileus is Christ's divine appointment, so the Church thinks that it should have a say in how the emperor conducts himself. If Michael alienates the Patriarch, he will have a dangerous foe.'

I did as Psellus recommended and spent the next month as a dutiful member of the Hetaira. Apart from the usual round of ceremonies, there was really very little work to do now that the Pechenegs were responsible for the emperor's personal safety. Former Life Guards gave a wide berth to the Pechenegs, whom

we judged to be little more than professional cut-throats unworthy
of the tradition of the Hetaira. Their loyalty was only to Michael
himself, while our Varangian tradition had been to serve whoever
was the legally recognised emperor. In consequence I had ample
time to spend with Pelagia, and I must admit that I was finding
her style of life increasingly agreeable. Like many people who
have worked their way from humble beginnings, she knew how
to run an efficient household. As a former baker's wife, she had
clear ideas about what should be served at her table, whether it
was the quality of the ingredients or the way the food should be
cooked. Never in all my life had I eaten so well. Her kitchen staff
prepared poultry marinated in wine and stuffed with almonds,
served caviar followed by fresh cuts of sturgeon, wild game
cooked in olive and garlic, and rich casseroles of pigeon. Most
meals concluded with something sweet flavoured with cinnamon,
Pelagia's particular favourite. After such banquets I found it
necessary to stroll in the garden to aid my digestion, as my
stomach was protesting so noisily. One afternoon Pelagia made a
joke of it.

'You should make a living in the market. Set up your pitch
among the snake charmers and the showmen with their performing
dogs, and tell fortunes as a stomach talker. They claim that their
rumbling guts speak of the future in the same way the brontolo-
gists say that they can interpret the meaning of the thunder claps.
Mind you, with the din your stomach makes, I'm not sure to
which group you should belong.'

'Where I come from,' I answered huffily, 'we believe that
thunder is nothing more than the sound of one of our Gods
driving his chariot through the sky. It doesn't signify anything.' I
belched as discreetly as possible. 'But we do believe it is possible
to read the future in dreams or by reading signs in the sky, the
movements of birds and smoke, or by casting certain sticks carved
with mystic signs.'

'Civilised or barbarian, everyone believes in the significance
of dreams,' observed Pelagia, trying to placate me. 'Entire books

have been written about how to do it, though I've never read any of them.'

'There was a time when I used to dream a lot,' I told her. 'And I had the occasional vision which foretold the future, though this was difficult to interpret. Yet since I arrived in Constantinople, I've not had a single prophetic vision, and it's only after a particularly rich meal like that roast peacock with pistachio sauce we had yesterday that I have even dreamed.'

'And what was in that peacock dream?' Pelagia enquired, grinning.

'More a nightmare, really,' I said. 'The Varangians were back on duty as the Life Guard, instead of the Pechenegs, and we were escorting Michael to the throne room. They were all there – the empress Zoë, his uncle Constantine, even the Orphanotrophus. They all stood around and stared at us. They were looking at the state of the Basileus's robes. I remember thinking to myself that the vestitores who dressed him were playing a joke. They had given him to wear a chlamys, the imperial cloak, which was in rags. It also needed a good wash—'

I stopped in mid-sentence because Pelagia had laid her hand on my arm. 'Don't go on,' she said quietly but firmly, 'I don't want to hear any more.'

'Nothing much happened after that in my dream.'

'I know next to nothing about oneirokritika, the science of interpreting dreams,' Pelagia murmured, 'but I do know that the appearance of the Basileus wearing a dirty or threadbare chlamys means the end of his reign is at hand.' She paused. 'Perhaps even the collapse of his dynasty.'

EIGHT

FIVE WEEKS AFTER the elimination of the Orphanotrophus, Michael lashed out once more. A platoon of his eunuch guards burst into the gynaeceum, sheared off Zoë's hair, and forced the empress to put on a nun's black habit. Then they bustled the old lady out of the palace and hurried her down to the Bucephalon harbour where a ship was waiting to carry her to the Prinkipio Islands, half a day's sail away and a traditional place of exile for unwanted members of the royal family. There the Pechenegs handed Zoë over to a nunnery.

The kidnap would have been successful if Michael had not over-reached himself. Alexis the Patriarch had long dabbled in politics and was known to be a supporter of Zoë, whose marriage to the previous emperor he had solemnised. Michael, intending to remove any potential source of dissent, sent four Pechenegs to lure Alexis from the monastery of the Studius. They took a gift of gold and an invitation for Alexis to attend a meeting with the Basileus. The intention was that the gold would lull the Patriarch's suspicions that he might be the next victim of Michael's megalomania, but it had the opposite effect. Alexis fled the monastery, and instead of going to the rendezvous, where Michael had an assassination squad of eunuchs waiting, he went to the church of Hagia Sophia, summoned the senior officials of the administration, and denounced the Basileus as unworthy of the throne.

The first that I and the other Varangians idling in our guardroom knew of these events was when we heard the bells. It began with the great bell of Hagia Sophia sounding out an urgent alarm. Then, as the news spread across the capital, dozens of monasteries and churches joined in. The noise was extraordinary, a massive, constant tolling that reverberated through the city, rolled out across the suburbs, and grew louder and more insistent. The walls of the guardroom seemed to vibrate with the noise. Such a signal was given only when Constantinople was under dire threat, and the citizens poured out into the streets to demand what was happening. The Basileus, they were told by their priests, had tried to kill the Patriarch, and had banished Zoë, representative of the true line of emperors. The Basileus was wickedness personified, and unless he was curbed, he would bring ruin on the city.

The citizenry were puzzled and anxious, not knowing whether to believe the priests or stay loyal to Michael. Some went to the churches to enquire further and to pray; others flocked towards the Great Palace to demand an explanation from the emperor. He sent his most senior representative, the sebastokrator, to address them in the Forum of Constantine and, because the Pechenegs were held back to protect the emperor himself, the sebastokrator took with him a Varangian escort. Halfdan, myself and twenty others marched along the Mese to the Forum with the sebastokrator in our midst and the clamour of the bells pounding in our ears.

The great square of Constantine was packed when we arrived. I saw shopkeepers, ironworkers, beggars, cutlers, carpenters, tilers, masons, stevedores and fishermen. There were also a surprisingly large number of women and children.

The sebastokrator stood on a mounting block and began to address the crowd, shouting to make himself heard over the noise of the bells. His listeners were attentive, though sullen. Zoë the empress had been banished, he shouted, because she was a poisoner. It was better that she was placed where she could do no further harm. Listening, I thought to myself that it was possible that Zoë had poisoned poor bloated Romanus, whom I had seen drown, and that she had done away with her second husband, Michael, whom I had also witnessed dying agonised in the monastery. But claiming that Zoë was involved in a plot to poison the present Basileus seemed highly unlikely.

The sebastokrator ended his announcement and was met with silence. This was more worrying than if the crowd had jeered or scoffed. Only the clanging of the bells sounded.

Beside me Halfdan said quietly, 'Tell him to get down from the mounting block and begin walking back to the palace. He must move calmly and without haste and make it seem as if he has completed his assignment. If he does that, we can protect him. But if he shows any panic, the crowd may turn nasty. There are not enough of us to hold them off.'

I translated Halfdan's instructions and the sebastokrator followed them scrupulously. It was only a short distance back to the palace, but at any moment I expected to feel the thud of thrown stones on our unprotected backs. For the first time I regretted that the Varangians did not carry shields, and I began to appreciate just how menacing a crowd can be. The main gate of the palace, the Bronze Gate, opened a fraction to allow us in, and Halfdan let out a sigh of relief as we slipped inside.

'The Basileus had better do something, and quickly or we'll have a full-scale riot on our hands,' he said.

Michael's response was to reverse his policy towards Zoë. No sooner had the sebastokrator reported the crowd's mood than a squad of Varangians was detailed to accompany a high official of the chancellery to the Bucephalon harbour. A guard boat rushed them to the Prinkipio Islands, where the grovelling official explained to Zoë that her 'son' desired her to return to the city as he needed her advice.

As we waited for Zoë's return, we became aware of increasing disturbances in the city. Frightened messengers arrived with reports of gangs of looters on the prowl: the marauders were selecting the town houses of those who were most closely associated with the Basileus. The largest mob had laid siege to the palace of the emperor's uncle and confidant, Constantine, who had been elevated to the rank of nobelissimus, second in seniority only to the Basileus himself. This worried us because a detachment of Varangians had been assigned to guard Constantine, and we wondered what was happening to our comrades. In mid-morning they joined us, several with cuts and bruises. Constantine had decided to abandon his palace, they said, and had asked his Varangians to escort him through the streets to the Grand Palace where he could join his nephew.

'What's it like out there?' asked one of my colleagues.

A weary-looking guardsman, with a deep gash over one eye where a stone had hit, shrugged. 'No one seems to know what's going on. The crowds are still disorganised. The only thing they do agree on is that the Basileus should not have mistreated Zoë. They're shouting that she is the true imperial line, and that Michael and his family are upstarts. The women in the mob are the worst. They scream and yell abuse. Apparently the staff from the gynaeceum has been spreading rumours that Zoë was beaten up by the Pechenegs. The crowd can't tell the difference between Pechenegs and Varangians. It was a woman who flung the stone that caught me in the face.'

'Is Zoë really the true imperial line?' someone asked. 'What should we do now? Seems to me that we don't owe any loyalty to the new emperor. He ditched us in favour of those beardless Pechenegs. Let them look after him.'

'Enough of that!' snapped Halfdan. 'The guard is always loyal to the emperor. As long as Michael is Basileus, we serve him. That is our oath.'

'And what happens if the mob decides someone else is the emperor? Whom do we follow then?'

'You follow orders,' said Halfdan. But I could see that many of my colleagues were uneasy.

That night we mounted double patrols on the ramparts and gates of the palace. It was an awkward place to protect because, having been expanded and altered over the centuries, it lacked a single defensive perimeter. The best defence, according to the Basileus's councillors, who hurriedly convened, was somehow to deflect the anger of the citizenry and prevent the mob from attacking. So when Zoë arrived back in the palace the following morning, Michael apologised to her for his earlier behaviour and then took her to show her to the crowd.

Crossing the footbridge which joined the palace to the hippodrome, Michael made his entrance in the imperial box with Zoë at his side. But if he thought this display would reassure the mob, he was mistaken.

The hippodrome could hold forty thousand people to watch the parades and spectacles held there. That day not a single seat was empty, and even the sandy arena where the chariots normally raced was packed. The crowd had waited since dawn for Michael to show himself, and the long delay had increased their discontent. When he finally appeared on the balcony, many in the crowd were too far away to recognise that it was Zoë at his side. Others, suspicious of the duplicity of the palace, believed that the old woman beside the Basileus was not the empress at all, but an impostor dressed up in the imperial regalia. Listening from the parapet above the Bronze Gate where Halfdan's company was stationed – the Pechenegs were on Life Guard duty and the bells were silent at last – I heard something which previously I had associated with a bungled circus act in the hippodrome: the sound of jeering interspersed with insults and cries of anger.

As the heckling continued, a movement in the courtyard below me caught my eye. A small group of gatekeepers, the manglabites, was heading towards the palace entrance. Something about their furtive manner told me that they were about to desert their posts. Halfdan noticed it too.

There was a confused shouting in the distance. The Basileus must have left the hippodrome and returned across the footbridge.

'Here they come,' warned Halfdan. 'Lars, take ten men and get down to the gate, make sure it is bolted and barred. Thorgils, you stay close by me. I may need a Greek speaker.'

When I next peered over the parapet, the front ranks of the mob were already milling about in the open space before the Bronze Gate. Most of them were armed with rocks and stones, crowbars and torches. Several, however, carried swords and pikes. These were soldiers, not civilians. The palace was facing a military mutiny as well as a popular uprising of the citizenry.

'We need archers, slingers and javelin men up here, not a squad of axemen,' muttered Halfdan. Once again, the veteran guardsman seemed to be taking charge in a palace crisis. 'Thorgils, go and find me someone in authority who can explain to us the overall plan of defence. Not a tablet scribbler, but a trained soldier.'

I hurried through the corridors and hallways of the palace. All around me there were signs of panic. Officials, still dressed in their formal costumes, were scurrying about, some of them carrying their personal possessions as they anxiously sought to find some way of leaving the building. Once or twice I passed a detachment of Excubitors, the Greek household regiment, and I was relieved that at least some of the local garrison were still loyal to the throne. Eventually I caught up with one of their Greek officers. Saluting him, I asked if he could send archers to the parapet above the Bronze Gate as the mob was getting dangerously close to breaking in.

'Of course,' he snapped. 'I'll send bowmen. Anything else you need?'

'Two or three scorpions would be helpful. If they could be positioned high up on the wall, they would have a good field of fire and prevent the crowd from massing in front of the gate.'

'Can't help you there,' answered the officer. 'There are no ballistae operators in the Palace Guard. Nobody ever thought they would be needed. Try the Armamenton. Maybe someone there can assist. I know they've got some scorpions stored there.'

I had forgotten about the armoury. The rambling Great Palace was like a city in miniature. It had its royal apartments, formal state rooms, chancellery, treasury, tax office, kitchens, silk-weaving workshops, and of course a major arms store. I raced back to the Bronze Gate, where Halfdan was now standing cautiously behind a battlement, looking down at the mob, which had doubled in size and grown much more belligerent

'Stand well back, Thorgils,' he warned. 'They've got archers down there, and some slingers.' An arrow clattered against the stone buttress.

'Can you let me have a dozen men?' I asked. 'I want to get to the armoury and see if I can bring up a scorpion or two.'

Halfdan looked at me quizzically. 'Since when did you become an artillery man?'

'I had a few lessons in Sicily,' I said.

'Well then, take as many men as you need. The mob has not yet got itself sufficiently worked up to launch a concerted attack.'

With a squad of a dozen Varangians at my heels, I headed towards the armoury. I hammered on the heavy double doors until a storekeeper pulled one of them open cautiously. He looked decidedly peevish. Doubtless he had hoped that he was in a safe retreat, well away from any trouble.

'I need weapons,' I blurted, out of breath.

'Where's your written order? You must have a signed authority from the archon strategos before I can issue any weapons.'

'Where can I find him?'

'Can't tell you. Haven't seen him all day,' said the storekeeper with an air of smug finality.

'This is an emergency,' I insisted.

'No paperwork, no weapons. That's my orders,' was the short answer I got.

I put my hand on his chest and pushed him aside.

'Here, you can't do that,' he objected, but I was already inside and looking around.

The armoury was generously equipped. I could see everything

from parade equipment with gilded hilts and coloured silk tassels to workaday swords and pikes. Against one wall was a stack of the small round shields used by light infantry.

'Grab as many of those as you can carry,' I told my men, 'and take them back up to the ramparts, and get some of those bows from that rack over there and as many arrows as you can handle. Tell Halfdan that there are plenty more bows and arrows if he needs them.'

Meanwhile I had spotted the heavier weapons in the far corner of the store. I recognised the wooden stocks, the iron winding handles, and the thick stubby arms of the bows of at least a dozen scorpions neatly arranged. Looped around a wooden frame were the special bowstrings made of animal sinew. Trying to recall exactly what I had seen in Syracuse when Nikephorus had shown me round his siege tower, and again during the battle at Traina, I began to select enough items to assemble three scorpions. To the strongest man in my squad, an ox-like Swede, I gave all three tripods to carry. To the others I handed out the remainder of the parts as well as two large bags full of iron bolts. I personally took charge of the trigger mechanisms, as they looked fragile and easily damaged.

'Hail to the new technicians,' joked Lars as my men laid out the items on the walkway behind the parapet and I began to experiment how they would fit together.

As it turned out, the scorpions were easy to assemble. Anyone who knew how to lock together the complicated joints in ship-wright's carpentry could do it, and several of my Varangians had that skill. Only the trigger mechanisms were puzzling, and it took one or two false attempts before I finally got them correctly installed and the scorpions were ready for use.

'Here, Thorgils, you get to release the first bolt,' offered Halfdan as he hoisted the completed weapon up on its tripod.

'No thanks,' I said. 'You wind up and pull the trigger. I want to watch and make sure that I have the tension right.'

Halfdan cranked the handle, drawing back the arms of the

bow, placed a metal bolt in its groove, took aim, and squeezed the trigger. To my satisfaction the bolt flew straight, though Halfdan had overcompensated for the angle and the metal bolt whizzed over the heads of the crowd and smacked into the facade of the buildings opposite.

'Powerful stuff, eh?' commented Halfdan contentedly. 'Still, if I was going to kill someone, I would prefer to do it from close-up, where I can see exactly whom I despatch.'

My satisfaction at assembling the ballistae was replaced by dismay. Looking down into the crowd, I saw Harald. Standing a full head taller than those around him, his long hair and moustaches were unmistakable. Then I identified Halldor and several others of Harald's war band right behind their leader, pushing their way through the crowd to reach the front rank. All of them were wearing helmets and carrying their axes. Obviously the mob had broken into the jails and released all the prisoners. The insurrection had also found a common scapegoat. The mob was chanting, 'Give us the Caulker! Give us the Caulker!'

'Don't fire into the crowd,' I begged Halfdan.

'Are you crazy?' he demanded. 'Why go to the trouble of providing these weapons and not use them?' He reloaded, swivelled the scorpion on its mounting and took aim. The chances that he would hit Harald were remote, but I removed his hand from the trigger.

'Over there to the left,' I said. 'That's Harald of Norway, and behind him, Varangians.'

'So they've broken their oath and joined the rebels,' grunted Halfdan.

'You can't shoot down your own people.'

'No,' said Halfdan. 'That would be cowardly. Hand to hand is the only way. They're traitors.'

He abandoned the scorpion and unslung his axe. 'Time for a sortie, men. Show them that we mean business,' he announced.

I watched the reaction of my comrades. They looked as if they were in two minds whether to follow Halfdan or ignore him.

There was an awkward pause, which was interrupted by the sound of feet on the stone steps leading to the parapet. A Greek officer appeared, a man I recognised vaguely from the siege of Syracuse. He seemed competent, and there was no doubt about what he intended. He gestured for us to leave the parapet.

'We're taking over now,' he said in Greek, and I translated for Halfdan's benefit.

'Ask him what he wants us to do,' Halfdan asked.

The Greek muttered something about the Varangians being held as a strategic reserve, and that we were to wait in the open courtyard behind the Bronze Gate in case a frontal attack was launched. Halfdan seemed disappointed, but obediently he led our platoon down into the courtyard.

'That does it,' said one of our men as we watched a file of Greek heavy infantry mount the stairway to take up the positions we had just left. 'That was a lie about needing a strategic reserve. They don't trust us. They think we will join up with our countrymen outside the palace and throw in our lot with the rebels.' Angrily he stumped over to a bench, dropped his axe on the paving slabs and sat down. 'I don't know about the rest of you, but I'm going to wait here until the Greeks sort out among themselves who is really running this place.'

I knew that the platoon agreed with him, and that in a few moments Halfdan would entirely lose his authority. I had always judged Halfdan to be a decent type, if unimaginative; to save his dignity, I said, 'Maybe I could locate someone in charge who can decide where we can be most useful. It will save time if Halfdan comes with me so that he can explain the tactical situation.'

Without waiting for a response, I set off for Psellus's office in the chancellery. He was the only person in the palace whom I trusted to give me an honest answer: something odd was going on. The mob outside the walls was hanging back, as if waiting for something, and I did not know what it was. The Greek infantry who had replaced us on the parapet had appeared strangely complacent. They were not as bellicose as I had expected, and I did not know why. Perhaps Psellus could explain.

Halfdan and I met him in the corridor long before we reached his office, and to my astonishment he greeted us as his saviours. 'The blessed Demetrios himself must have sent you,' he exclaimed. 'The Pechenegs have abandoned their posts and fled, every last one of them, just when the Basileus needed them most. Are there any more of you Varangians?'

'There are,' I said, 'but they are back near the Bronze Gate, awaiting orders, and frankly I'm not sure that they will obey them. Please tell me what is going on. Why aren't the household troops defending the palace more actively, and why hasn't the mob launched an all-out attack?'

'The emperor has renounced his title,' said Psellus urbanely. 'He wishes to retire to a life of peaceful contemplation. He is to become a monk.'

I must have looked dumbfounded, because Psellus went on, 'he has abdicated in favour of his "mother", the empress Zoë, and her sister, the empress Theodora.'

'But I thought that Theodora was in a nunnery.'

'Until yesterday evening,' said Psellus. 'The Patriarch Alexis suggested that she should renounce her vows and enter political life. She is, after all, born to the purple. To Theodora's credit she resisted the idea at first, but was eventually persuaded. The Patriarch crowned her empress a few minutes after midnight. I expect that she and her sister Zoë will be co-rulers of the empire of the Romans as soon as they can come to a suitable arrangement.'

'What about Michael? Where is he now?' My mind was in a whirl as I tried to grasp the sudden change in the politics of imperial rule.

'Close by, and that is why I am so pleased to see you and your colleague. Michael and his uncle, the Nobelissimus, are awaiting immediate departure to the monastery of the Studius.'

By this stage my mind was reeling. 'But isn't the Studius

monastery the residence of the Patriarch Alexis? And wasn't he the man who led the uprising against the Basileus?'

'Thorgils, for a barbarian you are unusually well informed. However, the Studius monastery is the only one which the former Basileus can reach without being molested by the mob, which, as you have observed, is baying for his blood. From the Bucephalon harbour he can reach the monastery by boat before the crowd knows that he has departed. I presume that you can handle a small boat.'

'Of course.'

'There will be only three passengers: Michael, his uncle Constantine, and a chamberlain. The rest of his staff will go on foot to the monastery, discreetly and in small groups, so that they can arrange Michael's reception. In recent weeks I have been privileged to act as the Basileus's private secretary, so I see it as my duty to intercede on his behalf with the new empresses and organise a smooth handover of the imperial government. As soon as I have their majesties' decision, I will come to the monastery with the news. In the meantime I know that I can trust you and your colleague to transport their highnesses safely to the Studius.'

So that is how it came about that I, Thorgils Leifsson, and my company commander, Halfdan, became a boat crew for the former Basileus, Michael V, as he evaded capture by the mob of Constantinople. It felt strange to be rowing a man who, only the previous day, had been considered semi-divine, so that even his closest attendants were obliged to wear gloves when approaching his presence in case they touched his consecrated flesh. Now he and his uncle, disguised as simple monks, sat an arm's length away in the stern of the small rowing boat we commandeered for the short journey. Their chamberlain was in the bows, directing our course as we picked our way between the mass of fishing boats and the cargo ships at anchor off the city. It seemed that all their crews were ashore, joining the insurrection.

Throughout our brief journey Michael kept his head down, staring silently into the bilge of the boat, and I noticed that water was soaking into his purple boots, which he had not yet removed. His uncle, by contrast, took a more intelligent interest in our surroundings. Surreptitiously I watched him as I heaved on the loom of the oar. There was no mistaking his resemblance to his brother, the Orphanotrophus. They both had the same deep-sunk eyes and shrewd gaze, and they shared an aura of knowing exactly how to set about obtaining what they wanted. What a remarkably talented family, I thought to myself. It had supplied an emperor, a Nobelissimus, and, in the Orphanotrophus, a gifted civil administrator. The mob was wrong to dismiss them as nobodies. The family were adventurers, certainly, but no more so than the giant Maniakes whom the citizenry adored. Only Michael the nephew, sitting in a fog of self-pity, had let them down. He had thrown away his inheritance through inexperience in the wielding of power and his unbridled ambition.

The chamberlain called out that we were to steer for shore. Glancing over my shoulder I saw that we were level with the Studius monastery. Its massive walls of red and grey brick loomed over the landing place, a complex of chapels and cloisters crowned by an array of tiled domes, each topped by a cross. The monastery had its own landing steps, and Halfdan and I grabbed on to the mooring chains as our passengers disembarked. By force of habit I refrained from reaching out and touching the ex-Basileus, even when he slipped on the weed-covered steps and nearly fell.

A reception party of monks and courtiers was waiting, and they ushered the two men away.

'Tie up the boat,' the chamberlain ordered, 'and accompany their highnesses. You may be needed.'

Halfdan and I followed the little group into the monastery and then on to the great chapel, entering through a side door half hidden within an angle of the wall.

I gazed around me with interest. The main worship hall was certainly impressive. Above my head rose a great dome, lined with mosaics. Staring down at me from within the vault was a gigantic image of the White Christ, gaunt and stern, with great dark eyes. He looked stiff and sad. In one hand he held his holy book; the other hand was held up in what I supposed was a gesture of blessing or admonition. The light from hundreds of candles in iron holders suspended by chains flickered across his severe expression. The dome rested on great pillars from which hung wooden boards painted with images of the White Christ's most famous followers. The windows were small and set high up in the building, and the shafts of light reached only the upper part of the huge chamber. At ground level illumination depended on many more candles set in huge candlesticks, some as tall as a man, some arranged in banks of at least a hundred at a time. The general impression was of darkness and shadow interspersed with pools of radiant light. The air smelled strongly of incense. At the far end of the church stood the altar, and on each side were yet more masses of candles, as well as two carved and gilded wooden platforms where I supposed the priests of the White Christ stood during their devotions. These two platforms were now occupied by several dozen courtiers, monks, and various bureaucrats. I was reminded of the audience who, in a market square, clamber up on carts to get a better view when jugglers or hucksters perform. They were all looking at Michael and his uncle Constantine as they crossed the floor of the church towards the altar itself.

'I claim the sanctuary of the monastery!' Michael cried out shrilly. He reached the altar and turned towards a monk standing a little in advance of his fellows. The man was, I presumed, the chief priest.

'I claim sanctuary,' Michael repeated, 'and wish to offer myself humbly to the service of our Lord.'

There was a long, long silence, and then the shadows all around the sides of the chapel moved. The walls, I realised, were lined with men. They had been standing there waiting silently, whether in respect or in ambush I could not tell. They stood three or four deep, and now they produced an exasperated sound, a

collective, angry muttering. Peering into the shadows I saw that
several hundred of the citizens of Constantinople were already in
the chapel. They must have been told, or guessed, where the ex-
Basileus and his uncle had been heading when they left the palace,
and they had got here before us.

Hearing the sound, Michael gave a frightened glance and
edged closer to the altar.

'Sanctuary,' he cried again, almost shrieking. 'I have a right to
sanctuary.'

Again came angry muttering, and Michael sank to his knees in
supplication and seized hold of the cloth that covered the altar.
His uncle moved to be beside him, but remained standing.

'Respect the Church!' cried Michael.

Then a man stepped out from the crowd. He appeared to be
a minor official, a city employee perhaps. Evidently he was a
spokesman.

'You are to stand trial for your crimes—' he began, but
Michael interrupted frantically, 'How dare you address me in this
fashion?'

Clearly he had forgotten that he was now meant to be a
humble monk. He looked round and saw Halfdan and myself
standing there.

'Guardsmen,' he ordered, his voice cracking with fear, 'protect
me from this lunatic.'

Halfdan took several paces forward and placed himself
between the cringing ex-Basileus and the leader of the crowd. I
followed him, thinking to myself how ridiculous it was for just
two men to attempt to serve as a shield. But for the moment, at
least, our presence was effective. The crowd held back, and to my
relief I saw Psellus enter the chapel by the main door and come
hurrying towards us. With him was a delegation of officials.

'With the authority of the empress Zoë,' he announced loudly
so all could hear, 'I bring an order for the detention of His
Highness Michael and the Nobelissimus. They are to be brought

to the palace for due judgement of their actions. They must not be harmed.'

'He'll only smooth-talk his way out of trouble. Let's deal with him now, our own justice,' an angry voice shouted from the back of the crowd. The onlookers stirred, closing in. Behind us I heard Michael's yelp of fear, and I sensed that the two groups of onlookers on each side of the altar were spellbound by the scene being played out before them.

Psellus was soothing. 'I assure you, your highness, no harm will come to you if you accompany us,' he told him. Then, addressing the crowd's spokesman, he said, 'I promise you that the people will have justice. The empress Zoë is discussing with her sister Theodora how best to restore peace to the city. The people, through their representatives, will be consulted before any decision is reached. For the moment it would be prudent for His Highness Michael and the Nobelissimus to be held within the palace.'

After some hesitation the crowd began to move aside so that the group of officials with Psellus could approach the altar. Michael was still petrified. 'They'll kill me if I leave the church,' he sobbed. 'I refuse to go with you. I won't get a fair trial.' Watching his craven response, I remembered how little mercy he had shown his uncle the Orphanotrophus, and thought to myself that though John the Eunuch might have been ruthless and menacing, he at least had had courage. His nephew was a coward.

'These two guardsmen will accompany us,' said Psellus. 'They will see you safely back to the palace. Just as they brought you here.' He glanced across at me. 'Thorgils, perhaps you and your colleague would be so good as to accompany us on the way to the palace.'

Reluctantly Michael released his grip on the altar cloth and rose to his feet. Then he and his uncle walked down the length of the chapel, surrounded by Psellus's delegation. I noted that several courtiers descended from their vantage point and joined our little procession. I guessed that they were loyal members of Michael's faction.

We emerged from the gloom of the chapel and into daylight, and I realised that it was mid-afternoon. The overthrow of the Basileus had taken less than three days from the moment he had unwisely sent his eunuchs to arrest Zoë until his desperate plea for sanctuary in the monastery.

We started along the broad avenue of the Triumphal Way leading to the heart of the city. I remembered how I had marched the route with the Hetaira, escorting the corpse of Romanus, and later to bid farewell to Maniakes's army as it left for the Sicilian campaign. On the first occasion the crowd had been silent; the second time they had been cheering and shouting encouragement. Now, the crowd was resentful. They pushed in on us from each side, shouting abuse and spitting. We had to thrust our way forward.

We had got as far as the open space called the Sigma, named because it had the same shape as the Greek letter, when I became aware of another agitated group elbowing its way through the crowd towards us. A few steps later I recognised its leader: Harald. With him were at least a dozen of his men, including Halldor. He was escorting a high official of the court, dressed in his formal silk robe of blue and white and carrying his badge of office, an ivory baton. He made a vivid contrast to the shabby figures of Michael and his uncle in their rumpled monks' gowns.

Harald and his men barred our path. We halted, and the crowd drew back to give us a little space. The brilliantly clad official stepped forward and opened a scroll. A silver and purple seal dangled from the lower edge.

'By the authority of their joint Augustae, Zoë and Theodora,' he began. 'Punishment is to be carried out on the former Basileus Michael and the Nobelissimus Constantine.'

Michael let out a shout of protest. 'You have no right. I was promised safe conduct,' he screamed.

From the crowd came a muted growl of approval.

'The punishment is to be carried out with immediate effect,' concluded the official, rolling up his scroll and nodding to his Varangian escort.

Four of Harald's men stepped forward and took hold of Michael and his uncle by their arms. Halfdan and I did not interfere. We were outnumbered, and besides, I felt exhausted. Events had moved beyond anything I could have imagined, and I was tired of the whole business. I no longer cared who held the reins of power in the Queen of Cities. As far as I was concerned, this was a matter for the Greeks to sort out among themselves.

Michael continued pleading and sobbing. He was writhing in the grasp of the two Varangians, begging to be spared. 'Let me go! Let me go! I was promised safe conduct,' he repeated over and over again. He knew what would happen next.

Later it would be said that Harald of Norway carried out the mutilation, but that was not so. The little group had brought their own specialist with them, and he had with him the tools of his trade. A small, rather effeminate-looking man came forward and asked for a brazier.

We waited for a short while before someone came back with a brazier of the common household sort normally used for cooking. Its embers were glowing and it was placed on the ground. The executioner, for that was his role, I now realised, placed the tip of a long thin iron bar in the centre of the fire and blew delicately on the embers. The crowd pushed around so closely that he had to ask them to move back to allow him space to work. When the tip of the rod was glowing red-hot, the little man looked up at his victims. He was expressionless. I remembered Pelagia's warning that the torturers and interrogators of the palace took a pride in their work.

Michael was in hysterics, thrashing from side to side, begging to be spared. His uncle Constantine, the Nobelissimus, calmly took a pace forward.

'Let me go first,' he said quietly. Then, turning towards the crowd, he said firmly: 'I ask you to step back a little further still, so that there may be sufficient witnesses to the fact that I met my fate with courage.' Then he calmly lay down on the paving slabs, flat on his back, face to the sky, eyes wide open.

I wanted to look away, but found that I was too appalled. The executioner came forward with his iron rod and deftly pressed the tip into Constantine's right eye. The man's body arched back in agony, and at almost the same moment the iron rod was dipped into the left eye. A little hiss of steam came with each movement. Constantine rolled over on to his front, his hands pressed against his sightless eyes. He let out a deep, agonised groan. Hands reached down to help him back on his feet. Someone had produced a silk scarf, which was quickly bound around his head, and I saw two courtiers, themselves weeping, support the Nobelissimus, who was unable to stand unaided.

The executioner now turned towards Michael. He was squirming in the grip of the two Varangians and blubbering with terror. His gown was wet where he had soiled himself. The executioner nodded, indicating that the ex-Basileus was to be forced to the ground and held there, face up. The two Varangians pressed Michael to his knees, then pulled him over backwards. Michael still flailed about, twisting and turning, trying to escape. Two more of Harald's men knelt down and took a grip of his legs, pinning them to the paving stones. The Varangians who held his arms pulled them out straight, then pressed down on his wrists so that he was pinioned in the shape of a cross.

Michael's howls had risen to a desperate pitch, and he whipped his head from side to side. The executioner was reheating the iron, blowing gently on the charcoal. When he was ready, he sidled softly across to the spread-eagled ex-Basileus, and, without bothering to clamp the head steady, he again made a double dart with the burning spit. A sound rose from deep within Michael's throat and burst out in a terrible howl.

The executioner stepped back, his face still expressionless, and the Varangians released their grip. Michael curled up in a sobbing ball, his arms wrapped around his head. Mercifully, his courtiers picked him up. Then they turned and carried him away, as the crowd, silenced by the terrible punishment, parted to let them through.

NINE

LIKE A SHIP BUFFETED by a sudden great wave, the empire of
the Romans heeled, almost capsized, then began to right itself
when the ballast of centuries of obedience to the throne made
itself felt. During the days which followed the blinding of Michael
and his uncle, there was widespread disquiet in Constantinople.
The citizens asked themselves whether it was possible that two
elderly women could run an empire. Surely the machinery of the
administration would stutter and come to a halt. Foreign foes
would then take the chance to attack the imperial frontiers. There
would be civil war. But as day followed day and nothing dire
occurred, tensions eased. In the chancellery, in the tribunals, and
in the myriad offices of state, the bureaucrats returned to their
records and ledgers, and the government of the empire resumed
its normal course. Yet not everything was quite as it had been
before. During the insurrection the mob had broken into the
Great Palace. Most of the crowd had hunted for valuables to loot,
but a small and determined band had headed for the archives and
burned the tax records, as those officials who came back to the
treasury discovered.

'Simeon the money changer suggested that we torch the files,'
Halldor told me in the guardroom where the Varangians had once
again taken up their duties. 'I doubt that Harald himself would

have thought of it, but Simeon sought us out during the uproar. He too had been released from jail by the mob, and he gave us directions as to where to find the archives.' And with a chuckle he added, 'It means, of course, that now there is no evidence against those accused of collusion with the tax collectors.'

'I'm surprised that you found time to destroy tax records when you were also carrying out the instructions to arrest Michael and the Nobelissimus.'

'There was time enough,' said Halldor. 'The sister empresses argued for hours over what should be done with the former Basileus. Zoë wanted him imprisoned, awaiting trial. But Theodora was all for having his eyes put out, and as quick as possible.'

'Surely it was the other way round? Theodora was a nun, or at least had been.'

'No,' said Halldor. 'Theodora was the bloodthirsty one.'

I murmured something about the idea that the Christians, especially the nuns and monks, were meant to practise forgiveness and charity, but that evening, when I crossed over to Galata to spend the evening at Pelagia's villa, my friend soon set me straight.

'You still don't understand, do you, Thorgils? When it comes to the pursuit of power, nothing matters to those who are really ambitious. Take the example of Araltes. You think so highly of him and you assist in every way you can. Yet he will stop at nothing to achieve his ambitions, and one day you may regret being so loyal to him.'

I was thinking to myself that Pelagia probably resented my allegiance to Harald, when abruptly she changed the subject: 'Next time you are on ceremonial guard duty, take a good look at the two empresses for me, will you? I'd be interested to hear what you make of them.'

I did as she asked, and at the next meeting of the supreme state council in the Golden Hall I made sure that my position in the circle of Life Guards was right beside the imperial throne. In fact there were now two thrones, one for each of the empresses,

and Theodora's throne was set back a fraction, signifying that
Theodora was very slightly junior to her sister. I could see that
court protocol had adapted remarkably smoothly to the novel
arrangement of twin female rulers. All the usual high functionaries
were present, dressed in their official robes of silk brocade and
holding their emblems of office. Standing nearest to the empresses
were their special favourites, and behind them were the most
senior ministers. Then came an outer ring of senators and
patricians, and finally, in the background, a group of ranking civil
servants. Among them, I identified Psellus who, judging by his
green and gold robe, was now a senior official of the chancery.

I took careful note of details to tell Pelagia. Zoë was more
plump than her sister, and had managed to retain a remarkable
youthfulness, perhaps as a result of all those ointments and
perfumes I had heard about. Her skin was smooth and unlined,
and it was difficult to equate the harassed supplicant whom I had
turned away from her husband's deathbed with the poised and
immaculately manicured woman who now sat on the throne in
front of me. Interestingly, when Zoë was bored she amused herself
by eyeing the more handsome men in the room, and so I judged
that she was still man-hungry. Theodora, by contrast, fidgeted as
she sat. Taller than her sister, she was rather scrawny, with a head
that seemed too small for her body, and I had the impression that
she was unintelligent and frivolous.

While I was wondering which of the two sisters was dominant
in their partnership, I heard Harald's name mentioned. The akolouthos, the commander of the Hetaira, was making a formal
request on behalf of spatharokandidatus Araltes. He had asked
permission to leave the imperial service. The logothete of the
dromos who was hearing the petition turned to consult Zoë, bowed
obsequiously and asked for her decision. Zoë had been gazing at a
handsome young senator, and I doubt that she even knew what
the subject was. 'Denied,' she said absently. The logothete bowed
a second time and turned back to face the akolouthos. 'Denied,'
he repeated. The business of the day moved on.

'Harald won't like that at all,' said Halldor when I told him
the decision that evening. 'He's heard that his nephew Magnus
has been declared King of Norway.'

'What difference does that make?'

Halldor looked at me as though I was a dimwit. 'Harald has
as good a claim to the throne as his nephew, probably better.
That's what all this has been about – the amassing of loot, the
gathering in of valuables. The money will be his war chest if he
has to fight for what he considers rightfully his. Sooner or later
he will seek his inheritance, and the longer he delays, the more
difficult it will be to press his case. My guess is that he will ignore
the government's decision and leave.'

'But where will he find the ships to take him back up the
straits to the Pontic Sea and along the rivers to Gardariki? ' I
objected. 'It is not like when he sent those three ships back with
the emir's ransom from Sicily. What's left of his war band is
now a land force, without ships. If he tries to leave without
permission, he'll be arrested again. Then he'll never get to claim
the throne.'

'They'll have to catch him first,' said Halldor stubbornly, but
I could see that he lacked a solution to the problem.

'Let me see what I can come up with,' I said, for something
told me that this was my chance to make myself indispensable to
Harald and win his trust for the future.

Psellus was so swamped with work that I had to sweeten the
chartularius of his office with a small bribe to give me an appointment.

'It's all very well having two empresses,' Psellus complained
when I finally got to see him, 'but it doubles the workload of the
officials. Everything must be prepared in duplicate. Every document has to be written out twice so that a copy can be sent to the
staff of each empress, but frankly neither woman seems much
interested in dealing with the chores of government when the
papers do arrive. They prefer the more frivolous aspects of their
role. It's very pleasant having so many banquets, receptions,

pageants and the like, but the administration moves very slowly, mired in honey, you might say.' He sighed and shifted the pile of paperwork on his desk. 'How's your friend the spatharokandidatos doing?'

'You've guessed correctly,' I said. 'My visit is about Araltes.' I lowered my voice. There was no one else in the room, but I knew that very little was truly private in the Great Palace. 'Araltes urgently needs to resign his post and leave Constantinople. It is very important that he does so. But he has been forbidden permission by Zoë. '

Psellus got up from his seat and went over to check that there was no one loitering outside.

'Thorgils,' he said seriously, 'it was one thing to suggest how Araltes might be cleared of charges for tax fraud. That could have been arranged with some judicious bribes. It is entirely another matter to connive at the direct disobedience of an imperial decision. It could lead to my impeachment and – at worst – the death penalty. I have no wish to be scourged, tied up in a sack and thrown into the sea.'

'I know,' I said. 'It gets worse. It's not just Araltes who should be allowed to leave. The surviving members of his war band – there are about eighty men – will want to depart with him. They've got what they came for. They've made their fortunes.'

Psellus sighed. 'That's outright desertion. Army regulations call for punishment by mutilation or death.'

'I know,' I said. 'But don't you have any suggestions as to how Araltes and his men can get away?'

Psellus thought for a while. 'Right now I don't have any idea,' he said, 'but I can assure you that if Araltes does succeed in leaving without permission, there will be a violent hue and cry. There will be a hunt for those who might have helped him. His close associates will be picked up and interrogated. You have worked with Araltes for several years now, and you would be the first to fall under suspicion. I suggest that if Araltes does leave the city, you make sure that you leave with him.'

'That's something that I've already been thinking about,' I said.

Psellus came to a decision. 'Thorgils, I promised that I would assist you. But this request of yours goes beyond anything I had expected. I have to protect myself. If the scheme fails and you, Araltes and the others are caught, I must not be traceable. If an opportunity for Harald's departure with his men presents itself, I will contact you, but not in person. That would be too dangerous. Even your visit here today is now a risk to me. I do not want you to come to this office again. Instead I will write to you, and that message will be the last you will hear from me.'

'I understand,' I said. 'I'll wait for your contact.'

'It may never arrive,' Psellus warned. 'Anything could happen. I may get transferred out of this office, or I may never see the opportunity for Araltes to slip away. And if the letter falls into the wrong hands, that would be a disaster for all of us.'

By now I had guessed what Psellus was leading up to. I remembered how Harald had used rune symbols as a private code to set up the ambush of the Arab pirate, anticipating that his letter would be intercepted.

'You will use code?' I asked.

Psellus blinked in surprise. 'As I've noted before, Thorgils, for a barbarian you are remarkably astute. Here, let me show you.' He reached for a sheet of paper and wrote out the Greek alphabet, arranging the twenty-seven letters in three equal lines. 'The principle is simple,' he said. 'One letter substitutes for another that falls on the same line but in the mirror position. Thus, the second letter on the first line, beta, is substituted with the second to last letter on the same line, eta. Similarly with the other letters. It's a very basic code, and any senior bureaucrat would recognise it immediately. But it would baffle a mere messenger who might open the letter and read it out of curiosity.'

'I understand,' I said. 'I'm very grateful.'

I HAD TO WAIT nearly five weeks for Psellus's coded message to arrive, and it was a bitter-sweet interval. As Psellus had remarked, the reign of the Augustae, the two empresses, was characterised by frivolity. It was as if the terrible events of the fall of the Basileus Michael had to be followed by a period of gaiety so that the people could expunge the memory of the rebellion. Apparently, when Halfdan and I had been taking the Basileus to the Studius monastery, hundreds had died in the streets during skirmishes between the rebels and the troops loyal to the Basileus, as well as among the bands of looters fighting over the spoils. Now the populace wanted to be distracted, and Zoë and Theodora dipped into the treasury reserves to pay for parades and spectacles in the hippodrome. They gave lavish banquets, and even allowed selected members of the public to visit the Great Palace and see its marvels.

This gave me the opportunity to repay Pelagia for her kindness and hospitality, and I showed her as much of the Great Palace as was permitted. As a commoner she was banned from the great apartments of state, of course, but I took her to see the private zoo with its collection of exotic animals, including a hippopotamus and a long-necked African cameleopard, and in the Tzykanisterion sports ground we watched a horseback tournament. Young patricians were playing a game which involved using long-handled mallets to hit a leather ball the size of an apple into a goal. The game bored Pelagia, but she was fascinated by the horologion, a Saracen-made contraption which calculated hours by measuring water draining from a bowl and opened and closed small doors from which carved figures emerged according to the time of day.

'Isn't it strange,' she commented 'that the palace tries to make sure that everything endures and remains the same as it has always been. Yet it is also the place that measures how time is passing. It is almost as if the palace believes that one day they will discover how time could be stopped.'

At that moment I should have told Pelagia that my own time

in that city might soon be coming to an end, that I would be leaving Constantinople. But I shirked the opportunity, and we went instead to visit the gynaeceum, where Pelagia's sister was waiting to show her around. I was forbidden from entering. As I stood in the courtyard of the beardless ones, the guardian eunuchs, I agonised that perhaps I had been too hasty in seeking Psellus's help in extricating Harald and the others from their service to the emperor. Maybe, instead, I should make my life in the Queen of Cities, just as Halfdan had done. I was now forty-two years of age, past the prime of life, and the attractions of Constantinople with its luxurious lifestyle and pleasant climate had a strong appeal. Pelagia had never remarried since the death of her husband, and the two of us had become very close, so there was every chance that she would accept me as her partner, if that was what I proposed. There was no doubt that life with Pelagia, whom I respected deeply, would be very agreeable. I would retire from the Life Guard, live harmoniously with her in the villa in Galata, and give up my ambition to restore the Old Gods in the northern lands. All I had to do was ignore Psellus's message, if it ever came.

I was on the verge of making this decision when Pelagia emerged from the gynaeceum. She was marvelling at the luxury with which Zoë had surrounded herself, yet dismayed by the tedium of life within the women's quarters. 'They eat their meals with golden forks in there,' she said, 'but the food must taste like the ashes of the living dead.' Her remark, following so closely on my thoughts about my dilemma, made me wonder if, by taking the more comfortable path, my life would become a hollow shell; and whether, should Pelagia ever learn that I had abandoned my deeply held ambition, she would blame herself.

Even so, perhaps I would have stayed in Constantinople had not Loki strained at his bonds. There was a shaking of the ground on the evening after Pelagia and I visited the Great Palace. It was only a minor tremor, scarcely felt in the Varangian barracks. A few statues fell from their plinths along the Mese, several apartment blocks were damaged, and the city engineers had to come with ladders and hooks the next day to pull down the structures that were too dangerous. But on the Galata side of the Golden Horn the damage was far more severe. Several of the new houses collapsed as a result of shoddy workmanship. One of them was Pelagia's villa. She had just returned to her house, and she and several of her servants were crushed. I heard of her death from her sister Maria, who came to fetch me the next morning, and the two of us crossed the Golden Horn to visit the scene of the calamity. As I looked on the tumbled ruins of her house, I felt as desolate as if I was standing on the edge of a great void into which Pelagia had disappeared and from which she would never return. Numbed, I was overcome by a profound sadness that someone so full of spirit had gone, and I wondered whether Pelagia, who had believed neither in the salvation promised by the White Christ nor in my Old Gods, now existed in some other world.

Her death broke the only real link that I had with the Great City, and persuaded me that Odinn had other plans for the remaining years of my life.

Pelagia's family gathered to settle her affairs, and from them I learned that she had been very astute in investing my guardsman's salary for me. Thanks to her I was now reasonably wealthy, even without my secret share of the emir's ransom and the salvage of the Arab pirate galea, most of which had already been carried northward in Harald's ships returning from the Sicilian campaign. The following week I went discreetly to see the financier, a member of the banker's guild, to whom Pelagia had entrusted the safekeeping of my funds and asked him if I could withdraw the money as I was thinking of travelling abroad.

'No need to do that,' he replied. 'If you carry too much coin, you might be waylaid and robbed. I can arrange for you to collect your money at your destination from my fellow bankers, if the place is not too distant.'

'Would the city of Kiev be too far?' I asked.

'Not at all. I could manage to have your funds made available to you in Kiev. We have been doing an increasing amount of business there these past few years, transferring money for the Rus traders who come annually to this city. Not all of them want to travel back burdened with trade goods, struggling to haul them back upstream over the portages. They get notes of credit from me, which they redeem in Kiev.'

The banker's assurance removed my worry that Harald's departure from Constantinople might be hampered by financial complications. He too could use the bankers to move his assets from Constantinople. Now everything depended on Psellus to come up with some scheme whereby we could escape.

His cryptogram, when it finally arrived in late May, was so terse that there were just six words. It read, 'Two ousiai, Neiron, peach silk, Nativity.'

The first part was clear to me. Ousiai are small dromons, about the size of our Norse ships. Each normally carries a crew of about fifty men and they serve as fast escort vessels. The Neiron was the naval arsenal on the Golden Horn, so presumably the two ousiai would be docked there at the time of the feast of the Nativity. But I was puzzled and disappointed by Psellus's mention of the Nativity. If this was the date when he thought Harald and his men would have their chance to leave Constantinople, then my friend was more of a cloistered bureaucrat than I thought. The Nativity, the birth of the White Christ, occurs in mid-winter, and surely, I told myself, Psellus knew that December was far too late for a departure from Constantinople. The sailing weather was atrocious, and by the time we reached the river leading towards Kiev it would be in flood or frozen over. We had to leave in the summer or early autumn at the latest.

The reference to peach silk was a complete enigma. I could see no connection with warships at the arsenal.

So I went to the House of Lights. This was the most luxurious shopping emporium in the capital. Occupying a prime site on the most fashionable stretch of the Mese, it stayed open day and night, its arcades lit by hundreds upon hundreds of candles. Only one item was on sale – silk. The precious fabric was available in every grade and style and colour, whether as lengths of cloth, as complete garments, or cut and part-finished ready to be sewn together. In all the known world the House of Lights was the largest single market for silk, and the market dealers there were among the wealthiest merchants in the city, as well as the most rigorously controlled. They were obliged to report every single transaction over ten nomisma in value to the eparch of the city so that his officials knew exactly where each length of material came from and to whom it went. If a foreigner wished to buy silk, the dealer was only allowed to offer the lower grades of fabric, and he was obliged to report his customer's departure from Constantinople so that his baggage could be searched for contraband. Failure to do so would mean that the silk merchant was flogged, his head shaved in public humiliation, and all his goods confiscated.

Mindful of this strict regime, I chose the most discreet of the silk merchants' shops in the House of Lights and asked to speak with the owner. A white-haired man with a sleek, prosperous appearance came out from a back room, and the moment he saw I was a foreigner suggested that we discuss our business in private, in a back alcove.

'I'm enquiring about the price and availability of good quality silks for export,' I explained.

He complimented me on my excellent Greek and asked where I had learned to speak the language with such fluency.

'In trade,' I answered evasively. 'Mostly the shipping business.'

'Then you will already be familiar with the restrictions forbidding me to sell certain categories of silk to those who are not resident in this city,' he murmured, 'but alternative arrangements can sometimes be made. Did you have any particular goods in mind?'

'Highly coloured silks make more profit for me when I sell them on. It depends what is available.'

'At this moment I have good stocks of dark green and yellow in half-tint.'

'What about other colours? Orange, for example? That's popular where I come from.'

'It depends on the depth of the hue. I can probably find a pale lemon orange, close to the yellow I have. But the more dye stuff used in colouring the material, the more difficult it is to obtain. And, of course, more expensive.'

'If I placed an order for a specific colour, could you prepare it for me?'

He shook his head. 'The law forbids silk dealers from exercising the craft of dyeing silk. That is a separate craft. Nor can I handle raw silk. That too is a separate profession.'

I adopted a disappointed look. 'I had particularly hoped to find peach-coloured silk, for a very special client. And I could pay a premium price.'

'Let me send someone to check.'

He called a servant, gave him his instructions, and while we waited for the man to return from his errand, he showed me various samples of his stock.

'I'm sorry to say,' reported the silk merchant when his servant came back with the information he needed, 'that peach-coloured silk will be impossible to obtain, at least for some time.' He looked knowing, and continued, 'There's a rumour that the Augusta Zoë is due to get married again . . . for the third time, can you imagine! The royal workshops are working at full stretch to produce all the garments and hangings needed for the ceremony, and peach-coloured silk is a major item on their list of requirements.'

'But I thought purple was the imperial colour?'

'It is,' said the silk merchant, 'and so too is deep red and those shades of violet which border on purple. All those hues are strictly reserved for the palace. Anyone making or selling such material would be in serious trouble. Peach-coloured silk is made with the same dyestuff that produces the forbidden shades. It is a matter of precisely how much of the dye is mixed with certain tinting herbs, the temperature in the dyer's vat, and other craft secrets. Because of this association, peach is considered to be very exclusive and is customarily sent as a present to foreign rulers to inform them of important palace events such as weddings or coronations.'

I sighed. 'How very disappointing. I don't suppose it is worth my waiting in the city for peach-coloured silk to become available again?'

'Preparing the gifts for the foreign potentates will not be a high priority,' the silk dealer said. 'The royal workshops will want to get all the ceremonial material out of the way first, then use up the last stocks of dye to make the peach silk for shipment.'

'And when might that be? I need to leave well before the celebration of the Nativity.'

'It depends which Nativity you mean,' he replied. 'I presume you are from Venice, or Genoa perhaps. In the west you celebrate the Nativity of our Lord, and so do we. But this city celebrates another very special Nativity, that of Mary, our protectress. And her Nativity falls in September.'

My sudden intake of breath must have puzzled the silk merchant, for I saw that I had given Psellus too little credit for his secret intelligence, and even as I hurried away from the House of Lights, I was busy recalculating how much time I had to prepare Harald's escape from Constantinople. If Psellus's information about the two galleys was correct, then I had three months to get everything ready.

IT COST ME five nomisma to bribe a clerk working in the dromos to keep me supplied with further details of the silk shipment as they emerged. Psellus must have had an excellent contact in the royal silk factory, because on June the eleventh Zoë did get married again – to a patrician by the name of Constantine who was acclaimed as the new Basileus the next day – and it was a little less than three months later that the corrupt clerk in the

dromos informed me that the thirty bolts of peach-coloured silk
were ready for despatch as gifts to the Caliph of Egypt. The silk
was to be taken there by the imperial envoy carrying the official
news of the acclamation of a new Basileus.

'According to my information,' I told Harald, 'two ousiai have
been ordered to the Neiron to pick up the silk and other gifts.
They are on standby to receive the imperial ambassador. He will
come aboard as soon as the chancery has prepared the official
letters announcing the coronation of the new Basileus.'

'You suggest that we seize the vessels?'

'Yes, my lord. They would suit your purpose. Ousiai are fast
and manoeuvrable, and they can carry you and your men up to
the Pontic Sea.'

'And how do you propose that we acquire these vessels? The
arsenal is heavily guarded.'

'My lord, you remember your mission to the Holy Land as an
escort for the architect Trdat?'

'Of course.'

'I suggest that you and your men present yourselves at the
gates of the Neiron as the escort for this new ambassador.'

I could see that Harald immediately liked the idea of this
deception. 'And what makes you think that the authorities in the
dockyard will be tricked?'

'Leave that to me, my lord. All I ask is that you and your
men act like a formal escort, and that you are ready to seize the
two dromons when the time is right.'

'That part of the plan will not be a problem.'

Never before had I forged an official document, but I had
retained the official orders I received when we had accompanied
Trdat, and now I used them as my model. I found myself thanking the Irish monks who had taught me penmanship in my youth
as I drew up an official-looking document stating that Harald and
his men were to escort the envoy bearing gifts to the Caliph of
Egypt. For paper I used a sheet of parchment which I purchased
from my contact in the dromos. I paid him another two nomisma

extra for the right colour ink – black for the text, red for the invocation to the Holy Trinity which is placed at the beginning of every official order. The ministerial signature I copied from my genuine original, and the seal with its grey silk ribbon I merely cut off and transferred. Finally I carefully folded the fake document with exactly the same creases, as I had heard that this was a secret method by which the clerks guaranteed the authenticity of a document.

Then, on the day before the feast of the Nativity of Mary, Harald, the remainder of his war band and I arrived at the main gate of the Neiron and requested permission to stow our gear aboard the two dromons. Fortunately the archon, the director of the dockyard, was absent as he was preparing for the feast day, and his deputy was too nervous to question why so many men were needed as an embassy escort. Also, Harald's imperious manner cowed him. The official barely glanced at the forged orders before handing us over to a junior assistant to take us to the dromons. We made our way past the shipwrights, riggers and painters, who glanced at us curiously, surprised to see so many foreigners within the arsenal, and eventually came to a short wooden pier where the two ousiai were moored. As I had anticipated, their crews had been given leave to prepare for the festival, and they had left their vessels in care of the dockyard. There was no one aboard.

'Sweeps and sails left on deck, thank the Gods,' muttered Halldor, looking around the vessels, and I realised that in my enthusiasm as a forger I had forgotten that the dromons might not be fully ready for sea.

'We'll stow our gear on board and stay the night,' I told the archon's assistant.

He looked surprised. 'Are you not attending the festivities tomorrow?' he asked.

'No,' I said. 'These men are unbelievers. Also the sekreton of the dromos informs me that the ambassador himself may arrive tomorrow evening, and we could be getting under way without delay.'

'But the regular crews are on shore leave,' the man objected.

'And if they are found to have neglected their duty, they will be reprimanded,' I added.

The dockyard assistant took the hint. 'Very well. I will make arrangements for additional fresh water and stores to be brought aboard tomorrow. But as it is a feast day, I cannot guarantee that it will be possible to provide all that is needed. I was not made aware that the ambassador would have such a numerous escort.'

'Do your best,' I assured him. 'We've brought enough rations with us to last the next few days.'

By mid-afternoon the activity of the dockyard was already subsiding. The sounds of hammering and sawing and the shouts of workers faded as the shipwrights left their tasks and went home early to prepare for the festival. Soon the only people left in the Neiron were the members of the fire watch, whose duty was to keep an eye on the highly combustible stores, and a night guard of about a dozen men who patrolled the slipways and quays.

Harald's men made pretence of settling down for the night aboard the two ousiai, but many of us were too nervous to sleep, and I worried that the night guard would become suspicious. Their patrol was random, and there was no way of anticipating their visits, so I told the young officer in charge that we would post our own sentries, as this was our custom, and persuaded him that his own men needed to come no closer than the foot of the jetty.

Everything now depended on the timing of our next move.

At the first glimmer of dawn, Harald quietly gave the order to unmoor our vessel from the quay. Astern of us, the second ousiai followed us. As silently as possible we pushed off from the pier and began to row out into the Golden Horn. We could feel the ripples slapping against the thin wooden hulls of the lightly built dromons. A fresh breeze from the north was raising waves in the straits outside, but in the sheltered waters of the great harbour the waves had little effect.

We were a long bowshot from the shore when a trumpet sounded the alarm from the Neiron behind us. The nightwatch had discovered we were missing.

'Put your backs into it!' roared Halldor, who was at the helm. 'Show those Greeks what real rowing is like.'

Each ousiai had a single bank of oars, identical to a longship, and Harald's Norsemen, two men to each oar handle, were relishing the return to their old ways. Harald himself was not too proud to seat himself on the oar bench nearest to the helm and row alongside his men.

'Row your guts out, men!' urged Halldor. From astern we could hear the shouts of the helmsman of the second ousiai following in our wake. Further in the distance was the clamour of alarm bells and more trumpet calls.

We picked up speed. The light was strengthening, and soon we would be in full view of anyone watching from the harbour walls. If the alarm was passed quickly enough, the signal mirrors on the harbour wall would begin to flash a message to the guard boats in the bay.

Halldor grabbed my arm and pointed ahead. 'Look!' he said. 'The chain is still in place.'

I squinted forward through the grey light of dawn and knew that my plan was in ruins. Directly across our path stretched a line of wooden rafts, evenly spaced, about fifteen paces apart. Low in the water, so that even the smallest wave broke across them, they bobbed and gleamed blackly. Hanging below them was the chain which closed off the Golden Horn each night and turned it into a lake. It was supposed to be removed at first light so that the harbour was open to traffic, and our way to the straits should have been clear, but I had failed to anticipate that, on the feast day of the Nativity, the chain-keepers would be slow in carrying out their duties. We were trapped.

Seeing my dismay, Harald left his oar handle to his neighbour on the bench and stepped up to the stern deck. 'What's the trouble?' he demanded.

There was no need to explain, I pointed at the line of rafts.

Coolly he surveyed the obstacle. 'How deep does the chain hang?' he asked.

'I don't know. The shoreward end is fastened to land, and it is floated out with the rafts each sunset.' In the days when I had stayed in Pelagia's house overlooking the bay, I had often seen the teams of workboats struggling out with the chain at dusk and closing off the harbour.

Harald looked up at the sky. There was enough light for us to see the links of the chain where they crossed each raft. 'What do you think, Halldor?' he said, turning to the Icelander.

'Can't say to be sure,' Halldor replied. 'Must sag a bit between each raft. Stands to reason.'

Again we heard alarm signals from the shore. A fire gong was being beaten, its clangour carrying unmistakably across the water.

Harald stepped to the edge of the steersman's platform and looked down the length of our ousiai. Ahead of him forty or more Norsemen were rowing steadily. They had the vessel moving sweetly through the water, so they had dropped the rhythm of the oar strokes to a measured beat. To an observer it might have looked as if they were relaxing their effort, but every man aboard knew that it was a waste of effort to tug dramatically at the oar handles. What was needed now was disciplined, powerful rowing to keep our vessel cruising forward.

'When I give the word,' called Harald, 'every man takes twenty oar strokes with all his strength. When I shout a second time, the oarsmen on the first five benches drop their oars, leave their benches and run to the stern. The others are to keep rowing. Is that understood?'

The labouring oarsmen looked up at their leader standing on the deck above them and nodded. Every last one of them knew what Harald had in mind.

The line of rafts was very close now. 'Get ready,' Harald warned.

I jumped down from the stern deck and took the place at the oar bench that Harald had vacated. Next to me sat a Swede, a scarred veteran from the Sicilian campaign. 'So they've finally got you at an oar handle, rowing and not scheming,' he grunted at me. 'That's a change worth waiting for.'

'Now!' shouted Harald, and we began to count our twenty strokes, roaring out the numbers before Harald shouted out again, and behind me I heard the clatter of oar handles as the men in the forward benches dropped their oars and ran back down the length of the galley. I felt the angle of the vessel alter, the bow rising as the weight of the extra men came on the stern. Three strokes later there was a grinding, slithering wrench as the keel of our little dromon struck the chain with a crash. In a few paces we came to a complete stop. The force of our collision had sent the galley sliding up on the hidden links; we hung there, stranded on the chain.

'Now! Every man forward!' yelled Harald, and all of us left our benches and scrambled into the bows. Slowly, very slowly, the galley tilted forward. For a moment I feared the vessel would capsize, as she teetered half out of the water. Then the added weight in her bows pulled her forward, and with a creaking groan the ousiai slid forward over the chain and into the open water on the far side. We all lost our balance, trod on one another, and grabbed for oars that were sliding overboard as we cheered with relief. We had forced the barrier, and now the open sea lay ahead.

As we settled again to the oar benches, we looked back to see our second galley approaching the chain. She followed the same technique. We watched the ousiai accelerate, heard the shout of her helmsman and saw the men jump up from the forward benches and run towards the stern. We could clearly see the bow lift, then the sudden tilt as the vessel struck the hidden chain and come to a halt, straddled across the links. Like us, the crew then ran forward and we held our breath as the vessel rocked forward, only this time the ousiai did not slip clear; she was too firmly stuck. Another command, and the crew, forty or more men, scrambled back towards the stern, then turned and threw their weight forward, striving to break the grip of the chain. The ousiai rocked again, but still stayed fast.

'Guard boats!' Halldor shouted, and pointed. Close to the shore where the chain was attached to the land, five or six harbour guard boats were putting out to intercept us.

Once more our comrades on the stranded ousiai tried to rock their vessel clear. This time their frantic effort brought disaster. As the crew applied their weight, first in the bow and then at the stern, the strain proved too great. Like a stick which breaks when overloaded, the keel of the ousiai snapped. Perhaps the vessel was older and weaker than ours, or less well built, or maybe by ill fortune the chain lay directly under a joint in her main timbers where the shipwrights had scarfed the keel. The result was that the ousiai cracked in half. The long narrow hull broke apart, her planks sprang open, and her men fell into the sea.

'Backwater with your blades,' called Halldor. 'We must save those we can.'

We reversed our vessel, and began hauling men from the water. Dragging them aboard was easy – our ousiai was built low to the water – but there was nothing we could do to reach those unfortunates from the stern of the shattered vessel; they had slipped into the sea on the far side of the chain. A few of them managed to swim and reach us. Others clung to the wooden rafts, and we collected as many as we could, but the guard boats were closing in and there was no time to save them all.

'Row on!' ordered Harald, and we began to pull away from the approaching guard boats.

'Poor bastards,' muttered the Swede next to me. 'I don't fancy their chances as prisoners . . .'

His voice died away as I glanced up.

Harald was standing on the stern deck, hard-faced and glaring down at us. The flash of anger in his eyes told us that it was time we shut our mouths, concentrated at the oar handles, and carried him towards his destiny.

TEN

WE ENTERED KIEV in great style. Harald led our column on horseback, dressed in his finest court robes from Constantinople and wearing the ceremonial sword with its gold handle and enamelled scabbard which marked his rank as spatharokandidatos. Behind him marched his war band, all in their best costumes and adorned with their silver and gold jewellery. A column of porters and slaves, loaded with the bales of peach silk and the other valuables we had stripped from the ousiai, brought up the rear. I too was on horseback, riding with Halldor and the other members of Harald's inner council. After our escape from the Queen of Cities, Harald had formally appointed me as his adviser. In return I promised to be his liegeman, to serve and support him as my superior lord, even to the day he took his rightful place upon the Norwegian throne.

'Cheer up!' Halldor said to me as we clattered through the city gate and King Jaroslav's guards cheered us. News of Harald's prowess had gone ahead, and the guards, many of them Norse mercenaries, were eager to lay eyes on the man who had been sending back such a mass of treasure for safe keeping.

I gestured towards the red-tiled domes of a large monastery on the hill ahead of us. 'I hadn't expected to see so much of the White Christ here,' I said morosely, for I was in low spirits.

'You'll have to get used to it,' said Halldor. 'I expect Harald will soon be getting married in a place just like that.'

His remark took me aback.

'Thorgils, you've forgotten that on his way to Constantinople, Harald asked for the hand in marriage of the king's second daughter, Elizabeth. He was sent away with a flea in his ear. Told to come back when he had riches and renown. Well, now he's got just that, and more. Elizabeth and her family are devout Christians. They'll insist on a wedding in the White Christ manner.'

I listened without enthusiasm. I had been congratulating myself that my appointment as councillor to Harald would give me the chance to shape his policies in favour of the Old Ways. Now, it appeared, I would find myself competing with the views of his wife and the retinue of advisers she would surely bring with her. The thought made me more depressed than I was already. Pelagia's death had hit me hard, depriving me of both a friend and a confidante, and on the way to Kiev I had been feeling more and more isolated amidst the often ribald company of Harald's followers.

'Then this is not the sort of place where I'll be comfortable,' I concluded. 'If I'm to serve Harald, I can be of more use to him in the northlands. I'll ask his permission to go ahead and prepare for his arrival in Norway. I can try to find out which of the powerful nobles might support him, and who would be against him when he makes his claim for the throne.'

'You'll be a spy again?' asked Halldor, to whom I had related my role as an informant for John the Eunuch. 'Harald will like that. He's always in favour of subterfuge and trickery.'

'Part spy, part envoy,' I answered.

Harald agreed to my proposal, and as soon as I had collected the money arranged for me by the banker in Constantinople, I headed onward with those of Harald's ex-Varangians who had asked to go home early. By the time Halldor and the others were celebrating the glittering wedding of the Prince of Norway to King Yaroslav's second daughter, I was back in the northlands where my own Gods belonged.

My first impression was how little had changed in the twelve years I had been away. Among the three main kingdoms, Norway and Denmark still regarded one another with suspicion, while Sweden stood aside and quietly fanned the flames of rivalry between her neighbours. Norwegian raided Dane and was raided in return. Alliances shifted. Leading families squabbled, and wherever Norsemen had seized land across the sea – in England, Scotland or Ireland – there were great magnates who nominally owed allegiance to an overlord in the homeland, but acted independently. Through these turbulent waters I had to plot a course for Harald when he returned.

I made a start by visiting the court of Harald's nephew, Magnus. He held the Norwegian throne, and also claimed the kingship of Denmark. I found him to be personable, energetic, proud, and shrewd beyond his years. He was only twenty-five years old, yet had won the affection of his people by his fairness and his habit of winning his battles against the Danes. Harald, I concluded, would find it difficult to dislodge the man his people called Magnus the Good.

I came to Magnus's court posing as an Icelander returning after service in Constantinople and wealthy enough to dawdle on the way. It was near enough to the truth, and no one questioned me too closely about my background. The only time I nearly dropped my guard was when I heard that the dowager queen Aelfgifu had died. She was the woman who had first taken me to bed. 'Good riddance, for all that she was the great Knut's first wife,' commented the man who told me of her death. 'Her husband sent her to us as co-regent, along with that callous son of hers. They weren't popular, and we drove them out. Can't say I'm sorry that she's gone.' His remark made me feel old. No one likes to think that their first lover is in the grave. Not when you remember their warmth and beauty.

IT WAS TO be nearly two years before I was able to tell Harald of my impression of Magnus, because King Jaroslav insisted that his new son-in-law stay on in Kiev for longer than Harald had intended. But I scarcely noticed the delay, for I had at last found a place where the Old Gods were revered, and I was happy.

I was travelling from Magnus's capital at Nidaros on my way to Denmark to assess the strength and character of Earl Svein Estrithson, who ruled there, and it was autumn. I had taken the land route over the mountain passes and reached the area known as Vaster Gotland. It lies on the border between Norway and Sweden, but is such a bleak and unforgiving region that no one really cares about the exact position of the frontier. It is a place of rock and forest, small lakes and shallow streams, and a large expanse of inland water – the Vaner Lake – which, like everything else, freezes over in winter because the climate is very harsh. I was on foot because the trail is difficult for horses and there is no fodder to be found. Nor did I have a servant to accompany me, but was travelling alone. Vaster Gotland has a reputation for outlawry, so I was beginning to wonder whether I was wise to carry so much gold and silver with me when I came across a memorial stone beside the track. On the rock was carved an epitaph to a lost warrior who, according to the runes, had ended his life in Serkland, 'the land of silk'. The mason who had cut the inscription was no rune master, for the gouges left by the chisel were plain to see, and the lettering was crudely done. Nor could I tell who was commemorated, for the rock had split away where the dead man's name had been written, and I could not find the broken piece. But I took it as a sign from Odinn, and after clearing away the undergrowth I buried half my hoard.

There were no villages along the trail, only an occasional farmhouse set well back from the path. The land was so poor and grudging that these dwellings were no more than small log cabins with roofs of wooden shingles and perhaps a shed or two. I was expecting to encounter the farmers returning home, as it would soon be dusk. But I saw no one. Whenever I passed a house, and that was rare enough, the door was shut tight and nothing stirred. It was as if the plague had struck, and everyone had retreated indoors or died.

The chill in the evening air warned of a cold night to come, and I had already caught a glimpse of a wolf in the forest, so I left the track when I saw the next house and went towards it, intending to ask for shelter for the night. I knocked on the heavy wooden door planks and called out. For a moment there was no response. Then, from deep within the house, a low voice said urgently, 'Go away! You disturb us! Go away!' I was as shocked as if someone had struck me in the face. The country folk had always been hospitable. That was their tradition. They enjoyed hearing a traveller's news and they appreciated the small coins paid for food and lodging. To turn away a stranger on a cold evening seemed unthinkable. I knocked again, more insistently, and called out that I was a traveller, on my own, hungry, and would pay for my lodging. This time I heard the shuffle of feet, and very slowly the door opened, just enough for me to see that the interior of the cabin was in darkness. Someone had covered over the small windows. From the gloom within, a voice said, 'Go away, please leave. This is not the right time to visit us.'

Something about the atmosphere of the place made me say, 'In the name of Odinn the Roadwise I ask for shelter.'

There was a long pause, and then the door pulled back a hand's breadth and the voice asked softly, 'Tell me, stranger, what is the name of the steed who westward draws night over the glorious Gods?'

The accent was local and strong, but the rhythm of the words was unmistakable. The man, whoever he was, was reciting lines of poetry. Long ago my tutors in the Old Ways had taught me the next verse, so I answered:

'Hrimfaxi's his name who draws the nights
Over the glorious gods
Each morning he dribbles down the flakes of foam
That brings dew upon the dales.'

The heavy door eased back, just wide enough to allow me to step inside, and the moment I had entered, it was closed behind me. I found myself in total darkness.

A hand took my wrist, and I felt myself carefully guided forward. Then the pressure of the hand indicated that I was to stop where I stood. I felt something touch the back of my knees, and knew that someone had placed a stool behind me. I sat down quietly. Not a word had been said, and still I could see only blackness.

There were people in the room: not many of them, though I could sense their presence. The floor beneath my boots was plain beaten earth. This was a humble home. I heard the rustle of clothing, light breathing. Then a point of dull red appeared a few feet away, close to the ground. Someone had uncovered an ember. I guessed that it lay in the family hearth. The glow vanished as a shadow moved between me and the fireplace. There was the sound of a person blowing gently on the ember, and then the shadow moved aside and I could see the hearth again. Now there was a small dance of flame in the fireplace, which gave just enough light for me to make out that there were half a dozen people in the room, three adults and three children, all dressed in the plain dun and brown garments of farming people. It was difficult to distinguish whether the children were girls or boys, but the adults were two women and a man. I guessed he was the person who had brought me into the house.

One of the women was moving towards the fireplace. She placed something on the ground in front of the hearth. It was a small bowl. She tilted a jug and I heard the splash of liquid. I sat completely still. Now I knew what was happening. This was the alfablot, the household's annual sacrifice to honour the spirits which live in every home. As landvaettir, they also exist among the trees and rocks and underground. They are the spirits of place, the ancient inhabitants who were there before men came, and they will be there long after men have gone. Their approval helps men prosper, their hostility brings ruin.

There were soft footfalls as the woman moved away from the fire, and her dark shape moved around the room, pausing in each corner. She held something. I guessed it was a small offering of food for the alfar.

I felt a nudge on my fingers. It was the rough crust of a hunk of bread. Then I was passed a wooden cup of beer. I tasted the bread. It was peasant's rye bread, coarse but wholesome. The beer was thin and watery. I ate and drank, taking care to move gently and carefully. Alfar are easily frightened away. I left a few dregs of beer in the cup, leaned forward when I had finished, and tipped the last few drops on the earthen floor. I knew that my offering had been observed by my hosts.

Not a word had been said from the moment that I had entered the house, and I knew that, out of respect for the spirits, all would be silent until daylight came. When the family completed their offerings, they retired to their communal bed, a wooden box against one wall, like a large manger. I wrapped myself in my travelling cloak and quietly lay down on the floor to sleep.

'WE ARE ALL pagans here,' were the first words of the farmer next morning. He spoke apologetically. 'Otherwise you would have had a kinder welcome.'

'Old Believers,' I corrected him gently.

He was a middle-aged man, unremarkable except for the bright blue eyes in his weather-beaten face and an unruly fringe of almost pure white hair around his bald scalp. He had the care-worn look of someone who laboured hard to support his family. Behind him his wife, a handsome woman who also showed signs of an exacting life, was washing the children's faces. The second

woman appeared to be her sister, for she had the same thick
reddish-brown hair and fine bone structure, as well as a graceful-
ness in the way she was collecting up the small offerings that had
been set out during the night. The milk that had been left in the
bowl for the alfr, I noticed, was poured back into the jug after a
few drops had been sprinkled on the hearth. There was no surplus
food in this household.

'You are a devotee of Odinn?' the farmer asked in a deep,
quiet voice. He was probing, wanting to know more about me
and to establish some sort of common ground between us. I liked
him.

'From childhood. I have followed Odinn since I was a boy.
And you?'

'Here we worship Frey. We are farmers, not warriors or
sailors. We need Frey's generosity.' I knew what he spoke of.
Frey is the God of fertility. He multiplies the seed that is planted
in the soil, brings the rain and warmth which ripens crops, and
makes good harvests. With Frey's help the cattle thrive, lambs
and calves are plentiful, sows farrow generously. Even the milk
we were drinking we owed ultimately to Frey's bounty.

'Last evening you invoked Odinn Vegtamr,' the farmer continued. 'Do you travel far?'

'Only as far as the Danish lands, if the rain holds off for
another week or so. I don't like squelching through mud.'

'Many berries on the bushes this year,' the man said. 'And the
swallows left early. Snow will come sooner than rain, I'd say. Not
that it means much to us in these parts. We don't travel except to
the great Hof, and it's a three-day walk to reach anywhere worth
visiting.'

'Yet I saw a memorial back along the road to a man who died
in Serkland. That's a great distance.'

There was a sudden tension in the room. The farmer looked
uneasy.

'Have you been to Serkland?' he enquired.

'I have, or at least close to it,' I said. 'I served with the emperor's guard in Miklagard, and he sent me to their Holy Land. That's close by. It's the place where the White Christ God lived.'

'Don't know about this Holy Land. We're too remote to see the White Christ priests. One of them did visit a few years back, but found us too set in our ways. He left and never came back.'

'Perhaps you were fortunate,' I commented.

The farmer seemed to reach a decision. 'It was I who cut that memorial stone,' he acknowledged. 'Did my best, though the work is rough. Should have picked a better rock. A corner broke off in the winter frost two years later. We wanted to have something to remember him by. He was married to my wife's sister.'

He glanced across the room towards the woman who had been cleaning up the hearth. She was standing still, staring at me, hanging on every word.

'News reached us, third or fourth hand, that he had died in Serkland. But there were no details. He had set out from here to make his fortune, and never came back. Vanished. We don't know anything of the place where he met his end, or how it happened. His name was Thorald.'

'I didn't know anyone by that name when I was in Miklagard,' I said, 'but if it will repay your hospitality, perhaps I could tell you what I know of Serkland.'

The farmer nodded to his sister-in-law, and she stepped closer. Her eyes were still fixed on me as I began to describe my time in the Hetaira, my visit to the Holy Land, and how I had met Saracens both as friends and enemies. It was a lengthy tale, and I tried to tell it briefly. But the farmer soon detected that I was leaving much unsaid, and he interrupted.

'There is so much we want to know. Would you not stay with us a few days and tell us your tale more fully? It would help Runa here.'

I hesitated. The family lived in such straitened circumstances that I was reluctant to impose myself on their kindness. But then the farmer, whose name was Folkmar, insisted, and I agreed to stay one more day.

It was among the best decisions of my life. That one day became a week, and by the end of it I knew that Folkmar's home was my haven. Nothing could have been a greater contrast to the sophistication and luxury of Constantinople with its broad avenues, well-stocked markets, and teeming crowds. There I had enjoyed the comforts of fine food, public bathhouses, and lavish entertainment on a scale unimaginable to my hosts in the harsh barrens of Vaster Gotland, where much of each day was spent in routine labour to achieve the basics of everyday life, whether drawing water, mending farm tools or grinding grain. Yet Folkmar and his wife were content to place their trust in the Gods, and in consequence there was nothing fearful in their lives. They were deeply fond of one another and their children; they lived simply and frugally, and they were sure of where they stood in relation to the land and the seasons of the year. Every time I accompanied Folkmar to his work in one of his small fields or to gather firewood in the forest, I saw how he respected the unseen spirits around him. He laid small tokens, even if they were no more than a broken twig or a leaf, on the isolated boulders which we passed, and if the children were with us he would insist they hushed their voices, and he forbade them to play games close by the sacred rocks. To him the deep forest was home to skogsra, female woodland deities who, if respected, would return a cow or calf that wandered from the meadow. If insulted, they would feed the stray to the wolves.

Folkmar's devotion to his main Gods, Frey and his sister Freyja, was uncomplicated. He kept their statuettes in his home, Frey with his enormous phallus, and Freyja voluptuous and sensual, but he knew little of their lore other than the popular tales.

'Cats,' he said. 'Freyja's chariot is drawn by cats. Just like a woman to be able to harness cats. That would be something to see. Hereabouts in mid-summer a man and woman dress up as

Frey and his sister and travel from farm to farm in a cart to collect offerings, but they are drawn along by a working nag.' He paused before saying, 'I'll be bringing those offerings to the Great Hof next week. Care to come with me? It means delaying your trip to Denmark, but Odinn has his own place in the Hof as well. It would be a chance for you to honour him.'

'How far is it to the Hof?' I asked.

'About ten days. Lots of people will be going. The king himself could be there.'

This time I did not hesitate. My trip to Denmark could wait. I had heard about the Great Hof from the Swedish Varangians I had met in Miklagard, who had told me about the festivals held near a place they called Uppsala where, since time out of mind, there had been a temple to the Old Gods. Here, in spring and just before the onset of winter, appeared great gatherings of Old Believers, who came in multitudes to make their sacrifices and pray for all the blessings that the Old Gods can bestow: health, prosperity, victory, a good life. The Swedish king himself often attended, because his ancestors traced their line back to Frey himself. I decided that after many years of living among the followers of the White Christ, now, at last, I could immerse myself again in the celebration of the Old Ways.

Folkmar was delighted when I agreed to accompany him, and our journey proved to be what the Christians would have called a pilgrimage. We were like a master and disciple as we trudged along and I answered his questions about the Gods, for he was keen to learn more and I was slowly coming to realise that my knowledge of the Old Ways was more profound than most possessed. I told him how Frey and Freyja belonged to the Vanir, the primal Gods who had at first resisted the Aesir under Odinn and fought against them. When peace was agreed, they had gone to join the Aesir as hostages and had been with them ever since.

'Pity the Norwegians and the Danes can't do the same. Make peace with one another, I mean,' Folkmar observed. 'It would put an end to this constant warring between them which does no one any good. I often think how fortunate it is that my people live so far out of the way. The quarrels of the outer world usually pass us by.'

'Perhaps that is why Frey and his sister chose not to live under Odinn's roof in Valhol. They have a space to themselves,' I answered. 'Frey has his own hall in Alfheim where the light elves live. And he and his sister have their special privileges. Frey is near equal to Odinn, and his sister in some ways is superior. After battle she takes half of those who have died honourably and brings them back to her hall, Sessrumnir, leaving Odinn and the Valkyries to select the rest. Freyja gets to make the first choice among the dead.'

'You would need to be a God to share power like that, never quarrelling over precedence,' observed Folkmar.

'I saw it done back in the Great City,' I said. 'Two empresses sharing the same throne. But I admit, it was unusual.'

'It's against nature. Sooner or later, there must be a contest for power,' said Folkmar. With his native shrewdness he had forecast what was to follow.

THE GREAT TEMPLE at Uppsala was worth our ten-day walk. It was the largest hof I had ever seen, an enormous hall of timber built close beside three large barrow graves which contained the bodies of the early kings. In front of the hof grew a huge tree, the very symbol of Yggdrasil, the world tree where the Aesir meet. This giant was even more remarkable because its leaves never faded, but remained green throughout even the hardest winter. To one side, clustering like attendants, smaller trees formed a sacred grove. These trees too were very ancient, and each was hallowed. On them were displayed the sacrifices made to the Gods whose images were within the Hof itself. Folkmar told me that at the great spring festival, the temple priests celebrated nine successive days of ritual, nine being their sacred number. Each day they emerged from the Hof and hung on the branches of the sacred trees the heads of the nine animals they had sacrificed to the Gods as proof of their devotion. Ritual demanded that each animal was a male, and that there was one from each type of living creature.

'Does that include human sacrifice as well?' I asked.

'In earlier times, that was so,' explained Folkmar, 'But no longer.'

He led me inside the Hof. Even though the autumn festival was of less importance than the spring celebration, the dark interior of the temple was crowded with worshippers bringing gifts. The builders of the temple had left openings in the high roof so that the daylight fell in shafts, illuminating the statues of the Gods. And today, despite the fact that it was cloudy, the three Gods seemed to loom over the congregation. Thor was in the centre – powerful, bearded, and holding his hammer aloft. To his right stood my own God, Odinn. Carved from a single enormous block of wood, and black with the smoke of centuries of sacrifices, Odinn squinted down with his single eye. To Thor's left stood Frey's image. This statue too was of wood, but brightly painted with the colours of the bountiful earth – ochre, red, brown, gold and green. Frey was seated cross-legged, a conical helmet on his head, one hand clutching his pointed beard, which jutted forward, the other hand on his knee. His eyes bulged. He was stark naked, and from his loins rose the gigantic phallus that was the symbol of the fertility he controlled, and also of physical joy.

Folkmar approached one of the Frey priests and handed over the package he had carried on his back all the way during our walk. I had no idea what the package contained, but knowing the poverty of Folkmar and his neighbours I doubted it was anything more than a few items of farmer's produce, yet the priest took the package as if it was of great value and thanked the farmer graciously. He beckoned to an assistant, and a moment later a small pig was dragged out from the shadows, and with a quick movement the priest cut its throat. The assistant already had a bowl in place, and as the blood drained into it, the priest took a whisk of twigs and, dipping it into the blood, flicked the drops towards the image of the God, then over Folkmar, who stood with bowed head.

I had expected the priest to set the pig's carcass aside, but instead he handed it to Folkmar and said, 'Feast well tonight.'

His duty done, Folkmar turned and began to leave when he remembered that I had not yet honoured Odinn. 'I am sorry, Thorgils, I did not think to keep something back that you could offer to your God.'

'Your people collected for Frey's honour,' I said as we moved through the crowd towards the soot-black image of the father of the Gods. 'It would not have been right to divert the slightest morsel of it elsewhere.'

We had reached the foot of Odinn's statue. It towered above us, twice the height of a man. The image was so old that the timber from which it had been carved was split and dry, and I wondered how many centuries it had stood there. Apart from the closed eye, the details of the God's face were blurred with age. I reached inside my shirt where my money pouch hung on a leather thong around my neck, then laid my offering at the God's feet. Folkmar's eyes opened wide in surprise. I had set down a solid gold coin, an imperial nomisma, worth more than all the farmer's worldly possessions. To me, it was a small token of my gratitude to Odinn for having brought me to Folkmar and his home.

'YOU SAY THAT you follow Harald Sigurdsson and are sworn to serve him,' said Folkmar to me that evening as we roasted the sacrificial pig, 'but it is too late in the season for Harald to arrive. The earliest he can be expected is in the spring. Why don't you spend the winter with us. I know that would please my wife and her sister.'

'First I must visit Svein Estrithson in Denmark so that later I can tell Harald what the man is like,' I answered cautiously, though Folkmar's invitation had forced me to acknowledge that perhaps I was not as solitary and self-possessed as I had always imagined myself to be. During the days I had spent with him and his family, I had experienced a sense of quiet harmony that I had never expected. Gazing into the flames of our cooking fire, I found myself wondering if my advancing years were having their effect, and whether the time had come when I should consider forsaking my rootless life and, if not settling down, at least having a place where I could stay and rest. So I allowed myself the luxury of calculating just how quickly I could complete my mission to Denmark and get back to Vaster Gotland.

Odinn must have favoured me because snow fell the very next morning and the ground froze hard. Travelling across a frozen landscape is far easier and quicker than in spring or autumn mud, and I made the journey to Denmark in less than two weeks' travel. I found that I neither liked nor trusted Svein Estrithson. He was stout, foul-mouthed and a great womaniser. He was also a powerful advocate for the White Christ, whose priests over-looked his lewd behaviour. For some reason, the Danes were very loyal to him, and rallied to his cause whenever Magnus's Norwegians threatened. I judged that Harald would find it almost as hard to dislodge Svein as to replace Magnus.

It was no hardship to cut short my visit and retrace my steps to Vaster Gotland. On the way there I stopped in a trading station to make some purchases and hire a carter. The man demanded a substantial sum to make such a long journey, but I was wealthy and his payment barely touched my store of ready funds. Thus, soon after I was once again back with Folkmar's family, a shout brought them to the door. Outside stood two small and sturdy horses with shaggy winter coats, their breath steaming in the cold air. Fitted to their hooves were the spiked shoes that had allowed them to traverse the icy ground as they dragged the sled that contained the furs, cloth, utensils and extra food that I now presented to Folkmar and his family as my guest offering.

Runa and I were joined as man and wife soon after the Jol festival, and no one in that remote community was in the least surprised. Runa and I had discovered that we were quietly suited, as if we had known one another for many years. We shared a mutual understanding, which neither of us mentioned because we already knew that the other was equally sensitive to it. In the confines of the little cabin our harmony occasionally revealed itself in a shared glance, or a half smile that passed between us. But more often it was simply that Runa and I were gladdened by each other's presence, and savoured the contentment that flowed from being together. Naturally Folkmar and his wife had noticed what was happening, and took care not to intrude.

Our wedding was not, of course, a marriage in the Christian rite, all priest and prayers. As a young man I had married that way in Iceland, and the union had been a humiliating failure. This time Folkmar himself performed the ceremony, because Runa and her sister had been orphaned at an early age and this left him as her senior male relative. Folkmar made a simple declaration to the Gods, and then, standing before the images of Frey and Freyja, took steel and flint, and, striking one against the other, produced a trail of sparks. It was to show that within each substance, stone and metal, as in man and woman, lived a vital element which, when brought together, provided life.

Next day he hosted a feast for our immediate neighbours, at which they consumed the smoked and salted delicacies that I had earlier provided, and toasted our happiness in mead made from forest honey and shoots of bog myrtle in place of hops. During their toasts, several guests gave praise to Frey and Freyja, saying that the Gods had surely arranged for Runa to marry me. The Gods had taken her first husband when he was far away in Serkland, they said, and from Serkland they had sent his successor. They were fulsome in their congratulations, and during the winter months several of them came to help to construct the small extension that was built on Folkmar's cabin where Runa and I had our bedchamber. I could have told them to wait until the spring, when I could hire professional builders and purchase costly materials because I was rich. But I desisted. I liked my haven and I feared to disturb its equilibrium.

From the outset Runa herself took great comfort from her sister's open approval of our union, and she went on to make me very happy. She was to prove to be an ideal wife, loving and supportive. On our wedding night she told me that when she heard of her first husband's death, she had prayed to Freyja, pleading that she did not wish to spend the rest of her life as a widow. 'Freyja heard my prayers,' she said quietly, looking down at the earthen floor.

'But I'm fifteen years older than you,' I pointed out. 'Don't you worry that you will again be a widow one day?'

'That is for the Gods to decide. Some men they bless with health and allow to live. To others they give a life of drudgery which brings them to an early death. To me you seem no older than men of my own age, for already they are half worn out by toil.' Then she snuggled down against me, and proved that Freyja was indeed the goddess of sensual joy.

I was so utterly content all that winter and the following spring that I might have set aside my promise to serve Harald had not Odinn reminded me of my duty. He did so with a dream that was both shocking and, as it turned out much later, a deception. In my sleep I saw a fleet of ships coming across the sea and disembarking an army whose commander sought to seize a throne. The leader's face was never visible but always turned away from me, and I took him to be my liege lord Harald, for the man was uncommonly tall. He boldly led his army inland, his troops marching across baked and barren fields until they were brought to battle by their enemy. The fighting was intense, but gradually the invaders were gaining the upper hand. Then, just on the point of victory, an arrow flew out from nowhere and struck the tall commander in the throat. I saw his hands go up – his face was still turned away – and I heard the breath whistle in his torn windpipe. Then he fell, dying.

I woke in a cold sweat of alarm. Beside me Runa reached out to comfort me. 'What is the matter?' she asked.

'I have just seen my lord Harald die,' I said, still shivering. 'Perhaps I can avert catastrophe. I must warn him.'

'Of course you must,' she agreed soothingly. 'That is your duty. But sleep now and rest, so that in the morning you have a clearer head.'

Next day she was just as sensible and made me repeat the details of the dream, then asked, 'Is this the first time that you have seen omens in your dreams?'

'No, there was a time when I had many dreams that hinted at the future if they were correctly understood. It's something that I have inherited from my mother. I hardly knew her, but she was a volva, a seeress gifted with the second sight. When I was in Miklagard among the Christians, such dreams were very rare, and certainly there was nothing so disturbing as what I saw last night.'

'Maybe your dreaming has returned because you are among people who still hold to the Old Ways. The Gods reveal themselves more readily in such places.'

'A wise woman once told me something similar. She herself possessed second sight and said I was a spirit mirror, and that I was more likely to have visions when I was in the company of others who also possessed the same ability. I suppose that being among Old Believers has the same effect.'

'Then you already know that we would want you to heed what the Gods are trying to tell you. You should seek Harald out and try to warn him. I am content to wait here for your return. I don't have to have second sight to know that you will surely come back to me. The sooner you set out, the sooner you will return.'

I left that same afternoon, taking the same eastward path that Folkmar and I had followed when we went to the Great Hof. On the third day I found someone to sell me a horse, and within a week I had reached the coast, and just in time. A fisherman mending his nets on the beach told me there was a rumour that a remarkable warship was under construction somewhere in the north, the like of which had never been seen before. The builders had been told to use only the finest timber and to install the best fittings, and that no imperfection would be tolerated. 'Must be costing someone a fortune,' said the fisherman, spitting towards his grubby little skiff as if to emphasise his point. 'Don't know who the client is, but he must be made of money.'

'Is the vessel launched yet, do you know?'

'Can't say as I do,' he replied, 'but it will be a sight to see.'

'I'll pay you to take me to see it.'

'Beats hauling on lines and baiting hooks,' he answered readily. 'Give me a couple of hours to pick up some extra gear and a bit of food and water, and off we go. Mind if my lad accompanies us? He's handy in a boat, and could come in useful. Breeze is in the north so it'll be rowing to start with.'

WE HAD BARELY cleared the bay when Harald's ship came into view, sailing southward and less than a mile offshore, and silently I thanked Runa for insisting that I hurried. Another couple of hours and I would have missed him.

There was no mistaking that it was Harald's ship. No one else would have required that his vessel be so extravagant and colourful. In later years, during frontier raids on the Danes, I was to sail aboard the largest vessel Harald ever commissioned, his *Great Dragon*, which had thirty-five oar benches, making her one of the biggest longships ever known. But that giant still does not compare in my memory with the vessel I saw that pleasant summer afternoon as Harald sailed to claim his inheritance. His longship was a blaze of colour. Immaculate display shields of red and white were slotted in the shield rack. The snarling serpent's head on the prow was gilded bronze, and flashed back the sun as the ship eased across the swells. A long scarlet pennant floated from her masthead, her rigging had been whitened, and the upper plank along her entire length had been decorated with gold leaf.

But that was not the reason why I knew for sure that she was Harald's ship. Who else would have ordered his sailmakers to use a cloth that, weight for weight, was as expensive as gold: every third panel of the mainsail had been cut and stitched from peach silk.

I stood up on the thwart of the fishing skiff and waved an oar. An alert lookout on the longship saw me, and a moment later the vessel altered course. Soon I was scrambling over the side and making my way to the stern deck where Harald stood with his councillors. I knew all of them – Halldor, his marshal Ulf Ospaksson, and the others.

'Welcome aboard, councillor. What do you have to report?' Harald demanded as if I had seen him only yesterday.

'I have visited both Magnus of Norway and Earl Estrithson, my lord,' I began, when Harald interrupted me.

'We have already met the Danish earl. He came north to ask help from the Swedes in his conflict with Magnus, and by chance we encountered him. How did he impress you?'

I paused, not wanting to sound pessimistic. But there was no getting round my opinion. 'He's not to be trusted,' I said bluntly.

'And my nephew Magnus?'

'My lord, he seems to be well regarded by his people.'

It was a tactless thing to say, and Harald rudely turned to look out across the sea, ignoring me. I suppose he felt that I was hinting he might not be so popular. Meekly I crossed the deck to join the other councillors.

Halldor commiserated. 'He needs someone to tell him the true facts from time to time.'

'There's more,' I said. 'I wanted to give him a warning, but now is not the moment.'

'What's the warning?'

'A dream I had recently, a portent.'

'You were always an odd one, Thorgils. Even when you first came to my father's house, my brothers and I wondered why he took you in and gave you such special treatment. Is it to do with your second sight? What have you seen?'

'Harald's death,' I answered.

Halldor shot me a sideways glance. 'How will it happen?'

'An arrow in the throat during a great battle.'

'When?'

'I don't know. The dreams are never precise. It could happen soon, or many years from now.'

'You had better tell me the details. Together we might be able to persuade Harald to avoid an open battle, if not now then at least for some time.'

So I told Halldor what I had dreamed. I described the fleet, the invading army, the tall man, the march across a dry land under a blazing sun, and his death.

When I finished, Halldor was looking at me with a mixture of relief and awe.

'Thorgils,' he said, 'my father was right. You really do have the second sight. But this time you have misinterpreted your vision. Harald is safe.'

'What do you mean?'

'It was not Harald you saw die. It was Maniakes, the tall Greek general who led us in the campaign in Sicily.'

'But that's not possible. I haven't seen Maniakes for years, and in all that time I've never given him a thought.'

'Why should you,' said the Icelander. 'You've been in the northlands these two years past and you could not know the news. A year ago Maniakes rebelled against the new Basileus. That man-eating old empress Zoë had got herself married for a third time and handed over most of the power to her new husband, and Maniakes tried to seize the throne for himself. He was commanding the imperial army in Italy at the time, and he led an invasion into Greece. That's the parched landscape you saw. The Basileus assembled all the troops he could muster, including the garrison of Constantinople, and marched out to confront him. The two

armies met – and it was on a hot sunny day on a barren plain –
and there was a great battle which was to decide the fate of the
empire. Maniakes has victory within his grasp, his troops had
the enemy soundly beaten when a chance arrow struck him in the
throat, killing him. It was all over. His army fled, and there was a
great slaughter. This took place just a few months ago. We heard
the news in Kiev just before we left to come here. Maniakes, not
Harald, was the man in your vision.'

I was dumbfounded and relieved at the same time. I remembered how very alike the two men had been in height and manner,
and that I had never seen the face of the dead commander in my
dream. It had all been a mistake: I had been spirit-flying. At
various times in my life I had been in the presence of certain
seidrmanna, the seers of the northlands who were capable of
leaving their bodies while in a trance and flying to other regions
far away. That was what had happened in my dream. I had been
transported to another place and another time, and there I had
seen Maniakes die. It had never happened to me before. I felt
bewildered and a little dizzy. But at least I had not made a fool of
myself in Harald's eyes by telling him of my fears.

Yet I failed to ask myself why Odinn had brought me to
Harald's ship, if indeed it was Maniakes's death I had seen. Had I
posed myself that simple question, matters might have turned out
differently. But then, deception was always Odinn's way.

ELEVEN

WHAT WAS IT like to be councillor to the wealthiest ruler in the northlands? For that is what Harald became in less than three years.

Initially he had to accept his nephew's offer to share the throne of Norway, but it was an uneasy arrangement and would certainly have ended in civil war, had Magnus not been killed in a freak accident when he was out hunting. A hare leaped up in front of his horse, the horse bolted, and a low branch swept Magnus out of his saddle. He broke his neck. The hare, like her cats, is another familiar of Freyja, so I thought at the time that the king's accident was a sign that the Old Gods were acting in my favour, because Magnus's death left Harald as the sole ruler of Norway. But I soon had my doubts when Harald's elevation to the undisputed kingship changed him. He became even more difficult and high-handed.

I measured his change through his treatment of Halldor. The bluff Icelander had been at Harald's side throughout his foreign travels, and in Sicily had received a face wound which had left him badly scarred, yet his record of loyalty did not protect him from Harald's vainglory. Halldor had always been outspoken. He gave his opinions without mincing his words, and the more powerful Harald became, the less he liked to hear blunt speaking, even from a favoured adviser. One example will suffice: during one of Harald's frequent seaborne raids on Earl Svein's Danish lands, Halldor was the lookout on the foredeck of Harald's longship, a position of honour and great responsibility. As the vessel sailed along the coast, Halldor called out that there were rocks ahead. Harald, standing near the helmsman, chose to ignore the warning. Minutes later the longship crashed upon the rocks and was badly damaged. Exasperated, Halldor informed Harald that there was little point in serving as a lookout if his advice was ignored. Angrily Harald retorted that he had no need of men like Halldor.

There had been countless incidents of a similar nature, but from that time forward relations between them cooled, and I was sorry to see how Harald took pleasure in baiting Halldor. It was a rule at Harald's court that every member of his entourage had to be dressed and ready for attendance upon the king by the time the royal herald sounded the trumpet announcing that the king was about to emerge from his bedchamber. One morning, to make mischief, Harald paid the herald to sound the trumpet at the crack of dawn, much earlier than usual. Halldor and his friends had been carousing the night before and were caught unprepared. Harald then made Halldor and the others sit on the floor of the banqueting hall, in the foul straw, and gulp down full horns of ale while the other courtiers mocked them. Another royal rule was that at meals no one should continue to eat after the king himself had finished eating. To mark that moment, Harald would rap on the table with the handle of his knife. One day Halldor ignored the signal and continued to chew on his food. Harald called out down the length of the hall that Halldor was growing fat from too much food and too little exercise, and once again insisted that the Icelander pay a drinking forfeit.

Matters came to a head on the day of Harald's coinage. This was the occasion each year on the eighth day after Jol festival when the king gave his retainers their annual bounty. Though his wealth was still vast — it took ten strong men to lift Harald's treasure chests – Harald paid Halldor, myself and his other sworn men with copper coin instead of the usual silver. Only Halldor was bold enough to complain. He announced that he could no longer serve such a penny-pinching lord and preferred to return home to Iceland. He sold off all his possessions in Norway and had an ugly confrontation with Harald, when he demanded that the king pay the proper price for a ship he had agreed to buy from Halldor. The whole sorry affair ended with Halldor storming into the king's private chambers and, at sword point, demanding that Harald hand over one of his wife's gold rings to settle the debt. Then Halldor sailed off for Iceland, never to return.

His departure saddened me. He had been a friend from the first, and I valued his good sense. But I did not follow his example and leave Harald's service because I was still hoping that Harald would champion the Old Ways, and, in some matters, Harald was living up to my expectations. He married again, without divorcing Elizabeth, his first wife. His new bride, Thora, the daughter of a Norwegian magnate, was a robust Old Believer. When the Christian priests at court objected, claiming that Harald was committing bigamy, Harald bluntly told them to mind their own business. Equally, when a brace of new bishops arrived in Norway sent by the Archbishop of Bremen in the German lands, Harald promptly despatched them back to the Archbishop with a curt message that the king alone decided Church appointments. Unfortunately for me, Harald also displayed Christian tendencies whenever it suited him. He refurbished the church where the bodies of his half-brother 'Saint' Olaf and his nephew Magnus lay, and whenever he dealt with the followers of the White Christ he made a point of reminding them that St Olaf was his close relative. It was to be several years before I had finally to admit to myself that Halldor had been right from the beginning. Harald was serving only one God – himself.

Yet I persevered. Life at Harald's court was the closest to the ideals that I had heard about when I was a child growing up in Greenland, and I reassured myself that Harald genuinely respected

the traditions of the north. He surrounded himself with royal
skalds and paid them handsomely for verses which celebrated
past glories. His chief skald was another Icelander, Thjodolf, but
his other poets – Valgard, Illugi, Bolverk, Halli, known as the
Sarcastic, and Stuf the Blind – were almost as deft at producing
intricate poems in the courtly style, whose quality Harald himself was capable of judging for he was a competent versifier
himself. For lighter moments he employed a court dwarf, a Frisian
by the name of Tuta, who had a long broad back and very stumpy
legs and who made us laugh by parading around the great hall
of the palace dressed in Harald's full-length coat of mail. This
armour had been specially made for him in Constantinople and
was so famous that it even had its own name – 'Emma'. Harald
himself always dressed stylishly, sporting a red and gold headband
when not wearing his crown, and on formal occasions the glittering sword that he had been awarded as a spatharokandidatos in
Miklagard.

Regrettably, the sword and mail coat were not the only
reminders of his days at the Basileus's court. In Miklagard Harald
had observed how to wield power pitilessly and to remove rivals
without warning. Now I watched as Harald eliminated one
potential threat after another, suddenly and without mercy. A
nobleman who grew too powerful was summoned to a conference
and rashly entered the council hall without his own bodyguard in
attendance. He found the hall in darkness – Harald had ordered
the shutters closed – and was murdered in the dark. Another rival
was promoted to command of Harald's army vanguard and sent
to lead an attack on a strong enemy position. Harald then delayed
his own arrival on the battlefield so the vanguard and its
commander were slaughtered. Before very long those who called
Harald a 'hard ruler' were outnumbered by those who knew him
more plainly as 'Harald the Bad'.

This, then, was the man I continued to serve faithfully, and
to whom I acknowledged myself as 'king's man' while I clung
stubbornly to the hope that he would stem the steady advance of

the White Christ faith and lead his people back to the happier days of the Elder Way. Had I been more honest with myself, I might have admitted that my dream was unlikely ever to be realised. Yet I lacked the courage to change my way of thinking. The truth was that my own life had reached a plateau and I was set in my ways. I was forty-six when Harald ascended the Norwegian throne, but instead of accepting that I was at a time of life when most men would have been considered to have entered old age, I still felt I might have a hand in shaping events.

And Runa was keeping me young.

For six months of every year, I put Harald's court behind me and went back to my beloved Vaster Gotland. I timed my arrival for mid-autumn when it was time to harvest the meagre crops grown in the rocky fields wrested from the forest around our settlement, and my return soon acquired its own small ritual. I would come home on foot and dressed in sombre travelling clothes, not my expensive court dress, and in a leather pouch I carried a special gift for Runa – a pair of gilt brooches worked with interlaced patterns to fasten the straps of her outer tunic, a silver belt, a necklace of amber beads, a bracelet of black jet cunningly carved in the likeness of a snake. The two of us would go inside the small wooden house that I had built for us close beside her sister's home, and, the moment we were away from curious onlookers, her eyes would sparkle with anticipation. Handing her the present, I would stand back and watch with delight as she unwrapped the item I had folded inside a length of coloured silk which later she would sew into trimmings for her best garments. After she had admired the gift, Runa would reach up and give me a long and tender kiss, then she would carefully put the item into the treasure casket that she kept hidden in a cavity in the wall.

Only after that reassuring welcome would I report to Folkmar and ask what farm work needed to be done. He would set me to cutting grain, helping slaughter and skin cattle for which we would have no winter feed, or salting down the meat. Then there was firewood to be cut, gathered and stacked, and the roofs of our houses had to be checked for wooden shingles that had come loose or needed replacing. As a young man I had detested the repetition and stern rigour of this country life, but now I found the physical labour to be reinvigorating, and I enjoyed testing just how much of my youthful strength remained, pacing myself as I worked, and finding satisfaction in completing the tasks allocated to me. In the evenings as I prepared to go to bed beside Runa, I would say a prayer of thanks to Odinn for having brought me from an orphaned childhood through battle, slavery and near death to the arms and warmth of a woman that I deeply loved.

To my surprise I found that my neighbours regarded me as some sort of sage, a man deeply learned in the ancient wisdom, and they would come to me for instruction. I responded readily because I was beginning to understand that the future for the Old Ways might not lie with great princes like Harald, but among the ordinary country folk. I reminded myself that 'pagan', the word the Christian priests used disparagingly to describe non-believers, meant no more than someone who was of the country-side, so I taught the villagers what I had learned in my own youth: about the Gods, how to observe the Elder Way, how to live in harmony with the unseen world. In return my neighbours made me a sort of priest, and one year I came back to find that they had constructed a small hof for me. It was no more than a little circular hut set in a grove of trees, a short walk from the house where Runa and I lived. Here I could sacrifice and pray to Odinn undisturbed. And once again Odinn heard me, for in the eighth year of Harald's kingship, Runa delighted me by informing that she was with child, and in due course she gave birth to a boy and a girl, both healthy and strong. We named them Freyvid and Freygerd in honour of the Gods who were also twins.

BEFORE THE TWINS had learned to walk, Harald sent me on a mission which was a foretaste of his grand ambition – nothing less than to become a second Knut by achieving mastery over all the Norse lands. He summoned me, alone, to his council room, and stated bluntly, 'Thorgils, you speak the language of the Scots.'

'No, my lord,' I answered. 'As a youth I learned the language of the Irish when I was a slave among them.'

'But the Irish language is close enough to the Scots tongue for you to conduct secret negotiations without the need for interpreters?'

'Probably, my lord, though I have never put it to the test.'

'Then you are to travel to Scotland on my behalf, to visit the King of the Scots, and sound out whether he would be willing to make an alliance with me.'

'An alliance for what purpose?' I dared to enquire.

Harald watched me closely for my response as he said, 'To conquer England. He has no love for his southern neighbours.'

I said nothing, but waited for Harald to go on.

'The king's name is Magbjothr, and he has held the throne of Scotland for fourteen years. By all accounts he's skilled in warfare. He would make a powerful ally. There's only one problem: he mistrusts the Norse. His father fought our Norse cousins in the Orkneys, when Sigurd the Stout was earl there.'

Harald's mention of Sigurd the Stout brought a twinge of pain to my left hand. It was an involuntary response to the familiar stiffness of an old wound.

'I fought at Earl Sigurd's side in the great battle of Clontarf in Ireland, where he died trying to overthrow the Irish High King,' I said, choosing my words carefully. I refrained from adding that I was the last man to hold aloft Sigurd's famous raven banner, and had received a smashing blow to my hand when the banner's pole was wrenched from my grasp.

'It's England's High King I plan to overthrow this time, with

Magbjothr's support,' Harald declared. 'Your task is to persuade
him to make common cause with us. There's a vessel ready to
take you to Scotland. It's only a two-day sail.'

I arrived in Scotland expecting to find Magbjothr at his
stronghold on the southern shore of what the Scots call the Firth
of Moray, but when I got there, his steward told me that the king
was on a royal progress around his domains, and not expected
back for several weeks. He added, 'The queen has gone with him.
May the Lord preserve her.' I must have looked blank because
the steward went on, 'She's been getting worse these past few
months, and no one seems able to help. And such a fine lady, too.
I'm not sure she's fit to travel.'

Finding that my spoken Irish was readily understood, I made
discreet enquiries and learned that the queen, whose name was
Gruoch, was suffering from some sort of mysterious illness. 'Elf
shot,' was how one informant put it, and another said flatly,
'Demons have entered her head.' Everyone I spoke to made it
clear that Gruoch was highly esteemed. Apparently she was a
direct descendant of Scots kings, and by marrying Magbjothr had
greatly strengthened his claim to the throne. Magbjothr was also
of royal blood, but had held the lesser rank of Mormaer of Moray,
a title equivalent to Earl, before he came to the throne by
deposing the previous king in circumstances that my informants
were reluctant to describe. Some said he had defeated the king in
open battle, others claimed that he killed him in a man-to-man
duel, while a third account hinted that Magbjothr had treacherously assassinated his king while he was his guest. Listening to
their conflicting stories, one thing became clear: Magbjothr was a
man to be reckoned with. Not only had he won the throne of
Scotland through violence, but he had also acquired his wife by
force of arms. Gruoch had been married to the previous Mormaer
of Moray, who was burned to death along with his retinue of fifty
men in a dispute with Magbjothr. What made the outcome all the
more remarkable was that Magbjothr had married the widow, and
then agreed that her son by her previous husband was to be his

heir. The King and Queen of the Scots, I thought to myself, must be a very unusual pair.

My route southward to find Magbjothr took me across a wild landscape of moor and rocky highland. Called the Mounth, the region was often swathed in mist and cut through with narrow valleys choked with dense brush and woodland. It was perfect country for an ambush, and I understood why so much of what I had heard about the quarrels of the Scots involved surprise attacks and sudden raids. When I finally caught up with the king, I thought he was wise to have installed himself and his entourage in an easily defended fortress. Sited on a hilltop with a clear view on all sides, the building was protected by a triple ring of earth banks topped with wooden palisades which, even as I plodded up the slope, were being reinforced by his soldiers.

I was greeted with suspicion. A sentry stopped me at the outer gate and searched me for hidden weapons before demanding to know my business. I told him that I had come on an embassy from Harald of Norway and sought an audience with the king. The soldier looked doubtful. No strangers were allowed into the inner citadel, he said. These were his standing orders now that the Northumbrians were threatening to invade across the border. I might be a spy for them. I pointed out that the Northumbrians' traditional allies were the Danes, and that King Harald and his Norwegians had been fighting the Danes ever since Harald came to the throne. 'That's as may be,' retorted the sentry, as he escorted me to see his captain, 'but as far as I'm concerned, all you Norsemen are alike. Bandits, best kept out of places where you don't belong.'

His captain cross-examined me before leaving me to wait in an antechamber, and it was only after a delay of several hours that I was finally ushered into the presence of a tall, soldierly looking man, perhaps a decade younger than myself, with a ruddy wind-scoured complexion and long yellow hair. It was the King of the Scots, known to the Norsemen as Magbjothr, but to his own people as Mac Bethad mac Findlaech.

'Where did you learn to speak our language?' he asked, tapping the table in front of him with the naked blade of a dagger. I guessed that the weapon was not just there for show. The king mistrusted strangers.

'In Ireland, your majesty. In a monastery.'

The king frowned. 'You don't look like a Christian.'

'I'm not. I entered the monastery under duress. Initially as a slave. But I never accepted the faith.'

'A pity,' said Mac Bethad. 'I myself am a Christian. How come you were a slave?'

'I was taken prisoner in battle.'

'And where was that?'

'At a place called Clontarf, your majesty.'

The rhythmic tapping of the dagger suddenly slowed.

'At Clontarf? That was a long time ago. You don't look old enough to have been there.'

'I was only a lad, not more than fifteen years old.'

'Then you would have known the Mormaer of Mar. He fought and died in that battle.'

'No, your majesty. I did not know him. I was in the company of Earl Sigurd.'

Mac Bethad looked at me, trying to judge whether I was telling the truth. Pensively, he continued to tap the knife blade on the pitted surface of the wooden table.

'I'm surprised,' he said, 'that Harald of Norway should send me as his spokesman someone who served Fat Sigurd. The Earl of Orkney was a mortal enemy to my father all his life. They fought at least three battles, and thanks to that magic banner of his, Sigurd always came out best. Then the Orkney men stole our lands.'

My first meeting with Mac Bethad had got off to a very poor start, I thought to myself. I would never make a successful diplomat.

'The banner was useless to Sigurd at Clontarf,' I observed,

trying to sound conciliatory. 'He died with it tied around his waist.'

'And how do you know that?' This time the question was aggressive.

'He took the banner from me when the fight was going against us, and no one else would carry it. He wrapped it around him, saying that the beggar must carry his own purse. Then he walked into the thick of the fight. To certain death. I did not see the moment when he fell.'

Yet again Mac Bethad was looking at me with disbelief.

'Are you telling me that you were Sigurd's standard-bearer, and yet you survived?'

'Yes, your majesty.'

'And you did not know the prophecy that whoever flew the raven banner in battle would be victorious, but the man who actually held the raven banner would die in the moment of victory?'

'I had heard that prophecy, your majesty. But at Clontarf it turned out to be wrong. My fate was different. The Norns decreed that I should survive and that the earl would be defeated.'

When I mentioned the Norns, Mac Bethad grew very still. The tip of the dagger slowed its rhythm and stopped. There was a silence. 'You believe in the Norns?' he asked softly.

'I do, your majesty. I am an Old Believer. The Norns decide our fate when we are born.'

'And at other times? Do they decide our fate in later years?'

'That I do not know. But whatever the Norns decree for us will eventually come about. We can delay the outcome of their decision, but we cannot escape it.'

Mac Bethad laid the weapon gently on the table. 'I was about to send you away without hearing the message you bring from Harald of Norway. But maybe your arrival here was also decided by Fate. This evening I would like you to meet with my wife and me in private. Maybe you can help us. You have probably heard that my wife is ill.'

'I am not a physician, your majesty,' I warned.

'It is not a physician that she needs,' said the king. 'Perhaps it is someone who can explain what seems to be against all reason. I am a devout Christian. Yet I have seen the Norns.'

This time it was I who fell silent.

THE ROYAL CHAMBERLAIN found a place for me to sleep, a small alcove scarcely more than a cupboard, close to the king's apartments, and left me to eat my midday meal with the garrison of the fortress. Listening to their conversation, I gathered that they were all members of Mac Bethad's personal retinue and that they had a high opinion of their leader's generalship. The only time I heard any doubt expressed was in reference to the queen. One veteran complained that Mac Bethad was so distracted by the queen's illness that he was paying insufficient attention to preparing his defence against the expected invasion. The Earl of Northumbria, Siward, had given sanctuary to two sons of the previous Scottish king, the man Mac Bethad had killed, and was using their claim to the throne to justify his attack.

When the chamberlain fetched me that evening and brought me to the king's private apartments, I was shown into a small room furnished only with a table and several plain wooden chairs. The light came from a single candle on the table, positioned well away from the woman in a long dark cloak seated at the far end of the room. She sat in the shadows, her hands in her lap, and she was twisting her fingers together nervously. The only other person in the room was Mac Bethad, and he was looking troubled.

'You must excuse the darkness,' he began, after the chamberlain had withdrawn and closed the door behind him. 'The queen finds too much light to be painful.'

I glanced towards the woman. Her cloak had a hood which she had drawn up over her head, almost concealing her face. Just at that moment the candle flared briefly, and I caught a glimpse of a taut, strained face, dark-rimmed eyes peering out, a pale skin and high cheek bones. Even in that brief instant the cheek nearest to me gave a small, distinct twitch. Simultaneously I felt a tingling shock as though I had accidentally knocked the point of my elbow against a rock, the sort of impact that leaves the arm numb. But the shock was not to my arm, it was to my mind. I knew that I was in the presence of someone with otherworldly powers.

It was a familiar sensation. I had experienced it whenever I encountered men and women skilled in seidr, the art of magic. Usually I reacted strongly, because there were times when I too was gifted with what the Norse call ofreskir, second sight. But this occasion was different. The power emanating from the woman in the cloak was unmistakably that of a volva, a woman with seidr ability, but it was disturbed and irregular. It came at me in waves in the same way that a distant horizon shimmers on a summer's evening with lightning. Not the harsh and shattering flash when Thor hurls his hammer Mjollnir, but the insistent and irregular flicker that country folk who live far inland say is the silver reflection of great shoals of fish in the ocean rising to the surface and reflecting off the belly of the clouds.

Again I noticed the woman's hands. She was twisting and rubbing them together as if she was washing them in water, not the empty air.

'People here know them as the three Wyrds,' Mac Bethad suddenly blurted out. There was anguish in his voice. 'As a Christian I thought it was just a heathen belief, a superstition. Until I met the three of them, dressed in their rags. It was in Moray, when I was still the Mormaer there, not yet king.'

The king was speaking of the Norns, launching directly upon the subject without any introduction. Obviously the topic had been preying on his mind.

'They appeared as three hags, clustered by the roadside. I would have ridden on if they had not called out for my attention. Perhaps if I had not stopped to listen, my wife would have been spared.'

'You saw the Norns in Moray?' I asked, filling the awkward

gap. 'They were seen nearby, in Caithness, at the time of Clontarf. Weaving a shroud and using the entrails of men as the threads. They were celebrating the battle's slaughter. When you saw them, what did they say?'

'Their words were garbled and indistinct. They were short of teeth and mumbled. But one of them was prophesying. Said I would become the king of the Scots, and warned me of treachery among my nobles. At the time I thought it was all nonsense. Trite stuff that any fool would dream up.'

'If they were indeed the Norns, that would be Verdhandi who spoke to you. She is that-which-is-becoming. Her two sisters, Urhr and Skuld, concern themselves with what is and what should be.'

'As a Christian I know nothing of their names or attributes. Indeed I would have paid no heed to their words, if Gruoch had not encouraged me.'

I looked again towards the hooded woman. Now she was rocking back and forth in her seat, her hands still twisting together ceaselessly. She must have heard everything we had said, but she had not uttered a word since I had entered the room.

'Gruoch is as good a Christian as I am,' Mac Bethad went on, speaking more gently. 'A better one, in fact. She is charitable and kind. No one could ask for a better consort.'

I realised, a little belatedly, that Mac Bethad truly loved his queen. It was an unexpected revelation, and it explained his present concern for her, even as his next words revealed how his love for his wife had ensnared them both.

'When I told Gruoch what the Wyrds had said, she too dismissed their prophecies as heathen babbling. But she did point out that I had a better right to the throne of Scotland than the weakling who held it – I mean my cousin, Duncan. She left unsaid that she herself is equally well born. Maybe that was not what she was thinking, but I imagined it was so. Her words made me determined to overthrow the king. Not for my own sake, though everyone knows that the stronger the king, the happier will be his realm. That's "the king's truth". For the sake of my wife I made up my mind that one day I would be seated on the sacred stone and acclaimed as the King of Scots. Then Gruoch would be a queen. It was her birthright, which was to be my gift to her.'

'And did it turn out as the Norns predicted?'

'I challenged King Duncan and defeated him in open battle. I was not alone in wanting him gone. More than half the other Mormaers and thegns supported me.'

'I have heard it said that the king was murdered while he was your guest.'

Mac Bethad grimaced. 'That's a well-rehearsed tale, a black rumour spread by those who would like to see one of Duncan's sons on the throne. They would be puppets of the Northumbrians, of course. Duncan was not murdered. He died because he was a poor tactician and a careless commander. He led his men into Moray to attack me, and his scouts were incompetent. They failed to detect the ambush we had set. After the battle I had the scouts executed for failing in their duty. If anyone was responsible for Duncan's death it was them.'

'And was it then that your wife fell ill?'

Mac Bethad shook his head. 'No. She is a king's granddaughter, and she knows the price that must be paid for gaining or maintaining power. Her sickness began less than three years ago. But it is getting worse, slowly and inexorably, and that is what I hope you may be able to explain, for I fear it has something to do with your Elder Ways.'

He turned to face his wife. She had raised her head, and the look which passed between them made it clear that Gruoch loved her husband as much as he loved her.

'I was too occupied with my duties as king to appreciate what was happening,' explained Mac Bethad slowly. 'After I gained the throne, she began to question why the Wyrds had appeared, and if they were no more than a heathen superstition, how it was that what they said had come true. The doubts preyed on her mind.

Our Christian priests told us that it was the work of the devil. They persuaded her that she had unknowingly become an agent of the dark one. She began to think of herself as unclean. That is why she constantly washes her hands, as you must have noted.'

'And did the priests suggest a cure?' I asked, unable to resist adding, 'They seem to think they have the answers to every human condition.'

Mac Bethad stood up and went across to where his wife sat. He bent and kissed her gently, then eased back her hood so he could reach down and remove an amulet hanging on a leather thong around her neck. As the hood fell back, I saw that Queen Gruoch must have once possessed a striking beauty. Her hair was unkempt and wild, but it was still thick and luxuriant and shot through with glints of reddish gold, though most of it was faded to a dull bronze. From her left temple a strange white streak extended back through her hair, giving her a strange and unsettling appearance.

Mac Bethad laid the amulet upon the table in front of me. It was a small tube of brass. I teased out the tightly rolled scrap of paper and smoothed it on the table so that I could read the words written there. They were penned in a combination of three scripts – runes, Greek and Roman lettering. '*In nomine domini summi sit benedictum*, thine hand vexeth, thine hand troubles thee, Veronica aid thee,' I read.

'The priest who prepared this note said that my wife should wear this close to her left breast,' explained Mac Bethad, 'and for it to be effective she must remain silent. But as you observe, it has had little effect. At least it is less harmful than the other cures that have been suggested. A different priest claimed that my wife's affliction could be controlled if I used a whip made of porpoise skin to beat her every day and expel the demons that have possessed her.' He grimaced with distaste.

I recalled the twitch that had passed across the queen's cheek, and remembered how the young Basileus Michael in Miklagard had trembled uncontrollably in the moments before his spirit had strayed. In Miklagard, too, ignorant priests had diagnosed devilish intervention. Other physicians, however, had been more practical. Long ago, in Ireland, I had seen a drui use herbs and potions to treat convulsions among his patients.

'There are no devils, nor dark elves in possession of your queen,' I assured the king. 'What is written on that paper is worse than foolishness. If you wish to ease your queen's suffering, throw away the amulet, let her speak when she wishes, and if she is distressed, give her potions to drink of warm vinegar in which henbane or cowbane has been soaked, or a light infusion of the plant called deadly nightshade.'

Mac Bethad paled. 'But those are plants known to be favoured by witches and warlocks – and the Wyrds,' he said accusingly. 'You are leading her towards that dark world, not away from it.'

I shrugged. 'I am an Old Believer,' I reminded him, 'and I find no fault in using them if they are effective.' As I spoke, I found myself wondering if Gruoch knew that she had seidr powers. And if she did know, whether she had suppressed or denied them because she was a Christian. If that was the case, the tension within her must have become insupportable.

'Will the medicine cure my wife, as well as ease her suffering?' he asked.

'That I cannot say,' I warned him. 'I believe that her spirit is in turmoil. Divided between the White Christ and the Elder Way.'

'The White Christ has been no help,' said Mac Bethad. 'Four years ago, when I was really worried about the queen's condition, I took her to Rome on pilgrimage. Sought out all the holy men, prayed, gave alms in abundance, but with no result. Maybe I should now turn to the Elder Way. If it cured my wife, I would give up my Christian faith, knowing that no harm can ever come to me.'

His words sent an alarm signal. I knew there was something not quite right.

'What do you mean by "that no harm will come to you"?'

'The final prophecy of the Wyrds was that I could not be killed by mortal man, and that my throne was secure.'

'And did they offer some sort of guarantee or proof?'

'They stated that I would not lose a battle until the wood of Birnam came to this stronghold. But Birnam is half a day's travel away. That is impossible.'

But I knew that it was possible. Even as Mac Bethad told me the prophecy, I understood that his kingship was doomed. Perhaps the country folk back in Vaster Gotland were right and I was some sort of sage, because I already knew that a prophecy of a moving wood had proved to be a sure sign of defeat to come. Travelling in Denmark some years earlier, I had come to a place known locally as the Spring of Carnage. Intrigued, I had enquired the reason for the name. I was told it was the spot where a king of Denmark lost his final battle to an enemy who advanced into their attack carrying the leaves and shrubs of trees to hide their numbers. The place where they had cut the fronds was still called the Deadly Marsh.

Composing my features to hide my consternation, I looked at the king of the Scots in the half darkness. There was no doubt in my mind that the prophecy of the Norns was an augury for Mac Bethad, not a surety. Odinn had allowed me a glimpse into Mac Bethad's future, but had denied it to the king. There was nothing that I could do to alter Mac Bethad's fate. It was his orlog, his destiny. I wondered what to say to him. I chose the coward's course.

'Be careful,' I cautioned Mac Bethad, rising to my feet. 'A single tree can destroy a king. Magnus of Norway who shared the throne with my liege lord Harald was killed by a single branch which swept him from the saddle. He too was a Christian.'

Then, burdened with a sense of foreboding, I said I was tired, asked Mac Bethad for permission to return to my chamber, and left the room.

Next morning I did not trouble to request for a second audience with the king, because I knew that any alliance I made between Mac Bethad and King Harald would prove futile. Instead I asked for permission to return to Norway for further consultations with my liege lord, and even as I was waiting on the coast for the ship that would carry me back to Nidaros, I heard that Siward and his Northumbrians had made a sudden strike across the border and overrun Mac Bethad's stronghold on the hill. I did not doubt that the advancing troops had carried branches from the wood of Birnam. Mac Bethad himself escaped the battle, and was to survive for two more years before he was hunted down and killed in the glens of the Mounth. How he was killed when he had been assured that no man born of a woman could kill him, I never found out. Nor did I hear what happened to his Queen Gruoch and whether she converted to the Old Ways or remained torn between the two faiths, tormented by her doubts.

'YOU COULD ALSO have warned Magbjothr that even the divine Baldr, whom the Gods thought was unassailable, was killed by a branch of mistletoe,' Harald observed shrewdly when I reported the failure of my mission to him.

His remark was typical of his familiarity with the Old Gods. Baldr was the most handsome of all of them. When he was born his mother asked all potential sources of harm that they would never hurt him. She obtained the promise from all things that might harm him – fire, water, disease, all animals, including snakes. She even asked the trees to give her their pledge. But she made an exception of the mistletoe, which she considered to be a plant too young and slender to be a risk. Confident of this protection, the other Gods amused themselves at banquets by pelting Baldr with rocks and stones, throwing spears at him and shooting arrows. Always the missiles fell short or were turned aside, until the trickster Loki made an arrow from mistletoe and gave it to Baldr's brother, Hod. Unthinkingly, Hod, who was blind, shot the arrow and killed his brother.

'Odinn the Wise One told us that it is better that men do

not know their fate,' I answered, and quoted a verse from the Havamal, the Song of Odinn:

> 'Medium wise should a man be
> Never too wise
> No man should know his fate in advance
> His heart will be freer of care.'

Harald grunted his approval of the verse, then dismissed me. 'Go back to your family in Vaster Gotland, Thorgils, and enjoy the rest of your days with them. You have more than discharged all your duties to me as a king's man, and I release you from that obligation. I will only send for you again if I can turn to no other.'

TWELVE

HARALD NEVER NEEDED to summon me again. When I did come
back to his court a full ten years later, it was of my own free will
and burdened with a sense of impending doom. I was in the sixty-
sixth year of my life, and I felt I had nothing left to live for.

The unthinkable had happened: I had lost Runa. She died of
disease when our peaceful corner of Vaster Gotland fell victim
to one of those petty but vicious squabbles which plagued the
northern lands. I was away from home on a trip to the coast to
buy a winter supply of dried fish when a band of marauders crossed
our previously tranquil territory, and of course they burned and
pillaged as they went. My brother-in-law fled with his own family
and Runa and the twins into the recesses of the surrounding forest,
so they all survived unscathed. But when they crept out of their
shelter and returned to our houses, they found the carefully hoarded
stocks of food had been looted. There was no time to plant a
second crop so they sought to lay in emergency supplies. I returned
home with my purchases to find my family anxiously scouring the
forest for edible roots and late-season berries.

We might have come through the crisis if the winter that
followed had not been so harsh. The snow came earlier than usual
and fell more heavily. For weeks we were trapped in our cabins,
unable to emerge or seek assistance, though our neighbours would

have been of little help for they too were suffering equal distress. The fish I had brought back was soon eaten, and I cursed myself for not purchasing more. All my hoarded wealth was useless if we could not reach the outside world.

Gradually we sank into a numbed apathy caused by near starvation. Runa, as was her nature, put the well-being of our children ahead of her own needs. Secretly she fed them from her own share of our dwindling rations and concealed her own increasing weakness. When spring finally came and the snows began to melt and the days lengthened, it seemed that all of us would survive. But then, cruelly, the fever struck. Initially it was no more than a soreness in Runa's throat, and she found difficulty in swallowing. But then my wife began to cough and spit blood, and to suffer pains in her chest and shortness of breath. In her already weakened condition, her body offered no resistance to the raging of the illness. I tried all the remedies I knew, but the speed of her decline defeated me. Then came the dreadful night – it was only three days after she showed the first symptoms – when I lay awake beside her and listened to her rapid breathing grow more and more desperate and shallow. By dawn she could no longer lift her head, nor hear me when I sought to comfort her, and her skin was dry and hot to the touch, yet she was shivering.

I went to fetch a bowl of fresh water in which to soak the cloth I laid on her brow, and returned to find she was no longer breathing. She lay as still and quiet as a leaf which, after trembling in the breeze, finally departs from the bough and drifts silently downwards to settle, lifeless, on the earth.

Folkmar and I buried her in a shallow grave scraped from the rocky soil. A half-dozen of our neighbours came to join us. They were little more than walking skeletons themselves, their clothes hanging loose on their bodies, and they stood in silence as I knelt down and laid a few mementoes of Runa's life beside the corpse in its simple homespun gown. There were a pair of scissors, the little strongbox in which she had kept her jewellery, and her favourite embroidered ribbon which she had used to hold back her auburn hair. Looking up at the faces of the mourners and the heart-broken twins, I felt totally bereft, and the tears were streaming down my cheeks.

It was Folkmar who comforted me in his down-to-earth peasant way. 'She never expected so much happiness as you and the children brought her in her final years,' he said. 'If she could speak, she would tell you that.' Then, solemn-faced, he began to cover the corpse with earth and gravel.

It was another week before Folkmar gently stated what he and his wife had decided even as they stood at Runa's graveside. 'We'll take care of the twins,' he said. 'We will treat them as our own until you can arrange something better for them.'

'Better?' I said dully, for I was still too grief-stricken to consider any course of action.

'Yes, better. You should return to Harald's court, where you have influence and command respect. There you can do more for the twins than anything which can be found here. When the time is ripe, maybe you can arrange for them to be taken into royal service, or perhaps fostered to a rich and powerful family.'

Folkmar's trust in my competence touched me deeply, though I doubted that I could achieve half of what he expected. Yet he and his wife were so insistent that I could not bear to disappoint them, and when the weather improved sufficiently I took the twins for a long and melancholy walk in the forest until we came to a dank clearing, surrounded by dark pine trees. There, as the melting snow dripped from the branches, I told my children the details of my own life that they had never heard before. I described how I had been abandoned as an infant and brought up by kindly strangers, and made my own way in the world. As intelligent youngsters do, they already knew where my talk was leading, and looked at me calmly. Both of them had inherited Runa's light brown eyes, and also her way of waiting patiently for me to reach the conclusion of my little speeches. As I groped to find the right words, I thought to myself how strange it must be for them to have for their parent a man who was old enough to be their grandfather. That wide gap in our ages was one reason why I felt I hardly knew them, and I found myself wondering what they really thought of me. Their mother had been the link between us, and once again the sorrow of her death nearly overwhelmed me.

'Both of you – and I as well – must learn how best to live now that your mother is gone,' I ended lamely, trying to keep my voice steady and not show my grief, 'so tomorrow I'm going to travel to the king to ask for his help. I will send for you as soon as our future becomes clear.'

They were the last words I ever spoke to them.

I arrived in Harald's new capital at Trondheim just in time to attend what was to prove the most important council meeting of Harald's reign. A sea-stained merchant ship had put in to Trondheim with news from London. On the fifth day of January the king of England, Edward, had died without leaving a direct male heir. The English kingdom was in turmoil. The English council, the witan, had elected the most powerful of their number to the vacant throne, but he was not of royal blood and there was much dissent. There were other claimants to the kingship, chief among them the Duke of Normandy, as well as the brother of the newly appointed king, who felt himself overlooked.

'I have as good a claim as any,' Harald stated flatly as his council gathered in an emergency session to discuss the situation. Out of respect for my grey hairs and my long service to the king, I had been asked to attend the meeting. 'My nephew Magnus was promised the kingdom of England by Knut's son and heir. When Magnus died, his claim passed to me as his co-ruler.' There was a silence. There were those among us who were thinking privately that Svein Estrithson in Denmark had an equal or even better claim because he was the great Knut's nephew. 'I intend to press for what is mine by right,' Harald went on, 'as I did for the throne of Norway.'

The silence deepened. All of us knew that the only way

Harald could pursue his claim was by force of arms. He was talking about waging full-scale war.

'Who holds the English throne now?' someone enquired tactfully. The questioner knew that it would give Harald a chance to tell us what he had in mind.

'Harold Godwinsson,' said Harald. 'He maintains that Edward named him as his heir while on his deathbed. But there is no proof.'

'That would be the same Harold who defeated the combined Welsh and Irish army last year,' observed one of Harald's captains, a veteran who had family connections among the Norse in Dublin. 'He's a capable field commander. Any campaign against him will need careful planning if it is to be successful.'

'There can be no delay,' declared Harald. 'With each month that passes, Harold Godwinsson makes himself more secure on the throne. I intend to attack this summer.'

'Impossible,' interrupted a voice, and I turned to see who was so bold as to contradict Harald so directly. The speaker was Harald's own marshal, Ulf Ospaksson. I had known him since our campaigns in the service of the Basileus, and he was the most experienced and canny of the king's military advisers. 'Impossible,' Ulf repeated. 'We cannot assemble a sufficiently large invasion fleet in that short time. We need at least a year in which to recruit and train our troops.'

'No one doubts your skill and experience,' answered Harald, 'but it can be done. I have the resources.' He was adamant.

Ulf was equally stubborn. 'Harold Godwinsson has resources too. He rules the wealthiest and largest kingdom in the west. He can raise an army and pay to keep it in the field. And he has his huscarls.'

'We will smash the huscarls to pieces,' boasted a young man, intervening. He was Skule Konfrostre, a close friend of Harald's son, Olaf, and one of the council's hotheads.

The marshal gave a weary sigh. He had heard enough of such

bravado in his days as a soldier. 'According to their reputation, one English huscarl is worth two of the best of Norway's fighting men. Think of that when you come up against their axes.'

'Enough!' broke in Harald. 'We may never need to face their axes. There is a better way.'

Everyone was straining to hear what the king had decided. It was another of Harald's rules that everyone had to stand while in the royal presence, unless given permission to be seated. Harald was sitting on a low stool while we stood in a circle around him. It did not make it any easier to hear what was being said.

Deliberately Harald turned his head and looked straight at me. I felt again the power of his stare, and in that moment I realised that Harald of Norway would never settle down to the quiet enjoyment of his realm nor abandon his grand design of being a second Knut. The death of the English king had been something that Harald had been waiting for. To the very last, the king was a predator at heart.

'Thorgils here can help,' he said.

I had no idea what he was talking about.

'If two claimants to the throne act together, we can depose Godwinsson and divide England between ourselves.'

'Like in Forkbeard's time,' said a sycophant. 'Half of England ruled by the Norsemen, the other half in Saxon hands.'

'Something like that,' said Harald dryly, though looking at him I knew him well enough to know that he was lying. Harald of Norway would never share the throne of England for long. It would be like his arrangement with Magnus for the Norwegian throne all over again. If Magnus had not died in an accident, Harald would have dispossessed him when the time was right.

Harald waited for a few moments, then continued. 'My information is that William the Bastard, Duke of Normandy, is convinced that Edward left the throne of England to him and that Harold Godwinsson is a usurper. My spies also tell me that William intends to press his claim, just as I will, by invading England. With Thorgils's help we can make sure that the two invasions are coordinated, and that Harold Godwinsson is crushed between the hammer of Norway and the anvil of Duke William's Normans.'

A glint of humour came into my liege lord's eyes.

'William the Bastard is a devout Christian. He surrounds himself with priests and bishops and listens to their advice. I propose to send Thorgils to his court as my emissary to suggest a coordination of our plans. Nothing would be more appropriate than to send Thorgils disguised as a priest.'

There was an amused murmur from the councillors. All of them knew my reputation as a staunch adherent to the Elder Faith.

'What do you have to say to this scheme, Thorgils?' Harald asked. He was baiting me.

'Of course I will carry out your wishes, my lord,' I said. 'But I am not sure that I will be able to pass myself off as a Christian priest.'

'And why not?'

'Though I had some training in a monastery when I was young,' I said, 'that was long ago, and in Ireland the monks followed a different version of the White Christ belief. Their way of worship has fallen into disuse. It has been supplanted by teachings from the All Father of the Christians in Rome, and by the new generation of reformers in the Frankish lands.'

'Then you must learn their ways and how to think like them so that you are mistaken for one of them. I want you to get close enough to William the Bastard so that you can form an opinion of him before you reveal your true identity as my ambassador. You must satisfy yourself that the Duke of Normandy will make a worthy ally. Only if you think that he will carry out his invasion are you to propose that he coordinate his attack with mine. Otherwise you are to maintain your disguise, and withdraw quietly.'

'And if I judge the duke to be a serious contender, what date should I suggest he launches his invasion?'

Harald chewed his lip, then glanced across at Ulf Ospaksson. 'Marshal, what do you recommend?'

Ospaksson still looked doubtful. Clearly he was uneasy at the idea of launching a major onslaught with so little preparation. I heard the reluctance in his voice as he set out his advice.

'We will need as much time as possible to raise an army, gather our ships and equip the fleet. Yet we cannot risk crossing the English Sea too late in the season when the autumn gales are due. So I would say that early September is as late as we dare leave it. But it will be cutting matters very short, and it will be impossible to supply the army once it is ashore in England. The distance from Norway is too great.'

'Our army will live off the land, just as it always has,' said Harald.

An image came into my mind of the dreadful famine that ravaged my home in the wake of the warriors. I took a deep breath and risked Harald's anger by asking, in front of the councillors, 'My lord, when I go on this mission for you I will be leaving my family and neighbours behind.'

Harald drew his eyebrows down in a scowl. I knew that he hated to be asked favours, and he had detected that I was about to ask for one.

'What are you trying to say? All of us will be leaving families behind.'

'The district where I spent the last four months is wracked by famine,' I explained. 'It would be a kingly act if you could send some assistance.'

'Anything else?'

'I have two children, my lord, a boy and a girl. Their mother died only a few weeks ago. I would be glad if they could benefit from royal favour.'

Harald grunted – whether in agreement I could not tell – before turning back to the matter of raising his army. Half of the levies of Norway were to assemble at Trondheim as soon as the harvest was in, every available warship was to be pressed into

service, a bounty would be paid to the smithies for extra production of arrowheads and axe blades and so forth. Only later did
I learn that, to his credit, he had arranged for three shiploads of
flour to be sent to Vaster Gotland, but that when his messengers
reached my home they found they had been mistaken for raiders,
and that Folkmar had disappeared. Last seen, he was heading in
the direction of the Thor temple at Uppsala, taking my twins with
him.

I spent the next two weeks trying to learn as much as possible
about the man on whom I was being sent to spy, and the more I
learned, the more I feared that Harald was overreaching himself
if he thought such a wily ally would cooperate. William the
Bastard attracted gossip like rotting meat attracts flies. His mother,
it was said, was a tanner's daughter whose heart-stopping beauty
had caught the eye of the Duke of Normandy, and their illegiti-
mate child was only seven when he had inherited the ducal title.
Against all expectations the youngster had survived the power
struggles over his inheritance because he possessed what the
Christians liked to call 'the devil's luck'. On one occasion a hired
murderer got as far as the boy's bedroom, and he awoke to see
his would-be killer struggling with his guardian, who had taken
the precaution of sleeping in the same room. The murderer cut
his guardian's throat but made such a commotion that he was
forced to flee before he completed his mission. Even William's
marriage was the subject of lurid description. Apparently he had
married a cousin, although his own priests had forbidden the
union as too close to incest, and, to add spice to the gossip, it was
rumoured that his bride was a dwarf who had borne him at least
half a dozen children. On one point, however, all the rumours
and speculation met: William of Normandy had shown himself to
be a master of statecraft. He had connived and fought until he
had secured his grip on the dukedom he had inherited, and now
he was the most feared warlord in France, as powerful as the king
of France himself.

This, then, was the man that my lord had sent me to evaluate and perhaps ensnare within Harald's grand design. It would be a dangerous assignment, and I was not at all sure that I still had the mental agility or the subtlety to act the spy. If I was to carry it off, it would only be with the help of Odinn, himself the great dissembler. It would be my last effort, and a distraction from the pain of losing Runa.

I began by acquiring my own disguise. I decided to wear the simple brown robe which would mark me as a humble monk. At Harald's court there were enough Christian priests for me to observe and copy their mannerisms, while the Latin I had learned in Ireland was more than good enough to mimic their prayers and incantations. The only dilemma I had was about my tonsure. Discreet enquiry among the priests revealed that the shape and manner of my haircut could be significant. Apparently the area of the scalp that was shaved, the length of remaining hair and the way it hung could indicate a White Christ devotee's background in the same way that the painted pattern on a shield indicates a warrior's allegiance. So I chose to have my head shaved completely of its last few remaining white hairs. If questioned, I would say that it was in honour of St Paul who was, according to the priest I interviewed, completely bald.

A cog took me from Norway south to its home port of Bremen and then towards the coast of Normandy, where I intended to disembark. This cog was a vessel that I had never experienced before, and I was ill at ease throughout the voyage. Designed for cargo carrying, the sides of the ship rose rather too high out of the water for my liking, and the bow and stern were made yet more clumsy by high wooden platforms. I thought the cog resembled a large barn that had somehow floated out to sea, though I had to admit that she was uncommonly capacious. The cog on which I sailed carried twice as much cargo as any ship I had ever travelled on, and as she waddled down from port to port I watched her hold fill up with stores that was clearly war material. There were bundles of shields, bales of sword blades, flax cloth for tent making, large quantities of ship-building nails as well as more humdrum gear such as boots, spades and bill hooks. Our ultimate destination was Rouen, Duke William's capital.

Njord the sea God, however, imposed a different outcome on our voyage. The cog loaded her final batch of cargo in Boulogne – a mixed consignment of metal helmets, tanned hides and pickaxes – and was working along the coast when, in the early afternoon, the weather turned against us. It was a typical spring gale when the sky swiftly darkens, clouds come scudding up from the west, and heavy bursts of cold rain spatter the sea with exploding raindrops. The sea, which had been a neutral blue-grey, turned a greenish black, and as the wind gathered in strength the swells began to mount and grow more violent until they toppled and broke. At first the cog's size and weight made her seem impervious to the deteriorating conditions, but eventually the waves which are Njord's servants gradually took control. Our Bremen skipper did his best to find shelter from the storm, but as luck would have it the gale had caught him at a point where he had no safe harbour to run to. So he ordered the sailors to shorten sail and tried to ride out the worsening conditions. Our deep-laden ship wallowed sickeningly as the waves rolled under her keel, and the wind buffeted the high bow and stern. It required all the steersman's skill to keep her riding to the seas, and it was impossible to prevent her drifting downwind as her slab sides acted as an unwelcome sail. As the wind shifted further into the north, I saw the skipper begin to look alarmed. He sent his crew below decks to fetch up the spare anchors from the bilges and get them ready on the heaving deck.

By now the rain was so heavy that it was impossible to see more than an arrow's flight in any direction, yet it was clear that the cog was being driven towards the unseen coast and into danger. I took care to conceal my own unease – priests are not supposed to be experienced mariners – but I noted how the waves were becoming shorter and steeper, and I suspected we were passing over shoals. That suspicion became a certainty when the churning of the waves began to throw up a yellow tinge of sand and mud. Once or twice I thought I heard the sound of distant breakers.

Then, abruptly, the rain stopped and the air around us cleared as if a hood had been lifted from our eyes. We turned to look over the lee rail to see where the wind had brought us. The sight brought an urgent command from our skipper. 'Let go all anchors,' he yelled.

Away to our port side, less than half a mile away, was a low shoreline. A beach of grey sand, glistening with the recent rain, sloped gently towards a ridge of dunes, and behind them rose a barrier of bone-white cliffs. To a landsman's eye it might have looked as if our cog was still far enough from land to be in deep water and safely clear of danger, but our skipper knew better. The gradual slope of the beach and the white crests of the waves between us and the shoreline told him that we had entered shoal ground. At any moment our vessel's keel might touch bottom.

The crew scrambled to carry out their captain's orders. Their greased leather sea boots slithered on the slippery deck as they wrestled the largest of our anchors, a great iron grapnel weighted with bands of lead, across to the side rail and heaved it overboard. The anchor rope flew after it, the first few coils disappearing quickly, but then suddenly slowing as the anchor hit the sea floor close beneath the surface.

'Jump to it!' bellowed the captain. 'Get the second anchor down.'

This time the anchor was smaller, a wooden shaft with a metal crossbar, easier to manage but less effective. It too was flung overboard, and by now the skipper had run forward and laid his hand on the main anchor rope. He was feeling its tremor, trying to sense whether the anchor itself had dug into the sea floor and was holding firm. His conclusion was evident as he shouted at the crew to throw out more anchors. 'Everything!' he yelled. 'She's dragging!' Desperately the crew obeyed. Four more anchors were tossed into the sea and their anchor lines made fast to strong points on the deck. But these emergency anchors were feeble affairs, the last one no more than a heavy rock with a wooden bar thrust through it, intended as a fang to bite into the sand.

All this time the cog was heaving up and down as each wave rolled under her hull, the anchor ropes went taut and then grew slack as the vessel worked her tethers, and the motion tugged the anchors treacherously across the soft sea floor.

There was nothing we could do but wait and hope that one or more anchors might take a firmer grip and halt our slithering progress. But we were disappointed. There came the deeper trough of a large wave, and we felt the keel of the cog thump down on the sand. Several moments passed, and then the vessel shuddered again, though the wave trough had been less obvious. Even the most inexperienced novice on our crew knew that our ship was being pushed farther into the shallows. Inexorably the gale drove the cog onward, and soon the shocks of the hull striking sea floor became a steady pounding. The cog was a credit to her shipwrights. Her stout hull stayed watertight, but no vessel could withstand such a battering for ever. The gale was showing no sign of easing, and each wave carried our ship a few inches farther towards her tomb.

Before long she was tilting over, the deck at so steep an angle that we had to cling to the rigging to prevent ourselves slipping into the sea. The cog was halfway towards her death. Even if her hull stayed intact, she would be mired in the shifting sands until she was buried and her timbers rotted. Her skipper, whose livelihood depended on his vessel, finally recognised that the sand would never let her escape.

'Abandon ship,' he called despondently, shouting to make himself heard above the grumbling of the waves which tumbled all around us.

When the gale had first hit us, our vessel's main tender – a ten-oared rowing boat – had been towing astern on a heavy cable, but when the cog struck the sands, the lighter boat had been carried ahead by the waves, the cable had parted, and our tender had been swept away. The remaining boat was a square-ended skiff, clumsy and heavy, suitable only for sheltered waters. The crew took axes and hacked away the low bulwarks to open a gap through which they pushed her into the seas. Even as the skiff slid overboard and hit the water, the breaking crest of a wave rose up and half filled her. The sailors shoved and jostled as they began to climb over the rail.

The skipper held back; probably he could not bear to abandon his ship. He saw me hesitating at the spot I had chosen. I was clinging to a shroud at the highest point on the vessel so that I did not tumble down the sloping deck. He must have thought that I was too frightened to move, and was hanging there, frozen with in terror.

'Come on, father,' he shouted, beckoning me. 'The boat is your only hope.'

I took a second look at the squabbling boat crew and doubted what he said. Gathering up the hem of my brown priest's gown, I tucked the material into the rope belt around my waist, waited for the next wave to crest, and the last the skipper saw of me was my flailing arms and naked legs as I launched myself out into the air and flung myself into the sea.

The water was surprisingly warm. I felt myself plunging down, then rolled and turned by the waves. I gasped for air and gulped down seawater, gritty to the taste. I spat out a mouthful as I came to the surface, looked around to locate the shoreline, and began to swim towards it. Waves broke over my head again and thrust me downward so that I was swimming underwater. I struggled to keep my direction. Another wave tumbled me head over heels, and I lost my bearings. As I came back to the surface, I squeezed my eyelids together to clear my vision, and my eyes stung with the salt. Once more I looked around, trying to realign myself with the shore, and caught a glimpse of the ship's small boat and its desperate crew. Four of the sailors were rowing raggedly, while the others bailed frantically, but their craft was dangerously low in the water. Even as I watched, a breaking wave lifted up the skiff, held the little boat there for a moment, and then casually overturned it, stern over bow, and flung the crew into the water. Most of them, I was sure, did not know how to swim.

Grimly I battled on, remembering my days in Iceland when I had taken part in the water games when the young men competed at wrestling as they swam, the winner attempting to hold his opponent underwater until he gasped for mercy. I recalled how to hold my breath, and so I kept my nerve as the waves crashed over me, trying to smother me, but also washing me closer to the shore. I was an old man, I cautioned myself, and I should dole out my last remaining strength like a miser. If I could stay afloat, the sea might deliver me to land. Had Niord and his handmaidens, the waves, wanted to drown me, they would have done so long ago.

I was on the point of abandoning the struggle when suddenly a pair of hands gripped me painfully under the shoulders and I found myself being hauled ashore, up the sloping beach. Then the hands abruptly released their grip, and I flopped face down on wet sand, while my rescuer, speaking in thickly accented Frankish, said, 'What shitty luck. All I've got is a useless priest.' At that moment I closed my eyes and passed into a haze of exhaustion.

A kinder voice awoke me. Someone was turning me on my back, and I could feel the clinging wetness of my monk's gown against my skin. 'We must find some dry clothing for you, brother. The good Lord did not spare you from the sea just to let you die of ague.'

I was looking up into the anxious face of a small, wiry man kneeling beside me. He wore a monk's habit of black cloth over a white gown, and was tonsured. Even in my exhausted condition I wondered to which monastic order he belonged, and how he came to be on a windswept beach, the scene of a shipwreck.

'Here, try to stand,' he was saying. 'Someone nearby will provide shelter.'

He slipped one arm under me and helped me rise to a sitting position. Then he coaxed me to my feet. I stood there, swaying.

My body felt as though it had been thrashed with a thick leather strap. I looked around. Behind me the waves still rumbled and crashed upon the sand, and some distance away I could see the wreck of our cog. She was well and truly aground now, lying askew. Her single mast had snapped and fallen overboard. Closer, in the shallows, the upturned hull of the ship's skiff was washing back and forth in the surge and return of the breakers. Occasionally, a large crest half rolled the little boat, and she gyrated helplessly. A group of about a dozen men was standing knee-deep in the sea, their backs turned towards me. Some were staring intently at the little skiff, others were watching the waves as they came sweeping towards the shore.

'No use asking them for help,' said my companion.

Then I noticed the two bodies lying on the sand, just a few yards away from the watchers. I guessed they were corpses of sailors from the cog who had drowned when the skiff capsized. When last I saw them, they were fully dressed. Now they were stripped naked.

'Wreckers and scavengers. Heartless men,' lamented my companion. 'This is a dangerous part of the coast. Yours is not the first ship to have come to grief here.' Gently he turned me around, and helped me stumble towards the distant line of cliffs.

A fisherman took pity on us. He had a small lean-to against the foot of the cliffs, where he kept his nets and other fishing gear. Over a small charcoal fire he heated a broth of half-cured fish and onions, which he gave us to eat while I sat shivering on a pile of sacks. A cart would be coming shortly, he said. The driver was his cousin, who passed by at the same time each day, and he would carry us into town. There the church priest would assist us. Listening to him, I found I was able to follow his words as they were mainly of the Frankish tongue, though mixed with a few words I recognised from my own Norse, as well as phrases I had heard when I lived in England. With my companion, I conversed in Latin.

'Where am I?' I asked the fisherman.

He looked surprised. 'In Ponthieu, of course. In the lands of Duke Guy. By rights, I should take you to his castle at Beaurain and deliver you as sea flotsam. Everything which is washed up by the sea is the duke's by right. That's the law of lagan. But I wouldn't be thanked for that, not since that business with the Englishman. The one who's now scrambled on to the throne over there, though he has no right. '

Odinn had a hand in my shipwreck, I thought to myself. The broth was warming me and I could feel the strength beginning to seep back through my limbs. 'What's his name, this Englishman?' I continued to enquire through lips that were painfully cracked and tasted salty.

'Harold Godwinsson,' answered the fisherman. 'He was cast up on the shore, just like you, along with half a dozen of his attendants. We get a dozen or so ships wrecked here every year, always on a north-west gale. He was a nobleman all right, anyone could see that from his fancy clothes. Even those plunderers, the wreckers, knew that they would have to take a care. No knowing what would happen if they messed about with the castaway. Too rich a fish altogether. Might stick in their gullets. So straightaway they took him to the duke, expecting a reward, though little good it did them. The duke stowed the man and his attendants in his dungeon while he made some enquiries as to who he was, and when he found out how important and wealthy he really was, he sent a ship over to England – my oldest brother was the first mate on her – asking for a good fat ransom. But our duke got no more profit out of it than the wreckers. Word of the castaway reached William the Bastard, and before you know it, a gang of his men-at-arms is on our doorstep telling our duke that he has to hand over the captive, or his castle will be torched and his head will be on a pole. Not a threat you ignore if Bastard William is behind it. Also he's Duke Guy's overlord, so he had a right to tell him what to do. So this captive is released from the dungeons, dressed up in a new set of finery, and the last we saw of him he was being escorted off to Rouen as though he was William's long-lost brother.'

The fisherman hawked to clear his throat, turned his head and spat a gob of phlegm accurately through the door of his shack. 'That's my cousin now, coming along with the ass and cart. You better get moving.'

'Bless you,' said my companion. 'Thrice bless you. You have done a Christian act today, for which God will reward you.'

'More than the duke would. He's a mean sod,' commented the fisherman sourly.

The little cart made slow progress. Its ill-shaped wheels wobbled on a single axle, and the vehicle lurched and slewed as it bumped across the tussocks of sea grass. I felt so sorry for the struggling donkey that I slid down from the pile of damp and smelly nets and walked beside the tailgate, holding on to the cart for support. I must have given the impression that I had recovered from my near drowning, because my companion could no longer restrain his curiosity.

'How came you to be upon that ship, and what is your name, brother?' he asked.

I had been expecting the question and had prepared what I hoped was a satisfactory reply.

'My name is Thangbrand. I have been preaching in the northern lands on behalf of our community in Bremen, though I fear that the word fell on stony ground.'

'Bremen indeed. I have heard that the bishop there holds authority over the northern kingdoms. But you are the first of his people that I have met.'

I relaxed. I doubted there were any survivors from the shipwreck who could throw doubt on my story.

'But you did not say why you were aboard the boat that wrecked.'

'The bishop sent me to seek out more recruits for our mission.

The northerners are a stubborn people, and we need help if we are to succeed in spreading the word of our Redeemer.'

My companion sighed. 'How true. Minds and ears are often closed to the magnificent and awesome mystery. Truly it is said that Christ was facing westward when he hung from the cross. All can see how in that direction the word of God has spread most easily. His almighty right arm pointed to the north which was to be mellowed by the holy word of the faith, and his left hand was for the barbaric peoples of the south. Only the peoples of the east are condemned, for they were hidden behind his head.

'And you, brother, how came you to be on the beach in my hour of need?' I asked, anxious to turn the conversation away from my own background and learn more about my pious companion.

'My name is Maurus and I am named for the assistant to the teacher of the Rule. I come from the region of Burgundy where its governance has long flourished.'

Baffled by his reply, I remained silent and hoped that he would provide a few clues as to what he was talking about.

'I was on my way to the Holy and Undivided Trinity to present to Abbot John a chronicle which celebrates the life of his predecessor, the saintly Lord Abbot William. I do this on behalf of the chronicler himself as he is no longer able to travel due to advancing years and ill health.'

'And this chronicler?'

'My mentor and friend, Rudolfus Glaber. Like myself he is from Burgundy. For years he has laboured compiling and writing a Life of Lord Abbot William. In addition he has written five books of Histories to relate the lives of the other important men of our time. Even now he is engaged in writing a sixth book, for he is determined to leave a written record for posterity of the many events which have occurred with unusual frequency since the millennium of the Incarnation of Christ our Saviour.'

I took a closer look at Maurus. He was, I guessed, somewhere between forty and fifty years old, small and sinewy, with a brick-red complexion that was either scorched by long exposure to the sun and wind or was the result of too much strong drink.

'Forgive me for my ignorance, brother,' I said, 'but this Rule you mentioned. What is that?'

He looked mildly shocked by my ignorance. 'That the brethren of a monastery obey one common will, are equal in agreement, and work and follow a uniform way of prayer and psalmody, eating and dress.'

'That makes them sound like soldiers,' I commented,

He beamed with approval. 'Exactly, servant soldiers of Christ.'

'That is something I would like to see.'

'You shall!' Maurus said enthusiastically. 'Why don't you travel with me to the Holy and Undivided Trinity? The monastery is second only to my own monastery of Cluny for the renown of its strict rule and discretion, the mother of virtues.'

It was precisely what I hoped he would say, because to travel in the company of a genuine priest would be excellent camouflage. His next words were even more encouraging.

'The monastery is at Fécamp, in Duke William's lands.'

THIRTEEN

IT TOOK US a week to reach Fécamp, walking by day and taking rides on farm carts when they were offered. At night we stayed with village priests, and twice we slept under hedges as it was now early summer and the night was mild. Throughout our journey I looked about me, trying to assess the resources which might allow Duke William to launch an invasion of England. What I saw impressed me. The countryside was fertile and well farmed. Rolling hills were cultivated for large fields of wheat, and every village was surrounded by carefully tended orchards. There were also large tracts of forest, mainly oak trees, and frequently we passed groups of men carrying saws and ropes, or we heard the sound of axes in the distance and encountered timber wagons drawn by oxen and piled high with raw logs, sawn baulks of wood, and the crooks and roots of large trees. I could recognise boat-building timber when I saw it, and I noted that the timber cargoes were all heading north, towards the coast of what the local people called 'the sleeve', the narrow sea separating Frankia from England.

Several times small groups of heavily armed men passed us. The weapons they carried looked well cared for, and I guessed them to be mercenary soldiers. Eavesdropping on their conversation as they passed, I identified men who came from Lotharingia,

Flanders, and even Schwabia. All of them were seeking hire by Duke William. When I commented on this to Maurus, he grimaced and said, 'Just as long as they keep their swords sheathed while they are among us. With the Duke you never know. He has brought peace to this land, but at a cost.'

We had reached the crest of a low hill and were beginning our descent into the far valley. In the distance a small walled town straddled the banks of a river.

'I once passed through a town just like that one over there,' Maurus recalled sombrely. 'It was border country, and the townsfolk had made the mistake of denying the duke's authority. They gave their allegiance to one of his rivals, and quickly found themselves under siege from the duke's men. They thought their walls could not be breached and compounded their error by insulting the duke himself. Some of the bolder citizens stood on the town walls, jeering and calling out that the tanner's daughter was a whore. The duke tightened the siege, and when food within the town ran out and a delegation of burghers came to beg for clemency, he had their hands cut off, then had them hanged from a row of gibbets erected opposite the main gate. The town surrendered, of course, but he showed no mercy even then. He gave his soldiers leave to put the place to the sack, then to set it on fire. There were only ashes and blackened house frames when I passed through.'

Duke William the Bastard, I thought to myself, was a match for my lord Harald when it came to being ruthless.

'Did not the town priests intervene, asking for their flock to be spared?' I asked.

'There is God's mercy, and the duke's mercy,' stated Maurus bleakly, 'and the sins of the earth can rise even to the heavens. The calamities we have suffered since the millennium of the Incarnation of Christ our Saviour are a sign that we have strayed from the path of righteousness.'

'It is true that there has been famine in the northern lands,' I commented, thinking of Runa's pitiful death.

'Famine, and worse, is our punishment,' said Maurus gloomily. 'My friend Glaber has written of it. For three years the weather was so unseasonable that it was impossible to furrow the land and sow crops. Then the harvest was destroyed by floods. So many died of hunger that the corpses could not be shrived in church, but were thrown into pits, twenty or thirty at a time. In their desperation men and women began to dig up and eat a certain white earth like potter's clay which they mixed with whatever they had by way of flour or bran to make bread, but it failed to allay their hunger cravings. Others turned to eating carrion, and to feasting on human flesh. Travellers like ourselves became victims of brigands who killed us in order to sell our meat in the markets. One trader even sold human flesh ready cooked. When arrested, he did not deny the shameful charge. He was bound and burned to death. The meat was buried in the ground, but another fellow dug it up and ate it.'

Maurus paused, and for a moment I wondered if he was imagining what human flesh tasted like, for I had noted that he paid the closest attention to his food and drink. Even in the humblest home he would encourage the housewife to improve her dishes with sauces, and he was constantly complaining about the standard of cooking in Normandy which, if he was to be believed, compared unfavourably with what he was accustomed to in Burgundy.

'But that is all in the past,' I ventured. 'Today the people look well fed and content.'

'We must not ignore portents which foretell a great tragedy,' Maurus responded. 'In a certain town in Auxerre, the wooden statue of Christ in the marketplace began to weep tears, and a wolf entered the church, seized the bell rope with his teeth, and began to toll the bell. And you can see for yourself the blazing star which appeared in the night sky in late April, and now burns every night, moving slowly across the heavens.'

Years earlier my teacher, a learned drui in Ireland, had told me about this wandering star and predicted its appearance. But to have told that to Maurus would have made it seem that I had learned witchcraft, so I said nothing.

'The world is tainted with blind cupidity, extreme abominations, thefts and adulteries,' he continued. 'The devil's assistants show themselves boldly. I myself have seen one. In my own monastery in Burgundy, he appeared to me in the form of a mannikin. He had a scrawny neck, jet-black eyes and a lined and wrinkled forehead. He had a wide mouth and blubbery lips, and pointed hairy ears under a shaggy mop of dirty hair. His lower legs were covered with coarse brown fur and he dribbled. He shrieked and gibbered at me, pointing and cursing. I was so terrified that I ran into the chapel, flung myself face down in front of the altar and prayed for protection. Truly it is said that the Antichrist will soon be set free, because this foul mannikin was one of his harbingers.'

But when we reached Fécamp and the monastery of the Holy and Undivided Trinity, it seemed to me that Maurus's fellow monks did not share his pessimistic view of the future. They were busy refurbishing their church in a manner clearly intended to last for years to come. The huge building swarmed with stoneworkers, labourers, carpenters, glaziers and scaffolders. The central feature was the tomb of the Lord Abbot William, whose Life had been written by Rudolfus Glaber. It was the scene of miracles, so a monk told me in hushed whispers. A ten-year-old boy, gravely ill, had been brought there by his despairing mother and left before the tomb. The child, looking around, had seen a small dove sitting upon the tomb, and after watching it for some time had fallen asleep. 'When he awoke,' the monk told me, 'he found himself perfectly cured.'

His pious tale was of less interest to me than the cloister gossip. The monks of the Holy Trinity were remarkably knowledgeable about what was going on in the duchy. They had their informants everywhere, from the smallest hamlets to the ducal court itself, and they discussed avidly the war preparations that Duke William was making – how many ships each of his great lords was expected to supply, the number of men-at-arms needed if the venture was to be a success, the quantity of wine and grain being hoarded in great bins, and so forth. The monks were very enthusiastic about the forthcoming campaign, and listening closely I discovered why: the monastery of the Trinity owned rich farmlands in England, and after Harold Godwinsson took the throne, they had ceased to receive any income from their property. Now they wanted Duke William to restore what was theirs, once he had supplanted Harold as king of England. The monastery had even pledged to supply Duke William with a warship for his fleet, paid for from the monastery's ample funds.

I commented to Maurus that some might see it as a contradiction for the house of God to be providing instruments of warfare, and he laughed.

'Let me show you something which is an even more useful contribution to his campaign. Come with me; it is only a short walk.'

He led me out of a side gate to the monastery and down a rutted lane until we came to an orchard. Unusually, the orchard was surrounded by a strongly built stone wall.

'There!' he said, pointing.

I peered over the wall. Grazing under apple trees were three extraordinary animals. I recognised that they were horses, but they did not look like any horses that I had ever seen before. Each animal was broad and heavy, with short muscular legs like thick pillars, and a back as broad as a refectory table.

'Stallions, all three of them,' explained Maurus approvingly. 'The monastery will donate them to William's army.'

'As pack animals?' I queried.

'No, no, as destriers, as battle chargers. Each can carry a knight in full armour. There is not a foot soldier in the world who can withstand the shock of a knight mounted on a beast like that. Our monastery specialises in the breeding of these animals.'

I thought back to the incident outside the walls of Syracuse when I had witnessed Iron Arm, the sword-wielding Frankish knight, use his brute strength to destroy a skilful Arab rider mounted on an agile steed, and I had a vivid picture of William's heavy cavalry mounted on their destriers, smashing down a shield wall of infantry.

'But how will William manage to transport such heavy animals on his ships and land them safely on the English shore?' I asked.

'I have no idea,' admitted Maurus, 'but there will be a means, that's for sure. William leaves nothing to chance when he wages war, and he has expert advisers, even from this abbey.' I must have looked sceptical, for he added, 'Do you remember meeting the monastery's almoner yesterday? He sat near us during the evening meal in the refectory, the gaunt-looking man with three fingers missing from his left hand. That's a war wound. Before he entered the monastery, he was a mercenary soldier. He's a member of Duke William's council and helps in planning the invasion. The monastery owns a parcel of land on the coast of England, just opposite the shortest sea crossing. It will be an ideal spot for William's troops to come ashore, and the almoner – his name is Regimus – will accompany the fleet so he can point out the best place to beach the boats carrying our troops and, of course, the heavy horses.

I was thoughtful as I walked back to the monastery. Everything I had heard about the Duke of Normandy indicated that he was serious about invading England, and that he was preparing his campaign with close attention to detail. I had the impression that when William the Bastard decided on a course of action, he followed it through and made sure that it was a success. It was not 'devil's luck' which had brought him this far; it was his determination and shrewdness, coupled with his ruthlessness. My earlier misgivings that Harald might be foolhardy in seeking an alliance with William came seeping back. And this time I also had to ask myself whether I too was being rash in involving myself so closely with these Christians who seemed so self-confident and pugnacious.

I made my excuses to Maurus, telling him that I intended to

travel onward to Rome carrying the bishop of Bremen's request for more priests to be sent to the northern lands. Maurus was content to remain at Fécamp, and now that I had had the experience of travelling with him, I was more confident in my disguise as an itinerant preacher for the White Christ. However, when I left the monastery early on a bright summer morning, I did make one important adjustment to my costume. I stole a black habit and a white gown from the laundry, leaving in their place my travel-stained robe of brown. From now on, I would pretend that I was a follower of the Rule.

Looking back on that theft, I realise that it was perhaps another sign that I was now too old to be a successful spy, and that I was becoming careless.

I needed a private audience with the duke at which I could propose the alliance with Harald of Norway, but I had failed to take into account how difficult it would be to gain access to him. William would be fully occupied with his invasion plans, and far too busy to listen to a humble priest, and his bodyguards would be suspicious of strangers, fearing that they were hired killers sent by the duke's enemies or even by Harold Godwinsson in England. So, recklessly, I had devised a stratagem which I hoped would lead to a meeting with the duke and only a handful of his closest advisers. This hare-brained scheme arose from a remark made by one of the monks at Fécamp. When Maurus had described how he found me half-drowned on the beach, the monks had told us that Harold Godwinsson had spent several months at the duke's court after a similar accident had befallen him. There Harold had been treated generously, and, in return, he had sworn allegiance to the duke and promised to support William's candidacy for the English throne. 'Godwinsson treacherously broke his oath by seizing the throne for himself. He is a usurper and needs to be exposed,' asserted one of the monks. 'There is a brother at the monastery in Jumieges who is writing a full account of this act of perfidy, and he will soon be presenting it to Duke William, just as brother Maurus here has brought to us the Life of Lord Abbot

William, lovingly prepared by his friend Rudolfus Glaber in Burgundy. Duke William keenly appreciates those who write the truth.'

Thus, when I reached the duke's palace at Rouen, I pretended I was on my way to its chapel, but then swerved aside and found my way to the anteroom where his secretaries were hard at work. Standing there in my black habit, I said that I wished to meet the duke privately on a matter of importance.

'And what is the subject that you wish to discuss?' asked a junior secretary cautiously. From his expression I judged that, but for my priestly dress, I would have been turned away on the spot.

'For many years I have been compiling a history of the deeds of great men,' I answered, allowing a sanctimonious tone to creep into my voice, 'and Duke William's fame is such that I have already included much about him. Now, if the Duke would be so gracious, I would like to record how he came to inherit the throne of England, despite the false claims of his liegeman Harold Godwinsson. Then posterity can judge the matter correctly.'

'Who should I say is presenting this request?' said the secretary, making a note.

'My name,' I said, unblushingly, 'is Rudolfus Glaber. I come from Burgundy.'

It took three days for my request to filter through the levels of bureaucracy which surrounded the duke. I spent the interval observing the preparations for the forthcoming campaign. Not since my days in Constantinople had I seen such a well-managed military machine. A space had been cleared in front of the city wall where, in the mornings, a company of bowmen practised their archery. Their task would be to pin down the enemy formations under a rain of arrows until the mounted knights could deliver their charge. In the afternoons the same practice ground was used for infantry drill.

A little to the north of the city was a grassy field where I watched the manoeuvres of a large conroy, a cavalry unit contributed to the duke's army by the Count of Mortagne. The Convoy numbered about a dozen knights accompanied by an equal number of squires or assistants. All wore chain mail, but only six of the knights were mounted on the heavy destriers. The others rode horses of a more normal size, and so they were practising how best to coordinate their attack. The lighter cavalry cantered their horses up to a line of straw targets and threw their lances, using them as javelins. Then they wheeled away, leaving their comrades on the heavy horses to advance at a ponderous trot so that their riders could run the targets through with their thicker, weightier lances or slash them to shreds with long swords. When this part of the exercise was over, the light cavalry dismounted, laid aside their metal swords and were given practice weapons with wooden blades. The conroy then divided in two and fought a mock battle, cutting and hacking at one another under the gaze of their leaders, who from time to time shouted out an order. At that moment one side or the other would turn and pretend to flee, drawing opponents forward. Then, at another shouted command, the fugitives would halt their pretended flight and the heavy cavalry, who were still on horseback and waited in reserve, lumbered forward to deliver the counter-blow.

While this was going on, I quietly sauntered forward to take a closer look at one of the battle swords that had been laid aside. It was heavier and longer than the weapons I had seen when in the emperor's Life Guard in Constantinople, and it had a groove down the length of the long straight blade. There was also an inscription worked in bronze lettering. I read INNOMINIDOMINI.

'Very appropriate, don't you think, father?' said a voice, and I looked up to meet the gaze of a heavily muscled man wearing a leather apron. No doubt he was the armourer for the conroy.

'Yes,' I agreed. 'In the Lord's name. It seems to be a fine blade.'

'Made in the Rhine countries, like most of our swords,' continued the armourer. 'Quality depends on which smithy makes them. The Germans turn them out by the dozen. If the blade snaps, it's not worth repairing. You only have to prise off the handle grips and fit a new blade.'

I remembered the consignment of sword blades taken aboard the cog before she wrecked. 'Can't be easy finding a replacement blade.'

'Not this time,' said the armourer. 'I've served the count for the best part of twenty years, making mail and repairing weapons on his campaigns, and I've never seen anything like the amount of spare gear that is being provided – not just sword blades, but helmets, lance heads, arrow shafts, the lot. Cartloads and cartloads of it. I'm beginning to wonder how it will all fit on the transports – if the transports are ready in time, that is. There's a rumour that some of us will be sent to Dives to help the shipwrights.'

'Dives? Where's that?' I asked.

'West along. The gear that's coming in to Rouen is being shipped downriver. The boats themselves are being built all up and down the coast. Dives is where the fleet is assembling. From there it will strike at England.'

It occurred to me that Harold Godwinsson must know what was going on, and that the English could put a stop to the invasion by raiding across the sea and destroying the Norman fleet while it was still at anchor. William's transports would make easy targets. By contrast, Harald's Norwegian ships, now gathering at Trondheim, were too far distant to be intercepted.

I was just about to ask the armourer if Duke William was taking any precautions against an English raid when a pageboy arrived with an urgent summons to the ducal palace. My request for a meeting with the duke had been granted, and I was to go there at once.

I followed the lad through the streets and along a series of corridors into the heart of the palace, where Duke William had his audience chamber. My suspicions should have been aroused by the swiftness of my reception. The pageboy handed me over to a knight who acted as the doorkeeper, and within moments I was ushered into the council chamber itself, the doorkeeper at my heels. I found myself in a large, rather dark room, poorly lit by narrow window slits in the thick stone walls. Seated on a carved wooden chair in the centre of the room was a burly man of about my own height but running to fat, with a close-cropped head and a bad-tempered look on his face. I guessed him to be in his mid-forties. I knew he must be Duke William of Normandy, but to me he looked more like a truculent farm bailiff accustomed to bullying his peasants. He was eyeing me with dislike.

Five other men were in the room. Three of them were obviously high-ranking nobles. They were dressed, like the duke, in belted costumes of expensive fabric, tight hose, and laced leather shoes. They had the bearing and manner of fighting men, yet they were strangely dandified because they wore their hair close-shaved from halfway down their heads in pudding-bowl style, a foppish fashion which, I later learned, had been copied from the southern lands of Auvergne and Aquitaine. They too were regarding me with hostility. The other two occupants of the room were churchmen. In stark contrast to my plain black and white costume, they wore long white robes with embroidered silk borders at the neck and sleeves, and the crosses suspended on their chests were studded with semi-precious stones. The crosses looked more like jewellery than symbols of their faith.

'I hear you want to write about me,' stated the duke. His voice was harsh and guttural, in keeping with his coarse appearance.

'Yes, my lord. With your permission. I am a chronicler and I have already completed five books of history, and – with God's grace – I am embarking on a sixth. My name is Rudolfus Glaber, and I have travelled here from my monastery in Burgundy.'

'I think not,' said a voice behind me.

I turned. Stepping out of the shadows was a man wearing the same plain black and white costume as myself. My glance dropped to his left hand, which lacked three fingers. It was Regimus, the almoner of the monastery of the Holy Trinity at Fécamp. In the same instant the doorkeeper, standing directly behind me, clasped his arms around me, pinioning my arms to my sides.

'Brother Maurus never mentioned that you came from Burgundy, and you do not speak with a Burgundian accent,' said the almoner. 'The brother in charge of our laundry also reported that a gown and habit were missing from his inventory, but not until I heard about a mysterious black-clad monk here in Rouen did I deduce that you must be the same man. I had not expected you to be so bold as to claim you were Rudolf Glaber himself.'

'Who are you, old man?' interrupted William, his voice even harsher than before. 'A spy for Harold? I did not know he employed dotards.'

'Not a spy for Harold, my lord,' I wheezed. I could scarcely breathe. The doorkeeper was gripping me so hard that I thought he would break my ribs. 'I am sent by Harald, Harald of Norway.'

'Let him speak,' ordered William.

The painful grip eased. I took several deep breaths.

'My lord, my name is Thorgils, and I am the envoy of King Harald of Norway.'

'If you are his ambassador, why did you not come openly rather than creeping about in disguise.'

I thought quickly. It would be disastrous to confess that Harald had asked me to evaluate William's invasion plans before offering an alliance. That was true espionage.

'The message I bring is so confidential that my lord instructed me to deliver it privately. I adopted this disguise for that purpose.'

'You soil the cloth you wear,' sneered one of the exquisitely dressed priests.

The duke silenced him with an impatient wave of his hand. I could see that William demanded, and received, instant obedience from his entourage. He seemed more than ever like a bullying bailiff.

'What is this message that you bring from Norway?'

I had recovered my confidence enough to glance at William's attendants, then say, 'It is for your ears only.'

William was beginning to get angry. A small vein on the right side of his forehead had started to throb.

'State your message before I have you hanged as a spy or put to torture to learn the truth.'

'My lord Harald of Norway suggests an alliance,' I began quickly. 'He is assembling a fleet to invade the north of England, and knows that you are planning to land forces in the south of the country. You both fight the same enemy, so he proposes that the two armies coordinate their attack. Harold Godwinsson will be obliged to fight on two fronts, and will be crushed.'

'And what then?' There was disdain in William's voice.

'After Godwinsson has been defeated, England is to be divided. The south ruled by Normandy, the north by Norway.'

The duke narrowed his eyes. 'And where will the dividing line be drawn?'

'That I do not know, my lord. But the division would be based on mutual agreement, once Godwinsson has been disposed of.'

William gave a grunt of dismissal. 'I'll think about it,' he said, 'but first I need to know the timing. When does Harald plan to land his forces.'

'His advisers are pressing him to invade England no later than September.'

'Take him away,' said William to the doorkeeper, who was still standing behind me. 'Make sure he is kept in safe custody.'

I passed that night in a cell in the ducal prison, sleeping on damp straw, and in the morning I was encouraged when the same pageboy who had brought me to the palace reappeared to tell the guard to release me. Once again, I was led to the duke's audience chamber, where I found William and the same advisers already gathered. The duke came straight to the point.

'You may inform your lord that I agree to his proposal. My army will land on the south coast of England in the first or second week of September. The precise date will depend on the weather. My transport barges need calm conditions and a favourable wind to make the crossing. According to my information, Harold

Godwinsson has called out the English levies, and is presently
holding his forces on the south coast, so it is likely that he will
dispute our landing. Therefore it is important that King Harald
keeps to his programme and opens a second front no later than
mid-September.'

'I understand, my lord.'

'One more detail. You are to remain here with me. It may be
necessary to communicate with your king as the campaign gets
under way. You will act as our intermediary.'

'As you wish, my lord. I will prepare a despatch for King
Harald confirming the details. If you can provide a vessel, I will
send the message to Norway.'

That same day, feeling quietly satisfied that my mission had
been accomplished so easily, I wrote out a summary of what had
happened. To prevent William's secretaries tampering with my
report, I hid my meanings in phrases that only those who knew
the ways of skaldic verse would understand. Harald became 'the
feeder of eagle of sea of carrion vulture' and the Norman invasion
fleet was 'the gull's wake horses'. And when I came to write about
William himself, I buried my meaning even deeper, because I was
not complimentary about his character. He became the 'horse of
wife of Yggr' because Harold would know that Yggr's wife was a
giantess, and that she rode a wolf. Finally, to make doubly sure
that the letter was treated as genuine, I folded the parchment,
using the same system of secret folds which, in Constantinople,
would prove that the despatch was authentic and which was
known to Harald, and gave the letter to a mounted courier, who
took it to the Norman coast. From there a ship would carry the
despatch to Trondheim.

For the next five weeks my status at William's court was
ambiguous. I was neither a prisoner nor a free man. I was treated
as if I was a minor retainer in the service of William, yet
everywhere I was accompanied by an armed guard. All around
me the preparations for the invasion continued apace, and in early

August, when William moved with his retinue to Dives to begin the embarkation of his troops, I went with him.

The scene at Dives was the culmination of the months of preparation. The port lay at the mouth of a small river, and by the time I arrived almost the entire invasion fleet had mustered in the roadstead. I counted at least six hundred vessels, many of them simple barges specially designed to carry troops. Lines of tents had been erected on the beach, and the army engineers had built cookhouses, latrines and stables. Squads of shipwrights were putting the finishing touches to the transports, and there was a constant coming and going of messengers and despatch riders as the infantry and conroys mustered for their embarkation. I had wondered how the destriers, the heavy horses, would be loaded, and now I saw the method. The cavalry transports were brought up on to the gently sloping beaches at high tide, and anchored. The ebbing tide left the flat-bottomed barges stranded, and the carpenters then placed low ramps up which the horses were led – sometimes with difficulty – and then stabled in the barges with their feed and water. There the massive animals seemed content to stand and eat as the incoming tide refloated the vessels and they were warped out into the roadstead.

On the eleventh day of September the duke did have his 'devil's luck', because, just at the time he had promised his invasion, the wind turned into the south-west as a gentle breeze, and held. At dusk William summoned me to his command tent, and, in the presence of his commanders, gestured towards the northern horizon.

'Now you can tell your master,' he said, 'that William of Normandy keeps his word. Tomorrow we complete our loading and sail for England. You will be staying behind to make your final report.'

The following morning I watched the entire fleet raise anchor and, taking advantage of the flood tide, set out to sea. As I trudged back up the beach to where my guardian man-at-arms stood waiting, I felt I had served my liege lord well, and for the last time. When the opportunity came I would be king's man for Harald no longer, and I would return to Sweden and seek out my twins. I was feeling old.

The man-at-arms was content to dawdle. It was pleasant on the coast, and he was in no hurry to return to his barracks at Rouen, so we spent the next few days at Dives. The place, now that the fleet had sailed, had a slightly desolate atmosphere. The beach where the barges had loaded still showed signs of the departure, and there were traces where the tents had stood, piles of horse droppings, grooves left by the carts that had brought the stores, and charred marks where cooking fires had burned. There was an air of finality. The roadstead was empty. Time was suspended while we waited to hear what was happening with the invasion.

The weather continued fair, with bright sunshine and a light south-west breeze, and to pass the time I arranged with a local fisherman to go out on his boat each morning when he checked his nets. There, ten days after I had watched the Norman fleet depart, we were bobbing gently on the sea when I identified a familiar profile. A small vessel was beating down towards us. Hard on the wind, she was making slow progress, but there was no mistaking her origin. She was a small trading ship, Danish- or Norwegian-built. As she tacked her way into the roadstead at Dives, I was sure that she had come to collect me, and that Harald must have received my letter.

I asked the fisherman to row me across so that we intercepted the vessel before she made her landfall. Standing up in the fishing boat, I called out a greeting, glad to speak Norse once again. I was still wearing my stolen monkish gown, so the vessel's skipper must have thought it odd that a Christian priest spoke his language, but he spilled the wind from his sail and the vessel turned up into the wind so I could scramble aboard. The first person whom I saw on deck was Skule Konfrostre, the same young hothead who had boasted that the Norwegians would

smash the English huscarls. I was perturbed to see that he was
very agitated.

'Is everything all right with Harald's campaign?' I asked,
alarmed by his manner. 'Has he landed safely on the English
coast?'

'Yes, yes, our fleet crossed from Norway in late August and
safely reached the coast of Scotland. When I left him, Harald was
advancing down the coast. He sent me to find out what was
happening with the attack that Duke William promised. He has
heard nothing further.'

'You need not worry about that,' I said complacently. 'I
watched Duke William's fleet sail for England ten days ago. By
now they should be well ashore and advancing inland. Godwinsson is caught in a trap.'

Skule looked at me as if I had lost my wits.

'How is it, then, that only yesterday, as we passed southward
along the coast, we saw the Norman fleet lying quietly at anchor
some distance up the coast. The skipper knows the place. He says
it is a port called St Valery, in the lands of the Duke of Ponthieu.
They have not even crossed to England yet.'

I felt as if the deck had shifted beneath my feet. I, who had
thought to deceive Duke William, had been the victim of a much
greater deceit. Too late I thought back to the day that I had first
suggested Harald's plan for a coordinated attack. I recalled the
armourer who had met me at the practice ground and how he had
been so eager to tell me that Dives was the departure point for
the invasion, and how, once I had that information, I had quickly
been brought before the duke. To my chagrin I realised that my
disguise as a monk had been penetrated far earlier than I knew,
and that William and his advisers had thought up a scheme to
turn my presence to their advantage: I was to be used to conceal
the true direction and timing of the Norman attack. After I had
revealed myself as King Harald's envoy and suggested the coordinated campaign, William and his advisers must scarcely have
believed their good luck. They had duped the King of Norway

into landing on English soil to face Harold Godwinsson's army, while the Normans hung back and waited to make their landing unopposed. It would not matter who won the first battle – Harald of Norway or Harold of England – because the victor would be weakened when he came to face Duke William and his conroys.

'We must warn King Harald that he faces the English army on his own,' I exclaimed, queasy with the knowledge of what a fool I had been. Then, to hide my humiliation, I added bitterly, 'So now, Skule, you will learn what it's like to face the huscarls and their axes.'

William, Duke of Normandy, had used me as a pawn.

FOURTEEN

THE VOYAGE NORTHWARD to warn Harald was a misery for me. I spent my time regretting how gullible I had been, then tormenting myself by imagining how I should have seen through William's subterfuge. Worse, now that I knew the extent of the duke's guile, his next move was clear to me: Godwinsson would have his spies in the duke's camp, and the duke would make it possible for them to relay to their master the news that, for the time being, the Norman invasion was at a standstill. Thus, as soon as Harold was confident that the Normans posed no immediate threat, the English king would head north to beat back the Norwegian invaders. The prospect of what might follow a Norwegian defeat filled me with despair. From the day I had first met Harald of Norway long ago in Miklagard I had imagined him as the last, best champion for the Old Ways of the north. Often he had disappointed me, but he still retained an enduring quality. Despite his arrogance and his despotism, he remained the symbol of my yearning that it might be possible to restore the glories of the past.

'Our fleet crossed from Norway to the Shetlands late in August,' Skule Konfrostre confirmed as we journeyed, adding to my discomfort. 'Two hundred longships we were, as well as smaller vessels, the largest fleet that Norway could muster. Such a spectacle! Harald has staked everything on this venture. Before we set sail, he went to the tomb of his ancestor St Olaf and prayed for success. Then he locked the door to the tomb and threw the keys into the River Nid, saying he would not return there until he had conquered England.'

'If you are a Christian, my friend, you may well find yourself fighting other Christians,' I retorted grumpily. 'If Harald overwhelms the English, then his next enemy in line will be Duke William and his Norman knights, and they are convinced that the White Christ is on their side. The duke himself constantly wears a holy relic around his neck, and his senior army commander is a bishop. Mind you, he's the duke's half-brother, so I don't suppose he was appointed for his religious qualities.'

'I'm not a Christian,' said Skule stubbornly. 'As I said, Harald left nothing to chance. He did not forget the Old Gods either. He made sacrifices to them for victory, and he cut his hair and nails before we sailed, so that Naglfar will not benefit if we fail.'

I shivered at the mention of Naglfar, because the young Norwegian had touched on my darkest premonition. Naglfar is the ship of corpses. At Ragnarok, the day of the final dread battle when the Old Gods are defeated, Naglfar will be launched on the floods created by the writhings of the Midgard Serpent lying deep within the ocean. Built from the fingernails of dead men, Naglfar is a monstrous vessel, the largest ever known, big enough to ferry all the enemies of the Old Gods to the battlefield where the world as we know it will be destroyed. If Harald the Hard Ruler had trimmed his nails before sailing for England, then perhaps he foresaw his own death.

Our grey-bearded skipper's opinion only added to my dejection. 'The king should never have sailed in the first place,' he interrupted. 'He should have heeded the omens. Christian or otherwise, they all point towards disaster.' The skipper, like many mariners, was swayed by omens and portents, and my silence only encouraged him to continue. 'Harald himself had a warning dream. St Olaf appeared to him and advised him not to proceed. Said it would result in his death, and that's not all.' He looked at me, still in my black and white gown. 'You're not a White Christ priest, are you?'

'No,' I replied. 'I am a follower of Odinn.'

'Then let me tell you what Gyrdir saw on the very day the fleet sailed. Gyrdir's a royal officer, and he was standing on the prow of the king's ship, looking back over the fleet. It seemed to him that on the prow of every vessel was perched a bird, either an eagle or a black raven. And when he looked towards the Solund Islands, there, looming over the islands, was the figure of a huge ogress. She had a knife in one hand and a slaughtering trough in the other, and she was chanting these lines:

> 'Norway's warrior sea king
> Has been enticed westward
> To fill England's graveyards
> It's all to my advantage
> Birds of carrion follow
> To feast on valiant seamen
> They know there will be plenty,
> And I'll be there to help them.'

I felt sick to my stomach. I remembered the words of the message that I had sent to Harald. I had referred to him as 'the feeder of eagle of sea of carrion vulture'. I had meant that Harald was the sea eagle, the image that I had held of him from the day I had first set eyes on him in Constantinople. Now I realised that the words in my letter could be interpreted to mean that he was the one who would deliver the carrion flesh of his own men to the ravens and eagles. If so, I was the one who had enticed him and his men to his doom with my letter from Normandy.

'You said there were other portents?' I asked shakily.

'Several,' the seaman replied, 'but I can remember the details of only one. Another of the king's men dreamed it. He saw our fleet sailing towards land. In the lead was King Harald's longship flying its banner, and he knew that the land they were approaching was England. On the shoreline waited a great host of warriors, and in front of them was an ogress – perhaps it was the same one, I don't know. This time she was riding a gigantic wolf, and the wolf held a bleeding human carcass in its jaws as easily as a terrier grips a rat. When Harald and his men came ashore, both sides joined battle, and the Norwegian warriors fell in swathes. The ogress collected up their corpses and hurled them, one by one, into the mouth of the great wolf until its jaws ran with blood as the beast gulped down its feast of victims.'

Now I knew for certain that my own power of second sight, dormant for so many years, had returned. When I had composed my report in Normandy, I had referred to Harald as a sea eagle and hidden Duke William's identity under the guise of the wolf which the ogress Yggr rides. In doing so, I had touched unwittingly upon the future: every death among Harald's men would be sustenance for the wolf, the name I had chosen for Duke William. Failing to recognise my own augury, I now quailed at the prospect that my premonition would prove correct. Should William emerge victorious, I would have helped put on the throne, not a possible champion of the Old Ways, but a voracious follower of the White Christ.

Even the weather conspired to depress me. The wind stayed as a gentle breeze from the south-west, so our ship ran speedily up the narrow sea between England and Frankia. I knew the same wind was ideal for William to launch his invasion, yet when we passed the port of St Valery and our skipper took the risk of sailing closer inshore to look into the roadstead, we saw the great assembly of William's ships still riding quietly at anchor or securely hauled up on the beach. Clearly, the Duke of Normandy had no intention of making the crossing until he heard that Harold Godwinsson had turned his attention to countering the threat from Norway.

Thanks to that favourable wind we made a near-record passage, and my hopes of averting disaster rose when we encountered one of King Harald's warships. It was patrolling off the river mouth into which Harald had led his fleet less than three days before. There were a few shouted exchanges between the two vessels, and Skule and I transferred hastily to the warship. Her captain, understanding the urgency of our mission, agreed to navigate the estuary at night and row up against the current. So it was that, a little after daybreak on the twenty-fifth of September, I came in sight of the muddy river foreshore where Norway's massive invasion fleet lay anchored. To my relief, I saw that the fleet was intact. The river bank swarmed with men. Harald's army, it seemed, was safe.

'Where do I find the king?' I demanded of the first soldier we met on landing. He was taken aback by the urgency in my tone, and looked at me in astonishment. I must have made a strange sight – an elderly bald priest, the hem of my white undergown spattered with river mud, and my sandals sinking in the ooze. 'The king!' I repeated. 'Where is he?'

The soldier pointed up the slope. 'Best ask one of his councillors,' he answered. 'You'll find them over there.'

I slipped and slithered up the muddy bank, and hurried in the direction he indicated. Behind me I could hear Skule say, 'Slow down, Thorgils, slow down. The king may be busy.' I ignored him, though I was short of breath and painfully aware that my advancing years had taken their toll. I may have made a dreadful error in supplying false information to Harald, but I still desperately wanted to undo the harm I had done.

I saw a tent, larger and grander than the others, and hastened towards it. Standing outside was a group talking among themselves, and I recognised several of Harald's councillors. They were in attendance on a young man, Harald's son Olaf. Rudely I interrupted.

'The king,' I said, 'I need to speak with him.'

Again the anxiety in my tone took my audience aback, until one of the councillors looked a little more closely.

'Thorgils Leifsson, isn't it? I didn't recognise you at first. I'm sorry.'

I brushed aside his apology. It seemed to me that everyone was being fatally obtuse. My voice was quivering with emotion as I repeated my demand. I had to speak with the king. It was a matter of the greatest urgency.

'Oh, the king,' said the councillor, whom I now remembered as one of Harald's sworn men from the Upplands. 'You won't find him here. He left at first light.'

I clenched my teeth in frustration. 'Where did he go?' I asked, trying unsuccessfully to keep my voice calm.

'Inland,' said the Norwegian casually, 'to the meeting place, to accept hostages and tribute from the English. Took nearly half the army with him. It's going to be a scorching day.' He turned back to his conversation.

I seized him by the arm. 'The meeting place, where's that?' I begged. 'I need to speak with him, or at least with Marshal Ulf.'

That brought a different reaction. The Norwegian shook his head.

'Ulf Ospaksson. Don't you know? He died in late spring. Great loss. At his burial ceremony the king described him as the most loyal and valiant soldier he had ever known. Styrkar is the marshal now.'

Another chill swept over me. Ulf Ospaksson had been Harald's marshal ever since Harald had come to the throne. Ulf was the most level-headed of the military advisers. It was Ulf who had opposed the idea of the invasion of England, and now that he was gone, there was no one to rein in Harald's reckless ambition to be another Knut.

The blood was pounding in my ears.

'Steady, Thorgils. Easy now.' It was Skule behind me.

'I must speak with Harald,' I repeated. It seemed to me that I was wading through a swamp of indifference. 'He has to reshape his campaign.'

'Why are you so agitated, Thorgils?' said one of the other councillors soothingly. 'You've only just got here and already you're wanting to change the king's mind. Everything has been working out just as planned. These English troops aren't as fearsome as their reputation. We gave them a thrashing just five days ago. We advanced on York as soon as we had got off our ships. The garrison came out to fight, led by a couple of their local earls. They blocked our road, and it was a fair fight, though perhaps we had a slight advantage in numbers. Harald led us brilliantly. Just as he always does. They came at us first. Hit us hard with a bold charge against our right wing. For a while it looked as if they might even overwhelm our men, but then Harald led the counter-attack and took them in the flank. Rolled up their line in double-quick time, and the next thing they knew we had them penned up against marshy ground, and nowhere to go. That was when we punished them. We killed so many that we walked on corpses as though the quagmire was solid ground. The city surrendered, of course, and now Harald's gone off to collect the tribute and stores the city fathers promised, as well as hostages for good behaviour in the future. He won't be long. You might as well stay here until he returns to camp. Or maybe you would prefer to give your information to Prince Olaf, who will tell his father when he gets back.'

'No,' I said firmly, 'my message is for Harald himself, and it cannot wait. Can someone arrange for me to have a horse so that I can try to overtake the army?'

The councillor shrugged. 'We didn't bring many horses with us on the fleet – we needed the ship space for men and weapons. But we've captured a few animals locally, and if you look around the camp, maybe you'll find one that suits. Harald can't have gone far.'

I lost more time trying to locate a horse, and succeeded only in finding a starveling pack pony. But the scrawny little creature was better than nothing, and before the troops had finished their breakfast I was riding away from the ships and along the trail that Harald and his army had taken as they marched north.

'Tell him we need some good juicy cattle,' a soldier yelled after me as I left the outskirts of the camp. 'Something to get our

teeth into instead of stale bread and mouldy cheese. And as much
beer as he can bring back. This weather makes a man thirsty.'

The soldier was right. The air had a dry, still feel. The sky
was cloudless, and soon the heat would be intense. Already the
ground was cracked in many places, baked hard by the sun, and I
could feel my pony's unshod hooves hammering down on the
unyielding surface.

It was easy to follow the army's trail. The dust was churned
up where the foot soldiers had tramped along, and occasionally
there were piles of dung left by the horses that Harald and his
leading men were riding. Their road followed the line of a small
river, the track keeping to the higher ground on its left bank, and
on both sides the low hills were desiccated and brown from the
summer drought. From time to time I could see the footmarks
where men had left the track and gone down to the water's edge
to slake their thirst. I saw nothing of the soldiery themselves,
except at one place where I came across a small detachment of
men guarding a pile of weapons and armour. At first I thought it
was captured material left behind by the enemy, but then I
recognised that the weaponry and shields and the thick leather
jerkins sewn with plates of metal belonged to our own men. They
must have taken them off and left them there, under guard, as it
was too hot to march in such heavy gear.

The soldiers told me that Harald and his army were not far
ahead, and sure enough I saw them in the distance when I topped
the next rise and found myself looking across a bend on the river.
The army was waiting on the far bank. Side tracks converged on
the main road shortly before it crossed a wooden bridge, and from
there the main road continued on up the far slope and over the
crest of the hill, leading directly to the city of York. It was a
natural crossroads and I could see why the place had been chosen
for the assembly point where the men of York would bring their
tribute.

I kicked my pony into one last effort, and came down into the valley. A handful of Harald's troops had not yet crossed the bridge, and my haste attracted their curious glances as I scurried past. Most of the men were sprawling on the ground in the sunshine. Many had stripped off their shirts and were bare-chested. Swords, helmets and shields lay where they had casually put them aside. A score of men were standing in the shallows of the river, splashing water on themselves to keep cool.

I clattered across the worn grey planks of the bridge. For a moment I thought of dismounting. The bridge was in poor repair, and there were wide cracks between the planks, but the little pony was sure-footed, and a moment later I was riding up the slope of the far bank towards a knot of men gathered around the royal standard. Even if the flag, Land Ravager, had not been flying from its pole, I would have recognised the little group as Harald's entourage. Harald himself was visible, towering above most men. His long yellow hair and drooping moustaches were unmistakable.

I slid off the pony's back, stumbling as my feet touched ground. It had taken me half the morning to reach Harald, and I felt stiff and saddle sore. I brushed aside the bodyguard who tried to intercept me as I approached Harald and his little group. They too looked completely at ease. Doubtless they were contemplating the pleasant task of how best to divide up the spoils. Among them I saw Tostig, half-brother of the English king. Until recently he had ruled these lands as its earl, but had been deposed. Now he had thrown in his lot with Harald, anticipating that he would regain his former title.

'My lord,' I called out as I approached the little group. 'I am glad to see you well. I have news from Frankia.'

Everyone in the little group turned to look at me. I realised that my voice had sounded cracked and harsh. My throat was dry and dusty from my ride.

'Thorgils. What brings you here?' asked Harald. There was an angry edge to his question. He was staring down at me from his great height, obviously irritated. I knew that he was thinking

I had abandoned my responsibilities. He would have preferred me to stay in Normandy, to act as his intermediary in dealing with Duke William.

'I had no choice, my lord. There are developments which you must know at once. I could not trust anyone else to bring the news.'

'What news is that?' Harald was scowling.

I decided that I had to be blunt. I needed to shock Harald into changing his plans, even if it meant drawing down his wrath on me.

'Duke William has betrayed you, my lord,' I said, adding hastily, 'It was my error. He used me as a tool to deceive you. He made me believe that he had agreed to your offer, and that he would time his invasion to coincide with yours. But that was never his intention. His fleet has not yet sailed. He is deliberately hanging back, giving time for the English king to attack you.'

For a long moment Harald's expression did not change. He continued to scowl at me, and then – to my surprise – he threw back his head and laughed.

'So Bastard William deceived me, did he? Well, so be it. Now I know what he is like, and that knowledge will be useful when we meet face to face and decide who really takes the realm of England. I'll make him regret his treachery. But he has miscalculated. Whoever beats Harold Godwinsson will hold the advantage. There's nothing like a recent victory to put heart into one's troops, and the English will follow the first victor. As soon as I have disposed of Harold Godwinsson, I'll drive William of Normandy back into the sea if he is so bold as to make his invasion. When he hears of my victory he may even cancel his invasion plans altogether.'

Once more, I sensed that I was swimming against a tide of events, and there was little that I could do.

'Duke William will not set aside his invasion, my lord. He has planned it down to the last detail, trained his troops, rehearsed, and committed all his resources to it. He may have as many as eight thousand fighting men. For him, there is no going back.'

'Nor for me,' Harald snapped. 'I came to take the realm of England and that is what I'll do.'

I fell silent, not knowing what to say.

Tostig intervened. 'Harold is far away. He has to march the length of England if he is to meet us on the battlefield. In the meantime our army will grow stronger. As people hear about us they will join our cause. Many in this region have Norse blood in their veins and trace their line back to the time of great Knut. The English will prefer to throw in their lot with us than with a gang of plundering Normans.'

Somewhere near us, a horse neighed. It was one of the handful of small Norwegian horses which Harald had brought with him. They were sturdy animals, ideal for long journeys across bleak moorland, but by no means as powerful as the battle chargers that I had seen in Normandy. I was wondering how they would withstand a charge of Norman knights, when someone said, 'At last! The good burghers of York are finally showing up.'

Everyone in our little group looked westward, up the slope of the hill towards the unseen city. A faint cloud of dust could be seen beyond the distant crest. The horse neighed again.

The first figures to come over the brow of the hill were indistinct, no more than dark shapes. I wiped away the sweat that was trickling down into my eyes. The black and white costume of a follower of the Rule could be very hot on a warm day. I should find myself a light cotton shirt and loose trousers and get rid of the Christian costume.

'That's not a cattle herd,' commented Styrkar, Harald's new marshal. 'Looks more like troops.'

'Reinforcements from the fleet, sent up by Prince Olaf so as not to miss the division of the booty.' The speaker sounded a little resentful.

'Where did they get all those horses, I wonder?' asked a

veteran, a note of puzzlement in his voice as he stared into the distance. 'That's cavalry, and a lot of it.'

King Harald had turned and was facing up the hill. 'Styrkar,' he asked softly. 'Did we post any sentinels on the hill?'

'No, my lord. I did not consider it necessary. Our scouts reported only a few peasants in the area.'

'Those are not peasants.'

Tostig was also watching the new arrivals. More and more men, both mounted and on foot, were coming over the brow of the hill. The leading ranks were beginning to descend the slope, fanning out to make room for those behind them.

'If I didn't know otherwise, I would say those are royal huscarls,' said Tostig. 'But that's impossible. Harold Godwinsson would always keep his huscarls with him. They are pledged to serve the king and guard his person.' He turned to me. 'When did you say Harold would know that the Norman fleet was delayed and was staying on in Frankia?'

'I didn't say,' I replied, 'but my guess is that Duke William deliberately planted that information on Harold soon after he left Dives. That would be about twelve days ago.'

Styrkar was making his calculation. 'Let's say it was ten days ago, and then allow Godwinsson two days in which to consult his councillors and make his plans. That would give him a little more than a week to march north and get here. It's difficult but not impossible. Those troops could be led by Harold Godwinsson himself.'

'If it is Harold,' said Tostig, 'it might be wise to fall back to our ships and gather the rest of our forces.'

But Harald seemed unperturbed. 'Well, if it does prove to be Harold, then he's got here by forced marches, and his troops will be footsore and weary. That makes them ripe for slaughter.'

He gave a snort of confidence, and I could see how his faith in his own success as a military commander was unshakeable. In the past decade he had never lost a major fight, and now he was certain that his battle luck would hold. Godwinsson, as far as Harald was concerned, was offering himself for defeat. With growing dread, I knew differently. I recalled the details of my nightmare on the night before Harald returned from Kiev on his splendid ship with silken sails. I had dreamed of a great fleet and its tall commander struck down by an arrow at the moment of victory, and when I had voiced my fears, I had been told that I had seen the death of the Greek general Maniakes, Harald's near double. Now, far too late, the image sprang into my mind of the great assembly of Harald's longships drawn up on shore or lying at anchor in the shallows of the river just ten miles away. That spectacle, I knew with absolute certainty, was the true fulfilment of my dream. Yet again I had failed. Years ago I should have warned Harald about the macabre portent.

'If it is Harold Godwinsson, then we had better get the formalities concluded,' Harald continued. He looked about him, caught my eye, and said, 'Thorgils. You're just the man. You can be my herald in your black and white gown.' He smiled grimly. 'They won't attack a man of the cloth, even if he's a fraud. Ride out and ask for a parlay.'

Knowing that I was being swept along by events over which I had no control, I walked back to where my pack pony was hopefully nuzzling the earth, trying to find a few wisps of dried-up grass. I felt that I was no more than a puppet in some vast and cruel game being played out by unseen powers. My legs ached as I hauled myself back on to the wooden saddle and plucked on the rope reins. Reluctantly, the pony lifted its head and began to walk. Its legs, too, were stiff and painful. Slowly, almost apologetically, the little pony and I climbed up the slope. Ahead of us, more and more English foot soldiers and cavalry were appearing over the ridge and taking up their positions across the hillside. The Norwegians below me were no longer relaxing in the sunshine. They had scrambled to their feet and were searching for the weapons and shields they had laid aside. There was no sense of order or discipline. They looked towards Harald and his councillors, waiting for instructions, and they watched me on my pony slowly plod towards the hostile army.

I noted a cluster of banners among the English cavalry, and veered in that direction. As I rode along the front rank of the English line, the foot soldiers called out, asking what I wanted. I ignored them. Around the banners was a group of some twenty men. All were mounted. I made a mental note to tell Harald that many of the English troops now massing behind their leaders were also on horseback. That would explain how Harold Godwinsson had managed to travel so quickly and take us by surprise. At least a third of his force were cavalry, and I guessed that the remainder were levies that he had collected locally.

The gleam of a sword hilt caught my attention, a dull yellow glint among the riders. I looked again, and knew that the ranks of horsemen nearest the banners were royal huscarls, Godwinsson's personal force, the finest troops in England. Since Knut's time they had carried gold-hilted swords. Many of them also carried spears, while others had long-handled axes dangling from their saddles. I wondered whether they would choose to fight on horseback or on foot.

'King Harald of Norway wishes to talk with your leader,' I called out when I was close enough to the group around the banners for them to hear me distinctly. They were English nobles, all wearing costly chain-mail shirts and helmets decorated with badges of rank. Their horses were tall, strong-boned animals, not nearly as massive as the Norman destriers, but far superior to the smaller Norwegian horses in Harald's army.

I reined in my little pack pony and waited at a safe distance. I saw the group confer among themselves, and then half a dozen came forward at a trot. Among them a tall, heavily moustached man rode a particularly handsome chestnut stallion. There was something about his bearing, the way that he sat in the saddle, that told me at once that this was Harold Godwinsson himself, the king of England, though he was careful to remain among his companions as if he was just another rider.

'Tell King Harald that there is nothing of substance to discuss. But the King of England, grants him an audience. He may speak with the king's herald,' came a shout.

I was fairly sure that it was Godwinsson who had spoken. It was an old trick for a leader to pretend to be his own spokesman. Harald had often used it himself.

I turned and waved to Harald and his entourage, beckoning them forward.

The two groups, evenly matched in numbers, met midway between the two armies. They halted their horses, careful not to get within a sword's length of one another, and I thought to myself, as I watched them, how very similar they were. All were bearded and moustached, with hair that was mostly blond or light brown, and all of them seemed to be both haughty and suspicious as they eyed one another across the narrow gap. The main difference was in the shields they carried. Those of Harald's men who had wisely brought their armour carried round shields, brightly painted with war emblems, while several of the English riders held longer, narrow shields with a tapering lower edge. I had seen these same shields among Duke William's men and knew that on horseback they gave an advantage, for they protected a rider's lower leg as well as the vulnerable flank of his horse. It was another warning, I thought to myself, that I should give to Harald.

The exchange between the two groups was brief. The rider who purported to be the royal spokesman – more than ever I was sure that it was the English king himself – demanded to know with what purpose the Norwegian army was trespassing on England's soil. Styrkar, the royal marshal, replied for the Norwegians. 'King Harald has come to claim the throne of England which is his by right. His ally and companion, Tostig here, has come to claim what is also his by right – the earldom of Northumbria, of which he was unjustly deprived.'

'Tostig and his men may remain, provided they stay in peace,' came the answer. 'The King of England gives his word that he will be reinstated in his earldom. He will, in addition, grant Tostig one-third of the realm.'

Now I was sure that Godwinsson himself was speaking, for the speaker had made no attempt to confer with his colleagues. It also occurred to me that the parlay was no more than play-acting. Tostig must have recognised his half-brother, the English king, yet he was pretending that he did not know him. The entire meeting was a sham.

Tostig spoke up. 'And if I accept that offer, what lands will you give to Harald Sigurdsson, the King of Norway?'

Hard as a blow of a fist to the teeth came back the unrelenting reply, 'He will receive seven feet of English ground. Enough to bury him. Or more, as he is much taller than other men.'

The two groups of riders stiffened in their saddles. Their horses, sensing the sudden surge in tension, began to fidget. One of the English riders slapped his reins on his animal's neck to make the creature calm down.

To his credit, Tostig soothed the situation before it broke into open violence. 'Tell the King of England,' he called out, still keeping up the pretence that he did not recognise his own half-brother, 'that it will never be said that Tostig, the true Earl of Northumbria, brought King Harald of Norway across the sea in order to betray him.' Then he turned his horse and began to ride away down the hill. The parlay was over.

Kicking my pony into a trot, I hurried to rejoin Harald's group. I rode up behind Harald in time to hear him ask Tostig, 'Who was that who spoke for the English? He had a deft way with words.'

'That was Godwinsson,' Tostig replied. Harald was obviously taken aback by the answer. He had not intended to compliment his rival.

'Not a bad-looking man,' he acknowledged, then drew himself

to his full height so he sat very tall in the saddle, and added, 'but a little puny.'

On the threshold of a battle, Harald's vanity was dangerous, I thought to myself. Combined with his self-belief, it could lead us into disaster. It was unlikely that he would compromise his pride by ordering a strategic withdrawal to the fleet. In his eyes, that would seem too much like an abject retreat.

We came back down the hill to rejoin the Norwegian troops with Styrkar shouting to our men that they were to fall back across the bridge and take up a defensive position on the far slope. At least our marshal was not blind to our danger. If we remained where we were, the English would be attacking us downhill. Nevertheless, our withdrawal was a scrambled affair, the men gathering up their weapons and converging on the little bridge with no sense of order or discipline. They jostled their way across the loose planks of the bridge in an untidy torrent, and made their way up the far slope where they began to regroup.

Seeing the backs of their enemies, the English forces took their chance to try to turn the Norwegian withdrawal into a rout. A detachment of their cavalry came cantering down the hill and closed with our stragglers. It was not a concerted attack so much as a haphazard onslaught to take advantage of the moment. I had already crossed the bridge with Harald and his entourage, and looked back to see a chaotic engagement unfold. Isolated bands of Norwegian warriors or single individuals were ducking and dodging as they tried to evade the lances and swords of the English horsemen. There were occasional shouts of defiance and whoops of anger as our men turned and tried to fight back against their mounted opponents. I could see that the English forces were relishing the advantage of surprise. They knew that they had taken the Norwegians completely unawares, and this gave them a powerful advantage.

As I watched the confused fighting, my attention was caught by an extraordinary sight. Slowly making its way through the skirmish, as if nothing out of the ordinary was happening, was an ordinary farm cart. It was the sort of vehicle which might be found in any modest farmyard, a simple wooden platform on two solid wheels drawn by a single horse. On the back of the cart were several sacks of grain, some barrels, and, bizarrely, several chickens trussed up and hanging head down in batches. I could only suppose that the carter was one of those engaged to bring supplies to the Norwegian army as part of the tribute from the citizens of York, and he had blundered into the fight inadvertently. Now he was petrified by the danger in which he found himself and too scared to react, while his horse between the shafts was an ancient nag, half blind and deaf. Even as I watched, the cart reached the approaches to the bridge, and the elderly horse stopped in puzzlement, gazing at the press of struggling men which blocked its path.

The last of the Norwegians' rearguard – those who had not been cut down by the English – had reached the bridge. They were more disciplined than their fellows, and had formed up in a squad which turned to face the enemy; now the men were retreating step by step. As they passed the stationary cart, one of the Norwegian fighters reached up and pulled the driver from his seat, sending the poor wretch flying. Moments later, the cart horse disappeared, as the bewildered animal, its harness cut, galloped away. A dozen hands grabbed the cart and wheeled it to the middle of the bridge, where it was overturned to act as a barricade to delay the English advance. Moments later the Norwegian rearguard was running up the slope to rejoin the rest of Harald's troops.

The overturned cart did not block the bridge completely: there was a gap between the cart and the bridge's edge barely an arm's span in width, but sufficient to allow a man to pass. In this opening a single Norwegian warrior now took up his stance, facing the enemy. He had a fighting axe in one hand, a heavy sword in the other. Who he was I would never know, but he must have know that his position was suicidal. He was making it clear that, single-handed, he would hold the gap until his own side had taken up their battle formation. He challenged the English to come forward and fight him. For a bleak moment I wondered if that lone warrior was not like myself, a forlorn dreamer defying the inevitable.

Still, the English hesitated. Then one of their cavalrymen rode out on to the bridge, his spear poised. But the moment the horse stepped on the loose planks, the animal shied and would go no farther. With an angry wrench of his reins, the cavalryman turned his horse and rode back to solid ground. A second rider attempted the bridge, but his mount also baulked. So it was an English foot soldier who advanced to accept the Norwegian's challenge. Judging by his long coat of mail, the Englishman was one of Harold's professional soldiers, a royal huscarl, and he advanced with a confident step, sword in hand, scorning even to lift his shield. It was his fatal error. He was not yet within reach of the Norwegian when, without warning, his opponent flung his axe. The weapon whirled across the gap and struck the huscarl in the mouth, felling him instantly. With a satisfied whoop the Norwegian ran forward, bent down to retrieve his weapon and, moments later, was running back to take up his position once again. There he clashed his sword and axe together defiantly, daring the next to come forward and fight him.

Three more times an English huscarl accepted the challenge, and each time failed to clear the passage. The Norwegian champion was a master of hand-to-hand fighting. He killed one challenger with a sword thrust through the body, decapitated the second with a swiping back-handed axe blow that seemed to come from nowhere, and deftly tripped up the third attacker who had come close enough to grapple with him, then pushed him over the edge of the bridge into the river below. Each encounter was met with groans or cheers by the two armies watching the spectacle from each side of the river, and for a time it seemed that the Norwegian champion was invincible.

'He can't hold out for ever,' someone beside me muttered.

'Eventually the English will bring up their archers and shoot him down.'

'No,' countered another voice. 'The huscarls want to claim the victory for themselves. They won't let some common bowman take the credit. Look there, upstream.'

I glanced to my right. Drifting down the river on the gentle current was a small boat. Little bigger than a washtub, it was a humble punt that some farmer would use to paddle his way across the river rather than make a detour to reach the bridge. In the boat sat an armoured English huscarl, his weight almost swamping the little craft, and he was paddling with his hands to keep the boat in mid-river where it would pass directly under the Norwegian's position.

'Look out, beware to your right,' someone shouted, trying to warn the Norwegian. But our champion was too far away to hear, and the cluster of huscarls on the far end of the bridge had already begun to set up a deafening chant, beating rhythmically on their shields to drown out the sound of any warnings. As the little boat neared the bridge, two huscarls stepped out from their ranks and began to advance deliberately towards the barricade. This time they took no chances. Both carried long shields, and they crouched down behind them to protect themselves from another axe throw. The Norwegian had no choice but to wait until they were within sword range, and then he struck, hacking down with his axe and sword hoping to beat down their guard. But the two huscarls stayed behind their shields, knees bent and deflecting the blows, only occasionally making a stabbing thrust with their own swords in counter-threat.

Helplessly we watched from our vantage point, knowing what would happen. The Norwegian's stamina was extraordinary. He continued to rain down blows on the two huscarls until the moment came when his opponents judged that the man in the boat was directly under the bridge. Then they rose up and hurled themselves forward. The Norwegian retreated back a pace so that he stood in the narrowest part of the gap between the cart and the edge of the bridge, and there he traded blows with his attackers. But it was exactly where they wanted him. Even as the Norwegian concentrated on fending off the huscarls' frontal attack, we saw the boatman grab one of the timbers supporting the underside of the ancient bridge and bring his little craft to a stop. Then he stood up, and, still holding on to the bridge with one hand he brought his spear up vertically and slid it through a gap between the planks. There he waited, the spear pointing upwards, while his comrades gradually pushed the Norwegian champion back to the precise spot. Then, suddenly, the boatman thrust upwards with his spear, the iron point driving straight into the Norwegian's crutch, unprotected by his long shirt of chain mail. The surprise attack spitted the Norwegian. He doubled forward, clutching at his groin, and one of his opponents took the chance to step forward and chop down with his sword at the gap below the helmet, killing his foe with a blow to the back of the neck. The fight was over, and even as the Norwegian body splashed down into the river, a squad of huscarls was running forward to lay hold of the upturned cart, drag it to the edge of the bridge, and heave it over.

Moments later the advance guard of Harold's army began to clatter across the open bridge and advance towards us, led by a file of mounted huscarls. Watching their confident approach, I recalled Ulf Ospaksson's words when he had tried to dissuade Harald from invading England. Then he had said that one English huscarl was reputed to be worth two of the best of Norway's fighting men. Now we would learn the truth of the dead marshal's warning.

FIFTEEN

'FALL BACK, MY LORD, fall back.' Strykar was still pleading with Harald. 'Let us make a fighting retreat. It is best we make our stand near the ships when the rest of our men have joined us.'

'No!' retorted Harald sharply. 'We make our stand here. Let the rest of our forces come to join us. Send riders to summon them. They must come at once or they will miss our victory.'

The look on Styrkar's face made it clear that he disagreed profoundly with Harald's decision, but he was in no position to argue with his king. The marshal beckoned to three of our few horsemen.

'Ride to the ships. Spread out so that at least one of you gets through,' he ordered. 'Ask Prince Olaf to send up the rest of the army and not lose a moment, or they may arrive too late. They must get here before dusk.'

The marshal glanced up at the sky. The sun was past its zenith, still blazing from a clear blue sky. I saw the marshal's lips move, and I wondered to which God he was praying. He lacked Harald's utter conviction that our ill-prepared army would survive the English attack, and when I had watched the three riders kick their mounts into a gallop and ride back along the trail we had taken, I took a moment to count how many horsemen still remained. There were fewer than fifty.

Harald, by contrast, was behaving with as much swagger and self-assurance as if he, not the king of England, held the advantage. He cut a regal figure in a cloak of richly ornamented blue brocade and his customary browband of scarlet silk to hold back his shaggy blond hair. To complete the dashing effect he was mounted on a glossy black stallion with a white blaze, a trophy from his victory three days earlier and the only blood horse in our company. But he was not dressed in Emma, his famous full-length shirt of chain mail said to be impenetrable by any weapon. Emma, like so much of our body armour, had been left behind with the fleet.

'Form shield wall!' bellowed Strykar, and the cry was taken up and passed along by the veterans in our army. Our men began to shuffle into position, shoulder to shoulder, the rims of their round, leather-covered shields overlapping. 'Extend the line!'

The marshal rode out a little way in front of our troops and turned to face the men. He was mounted on a tough little Norwegian pony, and was gesturing to indicate that the shield wall should be as wide as possible.

Suddenly Harald shouted, 'Wait!' He rode forward and, turning to face his men, he called out, 'In honour of this battle, I have composed a poem.' Then, to my mingled astonishment and pride, he proceeded to declaim:

> 'We go forward
> into battle
> without armour
> against blue blades.
> Helmets glitter.
> My coat of mail
> And all our armour
> Are at the ships.'

I found a lump was gathering in my throat. Not for a generation had any war leader in the northern lands been suffi-ciently skilled in the old traditions to be able to compose a paean on the eve of a battle. Harald was honouring a custom that had almost passed from use. It was a mark of his deep-felt longing to restore the glory of the Norse kingdoms, and for all his vanity and arrogance I loved him for it. Yet even as I felt the tug of admiration and remembered the oath which I had sworn to serve him, I knew in my heart that it was all a show. Harald was seeking to encourage his men, but the harsh truth would reveal itself when the arrows began to fly and the two armies locked in battle.

Harald was not finished. His horse was giving trouble, fidgeting and turning from side to side, so that there was a short pause while Harald brought his mount back under control. Then he shouted at his troops, 'That was a poor verse for such a momentous occasion! This one is better. Remember it as you fight!' and he proceeded to declaim:

> 'We never kneel in battle
> Before the storm of weapons
> and crouch behind our shields;
> So the noble lady told me.
> She told me once to carry
> my head always high in battle
> where swords seek to shatter
> the skulls of doomed warriors.'

When his words died away, a strange silence fell. Some of our men in the army, the older ones at least, had grasped the sombre import of Harald's words. From them came a low murmur. Others, I am sure, were not close enough to hear the king, while still more would have lacked the knowledge to understand the significance of his verse. Harald was warning us that we could be facing our final battle. For a moment there was a brooding lull, and from it emerged an eerie sound. A harp was being played somewhere in our ranks. Whoever had brought the instrument was a mystery. Probably it was one of those small light harps favoured by the northern English, and the harpist had picked it up on the earlier battlefield and brought it with him instead of his weapons. Whatever the reason, the first few clear notes hung in the air as a doleful lament. It was as if the harpist was playing a sorrowful tribute to our coming downfall.

As I and the army listened to the melancholy tune, it seemed as if the entire host was holding its collective breath. Not a sound came from the English lines. They too must have been listening. Then, cutting across the tune, came another sound, equally unexpected. In that hot, airless afternoon a single rooster crowed. The creature must have escaped from the toppled cart at the bridge, and now, for some unknown reason, it chose to let loose its raucous call, jarring across the plangent notes of the harp.

Once again Styrkar was bellowing at the top of his voice. 'Extend the line, extend the line. Wings fall back, form circle.' Slowly the flanks of our shield wall curved, the outer men stepping backward, glancing over their shoulders so that they did not trip, until our entire line had re-formed into a ring. In the first and second ranks stood those men who wore some of their armour, and all of our veterans. Behind them, within the circle, waited our archers and hundreds of our troops who were virtually defence-less. They wore no body armour, and some even lacked helmets. They clutched only their swords and daggers, and wore shirts and leggings, nothing more. When it came to a fight, they would be fatally vulnerable.

Harald and Strykar rode the perimeter, checking the shield wall. 'You are facing cavalry,' Styrkar called out. 'So remember, front rank direct the points of your spears at the riders. Second rank, plant the butts of your spears in the ground and hold them steady, aim lower, at the horses themselves. Above all, keep the line intact. Do not let the English break through. Should that happen, leave the king himself and our own horsemen to deal with the intruders. We will be waiting inside the ring behind you, ready to ride to any point where there is need.'

Harald and the marshal made the full circuit of our shield wall, and as they turned and began to ride in, preparing to take up their places, Harald's black stallion put its foot into a hole and stumbled. Harald lost his balance. He clutched at the animal's mane to steady himself, but too late. He lurched forward over the stallion's shoulder and tumbled to the ground while the startled horse danced away. Harald kept hold of the reins and pulled the stallion back to him, but the harm was done. The watching troops let out a groan, seeing the poor omen. But Harald laughed it off as he rose and dusted himself off. 'No matter,' he shouted, 'a fall means that fortune is on its way,' and rode into the shield ring. But many of his troops looked uneasy and afraid.

On my humble pack pony I found myself with the mounted force in the centre of our defensive circle. I glanced around nervously, looking for someone to lend me a weapon to carry. But everyone was preoccupied, watching the enemy. Harald, Tostig, Styrkar and two squadrons of perhaps twenty riders each were all we had to plug any breaches in the shield wall; all the rest of our army was on foot. By contrast the entire first wave of the English army now advancing against us was composed of mounted cavalry – huscarls armed with long spears and lances.

Perhaps the wild courage of the lone defender of the bridge had made the English cautious. Our battlefield was on an expanse of rough pasture sloping gently towards the river, open ground ideal for cavalry, yet the English horsemen appeared hesitant in their initial attack. Their riders came at us, cantering to within range, then thrusting tentatively with their spears at our shield wall before turning away and riding clear. There was no massed shock charge like that I had witnessed in Sicily when the Byzantine kataphract destroyed the Saracens, nor the crashing onslaught I had seen the Norman heavy horsemen rehearse. The English cavalry simply came, engaged, and then withdrew.

For a while I was puzzled. Why did the English not launch a mass attack? Harold Godwinsson must have seen that we had despatched riders to call up reinforcements from the fleet. As soon as the fresh troops arrived, the English would lose their advantage. The more I puzzled, the less I understood Godwinsson's tactics.

Only when the English cavalry had made their fifth or perhaps
the sixth probing attack, did I begin to grasp what was happening.
The English huscarls intended to wear us down. Each time they
rode up and engaged our front ranks in combat, several score of
our men were killed or badly wounded, while the English horsemen rode away virtually unscathed. Our shield wall was slowly
weakening as more of our reserves had to step forward and fill
the gaps. By forming a defensive ring, Harald and Styrkar had
lost the initiative. The English controlled the battlefield. They
were bleeding us to death.

As that long, cruel afternoon wore on, our circle slowly
contracted and the men within it grew more hot and thirsty under
the broiling sun. The English, by contrast, took water from the
river to quench their thirst and launched their attacks whenever
they wished. Soon they were riding right around the shield wall,
almost casually, selecting the weakest points. Our army was like a
wild ox in the forest surrounded by a pack of wolves. We could
only stand and face our foes, and present our best defence.

'Can't put up with much more of this,' said a veteran
Norwegian. He had been in the front rank and had fallen back
after receiving a lance thrust in his shield arm. 'Just give me a
chance to get close enough to those English horsemen, and I'll
make sure that they leave their bones here.' He finished tying the
makeshift bandage around his bleeding arm, and before he strode
away to take his place once again in the shield wall, he looked up
at me. 'You haven't got a flagon of water to hand have you, old
man? Some of the lads with me are truly parched.'

I shook my head. I was feeling tired and useless, too weary to
fight and burdened with the knowledge that my failings had
contributed to our predicament. Soon afterwards there was another
war cry, and once again the mounted huscarls were cantering
down towards us. This time, I noted, far fewer arrows flew
through the air to greet them. Our archers were running out of
arrows.

Suddenly Harald was in front of me. There was something

half-crazed about his appearance. He was sweating heavily, the perspiration running down his face, dark stains of sweat at his armpits. His black stallion was equally distraught: foam dripped from its mouth, and there was white sweat on its powerful neck where the reins touched.

'Styrkar!' Harald snapped, 'we must do something. We have to counter-attack!'

'No, my lord, no,' said the marshal. 'It is better we hold on, wait for the reinforcements to arrive. Only a few hours more.'

'By then we'll all be dead of thirst if not from the English spears,' said Harald, glancing towards the English huscarls. 'Just one good charge will smash the enemy.'

As he was speaking, his horse put down its head and tried to buck his rider off. In his frustration Harald snarled with anger and rapped the stallion between the ears with the flat of his sword. The horse only became more skittish, rearing and plunging, as Harald, who had already fallen from the saddle once that day, tried to control his mount. The members of his entourage scattered out of the way to avoid the highly strung animal. Only my small pack pony, still exhausted from our long ride, stood firm. Harald's stallion careered into us, and I was almost knocked from the saddle.

'Get out of my way,' Harald snarled at me. He was puce from anger.

Looking up into his face as I scrambled to my feet, I saw the battle gleam in his eyes. Harald was losing control of himself, just as he had lost control of the battlefield.

Just then there arose a great cry from our troops, a swelling roar of exultation. They were brandishing swords and axes above their heads as if in victory. Beyond them I could see the backs of the retreating English cavalry. Once again the huscarls' charge against the shield wall had been rebuffed, and they were pulling back. Whether at that moment it was Harald's anger, or a genuine misunderstanding by our men, or that their pent-up frustration simply boiled over, I shall never know, but the sight of the

English cavalry falling back was seen as a full retreat, and our shield wall erupted. Our soldiers, both veterans as well as raw recruits, broke ranks. They abandoned all discipline and spontaneously charged forward in a broken mass, chasing after the retreating English cavalry, shouting at them to turn and fight, then veering off to run at the English infantry where they stood waiting to engage in the battle. It was a disastrous error.

Even then, I think, Harald could have saved the day. He could have ridden forward, shown himself ahead of his troops, ordered them to re-form the shield wall, and they would have obeyed him. But just at that critical moment Harald's black stallion bolted. The panicked horse galloped straight ahead of the Norwegian charge, and it seemed to every man there that Harald himself was leading the assault. From that moment forward, the battle was lost.

I watched, aghast. I had seen William's Norman knights rehearse how to defeat the shield wall by pretending to flee, then turning on their disorganised pursuers as they were drawn out of position. But that had been practice, and what I now witnessed was real. The English cavalry stayed clear of the pursuing Norwegian infantry, and then swerved aside, leaving their own foot soldiers to take the brunt of the Norwegian onslaught. Harald's men had already been run off their legs when the Norsemen's charge burst on to the English levies, and the impact was irregular and ineffective. The two sides mingled in a seething mass of violence, the men hacking and stabbing and slashing at one another. There was no sense of purpose, only that both infantries were desperate to inflict the greatest damage on one another.

Harald himself stood out like a beacon in a sea of turmoil. Seated high on his horse, whose frantic run had been halted by the mass of men, he could be seen fighting like a berserk warrior from the ancient days. He had neither shield nor armour, but held a long-shafted, single-bladed axe in each hand, his favoured weapons since his days in the Varangian guard. He was roaring out in anger. Each of his axes would normally have required a

two-handed grip, but Harald was such a giant that he could wield
them one in each hand. All around him the English foot soldiers
were attempting to dodge his furious sweeping blows and, too
slow, were falling to his attack. I tried to calculate where Harald
was heading, and whether there was some purpose to his frantic
advance, but I could see no selected target for his wrath. The
English cavalry had withdrawn to one side and were regrouping,
waiting for the right moment to ride to the rescue of their
infantry. Among them I thought I recognised Harold Godwinsson,
but he was too far away for me to be certain. Harald himself was
oblivious to the gathering danger. His own battle flag, Land
Ravager, was nowhere to be seen. His standard-bearer had been
left far behind in the mad forward gallop.

Like hundreds of his own men, I looked towards Harald
himself, waiting for a signal telling us what to do. Without his
guidance we were lost. And as I did so, I saw the arrow fly.
Perhaps it was my imagination, but I was sure I saw a dark blur
skim over the heads of the struggling infantry, drawn fatally
towards the tall figure on the black stallion. It remains a moment
frozen in time for me: I saw the scarlet headband on Harald's
brow, the blue cloak flung back over one shoulder so that his
arms were free, and the two deadly axes rising and falling
remorselessly as he hacked his way through the press of soldiers.
His personal bodyguards had fallen back, hindered by the throng
of men, but even if they had been close to him they could have
done nothing to save their master. The arrow struck Harald in
the windpipe. Later I heard it said that Harald's war cry was cut
short into a single, choking gasp that turned to a bubbling grunt.
All I saw from a distance was Harald suddenly sway in the saddle,
stay upright for several heartbeats, and then slowly topple backwards, his tall figure disappearing into the chaos of the battle.

At that appalling moment, as those Norwegians close to the
dying king halted in dismay, Harold Godwinsson unleashed his
mounted huscarls at us. He sent them against our northern flank,
even as word was spreading across the battlefield that Harald

Sigurdsson was struck down. The news, which elated the hard-pressed English infantry, shocked our own embattled men. Not one of them had dared imagine that Harald the Hard Ruler would ever be killed in battle. He had seemed invulnerable. From a dozen major battles and countless skirmishes he had emerged alive and as the victor. Now, suddenly, he was gone, and there was no one to take his place. Our troops faltered.

The mounted English troops smashed into the demoralised Norwegian foot soldiers and shattered what little was left of their formation. The riders tore great gaps through the disorganised mob of our men, cutting them down as if they were huddled sheep. At first the huscarls used their spears as lances, but then they abandoned these weapons and drew their swords or unslung their axes because the slaughter was so easy. Our men were confused and defenceless. They attempted to parry the attacks with whatever was to hand – staves, clubs, their daggers – but it was futile against an armed huscarl mounted on his horse and swinging a heavy sword or the deadly long-shafted fighting axe. It was a massacre. The huscarls rode back and forth through our men like reapers clearing a field of standing corn, and those they left on their feet were set upon by the triumphant English infantry who rushed in to increase the carnage.

Weaponless, and still wearing my monk's gown, I sat on the little pony watching the disaster unfold. Despite all my forebodings, I was still unprepared for the extent of the catastrophe. This, I knew, was a defeat from which there could be no recovery. Never again would my people muster such a large army nor follow a leader with so much to offer us. This was annihilation, the final calamity, and I grieved to see Harald killed. But even as I mourned, I found consolation in knowing that the man to whom I had sworn allegiance would have preferred to die with honour on the battlefield than fade away, old and pain-racked, in his bed, knowing that he had failed in his great ambition to restore the greatest kingdom of the north. The disappointment would have embittered Harald for the rest of his days. I told myself that even in defeat, he had earned himself exactly what he would have wished: an honourable reputation that would never fade.

With that thought in mind I nudged my pony in the ribs and rode down the hill to retrieve Harald's body.

All my life I have known moments when a strange sensation of physical invulnerability comes over me. It is as if I am no longer aware of what my limbs are doing. My mind goes numb and I feel that I am advancing down a long, brightly lit tunnel where nothing can do me harm. That was how I felt as I rode forward on a tired pack pony that hot afternoon through the shattered fragments of a defeated army. I was vaguely aware of the crumpled corpses of our men lying on the ground, their blood and urine darkening the dust around them. Occasionally I heard the groans of the wounded. Here and there was a slight movement as some poor wretch tried to drag himself upright or to crawl away and hide. In the distance small bands of Norwegians were still putting up some resistance, but they were surrounded and outnumbered by their opponents, who were moving in to finish them. Somehow I was ignored.

I rode towards the last place I had seen Harald, the spot where he had toppled from his horse. A small cluster of men was gathered around something on the ground. They were bending over it, pulling and tugging. As I approached, my pony stumbled. Looking down I saw that it had tripped on a broken wooden pole, its end splintered. The flag attached to it was Land Ravager, Harald's personal standard. Nearby lay the body of his standard-bearer, a great gaping wound in his chest. He, like the others, had worn no armour. I reined the pony to a halt, got down and picked up the banner. Only a few feet of the pole remained. With Land Ravager in my hand I walked towards the group of men, leading the pack pony. Irrationally I thought that somehow I would be able to load Harald's corpse on the pony and ride back to the fleet, unscathed.

The men were English foot soldiers. They were stripping Harald's body of valuables. His fine blue cloak was already gone, and someone was tugging at the heavy gold rings on his fingers. Another man was pulling off a shoe of soft leather. Harald's body lay face up, a great dusty bruise across his cheek. The arrow that killed him was clearly visible. It had passed right through his neck. But that I had already dreamed.

'Stop that!' I croaked. 'Stop! I have come to collect the body.'

The looters looked up in surprise and irritation. 'Clear off, father,' said one of them. 'Go say your prayers in another place.' He unsheathed his dagger and was about to saw off one of Harald's fingers. Something clicked inside my mind and I passed from my distant reverie into sheer rage.

'You bastards!' I shouted. 'You defile the dead.' Letting go of the pony's reins, I raised the broken shaft of Land Ravager and struck at the looter. But I was too old and slow. Contemptuously he knocked aside the pole and I almost overbalanced.

'Clear off,' he repeated.

'No!' I yelled back at him. 'He is my lord. I must have his corpse.'

The looter looked at me narrowly. 'Your lord?' he said. I did not answer but took another lunge at him with the pole. Again, he knocked aside the blow. 'How come he is your lord, old man?'

I realised that I made a strange sight: an elderly priest in a long black gown, his bald pate showing stubble, and wielding a broken wooden pole. The other looters had moved away from Harald's corpse and were forming up in a circle around me. I was trembling with anger and exhaustion.

'Let me have the body,' I shouted. My voice was thin and wavering.

'Come and get it,' jeered one of the men.

I ran at him, using the pole as a lance, but he dodged aside. I pulled up and turned to see that his comrades had again taken up their positions around me and were laughing. I lunged again. The pole was heavy in my hands, and the long skirts of my monkish gown hampered me. I tripped.

'Over here, grandad,' taunted another voice, and I spun round to see someone dangling Harald's scarlet headband from the tip of his dagger. 'You'll need this,' he jeered.

The sweat was running down into my eyes so that I could scarcely see. I lumbered towards him and tried to snatch the headband, but it was whisked out of reach. I felt a thump in my ribs. One of my tormentors had struck me with the flat of his sword. I reeled away, trying to approach Harald's body. A foot reached out and I tripped headlong into the dust. The blood pounding in my ears, I picked myself up, and not knowing who or where I was striking, I swung Land Ravager in a circle, trying to keep my tormentors back. I heard their scornful laughter, then someone must have come up behind me and hit me, because I felt a terrible pain in my head as I slumped forward on my knees and then down on to my face.

Slowly everything began to go dark, and in the last fading moments something came into my mind which had been troubling me since the opening moments of the great battle. The hair rose on the back of my neck, and an icy cold shiver prickled my skin as the certainty came to me that the Old Ways were finally gone. As I slipped away into darkness, I recalled the prophesy of my own God, Odinn the All-knowing. He had foretold that Ragnarok, the last great battle, would be heralded by the sound of a harp played by Eggther, watchman of the giants, and that Gullinkambe the rooster, perched in Yggdrasil, the World Tree, would cry his final warning. Since the beginning of the world Gullinkambe had been waiting in the branches to announce the time when the forces of evil were unleashed and on the march. Together the two sounds, the harp and the rooster's crow, would herald the last great battle and the final destruction of the ancient ways.

SIXTEEN

TOSTIG RALLIED THE remnants of our army, so I was told later. One of our men picked up Land Ravager from where I lay on the earth, apparently lifeless, and brought the banner to Tostig, who was grimly fighting a rearguard action. He set up the flag as a mustering point, and those of our men who were still on their feet – less than a fifth of our original force – gathered there and formed a final shield wall. Seeing their plight, Harold Godwinsson offered them quarter. Defiantly, they refused. The English closed in and cut down all but a handful. Soon afterwards the Norwegian reinforcements from the fleet arrived, too few and too late. Most had made the same mistake of leaving behind their armour so that they could run all the faster from the ships. They appeared on the battlefield in small groups, disordered and out of breath. There was no doubting their courage, for they flung themselves on the English troops. The lightly equipped archers, first on the scene, did such damage that Godwinsson's troops quailed under the arrow storm. But when the archers had exhausted their stock of arrows, they lacked armoured infantry to protect them and were overwhelmed by the huscarls' counter-attack. The remaining stragglers of the relief force met a similar fate, finding themselves outnumbered by an enemy already flushed with triumph. By the end of that catastrophic day, the Norwegian force was virtually wiped out. The mounted huscarls harried the survivors back to the landing beach, where a handful saved themselves by swimming out to those ships which had been warped out into the river for safety. The remaining vessels were set ablaze by the victorious English.

I heard the details of the calamity in dribs and drabs, for I was on the point of death for many weeks and not expected to survive. A priest from York found me on the battlefield where he had gone the day after the great battle to pray over the dead. Scarcely breathing, I lay where I had fallen in the English battle line, and he presumed I had been with Godwinsson's men. I was brought back to York on a cart, along with the badly wounded, and nursed to health by the monks of the minster.

It took almost a full year for me to regain my strength because I had been badly hurt. There was a gaping gash on my skull – how I acquired it, I do not know – and it led my healers to suppose that my wits were addled by the blow. I had the good sense to encourage their error by pretending that I was not yet sound of mind and speaking little. Naturally I used the interval to watch and listen and acquire the information which allowed me to present myself as an itinerant priest swept up in Harold Godwinsson's lightning advance to the battlefield at a place called Stamford Bridge. This deception was made easier by my advanced years, for all the world knows that old people mend more slowly than the young, and later, when I made mistakes in my pretended guise, the errors were ascribed to an approaching dotage.

This prolonged convalescence gave me ample time to marvel at the gullibility of the monks of York. Not only did they think I was a devout and maundering colleague, but they readily swallowed the pap of misinformation fed to them in the official accounts of what had happened in the struggle for the throne of England. Frequently my tonsured companions would assert that all good Christians should give their unstinting support to the new king, William, because Christ had clearly shown himself to be on his side. Apparently William of Normandy – no one called him William the Bastard now – had disposed of Harold Godwins-son on the battlefield further south, in Hastings, just as effectively as Godwinsson had crushed Harald Sigurdsson nineteen days earlier. The proof of their God's favourable intervention, according to the monks, was that William's invasion fleet was held back on the north coast of Frankia by a headwind until 'by the grace of God' the wind changed to the south and allowed his barges to cross the sea unscathed to a landing unopposed by Godwinsson. I knew, of course, that 'the grace of God' had nothing to do with it. William the Bastard stayed on the Frankish coast until he knew his stratagem had succeeded and Harold had marched away to face the Norwegian army. In short, King William was not a virtuous believer rewarded for his piety, but a sly double-dealer who betrayed his ally.

But then, history – as is well known – is written by the victors, if it is written at all. It was with that commonplace in mind that I began to pen this account of my life which is now nearly at an end, and I suspect that Odinn himself had long prepared me for this task. It cannot have been entirely coincidental that I met the imperial chronicler, Constantine Psellus, when I was in the Varangian guard and observed his passion for telling an unvarnished history of the rulers of Miklagard. And I must admit that I enjoyed posing as a royal chronicler when I was on my way across Normandy to Duke William's court, even though that imposture was brief before I was exposed as a fraud. Now it amuses me that my deception is reversed: I find myself a genuine reporter of events, but one who writes in secret and cloaks his identity behind a monk's humility.

A question which has been puzzling me as I write my chronicle was answered as I composed these final pages. I used to wonder how the ways of the White Christ, apparently so meek, came to overwhelm the more robust tenets of my Elder Faith. Then, only yesterday, I was present when one of the local monks – it was the junior almoner – was recounting with breathless wonder how he had been in London and witnessed the court ceremony when a local magnate swore allegiance to the new sovereign, our pious and amulet-wearing William. The monk mimed the ceremony for our benefit: the solemn entrance of the nobleman, the king seated on the throne, the approach between ranks of courtiers, the bending of the knee, and the kissing of the regal hand. As the monk went down on his knees to illustrate the moment of homage, I noted the easy familiarity of his action. It was a gesture he repeated each day before the altar, and I recalled my lord Harald prostrate in submission on the marble floor before the throne of the Basileus, a ruler also declared to be a chosen instrument of that same God. Then I knew: the worship of the White Christ suits men who seek to dominate others. It is not the belief of the humble, but of despots and tyrants. When a man claims he is specially selected by the White Christ, then all those who follow that religion must treat him as if they are revering the God himself. That is why they go down in obedience before him. Often they even clasp their hands together as if in prayer.

This is a contradiction of all that the God is meant to stand for, yet I have witnessed how, among rulers of men, it is the truly ruthless and the ambitious who adopt the Christian faith, then use it to suppress the dignity of their fellows. Naturally this opinion would horrify the inoffensive monks around me, and some of them are genuine and selfless men. But they are blind to the fact that even here, within the minster, they bow the head in obedience to their superiors, whatever their quality. How different it was for those who followed the Elder Faith. As a sworn follower of Harald of Norway, as his king's man, I never had to bend the knee to him, either in an act of submission or to acknowledge his leadership. I only knew that he was more suited to rule than me, and that I must serve him as best I could. And when I was a priest of the Elder Faith among the Old Believers of Vaster Gotland, I would have been shocked if those who came to me to ask for guidance or to intervene with the Gods had believed that I was divinely appointed. I was judged only for my knowledge of the ancient lore.

So this is the ultimate power of the White Christ faith: it is a belief suited to despots who would curb men's independence.

I will never abandon my devotion to Odinn, though some might say he has abandoned me, just as he and the Gods have forsaken all those who followed the Elder Faith. Our world may have come to an end, but we never expected our Gods to be all-powerful and eternal. That sort of arrogance is reserved for the Christians. We knew from the very start that one day the old order would collapse, and after Ragnarok all would be swept away. Our Gods did not control the future. That was ordained by the Norns, and no one can alter the final outcome. While we are on this earth, each individual can only live his life to the best of his ability, strive to mould daily existence to best advantage, and never, like the unhappy Mac Bethad of the Scots, be duped by outward signs and appearance.

Still, it grieves me that the body of my king Harald was taken back to Norway and placed in a Christian church. He should have received a true funeral in the old style, been burned on a pyre or interred within a barrow grave. That is what I had in mind when I tried vainly to rescue his body from the battlefield. I know that it was an old man's folly, but at the time I was sure that the Valkyries had already carried away his soul to Valhol, or that Freyja's servants had selected him and he was now in her golden hall, Sessrumnir, as befits the warrior whom some are already calling the last of the Vikings.

I myself do not expect to go to Valhol nor to Freyja's hall. Those palaces are reserved for those who fell in battle, and – truth be told – I have never been a warrior, although I did my military training with the brotherhood of the Jomsvikings and have been present at the great battles: in Clontarf when the Irish High King fell, when the great Greek general Maniakes smashed the Arabs in Sicily, and of course at the bridge in Stamford. But I was never really a fighting man. When I took up arms, it was usually for self-defence.

The thought of Sessrumnir has reminded me yet again of the

twins, Freyvid and Freygerd. What has happened to them, I wonder? The last report I had was when their uncle Folkmar took them and fled for safety into the fastnesses of Sweden. It is too late for me to go to seek them, but in my bones I feel sure that they have survived. Once again I believe this is Odinn's wish. He taught that after Ragnarok, when all has been consumed by fire and destruction, there will be two survivors, twins who have sheltered beneath the roots of the World Tree and survived unscathed. From them will spring a new race of men who will populate the happier world that emerges from the ruins. With that knowledge I can console myself that my line may again bring the return of the Elder Ways.

So, in these closing days of my life, I am content to set down on paper my gratitude to Odinn for the guidance he gave me. Odinn Gangradr, the journey adviser, was always at my shoulder. He showed me many marvels: the glittering reflection of the great ice cliffs in the still waters of a Greenland fjord, the endless sweet-smelling pine forests of Vinland in the west, the Golden Dome of the great Saracen temple in the Holy Land, the slow curl of the early morning mist rising from the surface of the broad river which leads eastward from Gardariki, the land of forts. And, more important, Odinn also brought me to the company of women I loved, and who loved me – a young girl in Ireland, a maiden among the ski-runners of the north, and – in the end – to the embrace of Runa. How can the monks around me compare their lives to that?

I am still restless, even at my advanced age. When I was at my weakest and sat feebly in the herb garden next to the small infirmary, I would notice the high-flying birds passing overhead on their distant journeys, and wanted to rise and follow them. Now that my body is mended and I have reached the conclusion of my chronicle, I will add these final pages to the cache of writing that I have concealed within a secret hiding place in the thick stone wall of the scriptorium. When the opportunity presents itself, as it surely will if I keep my allegiance to Odinn, I will slip away from this minster and make a new life somewhere in the outside world.

Where will I go? I cannot be precise. That is not a vision that has been given me. All I know is that my fate was decided long ago, at the time of my birth, and by the Norns. They were kind to me. I have enjoyed my life, and even if I had been able to change its course, I would not have done so.

So I will leave this minster with a sense of happy expectation and my twins in mind. I will find a place where, in my final duty as a devotee of Odinn, I shall preach, and instruct my listeners that there will be a second coming of the Old Ways.

My lord abbot, If you will forgive this final notation, I must report that two years past our monastery received occasional reports of an unidentified preacher known locally as the 'the black priest'. This man established himself at a remote spot on the moors, and the common folk flocked there to listen and pay their devotions. It seems that he was greatly revered, though what he preached is unknown. Now he is seen no more, and it is presumed that he has departed this life. His parishioners, if they may be called that, come almost weekly to us to importune that we build and consecrate a chapel at the place of his hermitage. They say he was some sort of saint. I tremble at the possibility that with such an act we may be serving the Antichrist. But the people are most insistent, and I fear that if we spurn their request, they will be deeply vexed, to the detriment of our own foundation.

In this, as in all things, I seek your blessed guidance.

Aethelred
Sacristan and Librarian

extracts reading groups
competitions books new
extracts
discounts extracts
competitions
books new
events books
reading groups
extracts
new titles reading groups
interviews
reading groups
books events extracts
discounts
new books events
events new
discounts extracts discounts
www.panmacmillan.com
extracts events reading groups
competitions books extracts new